PRAISE FOR THOMAS H. COOK:

"Cook is an important talent, not simply a plotter but a prose stylist with a sensitivity to character and relationships that suggests Ross Macdonald . . . a storytelling writer of poetic narrative power. His crime fiction extends the boundaries of the form."

—*Los Angeles Times Book Review*

"Cook writes a prose that is sympathetic, commanding and chilling. He has twice been nominated for an Edgar Award. Surely it is time for the brass ring."

—*The Boston Globe*

"Cook's night visions, seen through a glass darkly, are haunting."

—*The New York Times Book Review*

"Cook has an eye as acute as any Nikon. And he knows how to write."

—*The Houston Post*

"Cook seems to know a lot about police work. He also knows how to weave a story that will make you sorry to see it end."

—*Chattanooga News-Free Press*

EVIDENCE OF BLOOD

THOMAS H. COOK

ZEBRA BOOKS
KENSINGTON PUBLISHING CORP.

Dylan Thomas, *Poems of Dylan Thomas* Copyright 1939 by New Directions Publishing Corporation. Reprinted by permission of New Directions Publishing Corporation.

ZEBRA BOOKS

are published by

Kensington Publishing Corp.
475 Park Avenue South
New York, NY 10016

First Zebra Books Printing: April, 1993

Printed in the United States of America

For
George Foy,
Jim Brodie and
Georgina Robillard—
Comrades in Arms.

The hand that whirls the water in the pool
Stirs the quicksand; that ropes the blowing wind
Hauls my shroud sail.
And I am dumb to tell the hanging man
How of my clay is made the hangman's lime.

—DYLAN THOMAS

One

He'd seen shadows of his own. Hers did not surprise him. It was only surprising how often they recurred, as if something in the mind still insisted that it had never really happened. Daphne Moore had seen one pass her bedroom window with something large and bulky in its hand. It had been tall and slender when Ellen Ferry had seen it glide swiftly across her closet door. Wyndham Knight had only glimpsed a head and shoulders as they skirted along the bright blue surface of her lighted, nightbound pool. Try as he had, he'd never been able to imagine what little Billy Flynn had seen.

"So you saw his shadow first?"

She nodded slowly, ponderously, as if underwater. "It came up from behind me. He was real close. Then he opened the door on the driver's side. He said, 'Get in. Get in, or you're dead.' Something like that. Then he came in after me, sort of pushing me in, you know?"

"Did he speed away?"

"No. He was going slow, like he didn't want to attract

attention, and he was doing everything like he'd really studied about it, very, very . . ." She searched for the word. He did his job, found it for her.

"Methodical?"

"Yeah, like that."

Her voice was weak, her eyes slightly diverted, a shy maiden reluctantly going over the unseemly details. He could sense her groping through the tale, hesitant, disordered, whole segments lost or out of sequence.

"I stayed in the frontseat, where he put me. I didn't know what else to do."

His pencil whispered softly as it glided across the lined yellow paper of his notebook. All around, the world seemed very still, despite the patter of the rain against her window, the sounds of traffic moving along the nearby street. It was a stillness that seemed to radiate out from her testimony in a cold, numbing wave.

Her eyes drifted to the window, then about the room, before finally returning to him. It was a gesture that reminded him of someone who could have been a nun, perhaps should have been a nun, secure in a cloistered life, beyond the reach of shadows.

"I was sitting up. I could see everything. It was at night. But I could see things."

She seemed mildly surprised by the fact that she'd never been pressed down onto the floorboard or locked in the trunk, that she'd been sitting up for the whole ride, as if she were his wife, sister, girlfriend. She considered it for a moment. "I saw people. It was dark, but we passed people walking down the road." She shrugged slightly. "But there was nothing they could do."

Kinley nodded. He'd heard this before, too, and always with the same tone of irony and unreality. *How could other people be so near, and yet so far away?* Patricia Quinn had passed three security guards as she was led down the corridor toward the room in which she would be slaughtered. Felicia Sanchez had seen her mother ap-

8

proach the house and peer toward the wrong bedroom window for a moment before going on her way. In those who survived their experiences of sudden, mortal danger, there was always a sense of being in and out of the world at the same time, a feeling that time had stopped, that everything had suddenly gone mute and motionless, except for the rope's flapping ends, the crack of the belt, the slight nudge of the muzzle.

"Did you talk to him?"

"I guess I did, but I don't know what I said. I guess I was asking him things. Like: 'Why?' Like: 'Why are you doing this?' "

She flicked a bit of ash into the small plastic ashtray on the table, and the gentle, retiring nun disappeared. Now she was just a jittery woman with dry skin and a Death Valley emptiness in her eyes. The universal victim. She could be a battered wife sucking at her broken fingernail or a factory worker slumped in a fat recliner. The falling ash would fall in exactly the same way, the mouth tighten into the same red scar. It was a look he'd seen a thousand times: the eyes closing languidly as if indifferent to the lash; the head drooping very slightly, ready for the axe; then, inevitably, the eyes opening again, though vacant and passionless, as if any remaining rage would be dismissed as self-indulgence, even by the drowsy reporter taking down the tale. *It's all ashes, ashes. Who really gives a shit about what happened to me?*

Kinley made his own stage move, pretending to write something in his notebook as he glanced about the room, taking in its small details. He had always assumed that if God was in the details, then Satan must be in them too, leering unrepentantly from a pile of tangled sheets or from behind a spent ring of masking tape. His experience had taught him that nothing betrayed the quirkiness of the mind more than the odd minutiae of crime: the pasteboard box Perry had laid Mr. Cutter on to keep him comfortable until he cut his throat; the can of deodorant

Whitman had taken with him to the Texas Tower, not wanting to offend; the little Christmas ornament Mildred Haskell had dangled out the door to coax in Billy Flynn.

As his eyes moved about the room, he could feel them gather in its small details. It had always been this way, his mind, a thing that feasted on the tiniest particulars. The apartment it inventoried now was a kingly banquet. There was a large, slightly faded doily on the boxy television. The lamp on top of it resembled a small mound of seashells or various other beach droppings, all of them glued together and polished to a glassy sheen. In a far bedroom, he could see part of the wooden bed frame, and a bit of the wallpaper behind it, English fox-hunting scenes, red jackets, horses, dogs. He remembered similar wallpaper in the little house where he'd grown up, only it had been a Southern scene, little girls in bonnets and hoopskirts dancing on a vast green lawn. Tara, his grandmother had called it, though always with that arctic smile.

Other walls, other rooms had suggested other things: the illuminated Christ that hung over Wilma Jean Comstock's bed (how fervently she must have prayed to it during the hours it took for Colin Bright to kill her); the pentagram in Mildred Haskell's dripping smokehouse (what must little Billy Flynn have thought?); the life-sized, semen-stained diagram of internal organs that Willie Connors had slept with before trying the real thing (had Wyndham Knight seen that?). He wondered what his grandmother would have called such adornments had she seen them as he had seen them, live, in living color.

His eyes returned to the witness. "Did he ever mention why he was doing any of this?" he asked.

She shook her head determinedly. "No, no, he never said anything like that."

Kinley brought his pencil to attention. "Okay, just tell me what happened after you got in the car."

"Right after he pushed me in. He made me do it." She looked away shyly, a nun again. "To myself."

Kinley noted the slight hesitation before the last two

10

words, and the barely perceptible sense of shame which accompanied them, all common victim reactions, a strange, irrational belief that nothing ever happened entirely by accident, that even the most horrible events had some kind of explanation, something you'd done to make it happen. *Maybe my hair was too loose, my sweater too tight; maybe that's what made him do it to me.*

"Play with myself. He made me do it. In the car while we were going." She took a long draw on the cigarette. Her foot began to tap at the floor in a soft, rapid beat. "He looked like he'd done it before, made girls do that."

"Did he say he'd done it before?"

If she said yes, he'd have to do more leg work, track down the possibility, however remote, that he had, in fact, done it before. He waited as she considered the question.

"No."

"You just had that feeling?"

"Yes. Just the way he did things. Like he'd done it before. Like it wasn't just something he was making up as he went along."

The "he" was Fenton Norwood, now resident number EG14679 at the Walpole Correctional Institute in Walpole, Massachusetts. At the time he'd abducted her, fall, 1974, he'd been twenty-four years old, a high school dropout and U.S. Army deserter roaming the Portuguese districts of New Bedford. As far as Kinley had been able to track down, Maria Spinola had been his first victim. Still, he needed to be sure.

"So he didn't actually mention anything about having done it before?"

"No."

"Did he tell you where he was taking you?"

"No, but we were on the highway. Going east. Southeast. Toward the Cape."

At the time of the incident, Maria Spinola had been sixteen years old. Now she was just over thirty, an alcoholic with an edgy manner, twice divorced, the mother of two children currently in her former husband's custody, her life is ruins, she claimed, because of what Fenton Norwood had done to her.

But as he looked at her, Kinley found he could not wholly accept the notion that Fenton Norwood was entirely to blame for Spinola's fate. He had seen too many other people like her, programmed for misfortune, as if there were a trapdoor at the core of their makeup. He had checked her school records, talked with her former guidance counselor. When Norwood had picked her up, she'd already been pregnant by a high school boy who periodically beat her, and Kinley suspected it had been her pregnancy that had probably prevented Norwood—the former Catholic altar boy, working through his own oblique moral gymnastics: murder one thing, abortion another—from killing her. In any event, her life had already begun to strike him as one of those for which no safe harbor was ever really available, a wingless and descending life that on one particular afternoon had simply drifted aimlessly toward a shadow.

For the first time she seemed to stiffen slightly, as if in a sudden surge of resentment. "I couldn't ever go to the Cape after what happened. I've never been to Cape Cod, you know? Not since that night. My whole life. Only a few miles away. But I can't go there." The momentary flash was quickly smothered by a thin, wet smile. "He didn't look like he could do what he did. Strange, huh?"

Kinley stared at Spinola, but saw Norwood instead, a pudgy pink face, bug eyes and fat lips. The ultimate disguise, Jack the Ripper in the body of Elmer Fudd.

She lifted her head slightly. "He should have killed me. Right there in the woods that night. In a way, he did."

But he didn't. All of that had come later. First the woman in the discount clothing store in New Bedford; then the little girl in Boston, the one he'd kept for nearly three weeks, walking her on a leash through the Commons the rainy afternoon before he killed her; finally two at a time, twelve-year-old twins vacationing at Nickerson State Park on the Cape. The one similarity had been in their looks, all of them with dark skin, eyes and hair. Once, when Kinley had pointed it out to Norwood, his fat face had gone blank for a few seconds before brightening with an impish grin. "Maybe I just like 'em slightly toasted," he'd said.

Spinola's resentment built a moment, then reached its crescendo in a sudden burst. "Just left me in the woods. All dirty, filthy. Just left me there, the bastard." She pulled in a long, exhausted breath, regained control. "Did you see the pictures?"

Kinley gave no indication of an answer, but he'd seen them, all right, the way he'd seen hundreds of others. Maria Spinola's were nothing special in the gallery of his mind. They showed a young girl in torn clothes, with a muddy face and wet, matted hair. The forest was apathetically beautiful behind her, and there was even a hint of the blue-green pond Norwood had planned to drown her in. As pictures, they were a long way from others he had seen: dark cellars fitted with chains, pulleys, eyebolts, jungles of rope, clothesline, straps and latches, miniature racks, pillories, dunking stools, and everywhere, in every vision, the shadows of hooks.

She shook her head despondently, reaching out for his tender word. "I sometimes wish he'd gone ahead and done his worst to me," she said.

Kinley looked at her distantly, remembering. *No, you don't. Believe me. No, you don't.*

Two

He took the five o'clock shuttle out of Logan and arrived at La Guardia less than an hour later. The cab ride to his apartment on the Upper West Side came to almost thirty dollars, and once there, he walked to his desk, pulled out his business expense notebook and recorded the amount precisely for the IRS. Precision was everything to him, and he often clung to it the way another might cling to a log in a maelstrom, as something fixed within the chaos. It gave him comfort to see all his notes in order, all his books in a neat row. And though he recognized his obsessive orderliness, with its accompanying mother lode of rock-ribbed discipline and self-control, as a mild form of compulsiveness, its exact source continued to elude him. It was one of his own shadows, he supposed, but one that had always served him well, ensuring that he would complete one book after another while others foundered in a seedy alcoholism or stumbled groggily from one domestic horror to the next. Whatever else could be said of a clean, unencumbered life, he often thought, it certainly was clean and unencumbered, and he had never felt the inclination to apologize for the choices he had made.

Even the simple arrangement of his desk for the night's work brought him a sense of stability and resourcefulness, and after he'd done it, Kinley fixed himself a scotch and slouched down on the small sofa by the window. He always allowed himself a few minutes of calm between the interview and its transcription, though this, too, was "working" time, his mind playing it all through again, from the moment Spinola had opened the door until the time she closed it, her small brown face continuing to watch him, as witnesses always watched him, warily from the shadows behind their windows, as if he were somehow as threatening as the ones who'd done them harm.

He looked at the digital clock on his desk. It was now almost seven o'clock, and the evening shade was falling over the streets below. He could hardly wait for it to deepen, since, in a way, he had always thought of night as his best friend. It was silent and unpeopled, a world of vastly reduced distractions. In the quiet he could let his mind do what it did best, retrieve and analyze, order and distinguish.

He was nearly finished playing back the interview with Maria Spinola when the phone rang. It was Wendy Lubeck, his agent, and for the next few minutes, Kinley listened as she related the details of a series of murders that had occurred in the Maine woods along the Canadian border. A publisher had asked if he might be interested in doing a book on the case, Wendy told him, and in response Kinley promised to think about it.

But he didn't. Instead, as he sat down on the sofa by the window, he thought about something else entirely, a place about as far from Maine as he could imagine, the northern Appalachian foothills of Georgia in which he'd been brought up by Granny Dollar, the maternal grandmother who'd taken him in after his parents had been killed in an automobile accident.

15

Granny Dollar had died only two months before, and since then he'd noticed his tendency to drift back to his past from time to time, quietly, unexpectedly, in those dead moments when his work left him, and he found himself alone in his apartment, wifeless, childless, with only Granny Dollar to remind him of the texture of family life he'd once known.

That texture had been very dense, indeed, it seemed to him now. She'd raised him in almost complete solitude, the two of them perched on an isolated ridge overlooking a desolate canyon, with nothing but the sounds of crickets and night birds to break the silence that surrounded them. Since that time he'd been a loner, and over the years, he'd come to believe that for people like himself, the true solitaires, it was better to have no one to answer to, wonder about, no one whose affections mattered more to him than the esteem he expected from the little Chinese woman who did his shirts: *Goo to see you, Missur Kahnley.*

He was working at his desk when the phone rang. He looked at the clock. It was just nearly seven-thirty, so he suspected it might be Wendy, still chewing at her idea. It could not be Phyllis, his oldtime drinking buddy, because she was on assignment in Venezuela. As for the type of woman other men spent so much time searching for, or trying to figure out, Kinley had long ago admitted that the Mythical She had either eluded him or he had eluded her. Instead, he dwelt in harmony with the dark-eyed murderesses of his work, admiring their coldly calculating eyes, the edge of cruelty and dominion which clung to their false smiles, their minds even more intricate, limitless and unknowable than his own.

The phone rang a third time, and he glanced at the message machine. He'd turned it off when he'd started to work, and now regretted it. There was no choice but to pick up the phone.

16

"Yes?" he answered curtly.

"Hello, Mr. Kinley?"

"Yes."

"It's Serena Tindall."

He thought it was odd that she'd said her last name, but he made nothing of it. "Hello, Serena," he said. "Are you in New York?"

"No, I'm at home," Serena said. "For summer break. I've been working at the high school."

"Your father's old stomping ground."

He heard her breath catch in that tense, briefly suspended way he'd often heard others pause before making the great plunge into their tragic tales. "It's about Daddy," she said.

"Ray? What? What is it?"

Her voice broke as she told him. "He died this afternoon."

He tried to continue with his transcription of the Spinola interview after talking to Serena, but found he couldn't, so after a while, he poured himself another scotch and sat down at the small desk by the window. On the hanging shelf just above it, he'd arranged all his books, as if he still needed solid, physical evidence of how far he'd come from where he'd started. Up north, he sometimes referred to his native region as "Deliverance country," but in his own mind, it had always remained "Ray's country."

Joe Ray Tindall.

Kinley turned on his computer, as if, with Ray gone, it was now his only completely reliable friend, and wrote out Ray's name. Including it among the body of data he'd accumulated in his work seemed to give it an honored resting place, and for a moment, Kinley stared at the name, his mind conjuring up the face that went with it. It was a large, broad-boned face, and Kinley could clearly recall the first time he'd seen it. He'd been standing in the crowded corridor of Sequoyah High, small, timid, aloof, not only the new boy in school, but the one who'd been singled out by a group of Yankee IQ researchers, branded "very superior" by their tests, and reported, almost like a dangerous alien, to the Sequoyah County Board of Education. The Board had subsequently pulled him from his mountain grammar school and rushed him down into the valley to join, at mid-year, the more advantaged freshman class of Sequoyah High School.

Ray had been the first person to speak to him there, an oversized boy clad in blue jeans and a checkered shirt, staring at him from across the hall, his eyes, as they always were, motionless and intense, as if taking aim before finally speaking to him.

You that freshman from up on the mountain?

Yes.

The one that's supposed to be a genius?

I guess.

Special tests and everything, you must be a whiz. My name's Ray Tindall.

Jackson Kinley.

Sounds like two last names. You give them to me in the right order?

Yeah.

You ever go hunting?

Yeah.

Maybe we'll go up to the canyon sometimes, shoot something.

Okay.

How about this Saturday? I'll meet you on the road to Rocky Ridge. Then we'll just head into the woods up there.

Okay.

Kinley peered at the name on the screen. He typed something else under it: ROCKY RIDGE. That's where they'd gone that first time. And as it turned out, it was also where they'd found Ray face down on the forest's

18

leafy floor. It was the only question he'd asked Serena beyond the usual ones about the funeral: "What was he doing down in the canyon?"

"I don't know."

"Who found him?"

"Some old man who lives up on the ridge."

"Was Ray on a case?"

"He was always on a case. That's just the way he was."

"What was it anyway?"

"I don't know. Something in the District Attorney's Office, I guess."

"No, Serena. I'm sorry. I meant, what killed him?"

"Oh. Well, it was probably his heart."

It had not been a soft heart, in the sense of great compassion or an infinitely extended understanding, Kinley thought as he continued to sit at his desk, still watching the computer screen, but it was a rich, difficult, complicated heart. There was something about Ray that could never be figured out exactly. Even the way he looked led you slightly off the mark. He had had wiry reddish-brown hair and a sallow complexion that easily burned in the summer sun. He had not been an intimidatingly large man, but when he came into a room, he seemed to shrink it just a bit. He had liked the woods but hated the water, loved fast cars but avoided planes, talked religion but never gone to church, read but rarely spoken of what he read. There had been something mysterious about him, something Kinley had noticed even that first day in the canyon, the way his eyes seemed to focus on something far away, unreachable even when he spoke of something near at hand, perhaps no further than a short walk into the woods.

There's an old house down here, but nobody lives in it anymore.

In the canyon? Where?

Not far from here. You want to see it?

I guess.

It's the perfect place. You can only find it if you really look hard.

Even now, it was impossible for Kinley to know why he'd followed Ray down the narrow, granite ledge and into the dark labyrinth of the canyon. He could remember the frothy green river that had tumbled along the canyon bottom, the sounds of its waters moving softly through the trees, even the unseasonably cool breeze that shook the slender green fingers of the pines, then swooped down to rifle through the leaves at his feet. It was his one great gift. He could remember everything.

And now he remembered that as they'd advanced on the house, the going had gotten rougher, the sharp claws of the briers grabbing at his shirt, low-slung limbs suddenly flying into his face like quick slaps to warn him back. The last hundred yards had seemed to take forever, as if the air had thickened, turned to an invisible gelatin which had to be plowed through as arduously as the bramble. It had taken them almost an hour to make it to the general vicinity of the old house Ray had spoken of, and by that time, Kinley remembered, the trek had begun to exhaust him, his legs growing more feeble with each step, his breathing more labored and hardwon, the old plague of his asthma snatching at his breath. It had been enough to rouse his new friend's concern.

Kinley, are you all right? We don't have to keep going.

How far is it?

Not far. Just through those last trees. Then we hit the vines.

What vines?

The ones around the house. Like a wall almost. You want to keep going?

Yes.

Okay, let's go.

The wall of vines had been exactly as Ray described it, a tall impenetrable drapery of coiling green that hung from the trees and sprouted from the ground simultaneously, its sticky shafts so covered with the dry husks of thousands of insects that in certain places the vines themselves appeared like lengths of tightly knotted rope. The very look of it, Kinley remembered now, had unnerved him so much that he'd actually drawn back, his breath now coming in short, agonized gasps.

I think we'd better stop, Kinley.

Why?

You need to get back. I think you may need a doctor.

No.

You can't really get to the old house anyway. There's no break in the vines.

But I want . . .

No.

Ray had said it just that firmly. There was to be no argument in the matter. They would go no further. Then he'd taken Kinley by the arm and led him away, the great wall of green disappearing behind him forever.

"Forever," Kinley whispered now, realizing that they'd never tried to find the old shack after that, but had simply let it sink, first from their conversation, then from their boyhood plans, and finally from their remembered hopes.

The phone rang again around ten. It was Serena again.

"I just wanted to tell you about the autopsy," she said. "My mother called to let me know, and I thought you might want to hear about it, too."

"Yes, I do."

"It was a heart attack," Serena said. "Massive. That's what the doctor said. Massive."

"So he died quickly," Kinley said before he could stop himself.

"And so young," Serena said. "I guess that's why they wanted an autopsy."

"Who did?"

"Mr. Warfield," Serena said, "the District Attorney, the man he worked for."

"Ray was working for the District Attorney's Office?"

"Yeah. He didn't run for Sheriff again. Didn't he tell you that?"

"No."

"Well, I guess he just got tired of it, decided not to run. That's when he took this job with the District Attorney."

"I see."

"Anyway, Mr. Warfield wanted an autopsy."

"It's probably a good idea."

"You know about this kind of thing, I guess. From your work, I mean."

"A little."

"He was a good man," Serena said. "I'm just sorry he had to die alone, way down in the canyon." She hesitated a moment, then added, "Looking for something, I guess. What do you think it was?"

Kinley shook his head silently. Maybe just a way through the vines, he thought.

Three

By mid-morning his travel service had made all the arrangements for his flight to Atlanta late that night. A rental car would be waiting for him there, and by midnight he expected to be back in Sequoyah, his hometown.

In the meantime, there was work to be done, and he spent the better part of the day doing it. First he transcribed his interview with Maria Spinola, reading it carefully once again as he typed it out. There was always a chance that something might be missed, a small detail that could bring a human touch to otherwise inhuman events.

As he read, he could hear Spinola's voice again as she'd said her last words to him: *Is he sorry*? She meant Norwood, was he sorry for what he'd done to her. He'd known what she wanted to hear, that Norwood was racked by nightmares, that his screams of remorse echoed through the cells and catwalks of Walpole CI, that his suffering was as Dante might have imagined it, burning skin, boiling eyes. Instead Norwood now munched sandwiches, watched television, and probably masturbated from time to time while feverishly remembering the pleasure he'd taken in raping her.

At the time, he'd wanted to give her the answer she needed, but found he couldn't, no matter how much it might have soothed her. It was a curious holding back of natural sympathies which he had long ago accepted as part of his character. For a time, he'd believed that it was his work that had drained them from him, the long trail of blood he'd followed, the pictures he'd seen, the even more desperate ones he'd imagined. He remembered a time early on, when a police sergeant had pulled out a carousel projector to try to find the slides that had been taken of the Comstock murders. He'd routinely aimed the lens at the opposite wall, projecting one picture after another onto it while he looked for the ones Kinley needed. What had flashed before him during the next ninety seconds was the whole terrible story of man's unspeakable misdeeds, a vision of random carnage so shocking that Kinley had actually glanced away, his eyes lighting on the old detective's face. It was a motionless, passive face, the large eyes blinking listlessly as the re-dtinted light from the wall swept over it, went black, then swept over it again, until the carousel had finally whirled to the slide he'd been looking for, and Wilma Jean Comstock's ravaged body hung from the white wall of the squad room, face-up, naked, arms outstretched across the barren field, eyes open, glaring, her mouth pulled down in a tortured grimace, and nothing but the old detective's voice to orchestrate her suffering. "Yeah, yeah, here we are, Mr. Kinley," he'd said as he handed him the small black remote with which he could turn the wheel himself. And he had taken the little black button and pressed it, moving through the slides, each image sinking in as the black wheel turned obediently, and the skin on his fingertip grew a bit more insensitive with each touch. As his heart had finally done, he suspected now, so that fifteen years later he could reply truthfully to Maria Spinola's

24

agonized question without blinking an eye: *Unfortunately, I think Norwood probably loves prison. For some people, it's not a punishment at all.*

The plane was almost an hour late in departing La Guardia, but after the initial tension he always felt on actually leaving the ground, Kinley was able to peer out the window and enjoy the lights of the city as the plane made its long, lazy circle before turning southward into the rural night.

Once the city had disappeared behind him, he ordered his nightly scotch and leaned back into his seat. The soft hum of the engines lulled him gently, but the nap he'd hoped for insistently eluded him. Instead, he found himself drifting back toward his youth, as if the plane were returning him to the granite cliffs and pine breaks in which he'd wandered, the little house perched at the canyon wall, the long afternoons of sitting on the old porch swing while Granny Dollar read to him from the only magazine she ever bought, the *Police Gazette*.

The tales had been gruesome, he remembered, and the accompanying photographs had been even worse, but his grandmother had always ended her reading with a decidedly reassuring remark. "What some people do," she'd always said, as if it was only "some people" who did such things, and that the house beside the canyon was far away from them, well beyond their deadly reach. It was only later he'd realized that it was her love that had somehow wrapped him in a strangely unthreatening atmosphere, despite the horror of the tales she read.

She had seemed such an irreducible part of his early life that even now it was hard for him to imagine her dead. It was Ray who'd brought him the news, the telephone ringing urgently only a month before, while he had been busily typing up his first interview with Norwood.

Hello, Kinley? It's Ray. Listen, I have some bad news for you. It's about Granny Dollar. She's dead. She was sitting on the porch, they said. Just sitting in her old rocker. Bolt upright, like she was tied to it.

He'd taken a plane home immediately, and now, after only two months, he was taking another one, his mind shifting anchorlessly from Ray to his grandmother, as if together they formed the single, tenuous line that still connected him to some part of life that was not drenched in blood.

The plane circled the Atlanta airport for over half an hour before touching down. It was an enormous terminal, but Kinley knew it well. His first trip had been almost fifteen years before, when he'd been writing his book on Colin Bright, the itinerant con-man who'd stumbled upon a farm family in southern Georgia one afternoon and killed all seven of them one by one over the next three days. It had been Kinley's first prison interview, and he could still recall how Bright had talked about the murders. He'd expected a dull, plodding mind, lumpishly stupid, with hooded eyes and slurred speech, a look and manner he associated with an earlier form of man. Instead, Bright had talked energetically and with immense detail about the final days of the Comstock family, how they'd wept and pleaded for themselves and each other while he moved among them with godlike power and demonic arbitrariness. "I discussed it with them," Bright said. "Who to do first, and how to decide. Maybe I should kill them in alphabetical order, I said, or maybe according to size, or, hey, maybe something even weirder then that, you know, like hair length, longest or shortest first, or who could keep their eyes open the longest without blinking, kill that one last, you know, or some crazy thing like that." The intelligence and cunning in his eyes, along with the boyish gleam which remained despite the fact that Bright was nearly fifty, was what had struck Kinley most powerfully about Colin Bright, the killer as a playful clown, murder as the ultimate prank.

26

In a way, Kinley thought now, as he lingered beside the moving conveyor belt of the baggage claim, Colin Bright had never completely left him. He suspected that, other than Granny Dollar, Bright had probably done more than anyone else to give shape and direction to his life. It had been Bright's eyes, their terrible intelligence, that had captured him, the pale light-blue irises and dark, bottomless pupils, the way they'd shot over to him at the very last minute, just as the black hood had been drawn over them seconds before his execution: *I would tell you everything, if I had the time.*

Within an hour, the lights of Atlanta and its far-flung suburbs were well behind him, and he could lean back in the seat of the rental car and enjoy the darkness of the countryside. It was a thick, almost palpable darkness, dense, silent, the sort he remembered from his youth. The long nights on the canyon rim had been made strangely rich and lovely by Granny Dollar's voice as she'd read to him from the *Police Gazette: The fiendish plot was conceived in the diabolical imagination of Mrs. Mildred Bell, the simple Iowa schoolmarm whose evil deeds have now been unearthed by Sheriff Davies (left) and Deputy Stowe (pictured above as they stand beside the excavation site.)*

There was something in that voice, he thought now, that had wound its way into him. It had been soft, hypnotic, musical, turning the most lurid words into a haunting and mysterious refrain. She had made crime a siren call, dark, alluring, irresistible, its roots ancient, marvelous and fabled, the ultimate quest for the ultimate detection.

He was still thinking about her as he crested the southern slopes of the mountain and headed on across its wide plateau. This was the land he knew best, the broad fields of corn that spread out in all directions, the swirling green rills and shallow, kudzu-choked ravines where he'd gone on his solitary rambles.

There was hardly a road or trail he didn't know, hardly a path he hadn't wandered down. And yet, there was also something that continued to distract and disorient him. He could never remember a time when he hadn't felt it, a sense of being an outsider, of yearning to get away. "You were born on the road," his grandmother had once told him. "It got into your system."

On the outskirts of Sequoyah, just before the mountain road took its long dive into the valley, he made a slow left turn and headed down a narrow dirt road to the small churchyard where his grandmother lay. It was a bright, cloudless night, and he had no trouble finding her stone. It was a short granite slab, pale blue in the moonlight.

As he stood over it, Kinley thought of what she must have looked like the day she'd been found, sitting straight up in the old wooden rocker on the porch, her long, iron-gray hair draped over her shoulders like a thick cotton shawl, her black eyes staring straight ahead, stricken and amazed, as Ray had described them when he'd called to tell him of her death.

She was just sitting there, Kinley, looking out over the canyon.

I see.

Anything I can do?

I don't think so.

What about her stuff, Kinley?

Stuff?

Well, word'll get around pretty soon about her being dead. And you know how it is with some of those people in the sticks up there—they might get into her things.

What do you think I should do?

Well, I could get everything boxed up this afternoon, put it all in storage at my place.

All right, Ray, thanks. I'd appreciate that.

Now she lay in the rocky earth, and Kinley could imagine the look of her body as it rested in the wooden casket. He'd seen enough pictures to know the full assault of decomposition. He knew that her eyes were now shrunken like raisins in the great crater of their sockets, that her lips had dried and blackened and turned to leather, that her scalp had cracked, allowing wisps of white hair to tumble softly to her chest. Ghosts were lithesome, graceful, beautiful compared to the truth of life's decay, the gradual desiccation of the flesh that Kinley had observed at every imaginable stage in its journey back to dust.

The Cherokee Hotel still stood at the center of Sequoyah's long main street, and from the dusty front window of his room, Kinley could see the old stone courthouse. Set on a sloping hill, it had towered over the town for decades, one great symbol of reason and self-restraint. Somewhere in its offices, Ray had worked through his last days.

After a while he turned from the window and began putting away his things. On top of the short chest of drawers by the closet, he deposited the laptop computer he'd brought along to fill up any idle time, then pulled his suitcase to the bed, and unpacked, carefully hanging his shirts and the one black suit he'd brought to wear at the funeral, before finally pulling himself into the bed.

He fell asleep almost immediately, and the dream settled over him a few minutes after that. He was moving through the woods, his small body plowing desperately through the heavy undergrowth, plunging blindly and at terrific speed into the impenetrable darkness. Someone was pulling him along, jerking his hand violently as he stumbled through the grasping bramble. He could feel the snare of the vines as they tangled around his bare legs, but the hand continued to wrench him forward mercilessly, dragging him toward the dark stone cliff. He could hear his own heart pounding frantically as he neared its jagged edge, pounding just as Maria Spinola's must

29

have pounded, he thought suddenly, as his eyes shot open and the icy breeze swept over him from the open window, and he saw her dark, stricken eyes fixed on the glimmering blue-green pond, felt her small hand squeezed painfully in Fenton Norwood's merciless grip as if it were his own.

Four

He'd closed the window, as well as the faded wooden shutters, but the morning light penetrated the uneven slats anyway, filling the room with a hard, bright light.

In the bathroom, his face looked a bit drawn when he glimpsed it in the mirror, checks slightly hollow, the wrinkles at the corners of his eyes a shade deeper. As for the eyes themselves, others had noticed that they sometimes took on a strange, animal urgency and inward penetration, as if they were looking backward rather than forward, the pupils aimed in the wrong direction, staring into the dark cavern of his skull. It was a peculiarity he's inherited from his mother. *Doll's eyes.* That's what Granny Dollar had always called them. *Doll's eyes. Like your mother's.* It was the only comparison his grandmother had ever made between him and his dead mother. Except for the day he'd left for New York, when she'd stood at the train, gray and silent, until she finally spoke: *You're like her.*

As to his father, Granny Dollar had never made any

31

bones about him. She'd labeled him a "no account" drifter and left it at that. If there'd ever been any pictures of him, he was sure his grandmother had long ago fed them to the fire in her stone hearth.

He took a quick shower, dressed and headed out onto the street. The morning air was cool and brisk, and as he made his way down the town's narrow main street, he remembered how he'd loved the fall best of all. In the mountains, early frosts had sometimes covered the ground with an eerie crystalline sparkle, and walking out into it, he'd often felt as if he'd been transported to another planet, a shimmering world where the grass was made of diamonds and the wind sang in a high, keening voice to the icy sky. Everything was cold and clear and gave off a feeling of utter isolation. It was a desolate, inhuman look that he'd never seen again until, many years later, he'd stared into Colin Bright's implacable blue eyes.

Was it a conscious decision?

You mean, did I think, "Okay, now, Colin, you've got to kill some people"?

Yes.

It never entered my mind one way or the other. Before I met them, they were dead. After I left them, they were dead.

Then it wasn't a decision at all?

No, Mr. Kinley. Just a way of life.

He had never forgotten those last five words, and in the end, he'd used them as the title for his first book: *Just a Way of Life.* Now, as he continued down the street, his eyes fixed on the small restaurant at the end of the block, he thought of the miles he'd traveled since that first inter-view, the cities he'd visited in his work: everything from the mean streets of Boston, Chicago and New York; to the flat rural byways of Indiana, Chicago and New York; to the flat rural byways of Indiana, where Mildred Haskell had finally, after many hours, strangled Billy Flynn; to the terrible desert wastes east of Los Angeles, arid little towns that squatted among the stones and cacti like something waiting for its prey. They were all alike, the places he knew. They had all been rocked by those sudden, instantaneous surges to "find a way out," as Colin Bright had described it, to soar for just one orgasmic moment on the broad red wing of your desolation. Ray had put it best: *Inside, Kinley, deep, deep down, everybody's always loaded for bear.*

The restaurant seemed to drift toward him, as if on a small gray cloud, and before he had even been able to calculate the distance to it, he found himself inside, seated comfortably in a booth by the window. A tiny, red-haired waitress approached him. She had a thin, bony face that made her look as if she'd already died and been buried hastily in a shallow grave.

"What can I gitcha this morning?" Her voice was homey, but with an edge, a drawl that looped around you like a noose.

"You have a menu?"

"Coffee, eggs, bacon, sausage, hotcakes. That's about it." She blinked rapidly, as if trying to bat a cinder from her eye. "Oh yeah, toast, buttered toast. With jelly, if you want it."

"Just coffee."

"Okay."

She streaked away from him, and while he waited for her to return, Kinley peered out at the deserted early morning street. Across the way, he could see the faded sign of Jefferson's Drug Store, the old soda fountain hangout where he'd often met Ray in the afternoon while the rest of the high school gathered at the more fashionable burger joint at the other end of town called Sally's-To-Go-Go, and which featured Sally's own specialty, something called Freetoe Pie, a mixture of soggy Fritos and canned chili that the varsity players particularly liked.

Ray had been a varsity player, too, but he'd never hung out with his teammates. Instead, he'd sometimes visited Warren Peacock, a ham radio operator who'd enlivened his day by listening to insurrectionary broadcasts from Castro's Cuba, and Dolly Pitts, a blonde whose slenderness bordered on anorexia, and who'd later moved to California to be remembered as Sequoyah's first and only hippie. Dolly was the last girl Ray had dated before he met and later married Lois Renshaw, a vaporous brunette from Minnesota who, Ray said, had come home from school one afternoon when she'd still lived in Minneapolis and found her mother hanging naked, like a slab of beef, in the coat closet by the front door.

I know it sounds like a yarn, Kinley, but she told me all about it.

Does she know why?

She says she has no idea. And you know, Kinley, this is the really weird part—and Lois told me this herself, so you know I didn't make it up—the weird part is that sometimes Lois wonders about the whole thing, you know, like maybe it wasn't really a suicide at all.

You mean that her mother was murdered?

Yeah, murdered. And get this, Kinley. Lois thinks maybe it was her father who did it.

It was precisely at that moment, Kinley remembered now, that Mrs. Dinker had walked into the drugstore, dressed, as always, in her long black coat, the lacy white handkerchief fluttering in her fist like a small bird she was squeezing brutally to death. He'd nodded toward her, and Ray had shifted slightly in his chair to see her, then returned his eyes to him, his face unexpectedly empty and forlorn. "It's better to know, don't you think, Kinley?" he'd asked. "No matter what the cost?"

Mrs. Dinker had never been granted the relief of knowing what had happened to her daughter, Ellie. Ellie had simply disappeared from the wooded path she'd taken up the mountainside that Friday morning, disappeared in her dark green dress, like something too well camouflaged to maintain its own identity within the dense, consuming foliage.

34

It's like she just dissolved, Kinley. Can people just dissolve?

Kinley had never answered Ray's question, but now, as the waitress returned with his coffee, and he watched the steam rise from it, dance its diaphanous, mystery dance for an instant, and vanish from the air, he thought he had an answer. *No, they can't. Something has always happened to them.* His mind recited the long list it had accumulated of the "disappeared." Riley Parker from his dry goods store. Sheila Benson from a park bathroom in Twenty-two Palms. Eliza Manchester from her crib, with nothing to reveal her fate but the two fragments of chipped paint they found on her windowsill. And Ellie Dinker, whose mother haunted the streets of Sequoyah, eyes vacant, rarely speaking, a presence wrapped in black, the terrible, tragic stand-in for her daughter's sleepless ghost. *Always, always, always. Something has always happened.*

He took a sip of coffee, hardly felt it as it went down, took another and another until the cup was empty and the waitress returned.

"Like a refill?"

"Yeah, thanks."

She returned with it shortly, along with a newspaper. "Comes with breakfast," she said as she plopped it down on the table.

Kinley was not surprised to see Ray's picture on the front page. In a town like Sequoyah, any man who'd been County Sheriff as long as Ray would have become a locally prominent figure.

In the photograph, he looked younger than Kinley remembered him. The deep lines that had begun to gather around his eyes and cut through the sides of his face were hardly visible, and his red hair had managed to conceal the gray that was sprinkled throughout it, but which could only be seen when the light was exactly right. It was hard to imagine him dead, even harder to think of him at the moment of death, stumbling through the brush, his hands clutching at his chest, his eyes popped in terror, the birds watching all of this from the bare limbs that streaked above him.

A short article accompanied the photograph. It was written matter-of-factly, and for anyone who might not have known, it detailed Ray's tenure as a Deputy Sheriff under Floyd Maddox, his later election as Sheriff after Maddox's death in 1974, and his decision not to seek reelection in 1990.

According to the article, Ray had died late on the afternoon of September 1. His body had been found by a resident of the canyon area. District Attorney William Warfield had subsequently ordered an autopsy.

Kinley folded the paper, returned it to the table in front of him and eased himself back in his chair. Outside, the town's one main street remained sleepy, perhaps comatose, compared to the noise and movement of New York, and he marvelled that Ray could have endured it for so long.

"That'll be fifty cents," the waitress said as she stepped up to the booth. "Do you want a receipt?"

Kinley thought of his tax records and decided that his trip home could not be counted as a business expense. "No," he said.

Five

He arrived at Ray's house at exactly eleven. He'd been there many times since they'd first met, the two of them sitting through the night in the wooden swing on the front porch and talking about everything under the sun. He'd spent so much time in and around the house during his last four years in Sequoyah that he'd finally come to think of it nearly as fondly as his grandmother's place on the mountain.

As a house, it wasn't much—small, wood-framed, with two tiny bedrooms and a living room not much larger. But it was as close as the Tindalls had ever gotten to an ancestral home, and because of that, Ray had given Lois just about everything else he had, all his savings, and much of the farmland he'd accumulated over the past fifteen years, in order to keep it in his family's name. Since the divorce, he'd lived there alone, wandering down its short, dimly lit corridors, or burrowing into the small office he'd fixed up for himself in what had once been Serena's bedroom.

Serena, herself, opened the door. She was now twenty, with Ray's red hair and penetrating green eyes. Even from behind the rusty screen, her skin gave off a soft white light.

"It's good to see you," she said quietly, as she swung open the screen door, stepped back and let him walk inside. "I'm glad you could come. You were the closest thing Daddy had to a brother."

Kinley drew her into his arms. She stood silently within them, her posture determinedly erect, unbending, a woman who'd fully inherited her father's rock-ribbed sense of dignity and self-containment.

He released her, and she stepped from his arms. "He's in here," she said as she directed him out of the small square foyer and into the living room. Sprays of flowers stood on green metal legs throughout the room, their sweet aroma almost suffocating in the enclosed space. The casket rested in front of the tiny brick fireplace, a massive metal vault which seemed to shrink the room around it.

"I decided to keep it closed," Serena said. "I think Daddy would have wanted it that way."

"Yes, I think so, too."

"Around here, people open them, but . . ."

"No, you're right," Kinley told her. "I did the same thing with my grandmother." He fixed his eyes on the casket. It was hard to imagine Ray inside, alone in the dark.

"I was here only a month ago," Kinley said. "We had a nice talk."

"When your grandmother died."

"Yes."

Serena kept her eyes fixed on the casket, but with a look that appeared slightly puzzled, as if she were trying to figure out exactly what lay inside.

Kinley looked at her solemnly. "You were the daughter he wanted, Serena," he told her softly. "He always felt that way about you. You know, that you were independent, ready to go it alone, the daughter he wanted."

Serena turned toward him. "We were always close. Very close. Except for the last few weeks. Something changed between us." She shook her head. "No, something changed in *him*."

Kinley shrugged lightly. "Well, a divorce, something like that, it always . . ."

"It wasn't just the divorce," Serena insisted. "It was Daddy. Something about him."

"He was always a little unusual, Serena."

"Something happened to him," Serena said firmly. "He didn't talk about it. But something definitely happened."

"Maybe just the middle-aged blues."

She shook her head determinedly. "No." She glanced about, as if looking for a more private place. "I don't know what to do," she said.

"About what?"

"Daddy. I want to know what drove him away from me."

"Look, Serena, sometimes you just have to . . ."

She shook her head adamantly. "It's better to know, don't you think? Better to know what happened?"

Kinley felt as if he'd been shot back in time, and he was once again in Jefferson's Drug Store, facing her father as he had the afternoon Ray had asked him the same question in the same determined voice. He thought of all the times since then that he'd actually found out "what happened," but had felt no better off for all he'd learned.

"I don't know, Serena, maybe it's not better," he said, an answer that he knew would disappoint her.

Lois arrived an hour later. She wore a plain black skirt and blouse, and looked considerably older than he remembered, as if time had suddenly swept down upon her, done its vulture's dance on her face and eyes.

"Hello, Jack," she said as she stepped over to him.

"Lois."

"How long's it been?"

"Four years, five? I'm not sure."

"Not exactly," Lois said. "I was at your grandmother's funeral."

"You were?"

"I came over, said hello."

"I'm sorry, Lois, a lot of that time . . ."

"A blur, I know," Lois said briskly. "It doesn't matter. I was always just 'Ray's wife' to you anyway."

As she walked away, Kinley wondered if what she'd said were true, if his mind had done its old trick of making people invisible. If so, there was nothing he could have done about it. He had long ago accepted the fact that his mind had its own postures and inclinations. So much so that he sometimes felt it hardly belonged to him at all, that it was something separate, a small gray animal curled up in his skull, peering out from behind his eyes, lurking there, alive and breathing in the dark, airless chamber.

Lois paused at the casket, then, without turning around, walked directly out of the house and into the backyard. From his chair in the living room, Kinley could see her there, her back to him as she stood half concealed by the slender tendrils of the enormous weeping willow that consumed the small backyard. For a moment, she stood very rigidly, her shoulders lifted, her head held slightly upward, as if she were watching the willow's shredded tent as it trembled around her.

A moment later, Serena joined her there, and even from a distance, Kinley could tell they were arguing, a struggle he assumed to be the last exchanges in an Oedipal war whose outcome no longer mattered.

Still, it was clear that the war went forward anyway, and as the seconds passed, it built steadily, the voices

40

growing louder, until Kinley could almost hear the words themselves. It only ended when Lois suddenly glanced toward the house, caught Kinley's silent, staring eyes, and lifted her hand to silence Serena. After that, the two of them walked back inside.

"Serena and I were just discussing the house," Lois said to Kinley as she returned to the living room. "I was trying to give her some advice."

"Well, you could rent it, I suppose," Kinley told them, already uncomfortable in the role of family advisor.

"No," Lois snapped. "I think she should get rid of it. Ray was able to keep it up. But for somebody like Serena, a single woman, living away at college, I think she'd be better off without it."

Serena stared at Kinley pointedly but said nothing.

"She needs to sell it," Lois said. "That's the best thing." She turned back toward the casket. "With him gone, there's . . ." She stopped, let her eyes drift back over to Serena. "There's nothing else to do."

Serena's face grew tense, but she did not speak.

Lois turned to Kinley. "Well, I guess I'll see you at the funeral tomorrow."

"Yes."

She offered him her hand. "Funerals. That's where we seem to have all our meetings."

Kinley shook her hand. "Lois, about last time . . ,"

"Don't worry about it, Jack," Lois said. "I've learned that when people forget you're around, they also stop bothering you." She smiled thinly. "Ray told me what you said, you know."

"Said?"

"Years ago," Lois explained. "When he told you about my mother's death."

Kinley said nothing.

"You were very matter-of-fact, just like always," Lois went on, her intensity building, set to explode. "Your theory was that I'd loved my mother and hated my father, and so I'd decided to make him a murderer."

41

"Yes, I remember that," Kinley said unemphatically, trying not to prime the powder.

"Well, you were wrong, Jack," Lois told him flatly. "I loved my father and hated my mother. But I still had the same suspicions. Can you imagine that?"

With that, she spun around, and headed for the door.

Almost as if moved by the hard waves of an aftershock, Kinley and Serena followed her, watching out the front window as she strode to her car, got in and drove away.

"She's one of those women," Serena said quietly.

"Those women?"

"The kind who never expect anything but hurt," Serena said. "Victims."

Kinley watched as Lois's car headed down the narrow, tree-lined street. He could see her head in silhouette above the driver's seat, a small, dark shape whose look reminded him so much of Maria Spinola that he wondered if some backwoods version of Fenton Norwood was already stalking her, perhaps toying with the lock on her back door.

By mid-afternoon the house was crowded with Ray's neighbors and associates. At first Ray's sister Millie was the only one he'd recognized. But as the hours of the wake passed, he found himself recognizing others, some of them from high school, a smattering of teachers and students, along with other local personalities whose faces he could recall, town figures of one sort or another, grocers, barbers. He could tell that quite a few of them had recognized him, as well. But that was not surprising, since the local paper had plastered his face on the front page every time a new book had been published.

By early evening the house was empty again, and Kinley and Serena walked out on the front porch and sat down in the swing. It was a cool evening, and Serena wrapped herself loosely in one of Ray's old sweaters.

"You didn't really have to stay in the house the whole day," she said.

"I wanted to," Kinley told her.

She smiled delicately. "He would have liked that. He believed in loyalty." She tucked her arm beneath his and let her head drift lazily onto his shoulder. "We used to sit out here when I was a little girl. Just like this. In the night. All snuggled up." She pulled away from him abruptly. "I can't believe he's gone."

"When it happens suddenly like that," Kinley told her, "it always takes some time to adjust."

Serena nodded. She seemed more composed than she'd been earlier in the day.

"When are you going back?" she asked casually.

"The day after tomorrow."

"You can stay here until then," Serena told him. "And I'll go to my mother's place."

"No, that's all right. Like I said, I have a room at the hotel."

"No, stay here," Serena insisted. "Daddy would have wanted you to."

He decided to do as she asked, and later that night he found himself alone in Ray's living room, his eyes watching the casket as it rested in its deep nest of swirling flowers. For a long time, his mind struck him as uncharacteristically blank, as if a kind of numbness had overtaken it, blocking out whatever pain he might otherwise have felt.

He stood up, walked out onto the porch and took in the cool night air. The night was closest to him, and he'd always felt more at home in dark places, the lightless horse stall in which Colin Bright had stacked the bodies of the murdered Comstocks, the small cramped smokehouse, where Mildred Haskell had performed her last experiment on little Billy Flynn, the damp cavern where her husband Edgar had later deposited those tiny, torn remains. Kinley had been in all those places and felt more at ease in them than any of the bright fields he'd flown over in his travels, or the green pastures he'd wandered in, his eyes roaming the grasses in search of that particular place where the earth had been turned up, the body finally uncovered and pulled up from its hidden vault. There was even something in the phrase "brought to light" that had always made him feel ill at ease, as if it were destined finally to drive back the vampire darkness in which he breathed far more comfortably.

After a time, he walked back into the house, and down the short corridor to the room that had been Ray's in high school, and which he'd long ago converted into a small, cramped office.

He stepped inside and closed the door behind him, as if to keep its interior hidden from eyes Ray would not have wanted prying into his private space. There was a small desk, gunmetal gray, with an ancient black type-writer and a single reading lamp. Several cardboard filing drawers had been stacked next to it, their sides bulging with the papers Ray had stuffed inside. Homemade wooden bookshelves took up the walls' remaining space, rising to the ceiling to make a kind of angular pit in which to house the desk. Books were stacked randomly on the shelves, bloating them out, forcing them to buckle, so packed and overburdened they looked as if they were about to snap beneath their heavy loads.

Ray had been the ultimate autodidact, the unschooled, self-educated dabbler in a hundred disparate fields. There were novels of every sort, collections of stories and liter-ary essays, along with works of history, biography, social science, assorted titles that had struck him at the moment. Only one shelf had the look of careful organization, and that was the one devoted to Kinley's books, each standing side by side, as if Ray had taken as much pride in them as Kinley had. One by one, Kinley took them down, read the old inscriptions he'd written year by year: *To my dear friend and fellow crime buff. To the only man whose nose remains with mine on the bloody path. To Ray, my tenth book for your fortieth year.*

When he'd read the last one, Kinley suddenly felt very tired. He walked over to the desk and slumped down in the small swivel chair. From that position, he could see a small rectangle of white paper which Ray had taped to the wall just above his typewriter. It hung in the gray shadow of the bookshelf which hung above the desk, and he had to lean forward and squint slightly in order to make out what it said. It was obviously a line which Ray had read in some kind of essay on mystery writing, an idea that had struck him so powerfully he'd actually taken the time to type it out and tape it to his wall:

> In an age of mass death, the mystery remains the final redoubt of romantic individualism in its insistence that one life, unlawfully taken, still matters so much within the human universe that the failure to discover how and by whom that life was taken contains all we still may know of romantic terror.

Kinley studied the quotation for a moment, his mind shooting back to the train station where Ray had brought him after his grandmother's funeral. There had been something strange in his deep green eyes that day, something Kinley had never quite forgotten. Later he had thought it might be loneliness, or family trouble, or perhaps nothing more than the sort of middle-aged despair he'd seen come and go in scores of his acquaintances. Now he wondered if Ray had been feeling something less ordinary than all that, and that if he'd looked deeper into his old friend's eyes that day, he might have glimpsed his longing for an answer.

Six

At Serena's invitation Kinley rode in the first car behind the hearse, with Lois and Serena opposite him, and Ray's sister Millie and her husband, Grady, at his side. A long serpentine procession followed along behind them, car after car in a twining line that stretched for nearly two miles up the mountainside to the spacious cemetery, where Ray was finally put to rest.

The service was longer than he'd expected, and while one of the local ministers droned on, Kinley found himself thinking again about the last time he'd seen Ray alive, his memory very vivid.

The rain had been falling in great gray sheets along the asphalt railway siding as he'd hopped aboard the northbound train. Ray had remained on the siding, looking up, his green eyes troubled, his voice tense and urgent as he'd spoken his last words before the train shuddered for an instant, then slowly, laboriously made its way forward, Ray trudging along beside it, as if intent on making a final point.

It's hard to sleep, Kinley.
You've always had trouble with that.
How about you?
I sleep fine.

Ray had smiled at Kinley's reply, an eerie, discomforting smile, as if his answer had been full of secret ironies. Then the smile had vanished as quickly as it had appeared, and Ray's face had grown very solemn again. Except for the eyes. They'd continued to search Kinley's face, as if looking for some code for an otherwise indecipherable text.

Kinley, are you . . . ?

It was precisely at that moment the train had jerked ahead, moving steadily faster as Ray had stepped up his pace, trotting beside it now, as if half determined to leap aboard.

Kinley, are you . . . ?

The train was advancing rapidly now, so that Ray was almost running to keep up with it, the rain exploding against his heavily moving body like crystal bullets, until at last, when he could no longer keep up, he'd simply stopped and watched silently as Kinley waved to him. "Bye, Ray," he'd shouted.

But Ray had never returned that last farewell, so that, as Kinley realized now, the preacher's voice a dull murmur in the background, their long friendship had ended with an unfinished and still unanswered question.

Kinley, are you . . . ?

Once the funeral was over, Kinley and Serena returned to the house on Beaumont Street. Kinley took a seat in the living room, his eyes fixed on the now empty space where Ray's coffin had rested only a few hours before.

"They're always moving," Serena said as she sat opposite him in the small, cramped living room. She nodded toward his hands. "Always moving."

47

He pressed them down on the arms of his chair. "It's an old habit. I've had it all my life."

"It's a grasping motion," Serena said, "the way your hands move." She smiled self-consciously. "I took this pop-psychology course in college. They talked about body language." She glanced toward his hands. "What you're always doing with them, it's called a grasping motion."

"Is that supposed to mean something?"

She shrugged. "It's just a nervous response."

"To what?"

She shook her head. "It was just pop-psychology. They didn't go very far into anything."

"I see," Kinley said, his eyes lingering on the bare area of floor where Ray's casket had once been.

Serena studied him a moment, as if unsure. "There's something I have to tell you." She hesitated. "I wasn't going to mention it, but I think I should."

"What is it?"

"Somebody went through Daddy's office the afternoon he died."

"How do you know?"

"Because when I came in the next day, it looked sort of different."

"Messed up?"

"Just the opposite," Serena said. "Straightened up. Everything neat and orderly, the way Daddy would never have left it." She stopped, waited for him to respond, then continued when he didn't. "And something else," she said pointedly. "You know that file cabinet in his office?"

"Yes."

"Several files were missing. Whole letters. Three of them: D, O and S. Everything in those files was gone. The folders were there, but there was nothing in them."

"Maybe there'd never been anything in them," Kinley told her.

Serena shook her head adamantly. "No, there had to have been."

48

"How do you know?"

"Because Daddy only made a file when he had something to put in it. There's no X or Z because he never had anything to file under those letters."

Kinley nodded.

"And I looked at the empty folders, too," Serena added, "the ones for D, O and S. They were stretched and cracked at the seam. I've worked in file cabinets long enough to know that that only happens when the files have had things in them. Usually lots of things, not just a few pieces, enough to weight the folders down."

"D, O, S," Kinley said softly. "Any idea what was in them?"

"No."

"Old cases? New ones?"

"It could have been either kind."

"Did he file things under names or subjects?"

"Both."

"That makes things a little complicated," Kinley said.

Serena waved her hand. "But that's the way he was," she said. "Complicated. That's why it bothers me, the missing files. They could have been about anything."

Later that night, Kinley found it difficult to sleep, so he wandered down the corridor to Ray's office and checked the files himself. In the yellowish light that came from the desk lamp in Ray's cramped office, he pulled out the upper file drawer to see if any other files were missing. They were all in place, all of them but the letters Serena had mentioned. He checked the file folders and noticed all the same things Serena had. There was no doubt that a great deal of material had once been in the folders, and that all of it was gone.

For a long time, Kinley remained in Ray's office, randomly fingering the remaining files, as if trying to soak up something of the spirit that had ruminated there, studying the crimes and misdemeanors of his native ground.

49

They seemed almost trivial, a world of petty larcenies and family squabbles that never soared toward the dark envelope Kinley pressed against continually in his own books. How could Dottie Adair's occasional forgeries compare with what Mildred Haskell had done to her neighbor's son, or Old Man Adams's public drunkenness to Colin Bright's demonic games?

Toward midnight, still unable to sleep, he left the office and walked into the living room. The smell of the funeral flowers lingered all around him, now sickeningly sweet, like the smell of something gone to ruin. To get away from it, he quickly pulled on his clothes and walked to his car, edging it quietly down the nightbound street so as not to disturb his less troubled neighbors.

He turned left at the end of Beaumont Street, then right again when he reached the town's main avenue. The shops and service stations were sleeping too, lights out, shades drawn, a world that looked as if it had been abandoned by everything but silence.

On a whim, he headed up the mountain, moving slowly along its narrow path, until he reached the top, then drove on until he found himself at the cemetery again. He walked across the flat green lawn to the little mound of earth where Ray slept through his first night in the ground.

He knelt down slightly, carefully edging himself away from the recently turned earth. If he'd had a prayer, he might have said it, but his long years of trailing the Colin Brights and Fenton Norwoods of the world had stripped him of any notion that a loving, guiding hand directed anything. If there were any hand at work, he sometimes thought, it was one that should have been severed before the world completed its first spin.

Still, it seemed a time for words, and so he said the only ones he could think of, the same ones he'd said that rainy afternoon as Ray ran alongside the train: "Bye, Ray."

He felt his fingers curl up in that grasping motion Serena had noticed, and it seemed to him that in some

50

way they were reaching for Ray, trying to grab a few strands of his red hair and pull him up out of the clay. It was an odd sensation, more powerful than anything he'd felt in a long time, and remarkably different from what he'd felt at his grandmother's burial. A month before, as she'd been lowered into the ground, he'd felt a curious relief. With his mother and father dead, she had been the final depository of his early history, and in a sense her own death had completed his journey toward isolation, had released him forever from all blood-based obligations. It was a feeling of liberation that Ray had been able to sense, Kinley remembered now, and as they'd walked out of the little cemetery together, Ray had glanced over, smiled his crooked, enigmatic smile, and said, "Well, it's over for you, Kinley."

Now, as he turned and walked back toward his car, Kinley found himself once again amazed at how intuitive Ray had been, and he wondered if Serena had inherited the same eerie skill, if perhaps her suspicions about the missing files were more than a distraction from her grief.

He was still considering it as he headed back along the winding mountain road that descended toward the valley. About halfway down, he stopped at the small scenic overlook the city fathers had recently erected for the benefit of Sequoyah's occasional tourists. From the railing that lined the steep precipice, he could see all of Sequoyah, like a body lying faceup before him, its slender backbone of roofs and spires spreading for several miles up and down the valley. It had changed very little since his boyhood, and he could still remember his grandmother's grim warnings about the kind of life that was lived there. "Not good for us," she had always told him. If Serena were right, he thought now, perhaps it had not been very good for Ray Tindall either, and he wondered if, after so many years, Ray might pose the same question he'd asked once in Jefferson's Drug Store: *It's better to know, don't you think, Kinley? No matter what the cost?*

Seven

As he sipped his coffee the next morning, standing thoughtfully over the sink in Ray's small kitchen, he decided to go about it exactly as he would have if he'd decided to write a book about Ray's death. He would rely on all the devices he'd learned through the years, and with a little luck, he might be able either to confirm Serena's suspicions or put them to rest. He would begin with the most fundamental data that could be gathered about Ray's death, see where it led, if anywhere, and then proceed to the next stage of investigation, or end it decisively, with no loose ends to flutter distractedly in Serena's mind.

He arrived at the District Attorney's office at nine sharp. It was on the third floor of the courthouse, but Kinley decided to take the stairs anyway, his old impatience driving him forward, invisible whips forever lashing at his back.

Warfield had not arrived at his office yet, but his assistant had, a small, very lean man, whose white bony hand felt like a clump of sticks when Kinley shook it.

"Bill Stover," the man said by way of introduction. "I'm the Assistant District Attorney."

Kinley nodded. "Jack Kinley," he said. "I was a friend of Ray Tindall's."

"You're the writer, aren't you?"

"Yes."

"Yeah, Ray talked about you once in a while."

Kinley smiled thinly. "I was wondering if you'd mind my taking a look at the autopsy report on Ray."

Stover looked surprised by the request. "Autopsy report?" he asked. "On Ray?"

"Yes," Kinley answered, his voice a little more stern, playing the part of the reporter who knows his rights and will not be denied.

"Well, I suppose it would be okay to show you that," Stover said hesitantly.

"I have Serena Tindall's approval," Kinley told him.

"Yeah, that's fine," Stover said. "I'll get it for you."

"And one other thing," Kinley added, stopping him in mid-turn. "I'd like to see the police report."

"Police report?" Stover said. "What do you mean? There was no investigation of Ray's death."

"Well, according to the paper, a couple of county deputies went to see the body," Kinley said.

"Yes, that's right," Stover said. "But . . ."

"They would have written up a report, wouldn't they?" Kinley asked. "It's standard procedure."

Stover shrugged. "Sure, but I don't think there'd be much in it."

"Photographs," Kinley said. "Initial observations. There's a place on the form for those, isn't there?"

Stover nodded. "I see you know your way around police work."

Kinley gave him a quick smile. "Cops always fill those lines in. Sometimes it's no more than a weather report, but there's always something. I've never seen it left blank."

"Now that you mention it," Stover said with a certain

studied amiability, "I don't think I've ever seen it left blank either."

"So, just those reports, and the autopsy," Kinley told him. "Then I'll leave you to your work."

"No trouble at all, Mr. Kinley," Stover said. "Come with me."

Kinley followed Stover out of the office and into a small witness room off the main courtroom.

"Just have a seat," Stover said. "I'll bring everything to you."

Kinley sat down behind the wooden table at the center of the room and waited. Outside the single small window to his left, he could see Sequoyah's main street as it stretched westward, the dark wall of the mountain rising high above it, silent, immense, the "place of spirits," as his grandmother had always called it, though whether she'd considered them good or evil had been a secret she'd taken with her to the grave.

"Here you are, sir," Stover said as he walked back into the room. He pushed a small manila folder across the desk toward Kinley. "That's all we have. As you know, there wasn't really any need for an investigation."

"Thanks," Kinley said.

"Fine," Stover said. "Take as long as you like. Court's not in session this week, so nobody'll be needing the witness rooms."

Once Stover had eased himself back out of the room, Kinley opened the manila folder and drew its contents onto the table. He read the autopsy first, coolly going over the details, mindful as he always was of the way its language reduced a human life to pounds and ounces. The first line set the tone, describing Ray as a "middle-aged Caucasian" who measured a certain number of centimeters and weighed a certain number of grams, his old friend's life reduced to its humble, nameless mass.

Still, the language had never bothered Kinley, and there were even times when he thought of it as being very much like himself, methodical, scientific, decidedly "matter-of-fact," just as Lois had described him. There was no room in an autopsy report for love or grief or pity, although from time to time, he'd noticed, a hint of feeling did emerge from the otherwise passive language. Words like "brutal" or "devastating" replaced the more often used "traumatic," as scientific objectivity fell away one adjective at a time.

Dr. Joseph Stark, the Sequoyah County Coroner, however, had shown no such lapses in Case Number 57343, JOE RAY TINDALL. His language had remained utterly controlled, and what it narrated was unquestionably a natural death. He had found no indication of external trauma on Ray's body, not so much as a scratch other than the small red ones which had occurred as Ray's face had slammed onto the ground. There were no puncture marks on his skin or "foreign substances" in his bloodstream or his stomach. By all appearances, he had died a healthy man, except for a problem with his heart, a massive infarction which had suddenly and solidly blocked the passage of blood from one chamber to the next and killed Ray Tindall as quickly and decisively as a shotgun blast to the chest. He'd only had enough time to fall to the ground and claw blearily at the earth for his few remaining seconds, a reflex that had resulted in a small deposit of reddish clay beneath his nails.

Kinley closed the coroner's report, took a quick breath, then went on to the police report he found in the same envelope. It was a simple, one-page form, what the police called an Incident Report, and it catalogued the few facts that were ascertainable without further investigation. According to the report, the Sheriff's Department had logged in a call at 3:30 P.M. It had been made by a man named Austin Phillips, who had told the operator that he'd found the body of a man in the canyon. The radio dispatcher had subsequently ordered Deputies Jerry Taylor and Herman Fitzgerald to the scene. It was Deputy Taylor who'd filled out the report.

According to Taylor, he and Fitzgerald had arrived at

Sims Grocery at 3:39 P.M., where they had found Mr. Phillips waiting for them. Minutes later he had led them down into the canyon, where they'd found Ray Tindall lying face down, one arm at his side, the other stretched out over his head. Once on the scene, the two officers had radioed for an ambulance, then surveyed the general area while they waited for it to arrive. During those same few minutes, Deputy Taylor had taken a few photographs with a simple Polaroid camera. The fact that he had done so was the only notation in the "Comments" section of the form. It was a plain, forthright notation. "As Mr. Tindall was an officer of the court, Deputy Taylor took several pictures of the scene for later use should they be necessary."

The pictures were clipped to the back of the report, and Kinley turned his attention to them immediately. There were five of them, each shot from a different angle. It was the usual way investigators moved, circling the body slowly, taking a shot every few steps, so that at the end of the process, the body had been photographed at 360 degrees.

The pictures showed exactly what the two officers had already described in their report. Ray's body was sprawled out over the dark pebbly ground just as they had noted, one arm at his side, the other flung out over his head as if he'd been reaching for something in his final, desperate seconds. He was fully clothed, and all his clothes were intact, no rips, tears, or any other signs of struggle. His shoes remained on his feet, and his reading glasses were still in his pocket.

Kinley glanced through the pictures a final time. From their background he could easily recognize the spot where Ray had died. He could see the huge gray stone they'd sometimes rested upon after rambling for hours along the canyon floor. But then, he thought, as he clipped the pictures back to the incident report, it would have been hard to find any place in the canyon they had not been together. The only thing that made it different was that this time Ray had gone alone.

He returned the pictures and report to the envelope and walked back into the District Attorney's office.

"Thanks a lot," he said as he returned the envelope to Stover.

"Mr. Warfield's in, if you'd like to see him now," Stover said.

"Maybe for just a minute," Kinley told him, "just to say thanks."

"Sure," Stover said. He pointed to an open door just across the room. "He's in there. You can just pop your head in."

Kinley did exactly that. "I just wanted to thank you for letting me read the report," he said without coming fully into the room.

Warfield looked up from behind his desk. He was a medium-sized man with a thickish build and small, nearly bald head, and he had the beleaguered, overworked look that Kinley had noticed before in rural civil servants.

"No trouble at all, Mr. Kinley," Warfield said. "Did you find what you were looking for?"

Kinley shrugged. "I wasn't really sure what I was looking for."

"Bill said you were interested in the autopsy and police report," Warfield said. He smiled. "It doesn't take a genius to figure it out."

"Serena had some questions," Kinley said.

"Really? What about?"

"She thinks a few things are missing from Ray's office, the one he had at home. Some files."

"What kind of files?"

"She doesn't know," Kinley admitted. "And neither do I."

"But the fact that they're missing, it's raised suspicions about his death? Foul play, I mean."

Kinley nodded silently.

Warfield leaned back in his seat. "Did you find any signs of that?"

"No."

Warfield looked at him gravely. "I would certainly want to know if you did, Mr. Kinley," he said. "I am the District Attorney after all."

"You'd have been the first person I'd have told," Kinley assured him, lying through his teeth, and yet not exactly sure who would have been the first person.

Kinley's assurance seemed to lighten Warfield's mood. "Well, that doesn't change the tragedy of it, though, does it?" he asked.

"No, it doesn't."

"You were close to Ray, I understand."

"We were old friends."

Warfield nodded sagely. "Well, the way it is now, with everybody rushing around, most people don't have old friends. They don't have time for them."

"Not many, that's true."

Warfield leaned back in his chair, now considerably more relaxed. "Well, if there's anything else I can do for you, I hope you let me know."

"I don't think there's anything," Kinley answered.

Warfield gave him a sweet, avuncular smile. "Well, if you need anything at all," he said, "we like to keep an open door to the public here in the office."

After leaving the courthouse, Kinley drove across town to his old high school, parked in its cramped parking lot, and made his way inside the building. The same hallways greeted him like faces from his youth, the trophy box at the front, the school flag draped on the far wall, the brass statue of the school mascot, a snarling bobcat, fangs exposed, claws ripping fiercely at the air. He could remember the first day he'd walked into the building, a mountain boy whose only reputation was that he lived with a crazy old woman and possessed an inexplicable brilliance that a ''bunch of Yankees'' had somehow discovered, and which everyone thought terribly, terribly important. For a time, the other kids had shied away from him, as if his mind were a flailing electric wire they wanted to avoid. Ray had been the only one to approach him, and as he lingered for a moment outside the school's office, he realized that the approach itself had happened in this very corridor, and that when he'd first glimpsed Ray's hulking figure, he'd thought him the dim-witted school bully who'd been sent to beat him up. He'd even flinched at Ray's first words: *You're the smart one, right*?

''You're Jack Kinley, aren't you?''

Kinley turned to see a tiny woman with blue hair and thick glasses. It was Mrs. Potts, his old English teacher; now close to eighty, she seemed hardly to have aged at all since his high school days.

''Mercy, Jack, what are you doing here?''

''I'm in town for a few days.''

''Oh, of course you are,'' Mrs. Potts said. ''For Ray's funeral, I bet.''

''That's right.''

''Well, mercy, Jack, you sure haven't changed much,'' Mrs. Potts said. She grinned impishly. ''You just reminiscing here, now?''

''Not exactly,'' Kinley said, then realized that he had very little to reminisce about for all his four long years at Sequoyah High. There'd been no love to set his heart ablaze, nor even that first frenzied sexual encounter. Instead, he'd graduated a stone-cold virgin, almost the same aloof, unapproachable senior as he had been a shy, remote freshman. Only Ray had been able to pierce the wall he'd built around him, flinging himself over it heedlessly and shamelessly: *You're the smart one, right*?

''Are you back for long, Jack?''

Kinley focused his attention on Mrs. Potts again. ''No, I don't think so,'' he said. ''Actually, I was looking for Serena Tindall.''

''Serena works up on the second floor,'' Mrs. Potts

said, "but if you'll wait right here, I'll go get her for you."

"Thanks, I'd appreciate that."

Serena came down the far staircase a few minutes later. She was wearing a light blue dress with a white collar, and reminded Kinley very slightly of Lois as she'd looked in high school, tall and willowy, but with something heavy about her, a figure slogging through the air, her fingers gripped brutally to a pencil as if it were a spike.

"I went to the District Attorney's Office this morning," Kinley told her. "I read the autopsy report. I read the police report, too."

Serena appeared to brace herself. "What did you find out?"

"He died of a heart attack, Serena," Kinley said flatly, "and unfortunately, there was nothing in any report to indicate a reason why he was in the canyon." He shrugged. "As to the files that were taken from his office, I really don't have any idea about that."

"All right, then," Serena said coolly.

Kinley touched her shoulder. "Sorry, but there just wasn't anything to go on."

Serena pulled away from him slightly. "I understand."

"So, the thing is," Kinley added hesitantly, "I thought I'd just do one more thing."

Serena looked at him quizzically. "What?"

"Talk to Dr. Stark," Kinley told her. "Sometimes the written autopsy's not the whole story, especially in a case like this, where there'd be no reason to look for anything strange. It's a long shot, but when you talk to people, they remember things."

Serena smiled appreciatively. "Daddy told me that he wanted you to have something of his," she said finally. "I have it in my car." She motioned him forward. "Come with me, I'll get it."

Kinley followed her to the car, then stood by silently as she opened the glove compartment and withdrew a thick book. It was a large book.

"It's in here," Serena said as she opened it.

Inside, Ray had pressed a small piece of brown forest vine.

Kinley picked it up and held it gently.

"He gave it to me a week ago," Serena said. "He wanted me to tell you that since you never made it there, he went and got it for you."

Kinley smiled softly, remembering their first adventure together.

"He never let anything drop," Serena said.

"No, he didn't," Kinley said, his eyes staring with a sudden unexplainable distance at the vine, as if his mind were drawing him away once again, reminding him of the perils of too much feeling. "Ray never forgot anything."

Eight

The coroner of Cherokee County was also one of its oldest citizens. When Kinley had first noticed his signature on the autopsy, he'd doubted it could be the same Dr. Joseph Stark who'd treated his sudden asthmatic attacks as a boy. But as the door to Stark's office opened, and he saw the old man rise slowly from behind his desk, he instantly recognized the dark eyes that had stared down at him in his youth. They were quiet eyes, but piercing as well, and Kinley had never really forgotten the curious way they'd seemed to watch him distantly from the other end of the long black stethoscope. Now, as the door swung open and Kinley stepped inside the doctor's office, he realized that they had changed very little. Stark's hair had gone silver and the skin of his face had slackened and turned pale, but the dark eyes seemed eternal, beyond the grip of time.

"Little Jack Kinley," the old man said, his voice now trembling slightly, the full lower lip pulled rudely downward at the left, so that Kinley realized that he must still be recovering from a stroke.

"Hello, Dr. Stark," Kinley said gently as he approached the desk. "It's good to see you again."

The eyes widened slightly. "Are you still a sufferer, my boy?"

Kinley looked at him quizzically. "Sufferer?"

"From those terrible attacks you used to have," Stark explained. "The asthma."

Kinley shook his head. "No, not anymore. I guess I finally outgrew it."

Stark looked pleased to hear it. "Not uncommon with that disorder," he said, "but I'm sure you know that as you grow old, you may come to be afflicted again." He shrugged softly. "The nature of things. Nothing to be done." He tried to smile, but the effort seemed to exhaust him. "Nature is not benign. We only like to think it is." He leaned back in his chair and folded his small hands over his old-fashioned white lab coat. "You are lucky to be alive, my boy," he said, almost wonderingly. "Do you remember that night?"

"What night?"

"So hot," Stark added. "A summer night."

Kinley shook his head.

"It was the first time I saw you," Stark said. "The attack, the one that was so bad. You were turning blue. You were holding your breath."

"Holding it?"

"You wouldn't try to breathe," Stark explained. "You were too exhausted."

Again, Kinley shook his head. "I remember lots of attacks, but not that one."

"You must have been about three years old," Stark told him. "And you were suffocating. Turning blue, like I said. It was terrible, the worst case I'd ever seen." His eyes took on a grave sense of concentration, as if memory were a pressure in his head. "The old woman brought

63

you in. I thought you were already dead. We tried an injection, but it didn't work. You wouldn't breathe, so I thought of something else, one last try. We put you in a car and drove as fast as we could. Your grandmother held your head out the window as we drove, so the air would be forced down into your lungs."

Kinley stared at him curiously. "I don't remember that," he said quietly, as if, for once, his mind had deserted him, an unexpected vacancy he found disturbing, as if he'd been betrayed. For a moment, he tried to recall the incident Dr. Stark had described, but found that his mind would not retrieve it for him, but simply left it like one of those fearful voids ancient cartographers had indicated on their maps: *Terra Incognita*. "I don't remember that particular attack," he said again.

Stark nodded contentedly. "Well, that's the glory of childhood," he said quietly. "You can forget such evil things." He shrugged helplessly. "Old men, on the other hand, we are doomed to remember everything." His head drifted slightly to the left, as if an invisible support had suddenly given way, and allowed the great white hill to shift. "Death was very close to you that night."

"Yes, I suppose it was."

Stark made a lunging motion with both hands, as if grasping for something invisible in the air. "Death was snatching at you," he whispered, "just like that."

Kinley stepped back reflexively, as if away from the grasping hands. His mind raced backward, gathering in the days and nights of his long affliction, but always returning empty of this particular brush with death. He fought to return to the present. "Actually, I came by to talk to you about another death."

Stark nodded but said nothing.

"The autopsy you did on Ray Tindall's body."

Stark motioned toward the chair in front of his desk. "Please, have a seat." He smiled delicately. "There's no rush. I only have a little bit of my practice left. Most people prefer a young doctor." Again, he shrugged.

"The nature of things." He lifted his slightly trembling hands. "They prefer a steady grasp."

Kinley sat down. "In the report, you're pretty clear about the cause of Ray's death," he began. "That it was caused by a heart attack."

"Yes, I am," Stark said. "There wasn't much room for doubt. It was massive. As massive as I've ever seen."

"Were you Ray's doctor?"

Stark nodded. "Yes, I was. All his life, I don't think he ever went to anyone else." Once again he lifted his hands. "They were still good enough for him."

Kinley kept his eyes on Stark's face. "His heart, you knew it had problems?"

"Oh, yes, certainly," Stark said. "I'd known it for a long time."

"How long?"

"In specifics, for several years," Stark said. "In general, since he was born."

"Since he was born?" Kinley asked. "What do you mean?"

"I knew his father, and Ray was like him," Stark explained. "You inherit that sort of thing, you know, maladies of the heart."

"So his was a congenital condition?"

"In a manner of speaking."

"And you'd been treating him?"

"As much as I could."

"What do you mean?"

"Not all patients are the same," Dr. Stark said. "Not all of them care about themselves."

"And Ray was like that?"

"Toward the end, he was," Stark said firmly. "I had warned him time and again that he needed to slow down. He was a smoker, and toward the end, he drank too much, as if he were trying to make things worse." He shook his head. "But even if he'd done everything I told him, took all my advice down to the last thing, I'm not sure it would have mattered in the end." He shrugged. "The fact is,

Ray Tindall was born to die pretty much when he did, and that's something not much can be done about." His eyes filled with a grim wonderment. "Every chromosome has a death certificate written on it."

Kinley was not so fatalistic. "Was he taking any medication?"

"No," Stark answered. "Just the opposite. He was doing everything wrong."

"Wrong?"

"Well, besides the smoking and drinking, he didn't need to be doing anything strenuous," Stark said authoritatively. "And look where they found him? Way down there at the bottom of the canyon." He shook his head with exasperation. "He didn't drive a car down there, you know. He had to have walked all the way." He looked at Kinley pointedly. "And you used to live up there, you know what that canyon's like."

Kinley leaned forward slightly. "Did he mention that he was going down there to you?"

"Absolutely not," Stark said. "If he had, I would have just pulled out a pistol and said, 'Here, Ray, just shoot yourself. It's the same thing, and it'll save us all the trouble having to hunt for you.'"

"And he knew that?" Kinley asked. "How dangerous it would be for him to go down there?"

"Sure, he did," Dr. Stark said. "I'd told him a hundred times that he ought to stay away from anything strenuous." He took in a long, slow breath. "In a way, Ray killed himself. Or at least, he might as well have. And he knew it, too." He shook his head wearily. "But what can you do with a man like Ray Tindall? Nothing. Just tell him not to do something, then sit back and watch him do it."

"Do you have any idea what he might have been doing down in the canyon?" Kinley asked.

The old man eased himself forward and firmly planted his elbows on the top of his desk. "Sometimes there are no answers for things like that," he said. "I've been coroner for a long time, and I've seen a few things I never could clear up." He tapped a single index finger at the side of his head. "The questions, they stay up here," he said quietly. "Always up here. Night and day." The eyes grew curiously intense, shining toward Kinley like two small gray lights. "You wonder what happened," he said very softly, almost in a distant whisper, as if he'd suddenly sunk into a daze. "But it's not for you to know."

He was tossing uneasily on the sofa in the front room, his mind locked in a vaporous half-sleep of floating shadows, when he heard someone's knock at the door. He rose sluggishly, his head still heavy as if filled with water, trudged to the door and opened it.

Lois stared at him from behind the gray metal veil of the screen. "I need to talk to you," she said edgily. "Right now, Jack."

Kinley opened the door and stepped aside to let her pass.

She walked directly into the living room, then spun around to face him. "What is this I hear about your staying around to look into Ray's death . . . or is it his life you're looking into?" She drove her right fist into her side. "What exactly are you looking into, Jack?"

Kinley tried to focus on her slender frame, but his eyes kept blurring, as if trying to block a clearer view. "You want something to drink, Lois?" he asked, stalling for time, waiting for his mind to regain its old control.

"Drink?" Lois asked. The offer seemed to strike her like a slap in her face. "No, Jack, I don't want a goddamn drink. I want to know what the hell you're up to. What is it? Tell me right now. I'm not leaving until you do. Other people may be intimidated by you, but I'm not. You need to understand that, Jack. I knew you when you were a wheezy little boy, and I want to know why you're sticking your nose in Ray's business."

Kinley walked into the living room and eased himself down on the sofa. "I was just checking a few things for Serena," he said wearily.

"Yes, she told me that much," Lois snapped. "What about, exactly?"

"How he died," Kinley said with a shrug. "What he might have been doing before that."

Lois let out a quick, exasperated breath. "I knew it. You want to solve something. The big-time writer's having a mid-life crisis. It's not good enough just to write about a crime, you've got to solve one."

Kinley rubbed his eyes, and suddenly she seemed to walk out of the blur, tall and slender and wired for explosion.

"There were a few things that were bothering Serena," Kinley told her. "I thought I might help her clear things up."

"Like what?"

"Well, for one thing, what Ray was doing in the canyon," Kinley said. "Nobody seems to understand that."

"Nobody?"

"Well, Serena, for one."

"And did you find that out?"

"No."

"All right, what else?"

"Well, according to Serena, somebody went through Ray's files after he died."

Lois looked at him knowingly. "Yes, someone did, Jack," she said hotly. "Me. I went through his files. Who did you think it was, some deranged killer?"

Kinley's eyes fell upon her steadily. "You went through Ray's files?"

"Yes, and I took what I wanted."

Kinley leaned forward slightly. "What did you take, Lois?"

Lois hesitated a moment. "I don't want you snooping into Ray's life," she said. "I have good reasons for that, believe me. Just don't do it. It won't help Ray, and it certainly won't help Serena.''

"What files, Lois?" Kinley demanded evenly. "I'm not doing this for the fun of it. If there's no reason for me to stay in Sequoyah, believe me, I'll be out of here tomorrow."

She looked at him snidely. "Still too good for it, huh, Jack?"

Kinley said nothing.

"That's what Ray thought, you know," she added. "That you were too good for it."

"Let's just say, I'll go as soon as I can," Kinley told her.

Kinley's last words seemed to assure rather than irritate her, and Kinley watched, astonished, as she calmly sat down in the large wooden rocker opposite the sofa.

"Look, Jack, Serena worshipped Ray," she said. "Absolutely worshipped him. I don't want anything to ruin the way she always thought about him."

"She said they'd grown apart during the last month or so," Kinley said. "That's one of the things that's bothering her."

Lois nodded. "Yes, I know."

"She needs to know why."

Lois looked at him imploringly. "She can't ever be allowed to know that, Jack."

"Do you know why?"

"Yes, I do," Lois answered. "It's the same reason I want you to go home and let this whole thing drop."

"What is it?"

"Serena's precious, oh-so-perfect father was having a love affair, Jack," Lois said. "It's what brought on the divorce a few months ago. We never told Serena. Ray really insisted on that. He was willing to give up everything for that." She shrugged. "Not that the marriage was ever such a great thing. It wasn't. But I loved him. He was a complicated man. I always knew that. But considering the pickings around here, Ray was the best thing around." She shook her head. "Anyway, when I found out he was dead, I came here and quickly snatched the files that might have had any reference to her, any letters, notes, anything." She smiled sadly. "Ray was such a pack rat, I knew he'd keep anything she ever gave him, and that he'd probably file it under her name, so I took all the files that had her initials in them."

"Which were?"

"Well, her full name is Sarah Dora Overton," Lois said matter-of-factly. "So those were the files I took."

"S, D and O," Kinley repeated.

"That's right," Lois said. She smiled grimly. "But, as it turned out, there was nothing about her in any of them. In the S file there was nothing but just old pictures of the town. Sequoyah, I mean. Ray fancied himself a sort of town historian, you know."

Kinley nodded.

"And the O, that was just a bunch of newspaper clippings."

"What about D?" Kinley asked.

Lois shrugged. "That one was empty."

Kinley nodded. "So there was nothing about this woman in any of the files?"

"No."

"So where is it?" Kinley asked. "The stuff about her?"

For a moment, Lois appeared off-balance, her own doubts rising, despite all her efforts to suppress them. Then her old resolve once again asserted itself, and her face grew very solemn. "I don't know, Jack," she began. "And I don't want to know." She glared at him determinedly. "It's enough that they're not here for Serena to find out about it all. And if you keep this up, this looking into Ray's death, you'll probably find out where his precious little love notes are, and when you do, Serena will find out about everything, too." She leaned toward him, her face softening almost to a look of pleading. "Please, don't do that, Jack," she said. "Serena thinks her father was a perfect man. Let her think it."

"Where does she live, Overton?"

Lois hesitated.

"It's easy to find out, Lois," Kinley told her.

Lois stared at him silently.

"Look, maybe she can put it all to rest," Kinley told her. "Maybe she can tell me where everything is. It's even possible that he'd gone down to the canyon to meet her. If she can clear a few things up, then I can do the same for Serena."

Lois still appeared doubtful. "Would you be that careful?" she asked.

"I'm not here to destroy a father's reputation," Kinley said firmly. "Particularly Ray's."

"All right," Lois said. "She doesn't live in Sequoyah. She lives up on the mountain. At the end of that same road where the cemetery is, the one where Ray's buried."

Kinley recalled the previous night when he'd been at Ray's grave, and his mind immediately did its miraculous trick of providing him with a fully detailed photograph. He saw the sweep of the cemetery with its crop of short, gray stones, then the wall of dark forest which lay beyond it, and somewhere deep within it, far in the distance, the small yellow light of a farmhouse near the mountain's rim. "Near the edge," he said. "She lives near the edge."

Lois nodded. "In more ways than one," she said.

Nine

The road narrowed after it passed the cemetery, curving sharply toward the mountain's edge, the undergrowth closing in around the car so that the yellow beams of its headlights seemed to be moving down a long green funnel. The dusty light that filtered through the surrounding trees and brush narrowed as the woods thickened, then suddenly diffused as he neared the black rim of the mountain.

Even from a distance, he could see where the great granite precipice stretched out before him, the night air spilling over it like an ebony waterfall. At the very edge, the road swung abruptly to the left, and he found himself headed down a narrow path which skirted the rim for nearly half a mile. At its end, he saw the small farmhouse he'd glimpsed the night before, wood-framed and unpainted, with a small swing on its slumped front porch.

He brought the car to a halt, shut off the lights and sat motionlessly behind the wheel. If this was the place Ray had come for love, he had chosen it well. It was small and remote, a place where he need fear only the gossip of the birds.

He got out of the car and headed toward the house. He was only halfway to its front steps when a woman stepped out onto the porch.

"I'm Jack Kinley," he said as he continued forward.

The woman had stopped before reaching the edge of the porch, her body in deep shadow.

"I'm looking for a woman named Sarah Dora Overton," he added quickly.

"I'm Dora Overton," the woman said. She stepped forward boldly, and the light from inside the house swept over her. She was very dark, her skin a color he would have called "Moorish" had he envisioned writing about her. Her hair was long, and he could see its reddish tint despite the subdued light.

He offered a quick, edgy smile. "You live quite a ways back."

The woman nodded crisply. "Always have."

It was a husky voice, but with a hard, unforgiving edge that reminded him instantly of other voices he'd heard in his work. Mildred Haskell's, for example, soft, but with a stony undertone, a voice that had made terrible demands: *All right now, boy, turn over on your back.*

As he continued forward, she looked at him piercingly, with eyes that matched the voice, and which probed him openly, like fingertips.

"What do you want?" she asked.

"Lois Tindall told me about you," Kinley began, "and I . . ."

"Lois Tindall doesn't know a thing about me," Dora said sharply.

"Well, she knew you were seeing Ray," Kinley said as gently as he could, removing any hint of judgment or accusation.

Dora stared at him coldly. "What difference does that make now?"

Kinley remained silent, concentrating on her eyes, black and merciless.

Dora took another step toward him, her whole body now in the light. "I didn't lie to Ray," she said firmly, "and I didn't let him lie to me."

"I don't think he would have tried," Kinley said.

He'd meant it as a compliment, but it hadn't worked. Instead, he could see her harden toward him.

"Ray's dead," she said flatly, closing the book on the matter.

Kinley remained in place. "I was Ray's friend," he said, giving the only credentials he thought she might respect.

"He talked about you sometimes," she said. "He would write to you, but you never wrote back."

"He told you that?"

Dora nodded slowly, her eyes growing less hostile. "Anyway, he's gone."

Kinley watched silently as she moved to the edge of the porch and leaned against one of its supporting posts. There was something in her presence that seemed too large for the small house. He had known other such presences, but it had always been a looming and gigantic malevolence which had dwarfed the basements, bedrooms and corridors they'd briefly occupied.

"He never mentioned you," Kinley said. "But then, we hadn't spoken very often in the last few weeks."

"He was old-fashioned," Dora said off-handedly, a casual relaying of information. "He kept things to himself."

"Yes, he did," Kinley said softly.

She shifted her eyes to the left and stared out over the edge of the mountain. "You never know for sure what's going on in someone else." She returned to Kinley. "Why did you come up here?" she asked.

"I'm not sure."

"Lois doesn't have to worry about anything," Dora

74

said. "Serena either. I'm not after anything Ray left behind."

"I don't think that's a matter of concern," Kinley said, his own words sounding formal to him, a lawyer's standard line.

"What's the trouble, then?"

"I guess Serena wants to know a little bit more about Ray," Kinley said.

"Not from me," Dora said determinedly. "Ray wanted it private, and that's how it's going to stay."

Kinley looked at her intently. "I guess I want to know a little bit more about him, too."

Dora thought a moment, as if trying to find exactly the right words. She only spoke when she'd found them. "I told Ray something, and he believed me. No one ever had believed me before." She smiled, but edgily. "It was a new experience for me."

"What did you tell him?"

"About my father," Dora said. "I think that in the end, he wanted to know as much as I did."

"Know what?"

The smiled opened slightly, as if against her will. "Ray used to say that there are two kinds of people, the ones who can sleep, and the ones who can't."

Kinley's mind replayed its tape of his last meeting with Ray: *Do you sleep well, Kinley?*

"Ray had problems sleeping, didn't he?" he asked.

"Toward the end, I guess he did," Dora said.

Kinley could feel his little notebook rustle slightly in his jacket pocket, as if it were a small animal rousing itself from sleep. "What was he looking for?"

She thought a moment, her eyes resting on him languidly. "I thought he might have told you."

"Told me what?"

She shook her head slowly. "I trusted Ray. But I don't know anything about you." A thin smile crossed her lips as she continued to study him. "You learn a few things,"

75

she said. "The lessons of the road, like Ray always said." The smile vanished. "The rest is bullshit."

He stared at her intently. "What was Ray doing in the canyon?" he asked again.

She glanced back into the house. "He liked it here," she said, "but he never felt comfortable."

Kinley shrugged. "It wasn't home," he said, matter-of-factly. "It never is."

She studied him a moment, as if trying to get a grip on some remote element of his character. "Ray said you were smart," she said. "He said you were a genius."

Kinley said nothing.

She stepped over to the door and opened it. "You want to come in?"

For a moment, Kinley hesitated, his mind suddenly rushing through all those other moments of hesitation he had studied in his books: little Billy Flynn at Mildred Haskell's smokehouse door; Wilma Jean Comstock at the edge of the woods; Kelly Pierce staring mutely toward the corridor's unlighted end. All of them had finally shrugged away their initial apprehensions. Now all of them were dead. Colin Bright had said it best, his gray hair gleaming under the prison lights, "old in his cynicism," as Kinley had later written, "but still youthful in his malice": *In the end, they always think, "Not me."*

Kinley felt his foot rise to the bottom step, stop there. "It's a little late," he said. "Are you sure?"

Dora remained in place, the door open, a rectangle of light motionless behind it. "Up to you," she said.

They think of the odds, and they say, "Not me."

He grasped the rail and pulled himself forward slowly. "All right," he said. "For a minute."

She turned, and he followed her inside. The living room was small, its wooden floor covered here and there by a few hoop rugs. A wobbly floor lamp stood between two unmatching dark-blue chairs, but it was an old upright piano that dominated the room.

"My mama's," Dora said. "Ray said you could play."

"A little."

"Go ahead," Dora said, almost as if daring him to prove it.

Kinley slid onto the stool and looked at the piece of sheet music that was already in place, then glanced back at Dora. " 'Someday My Prince Will Come,' he said. "Is this a favorite?"

"Ray brought it," Dora said, as she eased herself down in one of the blue chairs. "He liked it, but he always played it the wrong way."

"How do you want me to play it?"

She shrugged. "Well, do you think anybody's prince ever comes?"

Kinley shook his head. "No, I don't think so."

She smiled. "Then play it like that," she said.

He did. Slowly, haltingly, missing a note here and there, but with a long, disillusioned refrain that drifted out the door and over the edge of the mountain, disintegrating as it fell, so that not a single melancholy note of it ever reached the sleeping town below.

When he was finished, he looked up from the keys, stared directly into her eyes, and fired his question once again. "What was Ray doing in the canyon? Did it have anything to do with you?"

She did not seem at all surprised by the question. "No, I don't think so," she said. "There wouldn't be anything in the canyon that had anything to do with . . ." She stopped.

"Anything to do with what?"

"Ray was strange. He had his own way of doing things."

"But he was working on something, wasn't he?" Kinley asked urgently. "I mean, for you."

She nodded slowly. "Yes."

"What?"

"He was trying to find out what happened to my father," Dora told him. She paused a moment, and in those few seconds, the stony features of her face gave a bit, grew softer and more pliant as Mildred Haskell's never had. "Have you ever heard of Ellie Dinker?" she asked.

Ellie Dinker, Kinley thought, the lost daughter of the woman in black. "Yes, I've heard of her," he said. He remembered the afternoon in Jefferson's Drug Store, Mrs. Dinker's ghostliness, Ray's young eyes staring at her.

He shook his head. "Surely, after all these years, Ray wasn't trying to . . ."

Dora nodded determinedly. "Yes, he was," she said.

"But why?"

Dora smiled delicately. "To finally get some sleep, I guess."

Several hours later, as he lay awake in his bed, thinking back over everything Dora had told him during the preceding hours, he remembered a passage he'd written in his first book, and which, despite the academic archness of the language, still struck him as not too bad for a kid who still had a lot to learn:

The deepest of all human motivations are also those that move toward murder. They are buried in those contingencies of existence where the oldest and most rootless impulses still hold sway. In essence, murder is the radical insistence that the other is an obstacle it is permissible to remove. What follows is the most extreme and presumptuous claim one life can make upon the integrity of another.

Ellie Dinker.

His mind shot back to her from the lofty aerie of his more windy philosophical pretensions, and he heard

Dora's voice once again. It was low and husky, and he imagined Ray lying in her bed, listening to that voice, as he stared sleeplessly at the ceiling overhead while she narrated the story of her father's execution.

In the case of Charles Herman Overton, it had been by means of electrocution, and Kinley had had no trouble imagining how he had been strapped into the chair and assaulted with a searing jolt of electric power. He had seen the same thing happen to Colin Bright, and at Dora's very mention of electrocution, his mind had returned in full and excruciating detail to the only execution he'd ever witnessed. As if in a slow-motion reel, he saw Bright's body suddenly jerk forward and grow extremely taut, the skin drawing back along the bones, as if Bright's soul were trying desperately to escape the body in which it was imprisoned. The eyes popped out beneath their taped lids, a white froth gathered over the mouth, and a strange bluish smoke rose around him, danced for a moment in the light-green room, then vanished when the electricity was suddenly turned off. After that, Bright's body had slumped down, his head drooping very deeply, the muscles and tendons letting go, so that he appeared miraculously stricken with unbearable remorse, his head bowed heavily, as if weighed down by shame.

They executed Charlie Overton on January 4, 1955.

That was all she'd said before adding the fact that she'd been born only a few months before. He'd nodded quietly, then said: *And so you never knew your father?* To which she'd replied: *Only that he was innocent.*

But as he thought about it, Kinley was not so sure that Overton was innocent. The evidence against him, even as Dora had gone on to describe it, struck him as unbreakable in its thoroughness, much as he'd seen before in murder convictions, one detail piled on another until the mound of accumulated evidence was so great no jury could fail to see it. It rose like a mountain, massive, impenetrable to that small light which might yet have cast the shadow of a doubt. Once it had been constructed, the prosecutor only needed to point his finger in the same direction as the evidence pointed.

And that was precisely what Thomas Warfield had done in the fall of 1954. He had pointed his finger at Charles Overton and demanded that Ellie Dinker be avenged. He'd used words that Dora's mother had never forgotten, and that she had repeated in a morbid, bitter litany to her daughter:

That man took a child into the woods. That man forced her down upon the ground. That man took a tire iron in his hand and did an unspeakable thing to a young girl who was powerless to resist him. That man, there. That man, Charles Herman Overton, with malice aforethought, took Ellie Dinker's life.

Or had he?

Kinley got up, still thinking about all Dora had told him. He was certain that he had been able to remember all the details, and for a moment he simply let his mind play them back, as if it were a machine bound to him in service.

Once this silent, inner recitation was completed, he stood up, grabbed the laptop computer from its place beside the bed, carried it into Ray's office, plopped it down on his small metal desk and turned it on.

The high-tech light from the screen fell incongruously over the less modern means of information storage and retrieval upon which Ray had relied, hundreds of books, thousands of sheets of paper, dusty and cumbersome, relics of an older time. Compared to them, the sleek lines of the laptop appeared mercifully lean and uncomplicated.

He began by making a file for the computer menu. At first he didn't know what to name it. Then her face swam into his mind, and he typed out the file name: DORA. For a sub-file, he established the code OVER:TON for Dora's father, then proceeded to type everything he'd learned so far into it, all the details the prosecution had presented on behalf of Overton's guilt, as Dora had detailed them.

First, he listed them chronologically, moving through Overton's activities on the day of Ellie Dinker's disappearance.

CHARLES HERMAN OVERTON (Hereafter known as CHO)
Activities: 7/2/54
Caveat: Testimony of Dora Overton (9/5/91) not yet verified.
*indicates later verification from separate source.

1) Approximately 8 A.M., CHO leaves for his job at the Thompson Construction Company in Sequoyah.

2) At construction site, CHO works with Luther Lawrence Snow and Betty Gaines. Gaines will later testify that CHO complained of a stomach problem and left site at 12:30 P.M.

3) CHO seen talking to Ellie Dinker at approximately 12:40 P.M. by Luther Coggins.

4) Approximately 1:30 P.M., stalled truck is seen on mountain road by Seta Mae Williams. Both CHO and Dinker are gone.

5) Approximately 3 P.M. CHO arrives home on foot. He returns to the disabled truck immediately, fixes it, and arrives back at home forty-five minutes later. He does not leave home again until he heads for work the following morning.

These were the bare bones of Overton's day as Dora had laid them out. The crucial time was obvious. From approximately 12:40 until 3:00 in the afternoon, neither Overton nor Ellie Dinker had been seen. They had disappeared into the woods, and what had happened after that, the prosecution had contended, was murder.

Kinley leaned forward again and began typing a new heading.

CHO—PROSECUTION'S CONTENTIONS:

1) That CHO murdered Ellie Dinker between the hours of 12:30 and 3 P.M. on July 2, 1954.

EVIDENCE:

1) CHO unable to account for his whereabouts at the time of the murder, other than to say that he was walking in the woods, toward his home.

2) The fact that CHO was last person seen with Ellie Dinker.

3) The discovery (late on the afternoon of July 3) of Ellie Dinker's dress in the woods near the site where the two had been seen together.

4) The discovery on the morning of July 4) of Ellie Dinker's shoes beneath the front seat of Overton's truck.

5) The discovery (on the morning of July 4) of a blood-stained tire iron under the front seat of Overton's truck, stains which matched the blood type as it was recorded by the Sequoyah General Hospital on the birth records of Ellie Dinker as well as the records of her private physician, Dr. Joseph Stark.

Kinley stopped again, his eyes peering at the screen as he pondered the one important piece of evidence which the prosecution had never been able to unearth: Ellie Dinker's body.

It was what prosecutors called a "large item," something missing that was absolutely crucial to an air-tight case. It might be the murder weapon or the motive, but whatever it was, the absence of the "large item" always presented a problem. Not having a body in a murder case was one of the largest items a case could have, and Kinley had seen more than one case peremptorily dismissed for the lack of it.

According to Dora, District Attorney Warfield had escaped this particular pitfall by claiming that the substantial quantity of blood and hair found on Dinker's dress was enough of her body to merit a finding of murder. To buttress this contention, Warfield had displayed the dress during the course of the trial, carefully pointing out the enormous red stains and even offering Dr. Stark's testimony that such a large amount of blood could only have come from a life-threatening assault.

Still, there had been no body, and the question remained as to how and where Overton had managed to hide it.

Kinley went back over the time sequence. It was here that the laws of physics and the laws of time had to intersect. The accused had to be able to be at a certain place at a certain time if his guilt were to be proven. Overton had been seen with Ellie Dinker at approximately 12:40 P.M. Neither had been seen again until Overton had arrived home two hours and twenty minutes later.

So that was it. Two hours and twenty minutes to murder a sixteen-year-old girl, bury her, and walk back to his own house, a trip which Dora said would had to have taken at least an hour. This last hour reduced the time left for Overton to murder and then bury Dinker to a scant one hour and fifteen minutes. It was not a lot of time, but it was enough.

In the end, however, it was neither the undiscovered body nor the small amount of time available to Overton which had finally persuaded Ray to look into the case. Dora had made that completely clear just before Kinley had finally gotten up to leave her house on the mountain's edge. He'd already been halfway down the stairs when she'd called to him.

Kinley?

Yes.

The day before he died, Ray was pretty upset about something.

83

What?

I don't know, but he looked more troubled than I'd ever seen him.

But you don't know why?

He wouldn't tell me, but I knew it was something about this case.

How do you know that?

Something he said the last time I saw him. He was standing at the bottom of the stairs, just like you are now, and he looked at me very seriously, the way he could look serious, and he said, "This one's killing me, Dora."

What did he mean?

I'm not sure, but I think it had to do with all that he was uncovering, that there was something in it that was, I don't know, breaking his heart.

Ten

Breaking his heart.

It was a phrase Kinley's mind repeated continually as he made his way to the gray stone courthouse the next morning.

William Warfield was alone in his office when Kinley tapped at its open door. He looked surprised to see him, but offered a friendly smile anyway, though Kinley couldn't tell whether it was genuine or studied, a politician's waxy glow. He had seen other smiles, Mildred Haskell's the most memorable, sinister and gleaming, set off by the one gold tooth she'd used to attract her child victims: *Come in here, I got something to show you. Really. In my mouth.* Compared to that, Warfield's grin was the soul of harmless conviviality.

"Hello again, Mr. Kinley," Warfield said. "I thought you were headed back to the big city."

"I decided to stay awhile."

"Really? Why's that?"

Kinley nodded toward the large leather chair which sat in front of Warfield's desk. "May I sit down?"

"Be my guest," Warfield answered, then watched as Kinley took a seat.

"Actually, I'm glad for the opportunity to see you again," Warfield said.

"Why's that?"

"Because I failed to tell you before, but I've read a couple of your books," Warfield told him. "I found them quite interesting, especially the one on Colin Bright. That was your first one, wasn't it?"

"Yes."

"How did you happen to become interested in Colin Bright?"

"He killed an entire family," Kinley explained. "I wondered why a man would do something like that."

"Did you ever find out?"

Kinley thought of Bright for a moment, the lean face, gray hair, and piercingly blue eyes. He remembered the last line Bright had uttered at the end of their final interview. *You're lucky, kid, you'll never know.*

"No," Kinley said, his attention focused once again on Warfield. "No, I never found out."

"They don't often know themselves," Warfield said. "With some of them, there's just no inner life at all."

"Certainly one that's different from the ordinary," Kinley told him.

"Well, anyway, I found that book very interesting," Warfield said. "Bright was as evil a man as I've ever heard of."

"A sociopath, yes."

Warfield shook his head. "I sometimes wonder why we bother with such fancy modern names," he said. "I like nineteenth-century language better. You know what they would have called Colin Bright back then?"

"I guess not."

"They had a term," Warfield said. "A good one, too. 'Moral imbeciles,' that's what they called the Colin

Brights of this world. And that's what they are too, moral imbeciles.'' He paused. ''Or just evil, pure and simple.'' He looked at Kinley pointedly. ''Born that way. It's in their genes.''

Kinley nodded. ''Maybe so.''

Warfield's mood seemed to darken suddenly. ''Anyway, the last chapter, I remember that very well. The description of Bright's death. Very powerful. Was that your first execution?''

''Yes,'' Kinley said. ''And the last, too, I think. I don't expect ever to see another one.''

''Really, why not?''

''They're not very pretty.''

Warfield shook his head. ''No, that's where you're wrong, Mr. Kinley. They're beautiful. Majestic even. They're as close as we ever get to dispensing real justice. I mean, as the ancients imagined it.''

''The Code of Hammurabi,'' Kinley said.

''Ideas like that, yes,'' Warfield said. ''If you were a builder in ancient Babylon, and a house you built collapsed and killed the owner's son, do you know what would happen to you? *Your* son would be killed. Not you. Your son.'' Warfield's face seemed to harden almost imperceptibly. ''That is justice. Not like now, with everything one step removed.''

''Of course,'' Kinley offered cautiously, ''you have to get the right man.''

''Safeguards, yes,'' Warfield agreed. ''Many safeguards. Especially in a capital case.'' He shrugged, as if with disappointment. ''But we don't get many of those in a little district like ours.''

''Well, there was Charles Overton,'' Kinley reminded him.

Warfield's face turned solemn. ''Oh, yes, you're right. Charles Overton.'' He shook his head. ''My daddy was the District Attorney then. Thomas Warfield.'' His eyes saddened. ''We lost him last year. It came suddenly. Best way, I suppose.''

Kinley nodded. "And he prosecuted the Overton case?"

"Yes, he did," Warfield said. "Ellie Dinker." He smiled sadly. "You know, I can remember her mother very well. When I was growing up, she used to drift down main street. Like a ghost." He shook his head. "Probably never got over it," he added. "Her only child, you know."

"No, I didn't know that," Kinley said.

"That's one of the things that really got my father worked up about Overton," Warfield added. "You know, that he'd killed an only child, and the way Mrs. Dinker was carrying on about it."

"Was there a Mr. Dinker?"

"Not that I know of," Warfield said somewhat dismissively, as if the subject had begun to bore him. "Anyway, you were saying that you'd decided to hang around town a while longer."

"Yes," Kinley said. "As a matter of fact, it has to do with this same case. The Ellie Dinker murder."

Warfield looked at Kinley curiously. "That goes way back. Why would you be interested in that?"

"Because Ray was working on it."

Warfield looked surprised. "Ray was working on the Dinker case?"

"Yes, he was," Kinley said. "In his spare time."

"Why would he have been doing that?"

"He'd gotten to know Dora Overton, and she'd . . ."

Warfield looked at Kinley knowingly. "Well, that's not the first we've heard from Dora Overton," he said. "And her mother before her, I might add. They never accepted the jury's verdict, but that's not uncommon. Relatives believe whatever they want to believe, evidence or no evidence."

"Actually, that's what I'd like to take a look at, the evidence," Kinley said. "It obviously meant something to Ray, and so I think I sort of . . ."

"Are you sure it wasn't just Dora Overton who meant something to Ray?" Warfield blurted.

"Well," Kinley admitted hesitantly, "that might have been part of it. At least in the beginning."

Warfield shrugged. "Well, even so, it doesn't matter to me," he said. "Of course, I had no idea that Ray was looking into the Dinker case. But even if I had, I wouldn't have had any objection to it, just so long as he wasn't doing it on state time."

"Well, that won't be an issue in my case."

"No, of course not," Warfield said. He leaned forward, resting his elbows on the desk. "So, how can I help you?"

"I'd like access to the evidence and to the trial transcript."

"By evidence, you mean the physical evidence?"

"Yes."

Warfield nodded. "All right. That shouldn't be a problem."

"I'm even more interested in pictures and official records," Kinley added quickly, "and, more than anything, the trial transcript."

Warfield nodded casually. "We have all that. Of course, we can't really let it out of the building."

"I assume you have an evidence vault."

"Yes."

"And a little table in it?"

"Yes."

"That's all I'd need."

"Very well," Warfield said. "When would you like to begin?"

"Now," Kinley said bluntly.

Warfield looked at him pointedly. "Well, you certainly like to get things going, don't you."

Kinley knew no other response. "It's the only way to get them done," he said.

The transcripts were all contained in a large cardboard box which was stacked, along with scores of similar boxes, on a series of high metal shelves. Mrs. Hunter, the County Clerk whose office maintained the evidence vault, found it with very little difficulty.

"It's sort of high up," she said as she pointed to it. "Can you reach it?"

"I think so," Kinley told her, then reached up, grabbed the flap of the handle and pulled it forward into his arms.

"Probably pretty heavy," Mrs. Hunter said. "Don't strain yourself."

Kinley carried the box to the small wooden desk at the back of the room. "This is fine," he said. "Thanks."

She looked at him curiously. "You a lawyer?"

"No."

"Just poking into it? Like Old Lady Dinker used to?"

"Mrs. Dinker? When did she do that?"

"After the trial. After the execution. Even with all that over with, she couldn't let it rest."

"Why?"

"I couldn't ever figure that out, myself," Mrs. Hunter said. "It was strange, the way she kept poking at it. Like somebody stoking a dead fire, you know, trying to get it blazing again."

"Would you happen to know if she's still alive?"

Mrs. Hunter shook her head. "No, she's not alive anymore," she said. "She died a couple of years ago." She lowered her voice slightly. "In the state home."

"State home?"

"For the insane," Mrs. Hunter added. "She had some mental trouble."

"And so there are no Dinkers left in Sequoyah, I suppose," Kinley said. "Since Ellie was an only child."

"That's right. There's not even a house. The old Dinker place burned down."

"When was this?"

"Right before they put Mrs. Dinker away," Mrs. Hunter said. "She took to wandering around. I mean, people took her in, but I guess she just went off, you know, mentally, after the house burned down."

Kinley reached for his notebook. "Where was the house?"

"Right at the edge of the mountain," Mrs. Hunter told him. "Where the road starts to go up it." She turned toward the window and pointed toward the mountain. "There used to be a little house right up that way," she added. "It had pink siding. Mrs. Dinker always lived there. That's where the two of them lived. Her and her daughter, I mean."

Kinley remembered the house. It was hard to miss it going in or out of Sequoyah along the mountain road. It sat at the very base of the mountain, so close he'd often wondered if the front were the false façade for what was actually the mouth of a cave.

"When was the last time she did this 'poking around' here at the courthouse?" Kinley asked.

Mrs. Hunter's eyes rolled toward the ceiling. "Now, let me see, I been County Clerk for almost twenty-five years, and I guess it was about five years ago was the last time she came around." The eyes continued to search the ceiling. "So what does that make it? Let me see, well, that's about 1986, I guess."

"Over thirty years after the trial?"

"Yeah, that's about right."

"Did she say why she'd suddenly started looking into it again?"

Mrs. Hunter shook her head. "No, she never did. She just came up and said she wanted to look at whatever we still had on that case, and so we let her. Matter of fact, she sat right there at that same little table."

Reflexively, Kinley's eyes shot down at the table, then back up at Mrs. Hunter. "But she never said anything to you about what she was looking for?"

"No, sir, she never did," Mrs. Hunter replied flatly. "At least not to me. Mrs. Calhoun was the County Clerk then; she might have said something to her."

91

"Where would I find Mrs. Calhoun?"

"She's on a trip right now," Mrs. Hunter said. "But I can ask her about it when she comes back."

"Yes, thanks," Kinley said. "I'd appreciate that."

Mrs. Hunter's mind drifted back. "But I can tell you that something was eating at Mrs. Dinker, that's for sure." She considered it a moment. " 'Course something like that, losing a daughter, it'd be hard to let that go."

Kinley could see the evidence vault a few yards beyond him, his body already poised to shoot toward it. "Yes," he said. "It would."

Once Mrs. Hunter had returned to her desk outside the vault, Kinley set to work on the transcripts, using the method he'd developed over his years of reading them.

Every transcript began with a kind of dramatis personae of the significant figures in the case, a listing of all the witnesses called by either side in the order they'd been called. He knew that if Thomas Warfield had worked like most prosecutors, he would have presented his witnesses in a particular order, beginning with those whose testimony had to do with the discovery of the crime, moving on through those who had participated in the subsequent investigation, and finally bringing his case to a close with those witnesses whose testimony was designed to prove the defendant's guilt.

As Kinley read the transcript, he realized that Warfield had followed that method very carefully, calling Mrs. Dinker first.

According to her testimony, Martha Dinker had last seen her daughter at approximately twelve noon on Friday, July 2, 1954, when Ellie had headed up the mountain to visit a friend, Helen Slater.

WARFIELD: Now that was Friday, wasn't it, Mrs. Dinker?
DINKER: Yes, sir.

WARFIELD: Now Ellie, she was in summer school, wasn't she, Mrs. Dinker?

DINKER: Yes, sir, they was going to hold her back if she didn't go.

WARFIELD: But she didn't go to summer school that Friday, did she?

DINKER: No, sir.

WARFIELD: And although I'm sure we all remember about this, for the record could you tell us why Ellie wasn't in school that day?

DINKER: They wasn't having no school.

WARFIELD: And why was that?

DINKER: That was because it had been let out for Founder's Day.

WARFIELD: Which was scheduled for the following Saturday, isn't that right?

DINKER: Yes, sir, and they was going to dedicate the new courthouse, and they was cleaning the grounds around that, and decorating the town and all, and they wanted the kids to help, so they'd let out summer school.

WARFIELD: So she wasn't playing hooky, was she, Mrs. Dinker?

And so, as Mrs. Dinker related under Warfield's questioning, Ellie had decided to walk up the mountain to see a school friend, Helen Slater. The plan was to have lunch with her, then for the two of them to walk back down the mountain to help decorate the courthouse for the Fourth of July fireworks.

WARFIELD: Did you actually see Ellie head up the mountain?

DINKER: Yes, sir. I seen her go.

WARFIELD: Do you remember what she was wearing?

DINKER: A green dress and a pair of black shoes.

WARFIELD: What was the dress made of?

93

DINKER: Cotton.

WARFIELD: Was it dark green or light green?

DINKER: Dark green. And it had a little white lacy collar that I made for her.

WARFIELD: Mrs. Dinker, did you ever see your daughter again?

DINKER: No, sir.

WARFIELD: Mrs. Dinker, do you see this pair of shoes I have in my hand?

DINKER: (whimpering) Yes, sir.

WARFIELD: Whose shoes are these, Mrs. Dinker?

DINKER: Those are Ellie's shoes.

WARFIELD: How do you know that?

DINKER: By them shiny little buckles.

WARFIELD: Mrs. Dinker, did you ever see Ellie's green dress again?

DINKER: (crying) No, sir.

WARFIELD: Mrs. Dinker, do you see this dress I'm holding up to show the jury right now?

Martha Dinker had, indeed, seen that dress, and she went on to identify it positively as having been the one her daughter had worn the day of her death.

By eight that same Friday evening, Mrs. Dinker had begun to worry about Ellie, but since, as she put it, "kids is kids," she had waited until ten before acting on her concerns. She'd had no phone, she told Warfield, and so she'd walked the mile or so from her home to the Sheriff's Office. There she'd talked to Sheriff Maddox, who'd advised her to return home, after assuring her that he would alert all police patrols to be on the lookout for her daughter.

Maddox followed Mrs. Dinker to the stand. All during the night following Ellie's disappearance, he told the jury, the members of his department had kept an eye out for the missing girl. None of them had spotted Ellie by morning, however, and Maddox had begun to suspect that something very bad might have happened.

WARFIELD: So, in light of the fact that Ellie Dinker had not been located during the night, what did you do the next day, Sheriff Maddox?

MADDOX: I went up to Mrs. Dinker's house. I thought maybe the little girl had showed up. I figured since Mrs. Dinker didn't have no phone, maybe she wouldn't have been able to let me know if Ellie had come home.

WARFIELD: And what did Mrs. Dinker tell you when you arrived at her house?''

MADDOX: She was real upset. She'd already walked all the way up the mountain to the Slater girl's place, and the Slater girl had told her that Ellie never did come to her house.

WARFIELD: So Ellie Dinker never made it up to Helen Slater's house, is that right, Sheriff?

MADDOX: No, she never did.

WARFIELD: What did you do then?

MADDOX: I got started on a roadblock, just to see if maybe somebody had seen the Dinker girl going up the mountain.

WARFIELD: And someone had, isn't that right?

MADDOX: Mr. Coggins seen her.

WARFIELD: All right, now, you also had occasion to search the woods north of the mountain road, isn't that right?

MADDOX: One of my deputies did. Deputy Ben Wade.

WARFIELD: And what did he find?

MADDOX: (pointing) That dress you got in that bag there.

WARFIELD: The one Mrs. Dinker identified as Ellie's.

MADDOX: Yes, sir.

WARFIELD: Now we'll be hearing from Deputy Wade in a minute, but for the record, Sheriff, Wade brought that dress back down to your office, didn't he?

MADDOX: Yes, sir, he did. That's procedure.

WARFIELD: What did the dress look like?

MADDOX: Just like when you held it up.

WARFIELD: Bloody?

MADDOX: Just like you showed it.

WARFIELD: Were there any other signs of Ellie Dinker in those woods, Sheriff?

MADDOX: No, sir. We looked everywhere, but we couldn't find hide nor hair of her.

WARFIELD: All right, Sheriff, now, if you could, just tell us what happened after you found the dress. How did your investigation proceed?

It had proceeded just as Kinley thought it might, strictly by the book of rural law enforcement. A roadblock had been positioned along the mountain road to question any of the people going in or out of Sequoyah about what they might have seen the day before. As a police canvass, it had worked superbly. They'd found several people who'd seen things relevant to Ellie Dinker's disappearance, and one by one, as Warfield called them to the stand, they told the jury what they'd seen.

Luther Tyrone Coggins

WARFIELD: Now, Mr. Coggins, when the police stopped you at that roadblock, they asked you about Ellie Dinker, didn't they?

COGGINS: They asked about a girl in a green dress.

WARFIELD: Did they say her name?

COGGINS: No, sir, but I told them who I reckoned it was.

WARFIELD: And who was that?

COGGINS: Ellie Dinker.

WARFIELD: So you knew Ellie Dinker, did you?

COGGINS: I knowed her mother. She's on my peddling route. She always buys a few things from my truck.

WARFIELD: So what did you tell the police officer you spoke to at the roadblock?

COGGINS: I allowed as how I'd seen Ellie Dinker on the road. I told how she was wearing a green dress, and that she was standing next to a guy I knowed. They was by his old truck, and the hood was up on it.

WARFIELD: And what time would this have been, Mr. Coggins?

COGGINS: That would have been around twelve-forty, something like that.

WARFIELD: So you told the police that you'd seen Ellie Dinker with a man you recognized.

COGGINS: I sure did.

WARFIELD: Do you see that man in the courtroom here today, Mr. Coggins?

COGGINS: Yes, sir, I do.

WARFIELD: Could you point him out for the jury?

COGGINS: That's him, right there, sitting with Mr. Talbott.

WARFIELD: The man in the blue shirt?

COGGINS: Yes, sir.

WARFIELD: Your Honor, I ask that the record show that Mr. Coggins identified Charles Herman Overton, the defendant, being the man he saw with Ellie Dinker on the afternoon of Friday, July 2, 1954.

COURT: So ordered.

Even without turning to the next volume of transcript, Kinley knew who the next witness would be. Warfield was handling things just as prosecutors had always been taught, lining up his witnesses in such a way that each added bit of testimony moved the jury's mind just a little further in the direction of the defendant.

Officer Ben Wade

WARFIELD: And you heard Luther Coggins's testimony just a few minutes ago, didn't you?

WADE: I did.

WARFIELD: And was that a true and accurate report of what transpired between you and Mr. Coggins?

WADE: Yes, sir, it was.

WARFIELD: All right, sir. Now, could you tell the jury in your own words what action you took after hearing from Mr. Coggins?

WADE: I kept on with the roadblock for a while, then I went down and told Sheriff Maddox about what Mr. Coggins had said.

WARFIELD: And what did Sheriff Maddox do?

WADE: He said we'd look into it directly.

WARFIELD: And did you look into it soon after that?

WADE: We did early the next morning.

WARFIELD: But before that, you conducted a search of the woods north of the mountain road, isn't that right?

WADE: Yes, sir.

WARFIELD: Where was that search exactly, Deputy Wade?

WADE: In the woods up from Mile Marker 27.

WARFIELD: And that is a location directly north of where Mr. Coggins told you he saw Charles Overton and Ellie Dinker, isn't that true?

WADE: Yes, sir, it is.

WARFIELD: And what did you find in those woods, Deputy?

WADE: I found a green dress sort of hanging over a limb.

WARFIELD: Which you brought down to Sheriff Maddox, isn't that right?

WADE: Yes, sir.

WARFIELD: And what happened the next day, Deputy Wade?

WADE: That was Independence Day, and Sheriff Maddox and I went to check on what Mr. Coggins had said. You know, to ask Mr. Overton about it. But nobody was home. They'd all walked down to the courthouse for the celebration.

WARFIELD: You say, they'd walked. How do you know that, Deputy Wade?

WADE: Because Overton's truck was in the driveway.

WARFIELD: And did you have occasion to look in that truck, Deputy Wade?

WADE: Yes, I did.

WARFIELD: And did you find anything in that truck that

you thought might have a bearing on the whereabouts of Ellie Dinker?

WADE: Yes, sir. I found a tire iron wrapped up in cloth,
and it looked to me like it had blood and hair on it.

WARFIELD: Anything else, Deputy?

WADE: A pair of black shoes.

WARFIELD: And pursuant to your duties as a County Deputy, did you take these items?

WADE: Yes, sir. I took them right down to the Sheriff's
Office and handed them over to Sheriff Maddox.

Predictably, Warfield called Sheriff Maddox to the
stand a second time, then a series of court and law enforcement officials to establish that the chain of evidence
had never been broken, that once the shoes and tire iron
had been collected, none but authorized officials had
gained access to them.

He then moved on to the arrest of Charlie Overton,
something Maddox and two deputies, Wade and Riley
Hendricks, had carried out themselves.

Sheriff Maddox

WARFIELD: Where did you find Mr. Overton?

MADDOX: At his house on the mountain. We was waiting
for him when him and his wife come up the hill.

WARFIELD: What happened then?

MADDOX: Well, me and the boys sort of fanned out, you
know, in case he tried to run off. They got on either
side of him, and I just stood right there in front of
him, and I said, "Charlie, you know a little girl
name of Ellie Dinker?" And he didn't say nothing.
He just sort of went pale in his face, you know.

TALBOTT: Objection, Your Honor.

COURT: Sustained.

WARFIELD: Did you then arrest Mr. Overton?

MADDOX: They was a few more words between us, and
then I arrested him. He didn't put up no fight about

99

it. He just come on with us. His wife, she was crying and such as that, but Overton, he didn't offer no resistance.

Kinley stopped, noting, as he always did, those phrases which seemed to denote an emotional state that might otherwise have gone unrecorded.

No resistance.

He tried to arrive at an image of such passivity in his mind. He could see the men fan out around Overton, the Sheriff approach him, accuse him before his pregnant wife's astonished face, of murdering a young girl, and in the midst of all that, to offer no resistance.

He thought of Dora, the level look of her eyes as she'd related the events surrounding her father's trial the night before. Whatever Charles Herman Overton might have been, he was certainly a good deal different from his daughter, a man of no resistance whose daughter had not relented yet. He thought of Dr. Stark, of how he'd spoken of the wounded heart Ray had inherited from his father, and then of himself, wondering what secret defects he'd inherited as well, and which all his grandmother's solitary nurturing could do nothing to correct, and then of Dora, once again. For a moment he wondered what Ray must have thought of her after their first hours together. Knowing him as he did, Kinley knew that he must have thought of Lois and Serena, both of them sleeping comfortably in the valley, assured of his old-fashioned faithfulness, while he could feel that same solidity slipping away as he looked at Dora, listened to her tale, slipping away like earth moving helplessly downward, gathering mass and momentum as it hurled down the mountainside.

Eleven

It was nearly noon by the time Kinley finished the first few volumes of the transcript. By then he'd followed Warfield's witnesses through the early stages of the investigation, Overton's arrest, and the relatively small amount of forensic material which could be gathered in the absence of Ellie Dinker's body. Here, the testimony had come from Dr. Stark, and as Kinley sat in the small restaurant a few blocks from the courthouse, he reviewed the notes he'd taken as he'd read it.

According to Dr. Stark, Ellie Dinker had been a patient of his from the time he'd delivered her in his clinic on June 24, 1938. Although the Dinkers were a poor family, Dr. Stark said, they'd paid his fees either in small payments in cash, or more often, with vegetables grown in their backyard. It was a form of remuneration which Stark said he'd accepted since the Depression, but a practice, he'd added to the jury's amusement, that he did not wish to encourage in "these more prosperous times."

Still, he had continued to see Ellie Dinker through the

years, the last time only a month before her death, and in the process, he'd gathered a basic amount of data about her. For the purposes of the trial, the most crucial element within that data had been her blood type. It was B positive, Stark had told the jury, a relatively rare type that was shared by approximately eight percent of the general population. At that point in the testimony, Warfield had anticipated the defense cross-examination and had asked its most important questions himself. No, Stark had admitted in response, he could not say for sure that the blood on Ellie Dinker's dress was her own. He could only surmise that it could not be that of ninety-two percent of the remaining population. The exchange had been so suggestive of courtroom tactics in the mid-1950's that Kinley had written it down verbatim.

WARFIELD: So, scientifically speaking, you cannot positively identify the blood on Ellie Dinker's dress as being Ellie Dinker's blood, can you, Dr. Stark?

STARK: No, sir, I can't.

WARFIELD: But if you took a hundred people out of this courtroom here and gave them a blood test, the chances are no more than eight of them would have B positive, is that right?

STARK: Yes, that's right.

WARFIELD: And looking out over the courtroom, how many of these eight people are also wearing a green dress, Doctor?

STARK: I haven't counted the green dresses in the gallery, Mr. Warfield.

WARFIELD: Now, I know you're a scientist and a medical man, Dr. Stark. But would you also say that you have what we call around here regular walking-about sense?

STARK: Yes, sir, I think so.

WARFIELD: Well, let me ask you this, Dr. Stark. If I show you an animal that looks like a skunk and acts like a skunk and smells like a skunk, Doctor, using

your regular walking-about sense, what would you
say that animal is?

STARK: I'd say it was a skunk, Mr. Warfield.

WARFIELD: And if I show you a little girl in a green dress
who had B positive blood, and later I show you that
dress all ragged and bloody, and I tell you that the
blood on that dress was B positive, Doctor, whose
blood would you say was on that dress?

At that point Horace Talbott, Overton's attorney, had
predictably objected, and the court had sustained the objection. By then it had hardly mattered, of course, since
the jury had heard the question and guessed Stark's answer to be what they themselves had already surmised,
that the blood on Ellie Dinker's dress had come from her
body.

But where was the body? That was the question that
now moved restlessly about in Kinley's mind. Why
would Overton have hung the green dress in the tree for
all to see, then taken elaborate pains necessary to conceal
the body so effectively no one had ever been able to
locate it?

As he finished his hamburger and fries, Kinley well
knew that he could not have been the first person to ask
such a question. The initial stage of Overton's defense
would have had to confront the missing body, not only
as the incontestable physical evidence for the fact of Ellie
Dinker's murder, but also as the central illogical piece
in the prosecution's puzzle. Why would Overton have
bothered to hide a body and leave a dress flapping openly,
like a bloody pennant, in the trees above Sheriff Maddox's head?

"You must have thought about it," Kinley said urgently.

Horace Talbott nodded his great, bald head. Though
over eighty years old, Kinley could tell that he was com-

103

pletely lucid. He sat in an enormous woven tapestry chair, surrounded by plants, in the bright light of the solarium. Over his left shoulder, a mynah bird squawked from time to time, as if complaining of the heat, but Talbott seemed never to hear it, his dark brown eyes very steady as they stared toward Kinley.

"Did it bother you?" Kinley asked.

"Things that don't make sense always bother me, Mr. Kinley," Talbott said. "But as you told me, when you asked to see me, you are doing this for Miss Overton."

"That's right."

"And, like you, I would like to put that young woman's mind to rest," Talbott said. "Because of that, I wouldn't want to get into an explanation of her father's actions."

"Did you ever find an explanation?"

"Yes," Talbott answered confidently. "He was deranged. Many people are."

Kinley reached for his notebook. "In what way?"

Talbott gathered his thoughts a moment, then proceeded, his tone suddenly rather professorial. "Logic, sense, reason, these things exist only in the imagination," he said. "That's my conclusion on such matters." He brushed the fronds of a fern from the side of his face. "When you look for these things in human acts, they are often not present. What you see is reflex, improvisation, a sudden impulse that sweeps over someone." He shrugged. "There are things, Mr. Kinley, that are what I've learned to call 'pure acts.' You can't trace any reason for them, any pattern at all. They are what they are, and when people are overwhelmed by these things, they do what they do. Like I say, 'pure act.'"

"And you think the murder of Ellie Dinker was like that?"

Talbott nodded. "Charlie Overton was a quiet man. You'd have almost thought he was mute if you hadn't known better." The brown eyes narrowed. "But underneath, maybe there was a great upheaval in him. Who's

104

to say? Maybe for years he'd watched little girls go by and wanted to grab one, and have his way with her, and strangle her, or cut her up in little pieces. Then, all of a sudden, it rose up, you see, and he couldn't push his hands way down in his pockets anymore, or close his eyes real tight to keep the vision out, you know? So, the door popped off the hinges.''

"And he killed her?"

Talbott's eyes watched Kinley closely. "You have written about such people, haven't you?"

Kinley nodded. Mildred Haskell had been forty-three before she'd murdered the first time. Willie Connors had been fifty-one. Before then, they'd been nothing but the village seamstress who had a weakness for red shoes, the high school gym teacher who lectured his students on the joys of health.

"Did you know him before the trial?" Kinley asked.

"Very slightly."

"Then why did you defend him?" Kinley asked. "This was a pre-Gideon case. There would have been no court-appointed attorney."

"That's true," Talbott said. "But my connection was not with Mr. Overton. It was with his wife, Sarah."

"You knew his wife?"

"Very well," Talbott said. "She worked for me. Or should I say, for my late wife."

"In what capacity?"

"In a general capacity," Talbott said. "Mrs. Overton came in every day to help my wife." He glanced away for a moment, as if remembering his wife in a sudden brief glimpse, then returned his eyes to Kinley. "My wife was an invalid back then. She had polio. She became an invalid, and Mrs. Overton would come in and help out with things. She would cook and clean, and just generally do the chores. I got to know her. So, naturally, when her husband was arrested, she came to me."

"Did you ever believe he was innocent?" Kinley asked.

Talbott shook his head. "No, I always believed that he had killed Ellie Dinker."

"Why?"

Talbott looked at Kinley as if he were a small child defending the existence of the Tooth Fairy. "There was a great deal of evidence, Mr. Kinley."

"But the body," Kinley said insistently. "Why would he have hidden it?"

"I don't know."

"Did he strike you as insane?"

"No, not exactly," Talbott said. "Tormented. He did strike me as tormented."

"By what?"

"By poverty, Mr. Kinley," Talbott said authoritatively. "By a life of menial jobs, by having to shift around the local rich folks, by always having to be at their beck and call."

"So he was sullen, angry?"

"Yes," Talbott said. "And pent-up, too. Worn out by being pent-up, with no outlet." He thought for a moment. "Like a man who gets up on fire every morning and has to spend the rest of the day dousing himself with water, putting out the flames."

Kinley thought about Talbott's description for a moment. "Somehow, I don't see Overton as being like that," he said finally.

"Really?" Talbott asked. "And why is that? What do you know about him?"

"I just have a few impressions."

"Gathered from what source, may I ask?"

"His daughter."

Talbott smiled. "Dora Overton is quite an interesting woman," he said, "and lovely, too."

"We were talking about her father," Kinley reminded him.

For a moment, Talbott seemed at a loss for words, as if he'd moved into a trance. "Suddenly, you follow an impulse," he said finally. "I'm speaking of Charles

Overton now. You are attracted, and you follow that attraction. All the evidence may be in the other direction, but the need, you see, is not interested in evidence or reason or logic, or any of those higher forms we make so much of. The need is only interested in itself." He looked at Kinley. "Your current need, Mr. Kinley, is to pursue an old case." He pulled himself softly to the left and sat erectly in his chair. "Whereas, that day on the mountain, Charles Overton pursued Ellie Dinker." He smiled. "The only difference between Overton and you—or me, or anyone else for that matter—is that he had a very extreme need, and you, Mr. Kinley, have a safe and utterly common one."

Kinley started to ask another question, but Talbott rose suddenly. "I'm an old man now," he told Kinley as he walked toward the door of the room. "Everyone involved in that case is either old or dead."

"I understand that, Mr. Talbott, however . . ."

Talbott opened the door. "Either old or dead or . . ." He stopped, his face unexpectedly mournful. "Or beyond our grasp."

Kinley looked at him unbelievingly. "Are you kicking me out, Mr. Talbott?"

Talbott smiled, almost sweetly. "Yes, I am, Mr. Kinley," he said, "but as you can see, I am doing it politely."

Twelve

"Well, you're back," Mrs. Hunter said as Kinley walked into her office.

"I only broke for lunch," Kinley told her. "Is it all right if I go back into the vault now?"

"Oh, sure," Mrs. Hunter said. "It's all public record material, you know."

"Thanks," Kinley said. He turned, walked out of the office and headed back into the vault. He'd carefully returned the transcripts to their place on the shelf—a respectful practice he'd learned librarians and other bureaucrats devoutly appreciated—and now he retrieved them once again.

He'd already gone through three volumes of testimony, or, as he sometimes thought of it, two days of the trial. There were only six more volumes to go, and the very paucity of the transcript would have been enough to guess the date of the trial. Nine slender volumes could not even begin to contain a capital case transcript since the Supreme Court rulings of the sixties. Now, the *voir dire* testimony of prospective jurors alone required volumes of transcripts and days of courtroom time.

But the case of the *People of Georgia v. Charles Herman Overton* had taken only five days, a speedy trial, to say the least, but not uncommonly so for the time. It had not been an age of elaborate care for the rights of the accused, and certainly when overwhelming evidence reduced the presumption of innocence to little more than a pleasant legal concept, little time or public money had been devoted to protecting the more or less irrelevant rights of the accused.

Charles Overton had been treated as most men in his situation would have been treated in the small-town South of 1954, and nothing Kinley had read in the court record so far indicated that any but the usual standard had been applied to him. In fact, he had gotten more than most. He had been represented by counsel, a luxury few defendants would have been able to afford, and which Talbott had provided without charge because of his connection to Overton's wife. At least, Overton had been given a fighting chance to clear himself.

But not much of one, Kinley realized as he turned to the next volume of the transcript and began reading the testimony of Luther Snow, one of Overton's co-workers at the Thompson Construction Company. It was a hodgepodge of hearsay and conjecture to which Talbott had offered only fleeting objection, and which had done the prosecution the inestimably valuable service of establishing a motive for the murder of Ellie Dinker.

Luther Snow

WARFIELD: Do you see Charlie Overton in this courtroom today, Mr. Snow?
SNOW: Yes, sir.
WARFIELD: Would you point him out, please?
SNOW: He's the one setting right yonder beside Mr. Talbott there.

WARFIELD: Your Honor, may the record indicate that Mr. Snow has identified the defendant.

COURT: So ordered. Proceed.

WARFIELD: Now, Mr. Snow, you work with Mr. Overton down at Thompson's, is that right?

SNOW: Yes, sir.

WARFIELD: How long have you known him?

SNOW: About two years, I'd say.

For the next few pages, Snow went over the work he and Overton had done together during their time at Thompson Construction. For the last two years they'd been involved in the construction of the new courthouse, the very one in which the trial was being held, and which had only opened a few weeks before it began. Overton had worked as a general workman, doing everything from laying brick to light carpentry. Snow, on the other hand, had supervised much of the operation, from planning work schedules to handling the use of the site's heavy equipment.

SNOW: I dug the foundation, and I poured the cement for the whole place, everything from the flagpole to the courthouse steps.

WARFIELD: And did you and Mr. Overton sometimes take lunch breaks together?

SNOW: Yes, sir.

WARFIELD: And you sometimes talked to each other, isn't that right, the way men do?

SNOW: We talked a lot.

WARFIELD: Did you get the impression that Mr. Overton liked and trusted you?

SNOW: Yes, sir.

WARFIELD: And did he discuss what you might call his "private life" with you?

SNOW: Sometimes he did.

WARFIELD: In the course of those conversations, did you

110

get an idea of his state of mind on or about July 2, 1954?

SNOW: He was upset.

WARFIELD: What about, did he tell you?

SNOW: Well, Overton was real closed up. We talked sometimes, like I said, but he was real closed off.

WARFIELD: But you did mention his mood, didn't you, Mr. Snow?

SNOW: Yes, sir, I did. And the reason was, it was affecting his work. His mind was always wandering. He wasn't doing his job too good.

WARFIELD: So he looked distracted?

SNOW: What was that?

WARFIELD: Worried. Preoccupied. His mind on other things.

SNOW: That's right.

WARFIELD: And did you try to find out what the trouble was?

SNOW: Oh, yeah. I had to. Like I said, it was causing him to mess things up. His work was off. I can't put up with that.

WARFIELD: And could you tell us the substance of that conversation?

SNOW: Well, I asked him straight out. I said, "Charlie, what's going on? You're off your feed. You need to keep your mind on things."

WARFIELD: And what was Overton's response?

SNOW: Well, there wasn't much of a response. He just sort of looked at me. He didn't say anything. So, I went at him again, and kept at it until he finally told me what it was that was bothering him so much.

WARFIELD: So, he finally told you what was troubling him?

SNOW: Yes, sir.

WARFIELD: What was it?

SNOW: Woman trouble, that's what he said.

WARFIELD: Woman trouble? Were those his exact words?

SNOW: Yes, sir. That's what he said, that he was having woman trouble.

WARFIELD: And this woman trouble was the cause of his problems at work?

SNOW: That's what he said. That woman trouble was driving him nuts.

To this testimony, Talbott offered a very effective cross-examination, one that reduced Snow's remarks to the hazy, insubstantial mass they were.

TALBOTT: Now, Mr. Snow, you said that Mr. Overton expressed some confidences in you. I mean, talked to you about his problems?

SNOW: Woman trouble. That's what he said.

TALBOTT: And this was causing him some alarm, is that right?

SNOW: He was pretty upset over it.

TALBOTT: Did he give you the cause of that trouble?

SNOW: No, sir.

TALBOTT: Did he ever mention his wife?

SNOW: No, sir.

TALBOTT: So as far as you know, Mr. Overton said only that he was having trouble with a woman.

SNOW: Well, it was a little more than that. He was real upset about it.

TALBOTT: But he never said who this woman was, did he?

SNOW: No, sir.

TALBOTT: Did he ever mention Ellie Dinker?

SNOW: No, sir.

TALBOTT: To your knowledge, had he ever met Ellie Dinker?

SNOW: I wouldn't know about that.

TALBOTT: Well, you never saw them together, did you?

SNOW: No, sir.

TALBOTT: So all you know, Mr. Snow, is that Charlie

Overton said he was having trouble with a woman, is that right?

SNOW: That's right.

TALBOTT: Have you ever had any trouble with a woman, Mr. Snow?

SNOW: I guess so.

TALBOTT: Did you ever kill a woman?

SNOW: No, sir.

TALBOTT: Do you know any man who's never had any woman trouble?

SNOW: I guess not.

TALBOTT: I don't either, Mr. Snow, not a single one. Thank you.

The prosecution had rested its case with Luther Snow's testimony, and so after concluding his cross-examination, Talbott began the case for the defense.

His first witness was Dave Halgrave, another of Overton's co-workers at Thompson Construction, but, unlike Luther Snow, a man who thought of Overton as a friend.

TALBOTT: How long have you known Charlie Overton?

HALGRAVE: Since we was kids, I reckon. Thirty years, something like that.

TALBOTT: And you worked together, did you not?

HALGRAVE: I been at Thompson's for near on to twenty years now. Charlie come on about two years ago when we was hiring people to help build the courthouse.

TALBOTT: Would you say that you know Charlie Overton pretty well?

HALGRAVE: Well as anybody.

TALBOTT: Is Charlie Overton a killer, Mr. Halgrave?

(WITNESS LAUGHS.)

TALBOTT: Could you answer the question? We need a response for the court reporter.

HALGRAVE: No, Charlie ain't no killer. He ain't mean like that.

TALBOTT: Is it within his capacity to take the life of a young girl?

HALGRAVE: No, sir, it ain't.

TALBOTT: Even if that young girl was pestering him, Mr. Halgrave?

HALGRAVE: She could have been setting him afire, and he wouldn't have done her no harm. It ain't his way of doing things.

TALBOTT: Mr. Halgrave, did you see Charlie Overton on July 2, 1954, the day of Ellie Dinker's murder?

HALGRAVE: We was working together.

TALBOTT: In his statement to the police, Mr. Overton said that he'd gotten sick that morning and had had to leave the courthouse construction site. To your knowledge, was Charlie Overton sick on the morning of July 2?

HALGRAVE: Yes, sir, he was.

TALBOTT: You know this for a fact?

HALGRAVE: Well, I seen him throwing up.

TALBOTT: Where was this, Mr. Halgrave?

HALGRAVE: At the courthouse. He was over by his truck, and he was all bent over, and he was, well, you know, he was heaving up.

TALBOTT: You saw Charlie Overton vomiting beside his truck on July 2, is that your testimony?

HALGRAVE: Yes, sir.

TALBOTT: And shortly after that, he came to you and said he was sick and needed to go home, is that right?

HALGRAVE: Yes, sir.

TALBOTT: And what happened after that?

HALGRAVE: Charlie went home. He was white as a ghost.

TALBOTT: Thank you, that is all.

In his cross-examination, Warfield proved just as effective as Talbott had been, transforming words offered in defense to accusatory references.

WARFIELD: And you said you've known Mr. Overton almost all your life?

HALGRAVE: Yes, sir.

WARFIELD: And you consider him a good friend?

HALGRAVE: Good as any.

WARFIELD: Would you say that good friends often try to help each other, Mr. Halgrave?

HALGRAVE: I guess.

WARFIELD: That if a friend were in trouble, they might try to get them out of it?

HALGRAVE: I guess so.

WARFIELD: Would you say that a person who was on trial for his life, would you say that that person was in trouble?

HALGRAVE: 'Course they are.

WARFIELD: I'd like to go on to something else, if I may, Mr. Halgrave. You testified that Charlie Overton was not a violent man, isn't that right?

HALGRAVE: That's right.

WARFIELD: And that he was very sick on the morning of July 2?

HALGRAVE: He was throwing up by his truck.

WARFIELD: Yes, I heard your testimony. I believe you also stated that Charlie Overton . . . here it is in my notes . . . that Overton looked "white as a ghost." Were those your words?

HALGRAVE: That's how he looked, yes, sir.

WARFIELD: Mr. Halgrave, would you say that a man who was not normally a violent man, but who was planning on murdering a little girl in just a few hours, would you say that such a man might look a bit shaken?

TALBOTT: Objection, Your Honor.

WARFIELD: That he might look sick, that he might be . . .

TALBOTT: Objection!

WARFIELD: "White as a ghost"?

COURT: Sustained.

WARFIELD: No further questions, Your Honor.

Nor any need for them, Kinley thought, considering how effectively Warfield had dismantled the already frail vessel of Halgrave's testimony, turning positives into negatives in a case where there had been few positives to begin with.

Kinley flipped back to the beginning of the volume and let his eyes sweep down the witness list to make sure he'd read it correctly the first time, that Talbott had called only three witnesses on Overton's behalf. A quick glance confirmed his original conclusion. Only three witnesses to save Charles Overton's life.

He returned his attention to the transcripts and began reading at the Court's instruction to Talbott: *Call your next witness, sir.*

Thirteen

Her name was Betty Gaines, and almost from the moment he began reading her testimony, Kinley realized that she'd been a reluctant witness. Her answers came haltingly and with a strange, vaporous insubstantiality, as if she were testifying to the contents of a dream. It was the kind of testimony Kinley had become familiar with, and in his experience it had always signalled either that the witnesses were afraid of the testimony, or had some doubts about its veracity.

TALBOTT: You're acquainted with Charlie Overton, aren't you, Miss Gaines?

(WITNESS DOES NOT RESPOND)

TALBOTT: Miss Gaines?

GAINES: Yes, sir.

TALBOTT: Did you hear the question, Miss Gaines?

GAINES: Would you repeat it, please?

TALBOTT: I asked if you knew Charlie Overton.

GAINES: He works at Thompson's, like I do.

TALBOTT: And did you see him on the morning of July 2 at the courthouse construction site?

GAINES: It was a pretty day, I think. It was sunny.

TALBOTT: Why were you at the site that morning, Miss Gaines?

GAINES: I came down with the orders. Deliveries. Things come down there. Things are delivered.

TALBOTT: And the workers at the site, they have to be ready to unload these things, isn't that right?

GAINES: You got to be ready when things come around.

TALBOTT: And so you went down to the site to let the foreman know what deliveries he could expect on that day?

GAINES: I let Luther know.

TALBOTT: You spoke to Luther Snow, is that right?

GAINES: I gave him the orders, you know, what was coming.

TALBOTT: And while you were there, did you see Charlie Overton?

GAINES: Yes.

TALBOTT: Where did you see him?

GAINES: At the hole where the flagpole was going to be. The ground was still mushy-like, and he was complaining about it, 'cause it was going to be a week before it was dried out.

TALBOTT: So he was in front of the courthouse with the construction crew, that day?

GAINES: Yes, sir. They was lots of people there that morning, 'cause a lot was being done for the Independence Day thing.

TALBOTT: The celebration.

GAINES: Yes, sir.

TALBOTT: Charlie Overton was working at the courthouse that morning, wasn't he?

GAINES: Yes, he was.

TALBOTT: And Charlie came up to you, didn't he?

GAINES: Yes, he did.

TALBOTT: What did he tell you, Miss Gaines?

GAINES: He said, "I'm sick, ma'am. I think I got to go home."

TALBOTT: Did he look sick?

GAINES: Yeah, he looked sick.

TALBOTT: What happened then?

GAINES: I said "Well, you picked a good day for it, 'cause Luther says it's too wet to put the pole up anyway, so you better go on home and get some rest."

TALBOTT: And did he do that?

GAINES: Do what?

TALBOTT: Did you see him get in his truck and leave for home?

GAINES: Yes, sir. And the courthouse clock struck twelve-thirty.

TALBOTT: And did he look ill at that time?

GAINES: He looked the same that he looked when he talked to me.

TALBOTT: Thank you, Miss Gaines. Nothing more, Your Honor.

COURT: Any cross, Mr. Warfield?

WARFIELD: No, Your Honor. I have no need for it.

Kinley smiled. It had been a very shrewd move on Warfield's part. By telling the Court he had "no need" to cross-examine Betty Gaines, he had reduced her already weak testimony to complete insubstantiality in the jury's mind.

Talbott's last witness was Overton's wife, Sarah Ann Overton, and her testimony was brief and to the point. Under Talbott's questioning, she told the jury that she'd spent all of July 2 at home. She'd been in the last weeks of her pregnancy, and the terrible heat of mid-summer had made things very difficult for her. She'd found it necessary to restrict her movements drastically, and from the middle of June onward, she'd remained virtually a prisoner within her house. "Charlie just brought me what I needed," she told the court. "Food and things. But me, I just stayed home and sat out on the porch."

TALBOTT: And were you doing that on the afternoon of July 2, 1954, at around three in the afternoon?

OVERTON: Yes, sir.

TALBOTT: Did your husband come home at that time?

OVERTON: Yes, sir.

TALBOTT: What was he wearing, Mrs. Overton?

OVERTON: His work clothes.

TALBOTT: The same that he'd worn to work that morning?

OVERTON: Yes, sir.

TALBOTT: How did they look when he returned home at three that afternoon?

OVERTON: They looked a little dirty.

TALBOTT: Dirty how, Mrs. Overton?

OVERTON: They had some grease on them.

TALBOTT: Where was this grease, Mrs. Overton?

OVERTON: On the front of his shirt.

TALBOTT: Like he'd been lying under a . . .

WARFIELD: Objection, calling for a conclusion.

TALBOTT: Is that all that was on his shirt?

OVERTON: Grit, dirt. I noticed that.

TALBOTT: Where was this?

OVERTON: On the back of his pants and his shirt.

TALBOTT: As if he'd been lying on his back?

WARFIELD: Same objection, Your Honor.

TALBOTT: Where did your husband say he got this grit and grease?

OVERTON: From working on the truck. He said the oil pan had started leaking, and that he'd had to crawl under the truck to try to fix it.

TALBOTT: Had he fixed it?

OVERTON: No, sir. He left it on the road.

TALBOTT: When did he go back to fix it?

OVERTON: Just a little while after he got home.

TALBOTT: Now, Mrs. Overton. On the day the truck broke down, and your husband walked home, did you see any blood on your husband's clothes?

OVERTON: No, sir.

TALBOTT: Mrs. Overton, are you a Christian?

OVERTON: Yes, sir.

TALBOTT: Mrs. Overton, would you lie to Jesus Christ?

OVERTON: No, sir, I would not.

TALBOTT: Now, people, they'll say, "Well, sure, she's lying to save her husband." But that oath you took before your testimony, that was to God, wasn't it, and to his son, Jesus. That's the way you see the oath, isn't that right, Mrs. Overton?

OVERTON: Yes, sir.

TALBOTT: Now, I ask you again: Would you lie after taking that oath?

OVERTON: No, sir, I wouldn't.

TALBOTT: Mrs. Overton, I want to ask you again, was there any blood on your husband's clothes when he came home on the afternoon of July 2, 1954?

OVERTON: No, sir, there was not.

TALBOTT: No further questions, Your Honor.

This time Warfield had chosen to cross-examine the witness, but it was a decidedly gentle cross-examination, a style Kinley had seen before, and recognized as being affordable only to an attorney who had already won his case and did not want to risk it by alienating the jury with a cruel examination.

WARFIELD: You were very much in what we call a family way on July 2, weren't you, Mrs. Overton?

OVERTON: Yes, sir.

WARFIELD: And since that time, you've actually had that child, isn't that true?

OVERTON: Yes, sir. I had it two days after my husband was arrested.

WARFIELD: A little girl, I believe?

121

OVERTON: Yes, sir.

WARFIELD: Named Dora, I understand.

OVERTON: Yes, sir.

WARFIELD: Of course, in your position, with a newborn baby, I guess you have your hands full, isn't that right?

OVERTON: Yes, sir, I do.

WARFIELD: Is this your first child?

OVERTON: Yes.

WARFIELD: And being a good mother, you would want to be able to provide for that, wouldn't you?

OVERTON: Yes, sir.

WARFIELD: That's something a Christian is supposed to do, isn't it? Provide for the children. I mean, the Bible teaches that.

OVERTON: Yes, it does.

WARFIELD: And that would be very difficult without your husband, wouldn't it, Mrs. Overton?

OVERTON: Yes, sir, it would.

WARFIELD: You would like for Charlie to come home so he can help provide for this new child, wouldn't you?

(WITNESS DOES NOT RESPOND)

COURT: Answer the question, please, Mrs. Overton.

OVERTON: Well, of course, I would.

WARFIELD: Thank you, ma'am. No further questions.

With that final, understated civility, Warfield had ended the testimonial phase of the trial. The only things that remained were the summations, but as he glanced at the clock, then down at the substantial number of pages in Warfield and Talbott's closing statements, Kinley decided to wait until the next day before beginning.

On the way out, he dropped by William Warfield's office once again.

"Your father did a very good job," Kinley said as he peeped briefly through the open door.

Warfield could hardly be seen behind an enormous stack of papers. "That doesn't surprise me," he said.

"Did you ever see him work?"

"Lots of times," Warfield said. "He was the best pure trial lawyer Sequoyah ever produced." He smiled. "Of course, I'm a little prejudiced, I guess."

"I don't suppose you ever discussed the Overton case with him?" Kinley said.

"Not much about it, anyway."

"He never voiced any doubts?"

"About what?"

"Overton's guilt."

Warfield laughed softly. "Are you kidding? You've been reading the transcript. Do you have any doubts?"

Kinley shrugged. "In a murder case, I feel better when there's a body."

"Well, sure," Warfield said. "I'm sure my father would have felt better about that, too. But they had that bloody dress, of course, and there was no doubt that it was Ellie Dinker's."

"Did your father ever mention what he thought might have been done with the body?"

"You mean what Overton did with it?"

"Yes."

Warfield thought a moment. "Under water," he said finally. "My father pretty much felt that that was the only way Overton could have gotten rid of it. He thought he must have thrown it into the river."

"What river?"

"Rocky River," Warfield said, "the one that flows through the canyon. You know, out there where Ray Tindall died."

Fourteen

Lois arrived at the house on Beaumont Street only a few minutes after Kinley returned from the courthouse. She was wearing a gray suit, and looked more like a woman who'd just rushed up the streets of Manhattan than someone who'd lived in Sequoyah for almost thirty years. She had never lost her midwestern accent, and because of that, Kinley found her voice refreshing, a sudden reminder that other places existed beyond those he'd been reading about all day—narrow, tree-lined streets and forest paths, woods, canyons, a green churning river.

"I wasn't sure I'd catch you here," she said.

She was standing on the small front porch, still separated from him by the screen door, her face webbed by its slender metal squares, and for a moment she reminded him of Dora Overton, the same dark eyes and determined face, the same resilience and firmness that Ray had no doubt found attractive in both women.

"Since you've gotten so into whatever it is Serena's worried about, I wanted to show you what I took from

Ray's file cabinet," she added matter-of-factly. She lifted a large manila envelope toward him. "This should do a little to get her off that particular kick."

Kinley opened the screen door and took the envelope from her hand. "Thanks, Lois," he said as he drew the door closed again. "I'll read it tonight."

Lois did not move. "Well, I don't want to be pushy," she said, "but would you mind if I came in?" It was not a request.

"Of course," Kinley said. "I'm sorry. I didn't think you'd come by for a visit."

"I'm not mad at you, Jack," Lois explained. "I just want things laid to rest."

"I understand," Kinley told her as he stepped back to let her pass.

Lois walked directly into the living room and sat down on the sofa by the window.

"Want something to drink?" Kinley asked as he joined her there. "Not that I know where Ray kept his liquor."

"Over the kitchen sink," Lois said. "But, no thanks."

Kinley sat down in the small chair across from the sofa. "So, how are you doing?" he asked idly.

Lois drew in a quick, faintly irritated breath. "I won't be long, Jack," she said. "I just wanted to give you those files and tell you again that I don't want Serena to spend her life wondering what happened to her father. At least, as far as his death is concerned. As far as this other matter, I . . ."

"She won't hear about that from me," Kinley assured her. "I know how to keep things off the record. I'm sure Dora would want it that way, too."

Lois's eyes narrowed intently. "You talked to Dora Overton?"

"Yes."

"What did she say?"

"Nothing unusual," Kinley said.

"About her and Ray? The affair, you mean?"

Kinley nodded. "Yes," he said, then shifted awkwardly in his seat. "I don't know whether it matters to you or not, Lois," he told her. "But I think she cared a great deal for Ray, and he probably felt the same way about her."

Lois stared at him icily.

"Whatever it was between them," Kinley added. "It had to do with love."

"And that makes it okay?"

"I don't know about that."

"It's me. I'm the problem. Is that what you think, Jack?"

"About what?"

"About Ray and Dora," Lois said.

"I don't know about these things, Lois," Kinley said, "but I do think there was something between Ray and Dora that was . . . well, that wasn't just a . . ."

"Roll in the hay?" Lois interrupted sharply.

"That's right."

"And you know something, Jack, that makes it worse, not better," Lois told him. "It makes it a lot harder to take." She shook her head wearily. "You always think that love cancels out betrayal. All men think that. But it's bullshit."

Kinley shrugged. "People change, that's all I know. It happens all the time."

"Yes, it does," Lois blurted, "and more's the pity." Her eyes fled to the window and settled on the graying late-afternoon air beyond it. "Is that why you never married?" she asked after a moment. "Because people change?"

"I don't know."

Her eyes shot over to him. "Ray always denied it, but I never believed him. He said Dora was . . ." She smiled grimly. "Just a friend."

"He talked about her?" Kinley asked. "To you?"

She nodded. "Yes, he did. But not the real stuff. He said he was working on something for her, an old case. He made it sound like a job."

"He was working on something."

"What?"

"An old murder case."

She looked at Kinley questioningly. "Is that why he was down in the canyon?"

In his mind, Kinley saw Ellie Dinker's body rolling in the green waters of Rocky River, then sinking down, dissolving into an indistinguishable mass as the years passed, a condition Ray would no doubt have understood and thus found no reason whatsoever to search for her along the pebbly banks of the river.

"I don't think he would have expected to find anything about the Overton case in the canyon," Kinley said. "So far, I haven't found much of anything that would have led him down there."

"Found?" Lois asked. "You're working on it, too?"

"Yes."

"Why?"

"Because it was his last case," Kinley said. "That's the only reason I can think of."

"Can you talk about it?"

"I don't know very much," Kinley said. "So far I've just read the transcript of the trial. As far as I can tell, the case against Overton is pretty strong."

"Overton?"

"Yes, Charles Overton, Dora's father."

Lois sat back slightly. "He was a murderer?"

Kinley found himself giving in to the weight of evidence. "He might have been," he said.

"Who did he kill?"

"A young girl," Kinley said. "It was back in 1954."

"And they convicted him?"

Kinley nodded. "They executed him."

"Executed, yes," Lois said thoughtfully. "There was an article about that."

"Where?"

"In with all those clippings I found in one of Ray's files."

"Was there anything else in the file about the case?"

"Just what was in the O file," Lois said. "And to tell you the truth, Kinley, I was a little relieved. I didn't want to find love letters from Dora Overton. I mean, divorce or no divorce, you always feel a certain way."

"Yeah," Kinley said.

"Anyway, it's all in the envelope," Lois added, dismissing any further discussion of the case, her mind shifting back to Dora. "What's she like?" she asked. "What did Ray see in her?"

"I don't know her very well."

"But you're going to," Lois said. "I can see that in your face." She smiled. "I must say, I'm a little surprised in you, Jack."

"How?"

"Well, I wouldn't have expected you to come home and take up where Ray left off quite so . . . literally."

Kinley stared at her silently, and after a moment, she stood up and walked back out onto the porch. Kinley followed along behind her, the screen door closing softly behind him.

At the front steps, Lois paused and turned back toward him. "So, you're going to see Dora again?" she asked.

"Yes."

"Tell her I despise her," Lois said.

Kinley said nothing.

Lois glared up toward the mountain. "She knew him better, didn't she? Better than I did?"

"I don't know."

"He talked to her."

"Yes, I think he did."

Her face took on a strange resignation, as her eyes returned to Kinley. "The lover always gets the best of someone," she said quietly. "The dregs come home and go to sleep."

Kinley ate a quick dinner made up of what had been left behind in Ray's kitchen, a can of pork and beans and a few Vienna sausages, all of which he washed down with one of the three beers he found in the refrigerator.

While he ate, he watched the small black-and-white television which Ray had balanced precariously on one of the kitchen counters. It was tuned to Channel 3, a local access station which carried the latest news from Sequoyah and its surrounding communities. At the moment, a man dressed in green fatigues was tromping through a wooded area, glancing back toward the camera from time to time, as he commented on the local landscape.

As it turned out, Kinley finished his meal at the same moment the man on television brought his program to a close with a broad smile and a parting bit of homestyle instruction: "So, friends, this is Bob Burbank saying, 'Hey, look around you.'"

Kinley snapped the television off, washed the dishes, then walked down the short corridor to Ray's office, where he'd deposited the envelope Lois had given him an hour or so before.

The three files were arranged alphabetically, one on top of the other, a tribute to Lois's orderliness, and he opened D first, found it empty, just as she had said it was, then moved on to O.

It was a thick file, though not bloated, and Ray had arranged the papers inside it chronologically, beginning with various newspaper accounts of Overton's arrest on July 4, and ending with his execution at the state prison six months later, an event which was sufficiently newsworthy, Kinley noted, for the Sequoyah *Standard* to send one of its own reporters to cover it.

His name was Harry Townsend, and he'd covered the whole case, his byline under every story published by the *Standard*, from Dinker's disappearance to Overton's execution several months later. And in Kinley's estimation, he'd done a good job, not only in his individual pieces, but in the accompanying pictures he'd also taken while covering the case.

Ray had assembled the pictures in a kind of "order of appearance" format, beginning with Ellie Dinker and ending with a final photograph of Charles Overton as he was led away from the courthouse after he'd received his death sentence. All the incidental characters were present in the collection. Maddox and Wade posed in their recently pressed uniforms, Warfield and Talbott in dark, conservative suits beside the flagpole. Mrs. Overton, her head bound in a dark scarf, dodging Townsend's camera as she darted down the courthouse steps. Unlike Mrs. Overton, Dr. Stark and Mr. Coggins seemed grateful for the attention. As for Luther Snow and Betty Gaines, they appeared as direct human opposites: Gaines shy, looking away; Snow staring straight into the lens, as if daring it to expose him.

At the end, almost as a coda, Ray had clipped the last report on the case, Townsend's description of Overton's execution. To Kinley's surprise, as he read it, Townsend was no country hack. He'd read enough back-country journalism by then to know that "reporters" for such papers were often little more than town gossips with a literary itch. Townsend, however, was nothing like that, and his account of the execution of Charles Overton was fittingly solemn, with just enough graphic detail to evoke the scene without allowing it to cross the line into morbid titillation:

Charles Herman Overton, though only thirty-five years old on the cold, rainy day of his execution, looked much older than his years as he trudged slowly toward the unadorned metal chair where he was to die exactly four minutes and seventeen seconds later.

Overton appeared slightly disoriented as he glanced about, his eyes settling briefly on the group of witnesses that had gathered at the far side of the small concrete room before continuing their nervous, darting motion. He did not speak to anyone as he shuffled across the room, nor did he seem aware of the magnitude of the moment, and as the efficient prison staff went through the grim routine of straps and electrodes which must inevitably precede the act of execution, he seemed to shrink away, as if the air were being squeezed from his body. He stared straight ahead, made no further eye contact with either witnesses or prison staff, as the preparations continued, the guards moving through their assigned tasks with great speed and in complete silence.

Once harnessed to the machine, Overton remained upright and very erect as the metal skull cap was lowered over the shaved pate of his head. He blinked rapidly for a moment, then closed his eyes in a tight squint, as if in anticipation of the shock which was to come, or perhaps, to prevent himself the indignity of a scream.

His eyes did not open again in this world.

Not bad, Kinley thought, as his mind shifted suddenly to his own description of the death of Colin Bright. It had been very academic, it struck him now, a writing style that had been meant to please the English professors who would never read it, and which had adroitly stressed clever ideas over the terrible feeling of a carefully orchestrated and predetermined death, its grim mechanics of seared nerves. Harry Townsend, whoever he was, had done better than that, particularly in the lovely understatement of his last line.

His eyes did not open again in this world.

As he allowed himself to read the line again, Kinley had the sense that something was being loosened up in him, as if, against his will, he were being made to feel Overton's death as he thought Dora must feel it, and perhaps as Ray had come to feel it too, dark and tragic and unjust.

He stopped himself instantly, drew the cord tight again,

shoring himself up. Dark and tragic, that much still remained true of Overton, as it was probably true, it seemed to Kinley, of every human fate. But that left the final adjective intact. And so, Kinley wondered, as he closed the O file and turned to the S, flipping quickly through the irrelevant assortment of old town photographs Ray had assembled there, could it also be said that the death of Charles Herman Overton had been entirely unjust?

When he could answer that question yes or no, he thought as he turned off the desk light and headed for his bed, his work in Sequoyah would be done, and he could return to New York, to the small apartment which overlooked the upper reaches of Broadway, to the gentle rapture of untroubled sleep.

Fifteen

If the arguments for and against the death of Charles
Overton had ever existed in a concentrated form, Kinley
knew he was about to confront them as he drew the
transcripts down from the vault shelf the next morning.
Early in his work, he'd discovered the high drama which
inevitably accompanied even the most mediocre of the
closing arguments in capital cases. With so much at stake,
the arena of the courtroom became a place of mythic
struggle. The petty disputes which rang through the court
day after day suddenly gave way to a form of solemn
combat a Roman Emperor would have admired—fierce,
dedicated, and at times, as Kinley had noted more often
than he would have expected, strikingly poetic, as if
ordinary voices had suddenly been made glorious and
eloquent by the grave issue upon which they spoke:
whether or not a human being should be put to death.

Kinley had learned enough about Thomas Warfield's
courtroom style by the time he opened the trial transcript

to his closing argument to expect a fine performance. He was not disappointed.

For many pages, Warfield did what nearly all prosecutors found it necessary to do before making their final plunge into the lofty moral rhetoric with which their closing arguments would truly close. He had outlined his case again, massing one detail upon another, until the evidence stood before the jury like a great concrete finger pointing directly toward the defendant. Then, and only then, had he taken flight.

What is the evidence in this case? It is what it should be in a trial for murder. It is flesh and blood. It is in Ellie Dinker's blood on her dress. It is in the bits of flesh which clung to that tire iron Deputy Wade found in Charles Overton's truck.

The defense will tell you that we do not have a body. Mr. Talbott will tell you that we cannot even prove a murder has been committed.

Well, ladies and gentlemen of the jury, look at that dress as we show it to you now, draped across the chair before you. Look at the blood which stains it. Ellie Dinker was sixteen years old. Ellie Dinker was five feet tall. Ellie Dinker weighed ninety-three pounds when Dr. Stark weighed her only a month before her death. Look at the amount of blood on that dress, and tell me in your hearts if a body that small could sustain an injury so profound as to stain a dress the way this one is stained, and still live.

No, ladies and gentlemen, you know that Ellie Louise Dinker is dead. And the fact that Charles Overton to this day will not tell us where her body lies, that is a cruelty which he has inflicted upon Ellie Dinker's mother that is almost as evil as the murder itself. He could tell us where she is. He could let Ellie's mother give her only daughter a decent, Christian funeral. He could tell us. But he won't. He wants to save his life, and this is the only way he can save it. He can hope that you believe that because Ellie Dinker's body has never been found, that she is alive, living somewhere, probably in one of the world's great resorts.

Do you believe that?

Is Ellie Dinker in Paris? Is she in Rome? Is she having a wonderful time bouncing in the sea, climbing mountains?

No.

Ellie Dinker will never see Rome or Paris. She will never see the ocean or the mountains. She will never marry or have children of her own. All the opportunities of life, all its beauty and sweetness are lost to her. They were snatched from her by Charles Overton, and they can never be returned.

And you know why they can't be returned: In your hearts you know why.

Because Ellie Dinker is dead.

She is—to use the terms of the law in this case— she is unjustly dead.

You know what that means?

Unjustly dead.

It means she did not die by disease or accident. Unjustly dead.

It means that she did not die by negligence. Unjustly dead.

It means that she did not die in the service of her country.

Unjustly dead means that Ellie Louise Dinker was murdered.

And we may not have her body, ladies and gentlemen, but by the grace and intervention of a just and wrathful God, we do have her killer in this room with us today.

He is there. He is there.

I raise my hand and point him out to you.

He is there.

And ladies and gentlemen, I don't ask that you

135

*do to him what he did to Ellie Dinker. He put her
to death—remember the words of the law—he put
her to death unjustly.*

I will not ask you to do that.

I will ask you to do justice.

*I will ask you to put to death Charles Herman
Overton, not unjustly, the way he put Ellie Dinker
to death, but justly, as you have a right, and an
obligation, to do.*

I do not ask for vengeance.

I ask for justice.

I believe that you will render it.

Thank you.

It was good, Kinley thought as he turned the page, it
was very good. It had everything a rural Southern courtroom would have needed in the winter of 1954. It had
the high rhetoric and righteous fire that gave the whole
argument a fierce Biblical grandeur. And, as Kinley realized, it must have swept over the jury like a mighty
stream. In his mind, he could see the jurors nodding
sagely as Warfield made his long stride back to the prosecution table, their eyes following him in awe and wonder
before they finally slid distractedly over to where Horace
Talbott now rose to address them.

Warfield had fully anticipated defense's argument in
the case, but that anticipation had not served to warn
Talbott against making it. And in his closing remarks,
Talbott addressed the issue as relentlessly as if he'd never
heard Warfield raise it.

*You have a problem in this case. You don't know
where Ellie Dinker is. That's not a problem for me,
because I'm not being asked to put a man to death.
But you are being asked to do that. Mr. Warfield is
asking you to do that. He is asking you to forget
about the fact that you don't know where Ellie
Dinker is.*

Is she in Paris? I don't know.

Is she in Rome? I don't know.

And you don't know either, ladies and gentlemen of the jury.

And that is a very serious problem. Because you do not know for an absolute certainty that Ellie Dinker is dead. You can look at that dress until you turn blue, and you can look at the stains and think about how big or little Ellie Dinker was, what she weighed and her blood type and all of that, but it will not tell you for an absolute certainty that she is dead.

Is she running around in the ocean? I don't know.

Is she out mountain climbing? I don't know.

I don't have to know.

But you do have to know, ladies and gentlemen, because a man's life is dependent upon your knowing where Ellie Dinker is at this moment. Not tomorrow, and not yesterday, but where she is at this instant.

But since you do not know where Ellie Dinker is, I ask that you not send a man to death for killing her.

Thank you.

It had been short and sweet, Kinley thought after reading Talbott's closing remarks, but he had done all that was left for him to do by that point in the trial. Before that point, however, one considerably more important was so obvious that Kinley felt no need to jot it down: Why had Charles Overton not testified?

He remembered the passivity with which Overton had faced his arrest, and he wondered if such passivity might have been the result of a shock he was never able to overcome, a state he'd entered as the handcuffs were snapped in place, and which he'd lingered in from then until the moment he'd shuffled across the floor of the execution, still moving, it seemed to Kinley, like a sacrificial lamb. He'd seen that happen before, a strange, eerie calm after the wave of annihilating violence had passed. He thought of Bundy still filing his meticulous briefs during the final, dwindling hours of his life; of the Birdman of Alcatraz poring over volumes of ornithology; of Mildred Haskell's psychosexual texts, and last of Colin Bright, so peaceful in his captivity, monkish and serene, his soft blue eyes entirely motionless as he'd offered Kinley his bit of worldly wisdom: *Be careful. You don't always know who you are.*

He returned the transcripts to the box, then the box to its place on the top shelf. On the way out, he stopped at Mrs. Hunter's desk at the entrance to the vault.

"I wanted to thank you for letting me look through the transcripts," he said politely.

"Oh, no trouble," Mrs. Hunter said. She drew a pair of glasses from her eyes and let them dangle from a black cord around her neck. "Did you find what you were looking for?"

"Not exactly," Kinley told her, "but I made a start."

Mrs. Hunter smiled. "You know, I didn't know who you were at first."

Kinley looked at her quizzically. "Who I was?"

Mrs. Hunter shook her head shyly. "I mean, if you were the Jackson Kinley they write about in the paper sometimes."

Kinley nodded.

"Then Mr. Warfield told me, and I remembered seeing your picture from time to time," Mrs. Hunter added. "He said you came down for Ray Tindall's funeral."

"That's right."

"Wonderful person, Ray was."

"Yes."

"Wonderful person," Mrs. Hunter repeated idly. "Did you know him very well?"

"Not really. He kept to himself."

"Yeah, he did."

"I think he was sort of close with Mr. Wade, though."

138

"Mr. Wade?"

"He's the Chief Investigator for the District Attorney's Office," Mrs. Hunter said. "Ben Wade."

Kinley recognized the name immediately. "Ben Wade," he said. "Is he the same Ben Wade who worked for Sheriff Maddox back in 1954?"

"Yeah, he was with the Sheriff's Office back then," Mrs. Hunter said.

"And he's still around the courthouse?"

"Right upstairs," Mrs. Hunter said.

Kinley smiled quietly. It was one of the pleasures of working the rural outback, he thought, the fact that everything was so inextricably connected.

Sixteen

Ben Wade was now over sixty years old, but the large, robust body Kinley remembered from the newspaper photographs he'd found in Ray's file on the case was still very much in evidence. He sat behind a small wooden desk in a cramped office just down the hall from William Warfield's far more spacious one, and the blank walls and worn carpet suggested that he had little use, and no money, for the more luxurious taste of the District Attorney.

"You're Ben Wade, I believe?" Kinley said as he lingered at the open office door.

Wade's head lifted, and Kinley saw the web of red veins that lined his nose, and the moist, heavy-lidded eyes that peered gently in his direction, giving the unmistakable suggestion that a bottle of Old Grand-Dad could probably be found in his desk drawer.

"I'm Ben Wade," the man said. He leaned back slightly and drew in a long slow breath. He wore a white shirt, the sleeves rolled to the elbow, and Kinley could see a faint, purplish tattoo just above the right elbow, a sprig of vine coiled around a motto of some kind, but which he could not make out from his place beside the door.

"What can I do for you?" Wade asked.

"My name is Jack Kinley," Kinley began. "I was a friend of Ray Tindall's."

Wade nodded. "Good man, Ray. I liked working with him. I thought he might try to play the big shot, having been Sheriff before and all, but he didn't." He nodded toward a second wooden desk which was in the opposite corner of the room. "That's where he worked, in case you're interested."

Kinley's eyes swept over to the desk. It was almost a duplicate of Wade's, and just as marked by age and indifferent use, honed down to its function, the way Ray had often seemed honed down.

"Ray sort of kept to himself," Wade said, "but we got along pretty well."

Kinley returned his attention to Wade. "Do you mind if I ask you a few questions?" he asked.

"Questions?" Wade said, surprised. "About what?"

"Just about Ray," Kinley answered. "What he was doing the last few weeks of his life."

"Sure, I got some time," he said. "But I didn't follow what Ray was doing all that close."

Kinley walked further into the room and sat down at the small metal chair in front of Wade's desk. "I've been reading the transcript of the Overton trial," he said. "You remember it, back in 1954?"

Wade nodded, his face very still. "Yeah, I remember it," he said. "We don't have so many murder trials here in Sequoyah that you don't remember them."

"You must have been a young man when all that was going on," Kinley said.

"I'd just turned thirty," Wade said, "but I'd been around for a while by then." His eyes narrowed somewhat. "How come you're looking into that old case?"

"Because Ray was."

Wade looked at Kinley pointedly. "You know, before you get too deep in this thing, there's something you ought to know about Ray. And this is not for general circulation, of course, but it might explain a few things about why Ray was so interested in this . . ."

"He was having an affair with Dora Overton," Kinley blurted. "Yes, I know."

Wade's mouth tightened. "You got it." He smiled, a sage in his small arena of human connection. "Like the song says, 'looking for love in all the wrong places.'"

"That's what Ray was doing?"

"Well, Dora had a sort of a reputation here in town," Wade said. "You know what I mean?"

"Not exactly."

"Sort of living wild, you might say."

"She didn't strike me as the party type."

"Not exactly wild like that," Wade said. "More in her head. Wild ideas."

"Like her father's innocence?"

"Yeah, like that."

Kinley reached for his notebook. "You wouldn't mind if I took some notes, would you?"

Wade waved his hand casually. "Hell, no. Whatever you want."

"I just have a few questions about the investigation," Kinley said as he brought his pen to the notebook.

"Shoot."

"How did you first hear about the murder?"

"I got a radio call," Wade said. "From the dispatcher. We just had two radio cars in those days. Me and Hendricks, we handled most everything."

"Hendricks?"

"Riley Hendricks," Wade said. "He works over at South Side High School, in case you want to talk to him."

Kinley wrote the name down quickly, then continued with the interview, moving effortlessly into the style that

142

served him best, cool, matter-of-fact, a face that betrayed nothing but academic curiosity.

"And this radio dispatch," he asked. "What did it say?"

"That a girl was missing," Wade answered. "Said her name, you know, Ellie Dinker, said she was wearing a green dress and that her mother had last seen her going up the mountain toward Carl Slater's house."

"Carl Slater? Is that Helen Slater's father?"

"That's right," Wade said. "Ellie and Helen were high school friends, I guess. Anyway, she never made it to Helen's."

"Did you ever talk to Helen?"

"I talked to everybody up there, Carl and Helen, and Dottie, that's Helen's sister, and to Carl's wife, Cynthia."

"Are they all still around town?"

"Cynthia died about three years ago," Wade said. "Carl's in the state home up on Williams Road. Helen and Dottie are still around. Dottie's got a little sock store out in the factory district. Slater Socks, that's what it's called."

"And Helen?"

"She married a Foley," Wade said, "but when Carl got put in the state home, they moved into the old homestead."

"Where is that?"

"Up on Foster Road, where it always was," Wade said. "Same place Ellie Dinker was headed up to that morning Overton snatched her."

Again, Kinley carefully recorded the information for future use, ignoring Wade's clear belief that nothing had gone awry as far as the guilt of Charles Overton was concerned.

"And from your investigation," he said, "you learned that Ellie Dinker had never made it up to the Slater house?"

"Never made it, that's right."

143

"How far would that have been? From Ellie's house to Helen's, I mean?"

"Oh, five miles or so, if you took the road."

"Was there another way?"

"Through the woods," Wade said, "straight up the side of the mountain. It would be hard slogging in the summertime, but it could be done."

Kinley jotted it down in his notebook.

"Of course, she'd probably have taken the road most of the way up," Wade said, "then, once she topped the mountain, she could have cut a hard left and gone through the woods to the Slater place."

"Where is the Slater place, exactly?"

"Foster Road, like I said," Wade said. "Right at the end of it." He pointed to the window. "Hell, you can just about see it from the bottom of the mountain. It sits right on the edge up there."

Kinley thought a moment, his mind doing its service while he flipped back through the notes he'd taken of the trial testimony. "That's sort of strange," he said when he found the page he was looking for.

"What is?"

"Well, I was just looking at my notes on Mrs. Dinker's testimony," Kinley said, his eyes studying the open notebook. "And when Warfield asked her when she saw Ellie last, Mrs. Dinker said that she'd seen Ellie head out through the woods behind her house." He looked at Wade. "If Ellie were going to Helen Slater's, why wouldn't she have taken the road?"

Wade said nothing.

"Why would she have headed out into the woods behind her house?" Kinley repeated. "Instead of going in the other direction to the mountain road?"

Wade glanced quickly at the notebook, then back up toward Kinley. "Martha Dinker said that?" he asked. "That she saw Ellie going off in the woods behind her house?"

"That's what she testified to, yes."

144

Wade leaned back slowly in his seat. "I don't know," he admitted finally. "Because if she'd gone right up through the woods behind her house, she wouldn't have come nowhere around Carl Slater's place."

"They're not in the same general direction," Kinley said. "Not even close."

Wade shook his head. "No, they're not." He thought a moment. "Of course, old lady Dinker might have gotten it wrong." He smiled. "She's got a few loose screws too, you know?"

"You mean the dressing in black, haunting the town, all of that?"

"Partly," Wade said. "But she's also come back and forth to the courthouse a few times."

"Do you know why?"

Wade shook his head. "Sometimes she used to read the trial record, like you're doing. Then, after that, she'd just come and stand on the steps and stare out over the town."

In his mind, Kinley suddenly saw her, a black figure melodramatically set against the great stone edifice of the courthouse, silent, motionless, her face draped in the black netting that perpetually covered it, her hands tearing at a white, lacy handkerchief, unravelling it one slender thread at a time.

"They put her away about three years ago, you know," Wade said. "She died in the state nuthouse."

"Why did they put her away?"

"Well, she'd started raving about things," Wade said, "roaming around too. Especially after her house burned down. At night, sometimes. Just roaming around. People around town would come home and find her standing out in their yard." He shook his head at the preposterousness of it. "Hell, they even found her in the woods one time. An old woman, naked. Just roaming the woods out by the canyon." He shook his head. "Poor old thing. Judge Bryan had her committed after that."

"Judge Bryan?"

Wade nodded.

"Is that the same Judge Bryan who presided at Overton's trial?"

Wade laughed. "The very same. We don't have many judges in Sequoyah County," he said. "We can't shell out that kind of public money the way you rich folks can up North."

Kinley once again ignored the kind of jab he'd heard often enough in the past. Instead he noted the facts Wade had given him in his notebook, then, as he always did, drew his questions back to their original path.

"You said you talked to all the Slaters, and they hadn't seen Ellie. Is that right?" he asked.

"Yeah."

"What did you do after that?"

"Well, Sheriff Maddox had told me to go up to the Slaters," Wade said, "and I was through up there at around midnight, I guess, and after that I headed down the mountain road, just looking around, thinking the girl might be headed home. I didn't see her, of course, and so I checked back in at Headquarters."

"Your shift was over?"

"No, not quite, but I wanted to tell the Sheriff what I'd found out," Wade said. "It's what they call 'briefing' now, but back then we didn't have a word for it. We just came back and reported various things."

"Did anything else happen during your shift?"

"No," Wade said. "Nothing happened after that until we started to comb around the woods and I found Ellie Dinker's dress hanging in the tree."

"Was anybody with you?"

"No, and I was glad of it," Wade said. "Hell, if Riley'd been with me, he'd a turned white as a ghost. Swear to God, that boy would have run over to the nearest shrub and let go of his breakfast." He chuckled. "Riley just wasn't made of the right stuff for law enforcement, you know. He got out of it not long after the trial, and he was right to do it."

146

Kinley nodded. "What happened after you found the dress?"

"I called in to the Sheriff," Wade said, "and he came right out to where we'd found it."

"Where was the dress, exactly?"

"Sort of hanging on a limb."

"I know, I've seen the pictures," Kinley said.

"They're pretty good, those pictures," Wade said. "I took them myself. First time I'd ever used one of those instant cameras. I was a little surprised at how good the pictures came out."

"Yes," Kinley said quickly. "But I was asking about where the dress was in relationship to the mountain road?"

"About a half-mile off of it," Wade said. "There's a mile marker there. I think the number is twenty-seven, and where I found that dress, that's pretty much a beeline right up the mountain for about half a mile from there."

Kinley wrote down the directions, then looked back up at Wade. "What happened after that?"

"I gathered up the dress, and then me and the Sheriff searched the area, but we didn't find anything."

"Was there any indication of where the murder had taken place?" Kinley asked.

"The only thing we knew for sure was that it sure hadn't happened where we found the dress," Wade said.

"There was no blood in that area?"

"No blood, no broken plants or dirt and leaves messed with at all around that place," Wade said. "He'd carried her there from somewhere else."

"He?"

"Charlie Overton."

Kinley looked at him intently. "Did you ever have any reason to doubt that you had the right man?"

Wade shook his head.

"Ray did," Kinley said flatly.

Wade sat back slightly and folded his great arms over his chest. "Did Ray hear him confess?" he asked.

147

"Did you?"

"Yes."

"Why didn't you testify to that?"

"Because Warfield didn't ask me to," Wade said.

"Why not?"

"He read it over, and said it rambled too much," Wade said. "He claimed it was incoherent, that the jury would think Overton was a little nutty, and if they got to feeling sorry for him, they might let him off on that. He didn't want to raise that issue."

"But it was a confession?"

"It sure was," Wade said. "He made it in that little holding cell right there in Sheriff Maddox's office."

"Did you take it down?"

"Of course I did," Wade said, "not that it mattered. They never used it." Something struck him suddenly. "As a matter of fact, the only person who ever asked me for it after the trial was Ray." He glanced over to the empty desk. "He asked me where I'd put it, and I hunted around in my old files and came up with it."

"Do you know what he did with it?"

"Yeah," Wade said. "He put it in that top drawer. It might still be there, if you'd want to see it."

"Yes, I would," Kinley told him.

Wade pulled himself up and lumbered across the room to Ray's desk. "He put it right in here," he said as he opened the unlocked drawer. "Well, you're in luck," he added, as he drew the single sheet of paper from the drawer and handed it to Kinley.

Kinley looked at it unbelievingly. "Just one page?"

Wade shrugged. "He didn't have that much to say."

"Would you mind if I took it with me?" Kinley asked. "I'd like to give it a close reading."

"Like Ray," Wade said. "I saw him reading it several times."

Kinley folded the paper and inserted it in his jacket pocket. "Did he ever tell you anything he might have found out about the case?"

Wade shook his head silently, then returned to his place behind the desk. "No, he never said anything about it," he said, "but I could tell that it was getting to him. Or that something was." He smiled. "I figured it was Dora. I figured she was putting him through the paces, something like that."

"Ray never struck me as the type who'd put up with that," Kinley said.

"Me, neither," Wade said, "until Dora." The smile softened almost delicately, as if with a distant, wistful sympathy for Ray's plight. "But you know how things get turned around in a situation like that."

"Like what?"

"You know, like the song says," Wade told him, " 'When a man loves a woman.' "

Seventeen

It was late in the afternoon by the time Kinley left Wade's office. By now he realized that his stay in Sequoyah would be longer than expected, and so he drove down to his hotel, gathered up his few remaining articles, and checked out, the old man behind the desk eyeing him curiously, already amazed that anyone had stayed more than one night in a town he didn't live in.

Once back at Ray's house, he hung his clothes in the bedroom closet, then poured himself a scotch from the dwindling remains of the bottle Ray had left behind. It was still unseasonably warm for early September, so he walked out onto the porch and sat down in the swing. The first shade of evening was descending over the valley, and a bluish haze could be seen drifting slowly down from the mountain. Night had always fallen like this in Sequoyah, and as he watched the vaporous mountain haze tumble slowly, like an avalanche of clouds from the heights above, Kinley thought of all the times he'd sat with Ray, the two of them watching the same ominous advance. They had done it on their last night together, and Kinley could remember the few words they'd spoken on that particular evening, the sorrow of his grandmother's death still lingering in his mind, and Ray careful not to bring her up again, but to dwell on other, more distant observations.

Look at the mountain, Kinley. It's like cannon smoke.

What is?

The way the clouds come down.

Yes.

Clouds like that hung over the Wilderness Campaign.

That was a terrible battle.

Hung for days and days, part smoke, part water. "And the bullets fell like rain." That's what one of the old soldiers wrote.

Hard to imagine it.

It was then, at that precise moment, Kinley remembered now, that a strange restlessness had suddenly appeared on Ray's face, dark and lingering, like the clouds that were approaching from afar. "Hard to imagine, yes," Ray had said. "Like so many things."

Like so many things.

It was a short, cryptic remark, and Ray had added nothing to it. It had been uttered to the air, it seemed to Kinley as he recalled its precise tone, as if Ray were alone in the swing, as if he were talking only to his soul. At the time, Kinley had thought nothing of it, but now he wondered if it had come from some other part of his life, particularly the part that had to do with Dora Overton and her father.

He took a long sip of the scotch, placed the glass on the wooden floor beneath the swing, and drew out the confession Wade had taken from Ray's desk.

The brevity of it still amazed him. Now confessions went on for page after page, the police careful to record every imaginable detail to ensure that it was complete. In

1954, the police had moved through the world's pervasive lawlessness with far more confidence that what they said would be believed, or at least remain unquestioned. As a result, the confessions of their prisoners had possessed a frightening succinctness. He remembered Colin Bright's initial statement, one which he never amplified during his later trial, and whose more frightful details he had finally told Kinley himself for no other reason, as Bright himself had said, but that *it's you that's here.*

On the afternoon of August 7, 1954, I entered the home of William P. Comstock in Willisville, Alabama, and murdered five members of the Comstock family in this order and in the ways I'm putting down.

William P. Comstock—August 7—cut his throat
Danny Comstock—August 8—shot three times
Betty Comstock—August 8—stabbed several times, also raped
Keith Comstock—August 9—strangled
Wilma Jean Comstock—August 9—electrocution, also raped, front and back
This is what I did.

Sincerely,
Colin Bright

Although not as brief as Bright's statement, Charles Overton's was only slightly more detailed, and as he read it, Kinley tried to imagine the man himself, the long, dreary face he'd seen in the newspaper photographs, his posture, whether sitting or standing, always deeply slumped so that a sense of brokenness seemed to pervade every aspect of his character.

It was a sense that equally pervaded the written statement, despite the fact that it was not a verbatim rendering, but Wade's own summation of what Overton had told him. And yet, the same weariness and fatality rose from the account, a tone and style Kinley had seen before, most recently in Maria Spinola, the low groan of the perfect victim.

Written on plain, legal-sized yellow paper, it began with a brief commentary on Overton's background which consisted of information which Wade had gathered before extracting the confession.

Undersigned officer was told by Charles Herman Overton that he had lived in Sequoyah for the last twelve years. He had settled here after the war, and Mr. Overton stated that he was a veteran in the war and had been severely wounded in the European theater. Mr. Overton stated that he worked as a general laborer for Thompson Construction Company on Clermont Street in Sequoyah, and that he had been working on the new courthouse for the past year.

Mr. Overton said that he left work on the afternoon of July 2, 1954, because he was sick. On the way up the mountain, his truck broke down, and he was working on it when he saw a girl, later identified as Ellie Louise Dinker, come up the hill toward him. When she got to the road, Mr. Overton said that she came over to him, and that she began to talk to him, and that after a while, they went into the woods together.

Mr. Overton said that at some point while they were in the woods, he murdered Ellie Louise Dinker and threw her body in Rocky River and watched it float down the river and disappear over Spanish Falls.

After getting rid of the body, Mr. Overton said that he went home, then returned to his truck, fixed it, and went back home again, where he remained until he was arrested on July 4.

Mr. Overton said that he did not rape Ellie Louise Dinker, because he couldn't do that, but that he did

*kill her by hitting her with a tire iron. He said he
didn't know why he hung the dress in the trees, or
why he had killed the girl.*

*Mr. Overton said that this was a true account of
his crime and swore to the statement.*

*This statement was taken by the undersigned of-
ficer on July 4, 1954, at twelve midnight in the
holding cell at the Sequoyah County Sheriff's Department in Sequoyah, Georgia.*

> *Benjamin C. Wade*
> *Deputy*

Kinley folded the statement, laid it down on the swing
and headed back into the kitchen. He drained the last of
the scotch into his glass, then returned to the front porch
and sipped it quietly while the first evening shadows
gathered around him.

For a moment, he tried to draw on his own long experience with criminal violence, asking the questions that
experience had offered him as a way of testing the veracity of any particular rendering of a crime. Usually in
such cases, contradictions piled on contradictions, guns
exchanged hands, people shifted from one room to another, dialogue blew in the wind, randomly lighting on
first one mouth then another. Consistency was the great
goal of every investigator, but it was a harsh mistress,
elusive, demanding, at times utterly unreachable. Inconsistencies, either of character or circumstance, dogged
the trail of any investigator with the strength of character
necessary to look closely at a case. As he took the last
drink from his glass, he remembered Detective Ronald
Casey, the man who'd finally captured Colin Bright. He
had been Kinley's best official source, but even in a
case in which Bright's guilt had been incontestable, the
inconsistencies remained, and on their last meeting, with
the book nearly finished, Casey had finally voiced the
one that throughout the case had bothered him the most:

154

Why did Colin say he'd come up from Florida, Jack?
I mean, before he killed the Comstocks? Did he ever tell
you why he spun that particular yarn?

No. He always said he came up from Florida. He never
changed that.

No way, Jack. No way. That boy never saw a beach
or a palm tree in his whole shitty little life.

So the Florida story was a lie?

From top to bottom. He dropped a trail of bad checks
all over the South, but none of them were from Florida.

Why would he say Florida, then? What difference
would that make?

To this question, Casey, ancient in his gray hair, with-
ered skin and infinitely battered life, had given the only
reply his experience suggested to him. *It's like they say*
in the catechism about the Trinity, Jack, he said with a
wry, but oddly tormented smile. *It's a mystery.*

Kinley wondered if there were a few mysteries in
Charles Overton's statement, too. If there weren't any,
then why had Ray, as Wade had described it, "pored
over" the statement so many times. What had he been
looking for? Or had he sensed, as Kinley often did when
confronted with such documents, that something was
wrong, something missing or too often and pointedly
present, something indefinable at first glance, but which
might later rise suddenly like a red stain on the paper?

He unfolded Overton's confession and read it again,
this time with his notebook open, too, jotting notes for
any later discussion that might go on in his head.

In the first paragraph, he noted the scanty information
Overton had provided about his past. Was the war wound
a play for sympathy, or just a matter of information? Was
the comment about working on the courthouse a feeble
swipe at community involvement and social responsibility, the sort of self-serving detail Overton might have
used to gain Wade's sympathy?

In the second paragraph, Overton had continued his
tale of being sick at the courthouse construction site, of

having headed home, of having broken down on the way. If this part of his story was true, Kinley reasoned, then it was a confluence of small, insignificant accidents of health and mechanics that had finally served to generate a single, cataclysmic accident, the purely fortuitous meeting of Overton and Dinker on the mountain road. Such a meeting would have been likely only if Overton and Dinker had known each other and if Overton had had an illicit relationship with Dinker, why had he been unwilling to admit it in his confession?

The third and fourth paragraphs detailed the murder, the disposal of the body and Overton's movements after that, and the information was so spare of detail that Kinley circled it and made the notation *more here*, to indicate that he would need to speak with Wade again for additional questions.

The fifth paragraph had obviously been the result of Wade's questioning Overton at the time of his arrest. Kinley had seen enough of such statements to know where the investigator had pressed for more details. Although no tape had been made of the interrogation, Kinley could hear the dialogue in his mind, and for a moment he listened to it carefully, imagining its progress one question at a time. If Wade had extracted the details of the confession by leading Overton through the crime, in the way police officers had often done before the rules of evidence had changed, then Overton, as Dora had described him, would have fallen for it easily, the perfect victim, chewing obediently at the hook Wade cast toward him time and time again.

WADE: Now, Charlie, you've admitted killing Ellie Dinker, but let me ask you this. How did you do it?

OVERTON: How?

WADE: Yeah, I mean, what did you use?

OVERTON: Well, I . . .

WADE: I mean you did use something, right? I mean,

there was so much blood on the dress. Did you hit her with something? Did you have something in your truck?

OVERTON: I had a tire iron.

WADE: Did she struggle? I mean, she must have struggled, right?

OVERTON: Yes.

WADE: How did you stop her from struggling? Did you hit her?

OVERTON: Yes.

WADE: Did you do anything else to her?

OVERTON: You mean like . . .

WADE: I mean, before or after she was dead, you know?

OVERTON: No. No, I didn't do that. I couldn't do that.

WADE: All right, what did you do with the body? Did you bury it or throw it in the river or something like that?

OVERTON: I threw it in the river.

WADE: Then what?

OVERTON: Then I went home.

WADE: But what about the dress, the one we found hanging in the trees?

OVERTON: I just put it there. I don't know why.

WADE: Okay, Charlie, let me ask you this. Why did you kill Ellie Dinker?

OVERTON: I don't know.

As Kinley imagined it, the questioning of Charles Overton took on aspects of other cases he'd read or written about. In the co-ed murders in New York City, a defendant had drawn a crude floor plan of an apartment he'd never entered, described the color of the curtains in a room he'd never seen. If that kind of insistently leading police interrogation were possible in New York in 1968, he could not doubt that even greater abuses might have been carried out in the small-town South of 1954.

But that was in his mind, Kinley admitted immediately.

157

There was no written record of the questioning, but only Wade's brief, matter-of-fact and decidedly sketchy rendering of the results of the interrogation.

He glanced down at his notebook and quickly wrote out a command for himself: *Find out more about the interrogation. Press hard on this*.

He looked up again, the night now very deep around him. He could feel the first slight chill of autumn in the dark air, and he suddenly thought of Ray's body in the ground, colder than the earth, colder than the air, more distant from him now than the most distant star. He felt an urge to reach out to him across the great abyss, and even felt his hands twitch suddenly in their futile effort to drag him back from death, the fingers spreading, gripping, clutching in that motion Serena had noticed days before, as if reaching desperately for something whose departure all the hope and force of love could not delay.

Eighteen

Kinley was up early the next morning, the dawn light still filtering dustily into the single small window of Ray's back-room office as he sat down at the desk and began to assemble a preliminary guide for his investigation.

From his book on Colin Bright, he had learned that a true crime writer must gather and organize materials less like a journalist than a lawyer. The arrangement was critical to the final product. It had to be logical, sensible, each small element adding incrementally to the overall design.

Most critical of all, he'd learned that random interviews were fruitless, that scores of questions would be lost if the order of the interviews was flawed. Just as a good lawyer arranged the order of witnesses, a true crime writer had to order the list of sources he intended to contact. After a reading of the transcript, establishing what Kinley had come to think of as a "witness list" was the immediate order of business.

He placed the laptop computer on Ray's desk, opened it and turned it on. The soft blue light from the screen merged with the yellow dawn to give the room a strange greenish tint. It was a pleasant light, and for a moment Kinley felt as if he'd been swept into a forest grove, silent and primeval. As he continued to consider it, it struck him that at some point along the continuum of man's development, the first investigator must have appeared within that ancient forest, wrapped in animal skins, his hair filled with dried leaves and sprigs of vine, but an investigator nonetheless, probing the unfamiliar depths of some fellow creature whose death he was driven inexplicably to explain.

He blinked hard and returned to his senses, dismissing his own literary and philosophical fancies. The allure of such notions still struck him as the gravest pitfall which yawned before true crime writers such as himself, and he fought willfully to regain his mental balance against the aura of mystery and occult devotion which he could sometimes feel hovering about his work.

It was the actual work of writing which saved him from falling victim to his private ravings. Whatever the nature of his own fleeting exaltations, the work was not exalted, and after a single deep breath, he concentrated his attention on the notebook which lay open beside the computer, and the mythical Stone Age Sherlock Holmes vanished like the last frame of a B-movie dream.

Methodically, his mind now on a kind of professional autopilot, Kinley typed all the notes he'd taken in the courthouse vault, carefully arranging them in the same order in which the witnesses had been called and noting the date and time of the testimony.

It was nearly noon by the time he'd finished retyping the last of his transcript notes, then paused, his eyes lingering on the last entry.

It was Judge Bryan's remarks on the morning he pronounced sentence in the case:

COURT: Mr. Overton, do you have anything to say before the court pronounces sentence upon you?

160

OVERTON: No, Your Honor.

COURT: All right, sir. Well, Charles Herman Overton, the jury in the above entitlement has found you guilty of first degree murder. Accordingly, it is the judgment of this court that you be transferred to the Georgia State Prison in Reidsville, and that at that facility on January 4, 1955, and at an hour and in a manner prescribed by the laws of the State of Georgia, you suffer death by means of electrocution.

Then the gavel had sounded, Kinley knew, the hard knock of wood on wood echoing through the silent chamber, as the condemned man was led from the great hall, always led, the bailiff's hand upon his elbow, in a gesture Kinley considered more of comfort than restraint.

After a brief lunch made from the peanut butter and white bread he found in Ray's refrigerator, Kinley continued with his notes. For him, this tedious transcript always made for the most lackluster of his working days, the excitement of discovery already drained from the activity.

Now it was time to make a witness list, all the names that had emerged in the investigation so far, beginning with the actual trial witnesses, then expanding it to include every name that had been mentioned, no matter how peripheral the person's involvement might have been.

Once the names had been categorized, Kinley could decide on the order in which he thought it best to seek them out for questioning. Over thirty years had passed since the trial, and it had been his experience that such a span of time drew a long, dark line between the living and the dead. By the time he'd interviewed the surviving members of the Comstock family, only a scattering of aged aunts and adolescent cousins had remained to render the first shock of the murders as it had reverberated down the family line. His research for the second book had hit

161

similar dead ends, with Mel and Cora Flynn dead within three years of the day Mildred Haskell had invited their little boy into the smokehouse by the creek.

So it was biology more than logic which played the key role in setting up interviews, and as his eyes went down the witness list again, focusing particularly on those whose current fate he did not already know, they settled finally upon the witness who was most likely still alive despite the grim undertow of years: Helen Slater.

At the time of the trial, she'd presumably been the same age as her sixteen-year-old schoolmate, Ellie Dinker. In addition, Ben Wade had not only told Kinley that she was still alive, but precisely where she lived. His trial testimony had told him even more, and to renew his acquaintance with it, he called up the trial transcript file and scrolled down to the relevant passage:

WARFIELD: So, you went up to Carl Slater's place, is that right?

WADE: Yes, sir.

WARFIELD: And that would have been on July 3, the day after Ellie Dinker's disappearance?

WADE: Yes, sir. I drove up from the Sheriff's Office. It took about ten minutes, because Carl's place is way up yonder on Foster Road.

Kinley's mind recorded the spare detail of this part of Wade's testimony. For now, he had little else upon which to base his discussion with Helen Slater, but in the past he had discovered that the amount of information going into an interview was not necessarily indicative of the amount that could be gained during it. The interview itself was a subtle prying open of dark chambers, the light spreading in all directions once the door had been forced open.

He inserted his notebook in his jacket pocket and headed for his car. The sun was still high over the mountain, and as he glanced up at it, he recalled Foster Road very vividly. It was on the brow of the mountain, a slender dusty line, which skirted the edge of the mountain before it finally plunged over it and disappeared into the undergrowth that had covered its final few hundred yards since the last ill-fated iron mine had gone bust over ninety years before.

Foster Road, Kinley repeated silently in his mind. He and Ray had walked it many times.

To his surprise, the road had been paved since he'd last gone down it, and along its once isolated borders a few dilapidated house trailers and unpainted tract houses now stood in the surrounding woods. The old Slater place was at the very end of the road, and it seemed almost to totter uneasily at the brow of the mountain. As he approached it, he could see a long line of thick, gray clothesline cord as it dropped heavily beneath a weight of shirts, towels and plain white boxer shorts. A large woman in a floral house dress sat wearily on a washtub beneath the gently flapping clothes, her eyes following the path of Kinley's car until he brought it to rest only a few feet from her.

"Hi," Kinley said as he stepped out.

The woman nodded, a single beefy hand rising to shield her eyes from the mid-afternoon sunlight.

Kinley closed the door of the car and headed toward her slowly. "My name's Jack Kinley," he said. "And I was hoping you might help me out a little."

As he came nearer, Kinley focused on her face. It was unusually red, and her features were so puffy and rounded they seemed to close in on her eyes, squeezing them together until they finally appeared as little more than small slits.

"Back in 1954," Kinley said, "this was the Slater place."

The woman stared at him expressionlessly, with the kind of curious deadpan face he'd learned to expect from rural women, their features as shaved down as their lives.

"It still is the Slater place," she said.

Kinley looked at her closely, his mind comparing the face before him with one of the photographs from Ray's newspaper clippings collection on the case. It had shown a tall, strapping young girl in a loose summer dress, her hair tied in a wide ribbon. He could even remember the caption beneath it, a dramatic quotation from the girl herself: *She never made it to my house.*

"Are you Helen Slater?"

"Used to be," the woman said. "Until I got married. Name's Foley now." She let her head loll gently to the right, as if to take in the gusty mountain breeze that had swept over the brow of the mountain, driving a low scattering of fall leaves and forest debris before it.

Kinley smiled softly as he looked at her. The vibrant young girl in the photograph survived as little more than a shadowy after-image in the face before him now.

"Do you remember Ellie Dinker?" he asked.

The woman's eyes drifted back toward him as the breeze passed by and the little strand of graying hair it had pressed across her forehead came to rest. "Ellie Dinker?" she said, almost in wonderment, as if the name was a conjurer's command, an abracadabra which summoned back her youth. "Oh, yes, I sure remember Ellie."

"You went to school with her, didn't you?" Kinley asked.

"Yes, I did," Helen said without hesitation, almost brightly. She smiled. "Remember Ellie Dinker?" she asked rhetorically. "There's not a day goes by that I don't think about Ellie."

Kinley leaned into the slender pine that stood beside him, his hand already inching upward slightly toward the notebook in his jacket pocket. "Why is that?" he asked. "It's been a long time since she died."

"Because she was just the sort of person you don't forget," Slater said. "On fire, that girl. A real pistol."

"On fire?" Kinley asked, coaxing her along.

"Sort of wild," Helen said. "She had a tongue on her. She used to give people hell sometimes." The eyes drifted away a moment, lifting toward where a small wooden birdhouse hung idly in the trees. "She was mad sometimes," she added. "There was something in her that kept her steamed up."

Kinley indicated a small lawn chair, some of its loose folds flapping like the clothes above it. "Mind if I sit down?"

"Go ahead," Helen said. "I just sat down myself. Doing the clothes, that always gets me down."

Kinley drew the notebook from his jacket, his eyes still studying the woman before him, the devastation which time, work and long, uneventful hours had wrought. He had seen it before, of course, but it was always more poignant when a transcript or police report spoke of a vibrant, raw, perhaps rebellious young girl, and minutes later she was before you, old, or getting there, wearing down, all the glow smothered beneath unseemly layers of skin, the web of wrinkles, the wiry nest of gray hair, everything changed, inevitably and irrevocably changed, as it were, in an instant of tragically accelerated time.

"Did you ever get any idea about what she was mad about?" Kinley asked.

Helen thought a moment, her hands pressing the rounded folds that had gathered in her dress. "Not exactly," she said, "but I know that just before . . . ."She stopped, as if suddenly stricken mute, then continued, "Just before the murder, she was real mad. She was boiling over."

Kinley quickly scribbled the description into his notebook. "But you don't know why she was feeling like that?" he asked.

Helen leaned back slightly, so that Kinley suddenly caught a more youthful profile, sharp and strong and vigorous, Helen Slater in her awesome youth. "Ellie was more grown-up than the other girls," she said, as her eyes returned to Kinley. "She was in a hurry to grow up even more, and when you're like that as a girl, people sometimes don't like it much."

Kinley nodded. "Was there anyone in particular who didn't like her?"

Helen's eyes fell toward the notebook. "Why are you interested in knowing things like that?"

"I'm looking into her murder," Kinley told her. "I'm a writer."

"You're going to write about Ellie?" Helen asked, surprised, yet delighted as if in writing about her, Kinley was returning her, however fleetingly, to life. "You're going to write about her after all these years?"

"Maybe," Kinley said. "If there's something to write about."

Helen stared at him silently for a moment, as if evaluating a secret set of options. "Well, I guess I could tell you what I know," she said at last.

It was always like that, a quick, spontaneous breaking through of the more cautious bonds of silence. He'd seen it happen in witnesses, in public officials, in victims, even in those who'd done the dreadful things he'd recorded in his books. Mildred Haskell had begun to talk when he'd agreed to bring her a bag of freshly parched peanuts, and she had then sat in her chair for hours, reeling off the details of her gruesome inner world while popping the shells open one at a time in a gesture which Kinley thought must have resembled the way she's snapped apart the spine of little Billy Flynn. He'd glimpsed this same release in Colin Bright, at first so silent and withdrawn before the emergence from the mute and guarded chamber of his solitude. It had happened in an instant, the miraculous reversal of his former reticence for which he'd given only the slimmest and most arbitrary of reasons: *Because it's you that's here*.

"I know it's been a long time," Kinley said, gently

166

easing any of Helen Slater's remaining fears, "but sometimes a lot comes back all of a sudden."

"Not much ever left," Helen said. She rose laboriously, pulling herself up by grasping at the small stump beside her chair. "If it wasn't for a little bump on the mountain," she said, "you could almost see her house from here."

Kinley got to his feet. "Ellie Dinker's house?"

"Yeah," Helen said as she moved ponderously toward the edge of the mountain, raised her hand and pointed sharply to the left, angling down the mountain at what Kinley calculated as approximately forty-five degrees. "You go through those woods way down toward the bottom of the mountain, and if you went over that little hill, there, that's where you would have found Ellie's house if it hadn't have burned down."

"What happened after the fire?" Kinley asked.

"Well, Mrs. Dinker didn't have much of a place to go," Slater told him. "Ellie was her only child, and Mr. Dinker was long gone. Ora Fletcher took her in for a while, but she took to wandering off." She turned to the right and nodded down the long, narrowing road which finally disappeared over the mountainside. "They found her wandering around that old mine down there." She turned back toward him, her face oddly stricken, as if in embarrassment for her old friend's mother. "I even saw her hanging out behind my house once," she added, "just standing out there by the well." She shook her head at the thought of it. "Anyway, she was wandering around the town so much, they finally just took her off to the asylum. That's where she died."

Kinley nodded silently.

"She never showed up, you know," Slater added. "Ellie didn't."

"You mean, her body?"

"No, I mean that day she was supposed to come up here," Slater explained, "the day she died." She smiled sadly. "It was a Friday, and they'd let summer school

167

out for the parade. The town was full of kids that day. We watched the parade, then a lot of us went up to the courthouse. They were about finished with it, and old Mayor Jameson was making a speech.'' The smile nostalgic. "Everybody was there. All the big cheeses in town. The mayor, like I said. And Sheriff Maddox. The police chief and all the old courthouse crowd."

Kinley offered her his best professional smile, unwilling to halt the flow of memory, afraid that it might stop her tongue as well. "It must have been quite a celebration that day," he said.

"Oh, it was, it was," Slater said excitedly. "They were taking pictures in front of the courthouse. You know, for the paper. It was really something. Everybody was on the courthouse steps." Her eyes swept to the left and settled on the great gray edifice of the courthouse whose construction the town had been celebrating that day. "They'd just about finished all the work on the courthouse," she recalled. "There was still a lot of brick and wood and bags of cement scattered around, and the flagpole wasn't up yet, and the parking lot was full of old trucks, but otherwise, it looked real nice that day."

Kinley nodded, a bit impatiently. He was used to tangents, to the hard, steady pull of memory, but he also knew that there was a time when every witness had to be nudged back.

"And you were planning to go to the parade with Ellie," he said. "She was coming up here that morning."

Her eyes shot over to him. "Morning?"

"Yes."

She shook her head. "No, Ellie wasn't planning on coming up that morning," she said. "She was coming up late in the afternoon, and then we were going to go into town that evening for the fireworks."

"But you were already in town, weren't you?"

She nodded. "I came down early, to help with things," she said, "and Daddy was going to drive me back up so I could meet Ellie."

"Then you were going to walk back down to Sequoyah?"

"On foot," Helen said. "Because Daddy needed the truck."

"Carl Slater," Kinley said, a follow-up response which he routinely used as a lubricant to keep the flow of conversation going.

But the mention of the name had seemed to have an opposite effect, stopping her suddenly like a blockage in the heart. "My Daddy," she said quietly.

Kinley waited for more, but Helen continued to stare out over the rim of the mountain, her eyes fixed once again on the town below, the courthouse at its center, resting like a great gray tombstone on a rounded hill.

"Where was your Daddy that day?" Kinley asked finally.

She seemed to snap out of a trance. "After we came back up from Sequoyah, he went back down again," she said. "I guess he was headed down the mountain about the same time as Ellie was coming up it."

"But Ellie was walking," Kinley reminded her. "Wouldn't he have passed her on the road?"

"I guess so."

"He never mentioned that?"

"Mentioned?" Helen asked. "To who?"

"To Ben Wade, the deputy who questioned him," Kinley said. "He said he took the mountain road down toward Sequoyah, but he never mentioned seeing Ellie Dinker."

"Other people saw her," Helen said. "I remember hearing about other people who saw her."

"Yes, they did," Kinley told her. "I'm just trying to put a few things together that would help me figure out exactly where Ellie was at any given point on her way up here."

Helen shrugged. "Well, I don't know about where she was," she said. "I just know she never made it up here. So, after a while, I headed on down."

Kinley hesitated a moment, then decided to go ahead with the only question he'd actually had in mind at the time he'd decided to find Helen Slater. "Mrs. Foley, why would she have come up here at all?"

Helen looked at him oddly. "What do you mean? We were friends."

"But the plan was to meet up here, and then for both of you to go down to Sequoyah for the fireworks that night?"

"Yes."

"All the way back down the mountain?"

"Yeah, that's right."

"Well, wouldn't it have been more likely for you to meet at Ellie's house at the bottom of the mountain, than for her to walk all the way up here, then both of you go all the way back down the mountain?"

Helen's face took on a look of intense concentration, but she did not answer.

"Do you remember if there was any particular reason to meet at your house?" Kinley asked.

Helen continued to think about it. "Well, it was because Ellie wanted to do it that way." She seemed to be replaying the whole scene in her mind. "I said, 'Well, I'll come by your house around five, and we'll go to the fireworks.' That's what I told her."

"But she didn't want that?"

"No," Helen said. "No, she didn't. She said, 'I'll come up.' She said it real firm-like. 'I'll come up.' You know, like it's settled. There's no argument. 'I'll come up.' Just like that."

Kinley quickly wrote the words in his notebook, then glanced back up at Helen. "It's an awful long walk from the Dinker house to yours, isn't it?"

Helen nodded slowly. "Awful long," she said, almost to herself.

"And all uphill," Kinley added quietly.

"All uphill," Helen repeated thoughtfully, as if replaying the whole day in her mind.

170

Kinley hesitated a moment, then asked his final question. "And if you weren't supposed to meet until five, why did she leave the valley so early?"

Helen shook her head slowly. "I don't know," she said. "Ellie was a strange girl." Her eyes swept over to him. "And she was so mad," she added, "like something was eating her up."

Nineteen

In every case, the need finally emerged. As the data accumulated, one profound or incidental fact at a time, the mind lost its way, became entangled in the mesh of detail, and it became necessary to apply the first strategy ever invented to aid a finite intelligence.

He drew it slowly on one of the pieces of unlined paper he found in Ray's desk. Under the bright light of the desk lamp, he could see the lines as they merged or ran off in opposite directions, the simple wave of the mountain, a few parallel lines to indicate its sharp incline and rounded hills, a single curving thread to trace the course of the mountain road. At its zenith, Kinley drew in a simple square for the house of Helen Slater, and at its nadir another square, this one for the house of Ellie Dinker. After that, it was only a question of filling in the relevant times and people.

When finished, it was as plain and unadorned a map as Kinley's limited artistic ability could make it, and yet it was sufficient to point out the oddities and contradictions which the mind sometimes failed to see in a jumble of words and numbers.

Now carefully adding the details he'd accumulated from the trial transcript, Kinley tried to establish a time frame which would incorporate everything that had happened between the time Ellie Dinker had left her house, until the moment when, according to Mrs. Overton, her husband had returned home.

Once he'd established the times, he carefully printed the added information on the map, then studied it silently, listing one anomaly after another, first in his mind, then in his notebook under the same heading he'd used during all the years since he'd first established the practice by meticulously mapping out the house in which Colin Bright had slaughtered the Comstock family:

PLACE/TIME OBSERVATIONS:
1) Ellie Dinker appears to have headed in the opposite direction of Helen Slater's house at a time much earlier than necessary if she had planned to arrive at Helen's house by five in the afternoon.
2) Ellie Dinker appears not to have taken the mountain road until she reached it, along with Overton's disabled truck, when she emerged from the woods directly at Mile Marker 27.
3) Number 2 explains why Carl Slater did not see her coming up the mountain road, although he did pass Charles Overton's truck on the way down, according to a statement given to Deputy Wade almost a week after the murder.

Once Kinley had recorded these observations, he added the further questions which they suggested:

1) How long did it take Ellie Dinker to walk from her house to Overton's truck?
2) Where was she going when she left her house at the base of the mountain?

173

3) If Overton did not kill her, where did Ellie Dinker
   go after meeting him?

Kinley turned back to his notebook and flipped to the
pages where he'd recorded the critical elements of Sheriff
Maddox's trial testimony. Following Warfield's lead,
Maddox had answered the questions precisely and in the
logical order Warfield's examination had demanded:

WARFIELD: Now, Sheriff, did you have occasion to talk
   to Charles Overton after his arrest?
MADDOX: Yes, sir.
WARFIELD: When was this, Sheriff?
MADDOX: Well, I got in the backseat of Deputy Hen-
   dricks's car, and he drove us down to the Sheriff's
   Department in Sequoyah.
WARFIELD: And you were in the backseat with Overton
   at that time?
MADDOX: Yes, sir.
WARFIELD: And Deputy Hendricks was driving?
MADDOX: Yes, sir, he was.
WARFIELD: All right. Now, Sheriff Maddox, can you tell
   the court what transpired by way of conversation
   between you and Mr. Overton at that time?
MADDOX: Overton was denying everything, but he admitted that he had seen Ellie Dinker on the road. He
   said he didn't know her name. He said it was just a
   little girl in a green dress. He didn't know her name.
   He said as far as he could recollect, he'd never seen
   her before. They'd had a little talk, he said, and
   after that she'd left him and gone up the road a little
   ways.
WARFIELD: And this was the day of her murder?
MADDOX: The day of her murder, that's right. And he
   said that she was standing along the road there when
   his truck broke down.
WARFIELD: And what did he say happened at that time?
MADDOX: Well, when the truck broke down, he said he

174

pulled it over to the side there, and started to fix it, and while he was doing that, Ellie Dinker came over, and Overton told me that they'd had a little conversation, what you might say, a few words between them.

WARFIELD: Did he indicate to you what the nature of that conversation had been?

MADDOX: Well, nothing much to it, he said. She asked about the truck and that sort of thing, about what was wrong with it, how long it was going to take to fix it, that sort of thing.

WARFIELD: Just what you might expect then?

MADDOX: That's the way I'd describe her, yes, sir.

WARFIELD: Then what?

MADDOX: He told her what he thought was wrong with it, how long it would take to fix it, and just in general answered her back.

WARFIELD: And this innocent, everyday exchange, this was the full substance of their talk, is that right?

MADDOX: That was all they had to say.

WARFIELD: Then what, Sheriff Maddox?

MADDOX: Then Ellie Dinker walked away.

WARFIELD: Walked away?

MADDOX: Up the mountain a little ways.

WARFIELD: And that was the last Overton saw of her, according to his statement?

MADDOX: According to him, that was the last he saw of her.

WARFIELD: Just a little girl, heading on up the mountain, is that right, Sheriff?

MADDOX: That's how he described her, yes.

But that was *not* how Overton had described it, Kinley realized, as he glanced back over his notes, and was once again impressed with how important it was to copy the most relevant testimony verbatim, no matter how long it took or how unspeakably tedious it became.

Overton had never said that Ellie Dinker had walked

on up the mountain. In fact, he'd said something entirely different from that. According to Sheriff Maddox, he'd said that Ellie Dinker had "gone up the road a little ways," and Kinley knew that in common Southern parlance, such a phrase did not mean that Ellie Dinker had continued up the mountain and finally disappeared around a curve in the road or something else of that sort, but that she had "gone up the road a little ways" . . . *and stopped*.

In his mind it was not difficult for Kinley to visualize what had happened at approximately twelve-thirty on the afternoon of July 2, 1954, and for a moment he concentrated on seeing it exactly as he imagined Overton had seen it. The truck grinding to a halt, he'd pulled over to the side of the road, glanced up the mountain and seen a girl in a green dress as she stood across from Mile Marker 27 on the mountain road. He'd gotten out of the truck, lifted the hood and discovered that his oil tank was leaking. By that time, she was upon him, asking questions about what was wrong, how long it would take to fix it. While gathering his tools from the back of his truck, he'd answered her, then done what any shade-tree mechanic would have done to check the cause and severity of the leak. He had pulled himself under the truck, glancing to the right as he did so, his eyes locking for just an instant on a little girl who had gone up the mountain a little ways . . . and stopped.

For the few minutes following that last glimpse, Overton had gone about his business, his eyes concentrating on the greasy innards of his dilapidated truck, until, giving up on it at last, he'd pulled himself out from under it again, glanced once more to the left, and seen no one at all across from Mile Marker 27, because by then Ellie Dinker was gone.

Kinley turned on his computer and typed in another code, OVER:MYS, by which he identified its future contents: OVERTON: MYSTERIES.

He was about to type in the first entry when he heard

a soft knock at the front door. As he walked down the corridor toward the front of the house, he could see Dora standing on the front porch, its ghostly, bluish light washing over her eerily, giving her body an odd, vaporous look, as if she were slowly turning into steam.

"I don't have a telephone," she said as Kinley opened the door.

"Come in," Kinley said softly, then stepped back and watched as she walked past him and into the living room.

"You can still smell them," she said as she turned back to him.

"What?"

"The funeral flowers."

Kinley nodded. He had not noticed it before, and for a moment that obliviousness struck him as a somewhat alarming observation, as if he had avoided the life of the senses for so long that they had grown numb with disuse, atrophied like bound limbs.

"It's good to see you," he said quietly.

She glanced over toward the hearth. "That's where they put it, didn't they?"

Again, he looked at her quizzically.

"Ray," Dora explained. "His body."

Kinley nodded. "Yes."

She turned back to him. "I couldn't come to the funeral. It wouldn't have been right."

"Probably not," Kinley said. "Lois wouldn't . . ."

"I wasn't worried about Lois," Dora said, cutting him off. "I was worried about Serena."

"So was Lois," Kinley said. "She wants to keep it all a secret from Serena."

"You mean about Ray and me?"

"Yes," Kinley said. "She thinks it would somehow make Ray look like . . ."

"A man," Dora said, "a faithless man."

"That's about it, yes."

She looked at him evenly. "Well, he was, wasn't he?"

"In a manner of speaking."

Dora took a deep breath, as if drinking in the last fading odors of Ray's presence on earth. "I went to his grave, at least," she said, "late at night. After everyone was gone."

"So did I," Kinley told her. "It seemed like the right thing to do. It was his first night in the ground." He smiled softly. "We're primitive, you know. Primitive and superstitious. Magical thinkers. I guess we always will be."

Dora smiled. "Ray said things like that. We were dancing once. Well, not so much dancing as just swaying together to some music, and he said, 'You know why people love this?' And I said, 'No.' And he said, 'Because it's an old motion.' "

"Like the rocking of the sea," Kinley said.

"Swinging in the vines," Dora said. "That's how Ray described it."

Kinley nodded. "Would you like a drink?"

She considered it a moment. "Yes," she said finally, "I think I would."

By then only gin was left. Kinley went to the kitchen, returned with the bottle and two glasses, and poured each of them a shot.

"Well, to Ray," Dora said as she lifted her glass.

Kinley tapped his glass against hers. "To Ray," he repeated.

They drank, then sat down, Dora on the sofa by the window, Kinley in the plain wooden rocker that rested across from it.

For a moment, a silence fell over them, and in that interval, as Kinley let his eyes absorb her face and body, he imagined her with his old friend, the two of them nestled together, naked, drowsy, spent. It was always the manner in which he imagined love, not in action, but in aftermath.

"Have you found it?" Dora asked suddenly.

For a moment, he thought she meant love, had he found love, and the "no" of his reply was almost past

178

his lips before he realized that it was something else she was referring to, the proof of her father's innocence Ray had also tried to find.

"Not exactly," Kinley said, "but there are a few things I want to follow up on. Things I noticed in the transcript, and from asking around a little."

Dora took a slow draw on the glass, her eyes very dark and steady as they peered over its translucent rim. "What things?"

"I made a map," Kinley said. "From the way it looks, Ellie Dinker wasn't planning on going directly to Helen Slater's place when she left her own house at the bottom of the mountain."

"How do you know?"

"Because according to Martha Dinker's testimony, she didn't go in that direction," Kinley told her. "And she left very early, hours before she needed to be at Helen's."

"Where was she going then?"

"I don't know."

"Unless they'd planned to meet," Dora said. "That's probably what some people thought."

Kinley stared at her silently, an old technique which often forced the witness to elaborate upon his tale, to try harder to convince the mute, passionless observer that what he said was true. *Believe me. Believe me. Please, someone must believe me!*

But with Dora it didn't work. She only stared back at him, as sphinx-like as himself, the silence lengthening like a cord, stretching interminably, until Kinley felt the need to break it.

"Did you ever think that?" he asked, finally.

"That there was something between my father and Ellie Dinker?" Dora asked. "Absolutely not. He wasn't that kind of man."

"Faithless."

Dora shook her head. "Weak is what he was. Frightened. Of everything."

"How do you know that?"

179

"From his letters," Dora said, "the ones he wrote my mother."

"From prison?"

"No, from the war," Dora said. "From the hospital in Europe where he stayed after he was wounded. He never wrote her from prison." She took another quick sip. "He was dead before they killed him." A look of dreadful scorn rose in her face. "He died when I was still a baby," she said, "but I think if he'd lived, I might not have gotten along with him very well."

"Why not?"

"Because he was pathetic, and I don't like pathetic people."

It was a severe judgment, but she made no move to retract it.

"But he was also innocent," she added. "He didn't kill Ellie Dinker. He couldn't have done that. He was too weak." She took another quick sip from the glass. "If you read the letters," she added, "you'd see what I mean."

"Do you still have them?"

"Yes," Dora told him. "Do you want to see them?"

Sometimes, in his work, character was all he'd had to judge a crime, a criminal, a victim, nothing but the separate elements of their emotions which he gleaned from them like scrapings from an ancient cave, bits of color, a certain density, traces here and there of cowardice or fortitude, decency or nefariousness, the glint in Iago's eyes, Cassius's hungry look, Cain's uncertain step the day he slew his brother in the field.

"Yes, I'd like to see them," Kinley said.

To his surprise, she took them from the bag that sat in her lap. "I thought you might," she said as she handed them to him.

There were only a few of them, a slender stack crudely bound with rubber bands, military envelopes bearing the return address of a hospital in Belgium.

"Before the war, he might have been different," Dora

said as she drew her hand away from them. "My mother said he was." She looked at Kinley. "Stronger. Braver." She smiled. "Like Ray was."

So that was it, Kinley thought as his eyes settled upon her face, the Eternal Father. He wondered why, bereft of his own parents, he had never felt the need to look for them in others. But of course, there had been no need. His grandmother had swept into his life immediately, taking up the slack, filling in the empty space, nestling, cradling, providing.

"I was an orphan, too," he said quietly, solemnly, at last, gratefully, "but not for long."

Dora nodded crisply, her mind moving reflexively back to the matter at hand. "What's your next move?" she asked. "More witnesses, things like that?"

"I want to walk the route Ellie Dinker took up the mountain," Kinley answered.

"Why?"

"To time it," Kinley answered matter-of-factly, though he knew that timing was only part of it. The rest was something he could not explain, a searching for the mood of the day, the feel of the air, the play of light and shadows, the tone of imminence and fatality, of people moving helplessly toward a single searing instant of cataclysmic ruin.

"So you're going to walk the trail yourself?"

"Yes."

"From behind the Dinker house to where?"

"To where your father saw her still alive."

He could see something in her move toward him suddenly, as if a small piece of her spirit had crawled out of her body and floated toward him. She stood up quickly, as if to call it back. "I'd better be going," she said.

He rose and walked her to the door, opened it and let her step out onto the porch. Once there, she turned back toward him, her face very grave, yet somewhat questioning. "You're going to walk the trail tomorrow?"

"Yes."

"When?"

"In the morning."

She seemed to consider it a moment, before asking her next question. "Would you mind if I came along?"

"No."

"I wouldn't want to get in your way," she added tentatively.

"You wouldn't be."

For a moment, their eyes rested silently upon each other's before Dora's darted away, diving down toward the letters Kinley still clutched in his hands. "And when will you read those?" she asked.

"Tonight, probably."

She looked at him solemnly. "You work long hours," she said. "Don't you ever get tired?"

"Sometimes."

"What do you do then?"

Even before he answered her, he knew that for all its truth, his answer would strike her as absurd. "I work until I'm not tired anymore," he said.

Once she'd gone, Kinley returned to Ray's office, untied the letters Charles Overton had written to his wife during the war, and read them.

They were exactly as Dora had described them, the letters of a broken man, the sort Kinley had read by the hundreds, his "fans" reaching out to touch his shoulder, get his attention. *I read your book, Mr. Kinley, and I just had to write and tell you about what happened to me.*

What happened to me. In the vast number of letters he'd received since writing his first book, it had never been a war wound which had done the devastation. Instead, his nameless correspondents spoke of kidnappings, tortures, murders, of lost relatives found at last floating in the estuary, curled in the ravine, hanging from the trees. They wrote of the sudden, inexplicable rages that still swept over them without warning or relief, the terrible winds that blew forever across the desert wastes of crime.

Charles Overton's letters were different from these, very different. And Dora had caught their substance without compromise. They were the letters of one who had lost the will to live, who had been wounded so critically that more than his body had been devastated. The energy of life, its resilience and vitality, had been blasted from him, so that little remained but flesh in motion, a man going through the days until death came, like a friend, to take him to the oblivion he already desperately craved.

Now Kinley knew why Overton had crumpled at the first accusation and had finally trudged across the room to where the electric chair waited for him, like a mother with her arms outspread.

Twenty

She was waiting for him when he pulled up to the old Dinker place at the base of the mountain. She was wearing dark-blue pants, and from a distance, appeared almost like a soldier in uniform, erect, as if on guard against the enemy's advance.

"I'm off today," she said as Kinley approached. "That's why I can do this."

Kinley nodded, his eyes moving over the curve of Dora's shoulder, where he could see the old house's charred remains, a dark ruin amid a grove of pine.

"It wasn't much even then," Dora said as she turned toward it. "At least, that's what my mother told me."

Kinley stared at the house, its cement steps leading upward into nothing, the pile of black rubble jutting harshly from beneath a collapsed tin roof which looked as if it had gone to seed long before the fire.

"This is where we met," Dora said, as she continued to look at the devastated house. "Ray and I."

"Here?" Kinley asked.

"I had just come down one day," Dora went on, "following an urge, you might say. I was standing in the yard, and he pulled over. He was in his Sheriff's Department car." She smiled quietly. "He said, 'If you're thinking about buying this place, don't do it.' "

"Did he say why?"

"Because it's haunted, that's what he told me then," Dora went on, "haunted by Ellie Dinker." She turned toward Kinley. "I told him no, not by Ellie Dinker, by Charles Overton."

"Did he know what you meant?"

Dora nodded. "Yes, he did," she said. "His face got very serious. He'd been smiling before, you know, the way he could, like a kid. But he got very serious." She shrugged. "I guess that's when it started."

Kinley smiled quietly. It was a soft romantic tale, and he wondered why such a moment, leading as it did to such an experience, had never come his way. Perhaps, in the end, something his grandmother had once said to him was sufficient to explain it: *You give off a chill . . . like your mother.*

He felt his hand grasp for that invisible something which always seemed just beyond his reach, and he started to walk toward the house.

"Ellie left from the backyard," he said as Dora stepped up beside him. "That's what Mrs. Dinker said."

Moments later they stood in the backyard. It was a field of bare, muddy ground broken by small islands of gently undulating weeds and grasses which finally disappeared into the dense mountain forest that surrounded it like a huge green wall.

It was into that forest that Ellie Dinker had disappeared at around noon on July 2, 1954.

"She took that trail," Kinley said, his arm rising almost involuntarily, the lean index finger pointing toward a narrow break in the dense underbrush. He looked at Dora. "That's the first question," he said. "Why did she go in that direction, if she were heading for Helen Slater's house?" His arm drifted far to the left of the trail's entrance, then rose toward the distant crest of the mountain. "Helen Slater lives over there, beyond that hill. Ellie Dinker didn't go in that direction at all when she left that morning." He looked at her. "Why?"

Dora made no effort to answer him but followed along as Kinley moved further into the yard, his eyes doing the studied and precise inventory he had taught them to carry out, noting the scattering of wood, the broken metal swings, the covered well, the small smokehouse, its door hanging from a single rusty hinge, all the tiny, incidental items whose importance lay in the mood they set, the sense of loss or abandonment that rose from them like a barely whispered song.

"She took this trail," Kinley said when he and Dora reached the forest wall. He looked at his watch. "Seventwenty-four," he said. "All right. Let's go at a reasonable pace, and see how long it takes to get to the mountain road."

They entered the forest together, walking side by side until, as they continued on, the surrounding woods drew in upon the trail, narrowing it to a slender brown thread. The green shadows crouching in the distance seemed almost palpable, not so much areas of deepened color as breathing, watchful presences, the stuff of dreams and nightmares, the legions of the night whose snarls and groans Kinley remembered hearing as he tossed sleeplessly in his small room overlooking the canyon, his child's mind as fierce and wild as any of the creatures it invented.

After a moment, the slope of the mountain suddenly grew more radical, and he could feel his heart beating heavily in his chest, the breath in his lungs thickening, as it seemed, to the consistency of water, and he felt like a creature submerged in the suffocating, green slime which rested, heavy and motionless, on the surface of stagnant waters.

186

"Let's stop here," he said when the trail broke into an unexpected clearing.

"City boy," Dora said with a small smile. "You're not used to this."

Kinley glanced at his watch and made a mental note of the time, seven-forty-two, and fifteen seconds. "We'll go on in a minute," he assured her.

"She might have stopped here, too," Dora told him.

Kinley's hands reached for a slender, low-slung limb, as if grasping for it desperately to save him from a fall. "Yes, she might have," he said. "She'd have been walking for twenty minutes by then."

"And almost straight up," Dora added. Her eyes crawled up the mountainside. "To where my father waited."

"Except you don't believe that," Kinley reminded her.

"I know he couldn't have had anything to do with Ellie Dinker, if that's what you mean," Dora said. She looked at him pointedly. "Did you read the letters?"

"Yes."

"And?"

"He was broken, like you said," Kinley told her. "Did your mother ever tell you what the wound was? He never gives any details."

"His legs," Dora said. "That's where he was hit. Both legs, she said. He walked with a limp."

"More a shuffle," Kinley told her.

She looked at him curiously. "How did you know that?"

Kinley hesitated, wished he'd kept it to himself. "Well, I read a description of his . . . of his death."

"You mean, his execution."

"The writer mentioned how he walked," Kinley added.

Dora's face suddenly took on an attitude which entirely contradicted what she'd previously said about her father, his weakness, his cowardice, the natural role he had as-

187

sumed as spineless victim. In an instant, all of that was swept away, and amid the deep green shadows, her face miraculously grew even deeper, as if suddenly enriched by the love she still felt—would always feel—for her unknown father. Her eyes lifted toward Kinley, glistening slightly despite the shadowy light. "Why can't I let him go?"

"Be glad you can't," he told her.

"Why?"

He was not sure why, he realized, but only sensed that certain feelings should be a part of every life, and that if you never achieved the full range, certain losses were incurred, although he could not calculate exactly what they were.

"Why should I be glad?" Dora repeated.

Kinley thought of his own parents, dead, dead, dead. "Because you've come to know him a little," he said. "I never learned much of anything about mine."

She nodded. "Yes," she said. "Ray told me. A car accident when you were three years old."

Kinley felt his old uneasiness rise again, the uncomfortable sense that he was about to whine about his orphan state as he'd seen so many others do, using it to justify the things they'd later done: *If I hadn't been abandoned, I wouldn't have robbed, raped, killed.* It was an excuse he'd heard too often to feel anything for it but contempt.

"We'd better head on up now," he said, avoiding any further discussion of his own early life.

They began the long trudge up the mountain once again, Kinley in the lead, Dora close behind. He could hear her breathing almost as if it were his own, feel the shift of her feet on the ground behind him, and for a moment he thought that this must be what Ray had wanted most in his life, a companion in the forest, someone with you on the trail.

They reached the mountain road a half-hour later, and Kinley glanced at his watch. It was now seven minutes after eight, and after subtracting the brief pause on the way up, he calculated the approximate length of time it would have taken Ellie Dinker to make it from her house to the road.

"About half an hour," Kinley said as he looked up from his watch. "Which means that she would have gotten here at about twelve-thirty in the afternoon."

Dora nodded.

"And according to witnesses, your father left the courthouse at twelve-thirty on the dot," Kinley added. "Which means he would have gotten here at around twelve-thirty-five." He glanced up toward the mountain's crest, where he could nearly see the rim where he'd stood with Helen Slater only the day before, the two of them staring down toward Sequoyah, their eyes fixed on the great gray face of the courthouse. "It would only take another hour or so to climb the rest of the way up," he said. "It couldn't possibly take any longer than that."

Dora glanced up toward the mountain, but said nothing.

"She was supposed to meet Helen Slater at five in the evening," Kinley said. He looked at Dora. "Why would she have left her house so early?"

Dora shook her head. "I don't know."

"But she didn't go on up the mountain," Kinley added. "Or anywhere else for that matter."

"What do you mean?"

"If she got here by twelve-thirty, and your father didn't get here until twelve-forty-five or so . . ."

"Then she must have waited," Dora blurted.

"That's right," Kinley said. "For a good five or ten minutes. Standing along the roadside, like your father said she was." His eyes settled on a slender white column. "By that mile marker right there."

Dora looked at the marker. "Just standing there," she said, almost to herself, then glanced back at Kinley. "Why?"

Kinley shook his head. "That's what we have to find out."

189

She looked at him doubtfully. "Do you think you can?"

"I don't know, Dora."

"Ray couldn't."

"Maybe he just ran out of time."

She shook her head determinedly. "No," she said firmly, "he told me he'd come up with nothing, that there were no more leads to follow."

"When did he tell you that?"

"The day before he died."

"Did you believe him?"

Dora stared at him pointedly. "No, I didn't," she said. "I had the feeling he'd given up."

"Why?"

She shrugged slightly. "Maybe he got tired."

"Did he seem tired?"

"No."

"How did he seem?"

She considered it a moment, searching for the right word. "Lost," she said finally, "like he didn't know what to do."

Twenty-One

Kinley took his seat at Ray's desk, turned on his computer and typed in the relevant code: OVER:MYS.

Then he typed in the first series of questions under the heading: QUESTIONS CONCERNING ELLIE DINKER

1) Why did Ellie Dinker want to meet at the Slater house instead of her own, which would have been much closer to their ultimate destination, the courthouse in Sequoyah?
2) Why did she leave for Helen's five hours before she needed to?
3) Why did she move in a direction opposite to the one she should have taken if she'd been planning to go directly to the Slater house?
4) Why did she stop on the mountain road?

Once the questions had been recorded, Kinley returned to the only account he had of Ellie Dinker's whereabouts after leaving her house at the base of the mountain, Overton's initial statement to Sheriff Maddox.

He read it over carefully, then read it again, his eyes moving slowly from word to word, waiting for something to emerge that might give him a clue. Sheriff Maddox had been dead for several years, but as he went through the statement the Sheriff had given of his talk with Overton, he noted one particular reference to a third person in Maddox's testimony at Overton's trial:

WARFIELD: Now, Sheriff, did you have occasion to talk to Charles Overton after his arrest?

MADDOX: Yes, sir.

WARFIELD: When was this, Sheriff?

MADDOX: Well, I got in the backseat of Patrolman Hendricks's car, and he drove the two of us down to the Sheriff's Department.

WARFIELD: So you were in the backseat with Overton at that time?

MADDOX: Yes, sir.

WARFIELD: And Deputy Hendricks was driving?

MADDOX: Yes, he was.

Deputy Hendricks had been driving the patrol car as Overton and Maddox spoke about Ellie Dinker in the backseat.

According to Ben Wade, Hendricks had retired not long after the Overton trial, and now worked at South Side High School. Kinley glanced at his watch, his mind calculating the probable times for class breaks if things hadn't changed drastically since he'd been in high school.

He arrived at South Side High a few minutes later, walked into the office, and asked for Riley Hendricks.

"He's in class right now," the woman behind the desk told him.

"When will he be out?"

"That would be lunch period, at eleven-thirty."

"Could I leave a message for him?"

"Why sure," the woman said cheerfully. "I'll take it myself."

"Just tell him that someone would like to talk to him," Kinley said. "I'll be waiting in the faculty parking lot."

"You want to leave your name?" the woman asked.

"That's okay." He moved to the office door, then turned. "By the way, so I don't miss him, what kind of car does he drive?"

"It's a Chevrolet, I believe," the woman said, "a light green station wagon."

Kinley nodded. "Thanks."

Kinley walked out of the school, made a hard left and headed into the faculty parking lot. He could see the green Chevrolet sitting beside a large orange dumpster, and for the next few minutes he watched it casually, his eyes only occasionally glancing up toward the mountain, as if drawn there involuntarily.

After only a short time, he saw Riley Hendricks walk energetically out the back door of the school and head toward his car. He was smaller than Kinley had expected, leaner too, as if he'd been careful to keep his fighting weight despite the onslaught of late middle age.

From his position a few yards away, Kinley advanced toward him slowly, coming up from the right, just as Hendricks was opening the door to his car.

"Excuse me," Kinley said. "You're Riley Hendricks, aren't you?"

Hendricks turned to face him. "Yes, I am."

"I left a message for you at the school office," Kinley told him.

"You did?" Hendricks asked. "Well, I didn't go back to the office." He smiled sheepishly. "To tell you the truth, I stay out of the office as much as I can."

"I wanted to talk to you in private for a minute," Kinley said.

Hendricks gave him a wary, apprehensive look. "You do? What about?"

"An old murder case."

193

"Murder case?" Hendricks asked doubtfully, adding nothing else. "Well, who are you, if you don't mind my asking?"

"My name's Jack Kinley."

"Are you with the Justice Department or something?"

Kinley shook his head. "No, I'm a writer," he said. "I was a friend of Ray Tindall's."

Something seemed to catch in Hendricks's mind. "I see."

"Ray was working on the same case."

Hendricks said nothing.

"The Dinker case," Kinley added.

Hendricks stared at him stonily. "I didn't have much to do with that," he said. "That was Sheriff Maddox's doing."

"Doing?"

"He handled it," Hendricks said quickly, "not me."

"You mean the questioning?"

"I mean everything," Hendricks said flatly. "I was just a rookie in those days."

Kinley slowly drew the notebook from his coat pocket and opened it to Sheriff Maddox's testimony. "You drove the car when Maddox questioned Overton."

Hendricks nodded slowly, with a strange reluctance, as if the admission made him culpable.

"At the trial, Sheriff Maddox testified about what Overton said to him while you drove them down the mountain," Kinley told him. "Did you hear that testimony?"

"Yes, I did."

"You were in the courtroom?"

Hendricks nodded. "It was a big trial," he said. "There were big crowds. I guess I was as curious as anybody else."

Kinley glanced at his notes. "Most of the Sheriff's testimony is pretty routine," he said, "but I have a few questions."

Hendricks's eyes dropped down to the notebook, as if

in sudden alarm at what might be written within its small white pages. Then, suddenly, he looked back up at Kinley. "Look, why don't you get in my car, and we'll go for a little ride," he said. "Schools are gossip mills, you know, and people would be asking me a thousand questions if they saw me talking to a stranger."

"All right," Kinley agreed. "Where do you want to go?"

"Just get in with me," Hendricks said. He pulled himself in behind the wheel and waited as Kinley took a seat on the passenger side.

"My patrol car was like this," he said, glancing back toward the rear seat. "No safety glass between the driver and the people in back, like there is today."

"So you could hear everything."

Hendricks nodded silently, then started the car and drove it out of the parking lot.

"I was just a kid, really," he said as he drove south, "a real Dudley Do-Right type." He smiled. "Gung ho. Idealistic. The whole nine yards."

"How long had you been in the Department?" Kinley asked.

"A couple years," Hendricks said, "and nothing big had ever really happened. We busted a few bootleggers and vagrants once in a while, and there were always a few drunk and disorderlies to deal with." He shook his head. "But the Ellie Dinker thing, that was the first murder I'd ever worked." He took a quick left turn, heading east for two blocks, then turned right and cruised slowly along the base of the mountain, its high green slope rising like a massive wall above them. "It was all you heard about until we arrested Charlie Overton."

"Did you know him before that?"

"Who, Charlie?" Hendricks asked. "No, not at all. I mean, I knew who he was. He'd been working around the courthouse while they were building it. But as a man? No, I didn't know him."

The road continued to skirt the base of the mountain,

then came to the place where it intersected the mountain road. Hendricks brought his car to a halt. "I waited right here for Sheriff Maddox. That's what he'd radioed me to do. Then I saw his car pass, and I fell in behind him. Ben Wade was in the car with him."

"And they were going to Overton's house?"

"We all went right on up the mountain," Hendricks said as he eased his foot down on the accelerator and moved the car across the intersection into the small picnic area that rested near Sequoyah High. "We can stop right here," he said as he brought his car to a halt. "It's nice and shady," he added as he opened the door, "and there are benches."

Kinley got out of the car, followed Hendricks over to one of the picnic tables and sat down opposite him.

"I like to rest here in the afternoon," Hendricks explained. "It gives me peace."

Kinley opened his notebook again. "The Sheriff testified that Overton denied the murder."

"He did deny it," Riley said, "but later he admitted it."

"But that was several hours later. With Ben Wade."

"That's right."

"Did he give any indication of guilt when he was in the backseat with Sheriff Maddox?"

"No," Hendricks said. "He looked scared."

"Did Maddox give him reason to be?"

"You mean, was he rough with him?" Hendricks asked. "No. He was real gentle, as a matter of fact. He asked a few questions and Overton answered them."

Kinley looked at his notes. "This is the part of Sheriff Maddox's testimony I have a few questions of my own about," he said. Then he read the exchange:

WARFIELD: All right. Now, Sheriff Maddox, can you tell the court what transpired by way of conversation between you and Mr. Overton at that time?

MADDOX: Overton was denying everything, but he admitted that he had seen Ellie Dinker on the road. He said he didn't know her name. He said it was just a little girl in a green dress. He didn't know her name. He said as far as he could recollect, he'd never seen her before. They'd had a little talk, he said, he said, and after that she'd left him and gone up the road a little ways.

WARFIELD: And this was the day of her murder?

MADDOX: The day of her murder, that's right. And he said that she was standing along the road there when his truck broke down.

WARFIELD: And what did he say happened at that time?

MADDOX: Well, when the truck broke down, he said he pulled it over to the side there, and started to fix it, and while he was doing that, Ellie Dinker came over, and Overton told me that they'd had a little conversation, what you might say, a few words between them.

WARFIELD: Did he indicate to you what the nature of that conversation had been?

MADDOX: Well, nothing much to it, he said. She asked about the truck and that sort of thing, about what was wrong with it, how long it was going to take to fix it, that sort of thing.

WARFIELD: Just what you might expect then?

MADDOX: That's the way I'd describe it, yes.

Hendricks listened quietly until Kinley had finished, then nodded silently.

Kinley closed the notebook. "Is that what you remember Overton saying to Sheriff Maddox?"

"Yes, it is."

"Do you remember Overton saying anything else?"

"Nothing important, no," Hendricks said. "The ride was probably eight or nine minutes, no more than that. They didn't have time to say too much."

Kinley added nothing else, and for a moment Hendricks watched him, as if trying to decide what to say.

From across the bare, concrete table, Kinley could see something move behind Hendricks's eyes, shifting, darting, like a creature looking for a way out. He decided to give it seven seconds to find its own way before prying open a larger space with another question. He counted them off in his mind: *one two three four five* . . .

"Ray talked to me, you know," Hendricks said suddenly. "About three months ago. He had a few questions, too."

"Ray talked to you?" Kinley asked. "What questions?"

"He went over the same things you did," Hendricks answered. "He wanted to know if Overton had said anything else on the way to the courthouse."

"I see."

"Something bothered him about what Overton said," Hendricks went on. "Ray had been a cop a long time, and he could see things, situations, you know, in his head."

"Yes, I know what you mean," Kinley told him. "What did he see in this situation?"

"Well, you have this young girl on the side of the road," Hendricks began, "and a strange man pulls over in a beat-up old truck, and he gets out, and you're a girl there all by yourself."

"Yes?"

"Well, would a young girl go over to a man like that?" Hendricks asked. "And those questions she asked. Why *those* questions? I mean, about what was wrong with the truck, how long it would take to fix, stuff like that. I mean, why would she give a shit one way or another, you know?"

Kinley nodded.

"That's what bothered Ray," Hendricks said. "What Ellie Dinker did and said on the road, it didn't make sense. It didn't fit with the situation the way Ray imagined it." He paused a moment, the ferment still building slowly in his face. "And that made me remember something later," he went on. "I meant to tell Ray about it, but I waited, and so . . ."

"What did you remember?"

"Well, Overton described the Dinker girl just like the Sheriff said in court, the way she came over to him, and the questions she asked, but he also said that she looked strange, and I remember the word he used to describe the way she looked to him."

Kinley felt the tip of his pen press down onto the open notebook. "What word?"

"He said she looked 'nervous-like' " Hendricks said. "You know, jumpy."

Kinley quickly jotted the word down in his notebook, then looked back up at Hendricks. "Just her manner? Just the way she acted when she talked to him?"

"That's right," Hendricks said. "The way she looked to him, nervous-like."

"That's all?"

"I guess," Hendricks said softly as his eyes lowered somewhat, as if to avoid discovery. It was a movement Kinley had noticed many times on other occasions, and which had always signaled the presence of something more. In Colin Bright, it had been nothing more than the way his hand had suddenly inched forward toward Kinley's own hand, lingered a moment, then retreated. In Willie Connors, it had been something almost melodramatic, a trembling of his lower lip. Mildred Haskell had made no sign at all.

He looked at Hendricks steadily while his mind went through its bag of tricks, frantically searching for the one question that would set Riley Hendricks free as it had the others, whether guilty or innocent, cowardly or fearless, the one question that would penetrate the wall. After a moment, he found it.

"Ben Wade told me that you quit the Sheriff's Department not long after the trial," he said. "Is that true?"

Hendricks's eyes remained discreetly lowered. "Yes, it is."

"Did it have something to do with Charlie Overton?"

Hendricks's eyes lifted slowly and stared directly into Kinley's "No," he said. "With Ellie Dinker."

"What about her?"

"Her body," Riley said. "The one her mother wanted to find so bad."

"What about it?"

"Well, the way they sort of lost interest in it," Hendricks said. "I mean, I was no great cop, but one place seemed obvious to me."

"Where?"

"Well, we arrested Overton in his backyard," Hendricks answered. "And I remember that when I put the cuffs on him, I happened to glance over his shoulder, and I could see it plain as day, just like Sheriff Maddox could."

Kinley waited anxiously, but careful to keep himself in check.

"Well, there was a well back there," Hendricks said. "I could see it standing right in the middle of the yard."

Kinley nodded, his hand motionless on the notebook page as he listened.

"And nobody ever looked for Ellie Dinker there," Hendricks added. "Why not? It was the most obvious place."

It seemed so to Kinley, and the new information surprised him as much as it had always baffled Hendricks. "They never looked at all?" he asked.

Hendricks shook his head. "No. Never."

"How do you know?"

"Because it would have been me they'd have sent to do it," Hendricks explained, "you know, the rookie." He laughed, but with a curious edginess. "I mean, there's no way Sheriff Maddox would have climbed down some old muddy hole in the ground to look for a body. No way. He liked his uniform too much. He would have sent the new boy for sure."

"How about Ben Wade?" Kinley asked. "He wouldn't have sent him?"

Hendricks stared at him thoughtfully. "I don't know about Ben Wade," he said.

"Meaning what?"

"Meaning he was always sort of a mystery to me," Hendricks said. "But then, just about everybody is, don't you think?"

Kinley's mind raced through the catalogue of his acquaintances, editors, writers, all of them more or less transparent in the grand simplicity of their needs. It did not stop until it got to Ray, his face a black-and-white photograph. Except for the eyes, which Kinley's mind had eerily insisted on painting the same dark green as it had already imagined Ellie Dinker's dress.

Twenty-Two

Once again at Ray's desk, Kinley typed in the appropriate code: OVER:MYS.

The file flashed onto the screen, and Kinley scrolled down until he reached the questions he wanted:

1) Why did Ellie Dinker want to meet at the Slater house instead of her own, which would have been much closer to their ultimate destination, the courthouse in Sequoyah?
2) Why did Ellie Dinker leave for Helen's five hours before she needed to?
3) Why did Ellie Dinker move in a direction opposite to the one she should have taken if she'd been planning to go directly to the Slater house?
4) Why did she stop on the mountain road?

To the first four questions, he wrote a fifth, sixth and seventh:

5) Why did she approach Overton after his truck broke down?

6) Why did she ask him what was wrong with the truck and how long it would take to fix it?

7) Why did she appear "nervous-like"?

Once the questions had been written, Kinley let his eyes linger on them silently, doing what Ray had evidently done from time to time as well, imagining the scene, recording it like an invisible camera bearing down upon it from the overhanging cliffs.

In his mind, he could see Overton's truck as it slogged wearily up the mountain, laden with tools, dusty with the red clay of the courthouse construction site. Overton was behind the wheel, as Kinley now imagined him. He was sweating, his stomach churning uncontrollably as he fought to keep the old truck crawling up the mountain road.

But he had failed, and suddenly she was there in the distance, standing by Mile Marker 27 in her dark green dress, her head turning toward him as the truck ground to a halt on the weedy shoulder of the road.

Now the camera was outside, and Kinley could see the two of them on the mountain road. Overton was holding his stomach as he bent over the truck's steamy engine. Dinker was poised a few yards away, watching, waiting, until she began to move toward him, slowly at first, then faster until she was at Overton's side, her mouth twitching left and right as she fired her questions in a crisp, staccato voice: *What's the matter? Can you fix it? How long will it take?*

Overton, still clutching at his stomach to keep it from exploding, groaned his answers as he continued to lean under the raised hood of the truck, his eyes now peering blearily into the oil-splattered engine: *The motor's leaking. I have to find out how bad it is.*

In his mind, Kinley could see Ellie Dinker in her green

dress as she stepped away from the truck to watch nervously as Overton eased himself onto the pebbly earth, then pulled himself under the truck.

How bad is it?

Bad.

Can you fix it?

Now Overton was staring up into the worn metal innards of the engine. Oil was everywhere, everywhere, dripping from the engine block, oozing from the wide crack in the oil tank's ancient seal. All around him, like a thousand edgy, fluttering birds, Ellie Dinker's questions kept diving at him. *Can you fix it? Can you fix it?*

Overton's stomach heaved and bellowed, as his face grew taut under the relentless volley of her questions.

Can you fix it? Can you fix it?

To shut her up, he answered her at last: *I don't know.*

But his answer had not silenced her, and the questions continued to assail him: *How long will it take? Will it take an hour? Will it take half an hour? Will it take . . .*

Flat beneath the truck, his eyes staring achingly at the devastated engine, he had put it to her bluntly: *A long time.*

And after that, a silence must have descended upon them, Kinley thought, as he continued to envision the scene, a frozen instant before Ellie Dinker skirted away from him, her white legs moving rapidly through the weedy growth along the shoulder of the road, taking her away from Overton, away from the truck, past the white, pointed obelisk of Mile Marker 27, and "on up a little ways" as Overton had told Sheriff Maddox, "on up a little ways" . . . *where she stopped.*

Kinley's mind halted a moment, his eyes concentrating on all the small details of what he'd gathered so far about Ellie Dinker's last day on earth. He thought of her early departure, of the route she'd taken, one which would not have led her to Helen Slater's house, but straight up the slope of the mountain, where she would have reached the mountain road at—precisely at—Mile Marker 27.

He glanced at the list of questions he'd compiled under Ellie Dinker's name, then answered question three:

3) Why did Ellie Dinker move in a direction opposite the one she should have taken if she'd been planning to go directly to the Slater house?

Quickly, Kinley typed his answer under the question: *Because she was not going to Helen Slater's house. She was going to Mile Marker 27, which is directly in line with her path, and where she was seen standing when she met Charles Overton.*

Kinley's eyes moved up the screen's illuminated page and settled on questions one and two:

1) Why did Ellie Dinker want to meet at the Slater house instead of her own, which would have been much closer to their ultimate destination, the courthouse in Sequoyah?
2) Why did Ellie Dinker leave for Helen's five hours before she needed to?

He thought a moment, then typed the most reasonable answer to both questions: *Because she wanted to go up the mountain, rather than in any other direction, and because she needed time to go wherever it was she wanted to go, and to do whatever it was she wanted to do.*

Next Kinley moved quickly to the four remaining questions:

4) Why did she stop on the mountain road?
5) Why did she approach Overton after his truck broke down?
6) Why did she ask him what was wrong with the truck and how long it would take to fix it?
7) Why did she appear "nervous-like"?

205

For a moment he considered the possibilities. It was conceivable that one answer might fit all four questions. In his mind, he tried once again to reconstruct the events, this time from Ellie Dinker's perspective, rather than from Overton's.

He saw her standing by Mile Marker 27, standing idly, just as Overton had described her, in her dark green dress, her eyes turning suddenly to where Overton's battered old truck wheezed and rattled as it hauled itself up the mountain, the overheated engine gasping loudly, just before the truck drifted to the side of the road and came to rest on the littered shoulder.

As Kinley imagined it, she must have looked at the dusty truck, pausing for just a moment before she moved toward it, walking determinedly until she reached Overton's racked body as it slumped beneath the open hood.

After that, it was talking heads, Overton's slumped over the devastated engine, Ellie's beside him, her mouth at his ears, firing her questions one after the other, and then later, Overton under the truck, his eyes catching only brief glimpses of the small feet in the black shoes as they pranced about, pacing up and down, the young, girlish voice coming to him in short, nervous bursts: *What's the matter? can you fix it? how long? how long? how long?*

It was easy for Kinley to hear Ellie Dinker's voice now, as it had always become easy when he had released his mind like a dog in the woods, let it take him wherever the dreadful scent led, and in those weird and tragic moments, he felt the wildest region of his mind bloom with a sudden, relentless ardor, and he entered imagined landscapes, dark and smoldering and haunting, heard imagined voices, dim, shrill, full of rage, emptiness, longing, everything fully visualized in that powerful way his grandmother had taught him to imagine: *with your mind's fingertips, Kinley, with nothing between you and what you're after*.

206

For a time, he let his mind hold, trancelike, over the little scene on the mountain road, absorbing every nuance of sound and sight, before returning it to the brutal questions which still shone from the screen of his computer.

He read them over again, slowly, one by one, concentrating on each word, as the possible answers emerged, tossed about in his head, then settled to the ground with the fierce gravity of logic, and to all four questions, he typed in a single, unifying answer:

Ellie Dinker walked precisely from her house to Mile Marker 27 on the mountain road because it was a clearly visible landmark that could be easily designated as a place of rendezvous. She had not expected Overton's truck to break down in sight of the meeting place and had quickly rushed down to his truck in order to ascertain how long he would be broken down. Once she knew that Overton would not be leaving quickly, she had walked far enough up the road to make sure that when the missing person arrived, he would be far enough away to prevent his being seen by Overton. Within a few minutes, the missing person had, in fact, arrived, and Ellie Dinker had gone away with him . . . never to be seen again.

Never to be seen again, Kinley thought, as he read the paragraph again. Then he typed the eighth question:

8) Where is Ellie Dinker?

He'd barely removed his fingers from the keys when Riley Hendricks's motionless eyes swam into his mind, and he imagined himself not at some place that remained distant both in space and time, but another place entirely, one that was here and now.

207

Twenty-Three

It took a few minutes to assemble the tools he needed, but he'd finally managed to find everything in Ray's small, dusty garage. The rope had hung in a tangle beside the garage door, the rubber boots in the small closet adjoining the office. A pair of gray work gloves were in an old tool chest, and the flashlight in a kitchen drawer, nestled among a disorder of tape, pliers, matches, whatever else had been tossed haphazardly inside. Only the shovel had remained in its hiding place, so that in the end, he'd had to settle for the long garden hoe and small, sharp-edged spade he'd found near the disordered rope.

Night had already fallen by the time Kinley pulled himself into the car and headed up toward the Overton house. At the brow of the mountain, he turned onto the narrow road, edging the car through the near total darkness, his eyes occasionally glancing down the mountain slope to where the lights of Sequoyah still burned with their old radiance, the one he remembered from his youth.

Dora's house was dark, and the little gray car she'd

been driving when they met at the old Dinker place was gone. He looked at his watch, noted the lateness of the hour and wondered where she was, with what he recognized immediately as that little ache of fear and longing Ray had sometimes described in the early days when he'd found himself in love with Lois.

But it was not something Kinley had ever felt, and its curious, muted appearance now struck him as being oddly out of place among the graying hair at his temples, and the ever-darkening crescents that sometimes hung beneath his eyes. Because of that, he refused to give it more than the soft, passing nod its subtle emergence seemed to deserve.

Instead, he busied himself with his equipment. Methodically, he tugged on the large, ill-fitting boots, hoisted the rope over his shoulder, grasped the hoe, spade and flashlight and headed for the well.

It rested not far from the rim of the mountain, a circular wall of gray stone curving jaggedly around its black mouth. The central shaft had been covered by a sheet of now-rusted tin nailed to the posts that supported the arched roof of the well.

The nails which held the tin in place were badly weathered, and Kinley had no trouble dislodging them from the wood. Once free, he drew the tin sheet from the opening and let it slip quietly to the ground.

Now the dark shaft was fully exposed, and for a moment, Kinley leaned over into it, shining his flashlight toward the bottom. It was deeper than he'd expected, the yellow light diffusing as it swept down the narrow shaft until it disappeared altogether.

For a few seconds, he shifted the beam from wall to wall, as he looked for footholds along the shaft. There were very few, and because of that, Kinley understood that he would have to cling to the rope for long periods of time as he eased himself down toward the bottom of the pit. Carefully, he tied the end of the rope to one of the pines that stood nearby, then harnessed himself to the other end, crawled into the yawning shaft, released the hoe, and listened for a moment until he heard it splash into the water at the bottom of the shaft. From the time it took to fall, he calculated the distance to the floor of the well and began his descent.

The air seemed to thicken, congealing around him like a heavy, black liquid, and he could feel a sudden, irrepressible tension crawl slowly over him, tightening his skin around him, pressing in upon his bones. It was an odd sensation, and he found himself glancing upward from time to time, as if to remind himself that the earth above was still bright and clear. But the moon was no more than a smoky mass behind the nocturnal clouds, and so he let his eyes descend again, staring down toward the ever-darkening regions over which he hung.

As he continued downward, the circle of light that seemed to stare down from above narrowed steadily, until it appeared as little more than a distant tunnel.

He forced his eyes away again and concentrated on pressing his feet firmly against the side of the shaft as he lowered himself downward one step at a time. He could see his hands grasping fiercely at the rope, seize and release, seize and release.

As he continued his descent, the uneasiness within him, a predictable tension accompanied by an odd, unexplainable nostalgia, continued to build insistently, voices growing louder and louder as he neared their source.

It was as if something at the bottom of the pit were simultaneously calling him to it and warning him away, begging him to reveal it and crying out that he must not. For a moment, he stopped, his feet digging into the shaft's moist wall, while he dangled eerily in the blackness, his fingers pulsing along the long, gray rope. The darkness solidified around him so that he almost felt he could release the rope and drift back restfully onto its ebony bed, as if to hang there forever, in a lost suspension, his arms flung out, secure in the impenetrable darkness.

It's better to know, isn't it?

It was Ray's voice, and they were together again, moving through the woods, over the lip of the canyon and down onto its dense, green floor, moving faster and faster, until Kinley felt that it was only him moving, and he was a little boy again, and Ray was no longer leading him, but someone else, a hand dragging him through the undergrowth, his eyes following that hand, up the arm and shoulder to the tall, imposing blur that pulled him ferociously.

It's better to know, isn't it?

Now it was Dora's voice, and he was with her on the porch, and then in the tiny living room, his fingers dancing over the white keys of the piano, freed suddenly from the iron grip of repetitive motions, the lock of nerves that made them twitch and tingle, pull and grasp, as if the flight of music, its momentary exhilaration, was the only route to another sanctuary.

He heard himself gasp, and a burst of air shook the small tendrils of the roots that reached out from the circular wall, and he sucked in a long, deep breath, filling his lungs, expanding his chest, rushing air into his blood and along the complex system which led to his brain, clearing it with a sudden infusion of oxygen.

His fingers released their grip on the rope slightly, and he sank down again. He could feel a cool wave of air engulf him, sweeping upward, as if to drive back the yellow beam of the flashlight, while at his feet, the firm wall of the shaft grew moist and pliant, his boots now leaving faint tracks along the side of the well.

He stopped again and glanced down. He could see the bottom of the well at a distance of perhaps twenty feet, the handle of the hoe nosing up out of the water as it leaned against the dripping wall.

A sudden urgency overtook him, driving him down with an uncompromising command, and he gripped and released the rope, gripped and released it again as his feet plowed backwards down the wall.

He reached the bottom a few seconds later, and paused to get his breath, his eyes focusing upward into the darkness, while he continued to hang from the rope, his feet barely breaking the surface of the water. Above, the shaft looked closed, the moon swept from the sky, leaving nothing above but what remained below, a thick, watery blackness.

The urgency swept over him again, but this time more clear and definite, so that he was able to recognize its source.

"Kinley, are you . . ."

He heard Ray's voice again, saw his face wet with rain as the walls of the shaft were wet and dripping.

"Kinley, are you . . ."

"Afraid?" Kinley whispered softly, wondering if this had been the question Ray had never finished as he ran breathlessly beside the train.

His hands twitched, and he wrapped his fingers around the chrome handle of the flashlight to stop them. The light illuminated the fetid pool of green water beneath him. He released the rope again and took another backward step, the heels of his boots now breaking the surface of the water, then sinking beneath, deeper and deeper, as the water crept further and further up his ankles, knees, legs.

He gripped the rope more firmly, then drew his legs from the wall and let them dangle beneath him, flailing slightly in the water, the toes angled down, reaching for the first firm ground.

He brought them up again, took another backward step, then removed them, and began to dangle again, his feet still searching for the ground. Nothing. He tried again. Nothing.

He was almost waist deep in his crawl along the wall before the ground suddenly rose to press against his feet, and he slowly let go of the rope and stood upright in the well, the green water now only a few inches below his belt, cold and slimy as the other places he had been, ditches and ravines, swamps and ponds and estuaries, damp cellars and flooded basements,

212

streams, rivers, waterfalls, the last resting places of the unjustly dead.

He took the hoe, turned it upside down and began to tap its rounded end against the ground at his feet, nudging, prying, nosing into the muddy bottom. Years had passed since Ellie Dinker's death, but a body in decay still possessed a terrible stubbornness, an unwillingness entirely to disappear. It fought with stains sunk deep in cloth, flaps of black, desiccated skin, the brittle intransigence of bone. And Kinley knew that if Ellie Dinker's body had been thrown into the well, it would be there still, a lumpy, wormy mass, but a mass nonetheless, its gooey pile of amorphous flesh held in place by the webs and hinges of her bones.

Slowly, inch by inch, in tight circles radiating out from his feet, he prodded meticulously at the ground beneath him, the end of the hoe nosing through what he recognized as bits of wood, glass, metal, weedy islands of underwater plants. In the silence, he could hear the soft lap of the water as it licked at his waist or swirled around the gray shaft of the handle.

The process was grindingly slow, and by the time Kinley had moved the hoe several times along the outer wall of the well, he could feel his soggy clothes clinging to him sickeningly, the thick, stagnant water like a kind of glue binding cloth to flesh. He shook his head. Nothing. There was nothing.

He sank the end of the hoe into the strap at his back, grabbed the rope and began tugging himself upward, his feet slogging up the moist wall of the shaft.

As he rose, he could see his tracks before him, wet and dripping, the earth crumbling around them, the soft *plup, plup* of its reddish clay dropping from the shaft into the stagnant pool below.

The old urgency reared again, menacing and frightening, and he felt his grip tighten on the rope and his feet press deeply for a hold, then slip away as the dripping earth gave way.

He looked up, but saw nothing but the shrouded darkness. He drew the flashlight from his belt and aimed it upward, its beam shooting a steady stream of light up the narrow shaft. The ground above him seemed to tremble unexplainably, as if the beam itself had begun to gnaw into the earthen walls, dislodging steadily larger bits of dirt.

Kinley turned off the light and let it slip idly from his twitching fingers, as he grasped more desperately at the rope, tugging brutally upward, dragging himself forward toward the utter blackness overhead.

He could feel the ground rain down upon him, as if someone were shovelling earth into the shaft. He pulled himself upward against the falling earth, driving on through the torrent, head down, muscles bulged, the grip of his hands like vises on the slender rope.

His feet slid against the wet wall of the shaft, then slipped off entirely, dangling in the black air until he could reach the wall again. A steady throb of pain ran up his thighs and back, and each time he swung free, his grip on the rope tightened, his fingers like knots of flesh around the cord.

Still, he tugged and dragged at the rope as he fought to find footholds in the wall. He could feel his breath coming in quick, short gasps, see it in bursts of white mist in the chill night air, and for an instant, he thought of his life as something infinitely frail, something clinging to the limb while waves of fear rolled down its naked sides in small, icy streams of sweat.

Suddenly, he heard movement overhead, glanced upward and realized that he was near the top of the shaft. In the faint gray light he could see a figure staring down, the dark head poised at the entrance to the well. He felt a slight tremble in the rope, as if it were being sawed in two from above, the cuts coming rhythmically, the rope trembling with each pass of the blade as a body shudders with each pistol shot.

He pressed his feet to the side of the wall and dragged

himself upward frantically. Above, he could still see the lone figure staring down at him, motionless and demonic, as his grandmother had sometimes stared from her place above his head, eyes gleaming in the darkness.

"Help me," he breathed.

He saw the figure draw away, and he dragged at the rope, his feet whipping wildly in the empty air, as he dragged again and again, his feet no longer of any use, but simply great, soggy weights which hung in the blackness somewhere down below.

"Help me."

His hands twitching at the rope, grasping, grasping as he dragged upon it again and again, the eye of the shaft growing larger, as if he were tugging it mightily toward him.

"Help me," he repeated, then gave a few last furious pulls on the rope, his legs drawing up beneath him as his hands released the rope and he grasped wildly for the stone rim of the well, the tips biting into the hard rock, the nails scraping silvery patterns into its dry stone, the grip loosening even as he pressed it down again, his body edging back helplessly toward the dark pit.

"Help me," he said as he felt himself drift backward, sinking into the darkness, his hands suddenly breaking free of the stone, but still grasping, grasping.

Suddenly she was over him, leaning into the dark eye of the well, her long white arms reaching for him, holding him, drawing him up with a long, mighty pull that swept him over to the rope again, his hands wrapping around it with a sudden, unfathomable calm.

Twenty-Four

She wrapped him in a blanket, made a cup of black coffee, then watched him drink it as he sat beside a small electric heater in the living room.

"It was just a lead I was following," Kinley explained, "something Riley Hendricks said."

Dora said nothing, but only waited.

"He wondered why the police had never checked the well behind your father's house," Kinley added.

"So you decided to check it?"

"You have to eliminate certain possibilities as you go along," Kinley told her, the voice of the schooled professional now reasserting itself determinedly.

"So you thought my father might have dumped Ellie Dinker's body in the well?" Dora asked softly.

"I wanted to eliminate that possibility," Kinley answered weakly. "I mean . . ."

Dora raised her hand to silence him. "You don't have to explain." She stood up, walked to the window, glanced out quickly, then turned back to him. "Be-

216

sides, I'd already checked it," she said, "six years ago."

"You? Why?"

She leaned against the window, the dissolving glow from the lights in the valley rising in a faint aura from her shoulders. "Because of Mrs. Dinker," Dora said. "I came home one afternoon, and she was in the backyard. She was standing by the well, still wearing that black dress."

Kinley nodded but said nothing.

"I came up to her," Dora went on. "I thought she was crazy. There'd been a lot of talk. I didn't know what she might do." Her voice softened. "But she wasn't exactly crazy. Something else. Tormented." She paused a moment, as if attempting to get everything in order before going on. "She watched me come up to her," she continued finally. "And then she smiled."

"Smiled?"

"A strange smile, of course," Dora said. "You know, sort of taunting, as if she'd discovered my secret."

"Yes, I've seen that," Kinley said.

"Anyway, I said hello to her," Dora went on. "And she just pointed to the well, and she said, 'Is she down there?' Just like that. Then she asked the same question again, 'Is my little girl down there?'" She shook her head. "I didn't know how to answer that. It had never occurred to me that my father had killed Ellie Dinker, and so the well, what might be in it, that had never crossed my mind either."

"When did you look?"

"I did it right at that moment," Dora answered. "I thought it was the only way to prove to Mrs. Dinker that my father hadn't killed her daughter."

"So you went down into the well while she was there?"

"Yes," Dora said.

"Alone?" Kinley asked admiringly.

"Alone, yes," Dora answered matter-of-factly. Some-

217

thing in her earlier confidence seemed to give a bit. "Does that seem crazy?"

"Just unusual."

"I don't want to go nuts," Dora said. "I don't want to end up like Mrs. Dinker."

Kinley thought of all the ripped and blasted lives his work had brought him into, the empty chairs at the family table. He wondered why he'd never felt the same peril.

"Anyway, there was nothing down there, of course," Dora said, "and when I came up, I told Mrs. Dinker that."

"Did she believe you?"

"Yes, I think she did," Dora said. "She walked away, and that was the last time I spoke to her. I'd see her from time to time after that. She was always hanging around the courthouse. But I'd never spoken to her again."

She came toward him, gathered her skirt under her and sat down on the floor beside him. "Are you warm yet?"

He nodded. "Yeah, I'm fine."

She smiled quietly. "Ray was the first one to come along who was willing to help me on my . . ."

"Quest?" Kinley said.

Dora did not look amused by the grandeur of the word. "Reason to live," she said.

"If that's what it is, then it might be better if you never found out."

Dora shook her head. "No, it's not like that. If I ever found out who killed Ellie Dinker, it would be like being released from prison. Even if it turned out that my father really was the one who did it. Even that would release me." She turned toward him slowly, her eyes glowing in the red light of the heater. "Do you think he did?" she asked. "Do you think he killed that little girl?"

There was always a moment, Kinley knew, when judgment had to be rendered, sometimes in the presence of overwhelming evidence, sometimes on the basis of nothing more than a primitive intimation. "No," he said. "No, I don't think he did, Dora."

218

She seemed neither relieved nor surprised by his answer. "Ray didn't either," she said. "I think that's what it was between us."

"Not love?" Kinley asked.

Her eyes closed softly, then opened. "Maybe for him."

"And for you?"

Some slender rod in the great, unbending structure of her character loosened toward him, releasing a subtle confidence. "Sometimes, you just get tired of going to bed alone," she said.

Kinley's mind swept down the long chain of his nights, an indistinguishable landscape of interchangeable rooms, sentiments, people. "Yes," he said. "You do."

It had come upon them in an instant, lingered for a time, then departed. Kinley could feel his head pressed deep into the pillow beside her, his eyes watching the air beyond her bedroom window. In the early morning light, he could see the mists rising over the brow of the mountain, gray and billowy, as he remembered them from his home on the canyon.

She slept at his side, her dark face balanced on his shoulder, and as his eyes shot over to her, he felt a grave, nearly uncontrollable need to nudge her into wakefulness, so that he could tell her about his days with his grandmother in the small house, his long walks through the canyon depths, that first journey to the wall of vines, Ray's face like a ball of light in the deep green sea of the canyon floor, his voice full of a desperately whispered conspiracy: *no one could ever find you here*.

She shifted slightly, her cheek moving like a soft, brown cloth across his arm. He could smell her hair, her skin, feel the texture of her flesh, but the sensation was so new to him, so different from his past experience, that it came to him like an innovation, a sudden, revelatory instant within a process that was infinitely old and familiar.

219

She awakened with a start. "Sorry," she said. "I didn't think you'd stay all night."

"You didn't want me to?"

"I just didn't think you would. Ray never did."

"He had a wife."

"Even after that," Dora said, "even after the divorce."

"Well, there was Serena."

She shook her head. "It wasn't Serena. It was Sequoyah. It's too small for things like this."

She got up, drew on a long red robe and walked to the small window of her bedroom. "It may rain," she said idly as she stared out into the mist. "It's been a while. It's time for it to rain."

He pulled himself up slightly, pressing his back against the headboard as he watched her at the window. Her back was fully to him, so that he could see only the long fall of the robe, its red tide sweeping over her shoulders and plunging nearly to the floor.

"Dora," he said softly.

She turned to face him. "No," she said firmly, then pushed her hands out, a barrier between them. "It doesn't mean anything. It doesn't have to mean anything."

He looked at her accusingly. "That sounds like a line you've said before."

The hands retreated. "You'd better go now."

"Why?"

"Because that's the way it is."

"With people?"

"With me," Dora said. "I don't mean to be hard, but there's a kind of woman I can't stand. Hopeless, clinging. You know the kind?"

"Victims."

"That's right," Dora said. "I haven't made much of my life, Kinley, but I haven't become something like that, and I don't intend to start now." She nodded toward the floor, where his clothes lay in a tangled mass. "I'll let you dress alone," she said, then left the room, closing the door behind her.

He dressed quickly and headed into the other room. It was empty, and so he kept going, out onto the porch, then down the stairs to where he found her standing near the edge of the cliff, her eyes fixed on the town below.

She continued to stare out over the slope of the mountain. "You have to be careful, don't you?"

"About what?"

"Not to be trivial," Dora said.

"No one can ever be safe from a judgment like that," he told her.

"You can if you *do* something," Dora said.

"What do you want to do?"

She stared at him determinedly. "I want to find out who killed Ellie Dinker," she said. "I don't want to die in this fucking town without at least knowing *that*."

He looked at her coolly. "Does that explain last night?"

The sound of her hand as it struck him, he thought, must have echoed for a thousand miles.

Twenty-Five

No one had ever done that.

No one.

Ever.

At first he'd been unable to absorb it, the look in her eyes, the whirl of her arm, the blow on his face, slamming it to the right so that the whole fogbound valley had become an insubstantial blur. In the brief aftermath, he'd gone entirely numb, his eyes glaring at her in a smokey stillness, until she'd finally turned abruptly and disappeared into the house. After that, he'd had no option but to return to the house on Beaumont Street.

He slumped at the desk in Ray's office, took a deep, exasperated breath, and let his eyes move hazily along the line of books, then inch downward to settle on the computer's unlighted screen.

In a learned, unwilled gesture, he turned it on, then typed in the familiar code: OVER:MYS. When the file flashed onto the screen, he scrolled down, moving like a bird over the mysteries of Overton and Dinker, until the darkness at the end of the line flowed over the entire screen.

On its blank surface, he typed in the only heading that seemed possible for him at the moment:

QUESTIONS ABOUT DORA

For a few sluggish minutes, he tried to imagine exactly what those questions might be, but found that he knew so little about her, had done so little "research," that he had not even reached the point where he could formulate a list. She was not *his* in the way that certain things which swam about and included her now seemed to belong to him, facts and suppositions, the accumulated data of the Overton case.

He hit the delete key, instantly obliterated the last word, replaced it with another, then gazed silently at the new formulation:

QUESTIONS ABOUT THE INVESTIGATION

That was one thing that was incontestably his now, the investigation he'd mounted into the fate of Ellie Dinker. It was a part of him as much as it had ever been a part of Ray before him, or Dora before that, as much as it had been a part of Martha Dinker during those first apprehensive seconds when she had peered out at the darkening sky and wondered why her only daughter had not yet come home. It was his now, passionately his, and he would not let it go.

He found Ben Wade much as he had left him a few days before, his large frame hunched over the latest FBI reports.

"Makes for pretty rough reading," he said as Kinley came through the door.

Kinley nodded.

Wade laughed derisively. "Reading this stuff, you wouldn't think a guy could make it to the grocery alive."

Kinley smiled quietly, in no mood for levity. "It's a little overdone," he admitted dryly, "especially the crime clocks."

Wade chuckled. "Every two seconds a this, every three seconds a that. Makes the human condition look pretty grim." The laughter died away. "You work in this business long enough, you come to think the whole world's rotten to the core."

Kinley walked to the chair in front of Wade's desk and sat down. "I had a talk with Riley Hendricks," he said evenly, almost in a tone of accusation.

"Oh yeah? Does he still like teaching school?"

"We didn't talk much about it," Kinley said. "We talked about the investigation of Ellie Dinker's murder."

Wade remained silent, his eyes peering expressionlessly into Kinley's as if they were no more than two blue dots drawn on a white wall.

"About the well," Kinley said, letting the word drop like a heavy weight on Wade's battered desk.

"Yeah, that bothered him," Wade said languidly, "the way they never looked in the well." The hinges on his swivel chair creaked wearily as he straightened himself. "Riley kept thinking Dinker's body must be there, but nobody ever went to look for it." He fished a stick of gum from his shirt pocket, peeled off the wrapper and plunged it into his mouth. "We looked every damn place else, though," he added, "all through the woods, all up and down Rocky River. We drug it from the falls where Overton said he'd dumped it to what must have been as far as ten miles downstream." He shrugged. "We didn't find anything. Not a trace."

"But not the well," Kinley said. "You never looked there."

"No, we didn't."

"Why not?"

"The best I can figure, it just never entered anybody's

224

mind," Wade answered. "We'd go into Sheriff Maddox's office, and everybody would be there. I mean everybody. Me, the DA, half the Fire Department, even old Mayor Jameson a couple of times. I mean, everybody. And the Sheriff, he'd have his county map spread out across his desk, and he'd point at this place and that place, all the hell around, and he'd say, 'Look right here,' and put a little dot on the map, and off we'd go." He looked at Kinley helplessly. "But he just never put a little dot at the well in Charlie Overton's backyard."

"And you never mentioned it to him?"

Wade gave a low grunt. "Floyd Maddox wasn't the sort of man that a deputy made suggestions to." He tapped the side of his head. "We're not dealing with the smartest guy that ever lived, you know."

Kinley nodded. "I see."

Wade sat back, the mouth moving in slow circles. "Turns out it didn't matter, though," he said.

"What didn't matter?"

"Whether we looked in that well or not," Wade said. "Because the girl's body wasn't there."

"How do you know that?"

"Because Ray said so," Wade told him.

"I thought he didn't talk about the Dinker case."

"He mentioned the well one time," Wade said, "and the only other time was the day he died."

"The day he died?"

"That's right," Wade said. "It was the day they found him in the canyon. He came up the stairs. He was really out of breath, and he walked over to the desk there, and he unlocked the bottom drawer. I guess it must have been the one he kept all the Overton stuff in." He bent to the right and spit the gum into the garbage can beside his desk. "Anyway, he scooped everything out of it, scooped it all into a plain old yellow envelope. Then he looked over at me, and he said, 'It's just this Dinker stuff.' Then he said he was through with it and that nobody should talk about it."

"Nobody should talk about it?"

"Me. That I shouldn't mention it," Wade explained. "Like it was maybe a little embarrassing for him to have ever bothered with it in the first place."

"And this was Sunday?"

"That's right," Wade said. "I wouldn't have been here at all if I hadn't left the keys to my tool chest in my desk."

"Would anyone else have been in the courthouse that day?"

"On a Sunday afternoon?" Wade asked loudly. "You must be kidding."

Kinley let his eyes shift over to the desk in a slow, thoughtful motion that Wade caught immediately.

"Something bothering you, Jack?" he asked. "It's okay if I call you Jack, I hope?"

Kinley turned his attention back to Wade. "It's the secrecy," he said. "That's what bothers me. The way Ray was keeping everything to himself."

Wade shrugged. "If you want to look in that drawer, go ahead," he said indifferently. "Ray wouldn't have cared. He took the lock with him."

Kinley took Wade up on his offer without hesitation, walked to the desk and pulled out the drawer. There was nothing inside but a green folder identical to the ones he'd found in the file cabinet in Ray's office on Beaumont Street, but without any label of any kind.

"Too bad about Ray," Wade said quietly. "He was a first-class investigator."

Kinley turned toward him. "What time did you see Ray that day?"

"Around one-thirty, I guess."

"And he was found dead two hours later?"

"That sounds about right."

"In the canyon."

Wade nodded. "Must have gone directly there."

"Not quite," Kinley said.

"What do you mean?"

"Because whatever he took out of the drawer, it wasn't with him when he died."

"How do you know that?"

"The Incident Reports," Kinley told him. "They didn't mention anything but the body."

Wade's face grew very solemn, but he said nothing.

Kinley let his eyes rise toward the small square window in front of Ray's desk. He could see the slender gray flagpole on the courthouse lawn, the long gray steps where Martha Dinker had kept her vigil, and beyond them, the green slope of the mountain which rose like a great wall to shield the canyon from his view.

He was on his way down the corridor when he saw Mrs. Hunter rise quickly from her desk and approach him.

"Well, I wasn't sure I'd be seeing you again," she said brightly.

Kinley nodded politely.

"I wanted to let you know that I found an answer for you," Mrs. Hunter said.

"An answer?"

"You know, about Mrs. Dinker," Mrs. Hunter said. "About what she'd been interested in when she came and looked over the evidence in the case."

"Oh, yes," Kinley said, recalling an interest that seemed purely technical to him now.

"Well, Harriet Calhoun had been away for a few days," Mrs. Hunter went on. "But I finally got in touch with her last night, and she told me that every time Mrs. Dinker came to the office, she just wanted one thing."

"One thing?"

"Just one particular volume of the transcript."

"Did she remember which one?"

"Yes, she did," Mrs. Hunter said proudly. "It was volume four."

Kinley's mind did its job and called the volume up.

"Volume four," he said. "That was her own testimony."

"That's right," Mrs. Hunter said, "but she didn't read the whole volume, just one part of it."

"One part?"

"Just one page, Harriet said."

"Did she remember the page?"

A great glow of accomplishment swept over Mrs. Hunter's face. "Well, it turns out that Mrs. Dinker came here a lot, and she'd always get the same book, and she'd sit and read it, but she never would bring it back over to the desk. She'd just leave it open on the table."

Kinley nodded.

"And Harriet would always put it away," Mrs. Hunter continued. "And she said it was always open on the same page." She allowed for a single, dramatic pause, letting the suspense build. "Four-fourteen," she announced grandly. "Harriet remembered it very well."

"Four-fourteen," Kinley repeated softly.

"And I thought you might want to take a look at that page," Mrs. Hunter said.

"Yes, I would."

"Well, I've got it in my office," Mrs. Hunter said.

Kinley followed her into the office, then waited as she pulled out a desk drawer, allowed for another dramatic pause, then placed volume four into Kinley's waiting hands.

"I told Mr. Warfield that you were interested in this case," Mrs. Hunter said. "And he told me that since it's such an old case and no appeal coming, that you could just borrow the whole thing."

Kinley hugged the transcript to his chest. "Thank you."

Mrs. Hunter wagged her finger sternly. "But don't forget to bring it back," she said.

Kinley drove directly to Ray's house, strode back into the office and opened the transcript to page four-fourteen.

It was only a single page of neatly typed paper, but it had the look of an ancient text, a piece of revered parchment which had been studied again and again, the yellow stains of Mrs. Dinker's hands running over each word as if, like a blind woman, she'd had to read it with her fingertips. In his mind, he could see her in her black dress, hunched over the little metal table beside the door of the vault, growing older with the passing years, growing blind and deaf and mad as she read the single page over and over again, the page that Kinley now read for himself:

WARFIELD: Did you actually see Ellie head up the mountain?

DINKER: Yes, sir. I seen her go.

WARFIELD: Do you remember what she was wearing?

DINKER: A green dress and a pair of black shoes.

WARFIELD: What was the dress made of?

DINKER: Cotton.

WARFIELD: Was it dark green or light green?

DINKER: Dark green. And it had a little white lacy collar that I made for her.

WARFIELD: Mrs. Dinker, did you ever see your daughter again?

DINKER: No, sir.

WARFIELD: Mrs. Dinker, do you see this pair of shoes I have in my hand?

DINKER: (whimpering) Yes, sir.

WARFIELD: Whose shoes are these, Mrs. Dinker?

DINKER: Those are Ellie's shoes.

WARFIELD: How do you know that?

DINKER: By them shiny little buckles.

WARFIELD: Mrs. Dinker, did you ever see Ellie's green dress again?

DINKER: (crying) No, sir.

WARFIELD: Mrs. Dinker, do you see this dress I'm holding up to show the jury right now?

DINKER: (sobbing) INAUDIBLE

WARFIELD: Mrs. Dinker, is this the dress your daughter

was wearing when she headed up the mountain at twelve noon on Friday, July 2, 1954?

(THE WITNESS DOES NOT RESPOND)

WARFIELD: I know it's hard for you, Mrs. Dinker, but it's very important. This dress you've been looking at, the one I'm holding in my hands. Mrs. Dinker, is this the dress your daughter wore when she left home that Friday morning?

(WITNESS DOES NOT RESPOND)

WARFIELD: Mrs. Dinker?

(WITNESS DOES NOT RESPOND)

WARFIELD: Mrs. Dinker, please. I ask you, Mrs. Dinker, is this your daughter Ellie's dress?

DINKER: I ain't seen it since that day.

WARFIELD: Thank you. The witness is excused.

For a few minutes after his first reading, Kinley continued to focus his attention on the page, reading it carefully again. Then he closed his eyes and tried to imagine the scene in Judge Bryan's courtroom as the testimony was given. He could see Mrs. Dinker at the stand, speaking firmly in that way prosecutors hoped for, the plain, unadorned language and quick responses, *yes, sir, yes, sir*, suggesting a confidence that could only be engendered in the truth.

Then suddenly her composure had collapsed, and it was easy for Kinley to visualize the exact moment in all its wrenching detail. He could see Warfield as he stepped over to the prosecutor's table, his hands moving toward the box or bag strategically placed there for him, his words pealing over the courtroom crowd as he moved slowly toward his destination: *Did you ever see her dress again?*

Then the long white fingers Kinley had seen in the newspaper photographs crawled into the nondescript container, seized something, and began to draw it out slowly, holding it gingerly by the shoulders, so that it unfolded

230

fully as he lifted it, revealing the wide swath of blood that spread across its dark green front, the eyes of the jurors widening in horror as they gazed up at it, waiting for the District Attorney's next question: *Mrs. Dinker, do you see this dress I'm holding up before you now?*

It was then that she had broken, or faltered, her lips moving silently as if she were muttering something beneath her breath, a phrase or sentence which the court reporter had not been able to hear: INAUDIBLE

But Warfield had continued to press her insistently, his questions now coming one upon the other, ringing through the courtroom while he continued to hold the dress suspended in the air. *Is this the dress your daughter was wearing when she headed up the mountain on Friday, July 2, 1954?*

Again Mrs. Dinker fumbled, her eyes no doubt staring at the dress in the odd, lengthening silence which the court reporter recorded succinctly in a single, terse description: *WITNESS DOES NOT RESPOND.*

But Warfield had waited no longer than an instant before going on again, this time relentlessly: *I know it's hard for you, Mrs. Dinker, but it's very important. This dress you've been looking at, the one I'm holding in my hands. Mrs. Dinker, is this the dress your daughter wore when she left home that morning?*

Kinley opened his eyes, glanced down at the bottom of the page and let the transcript do the rest:

(WITNESS DOES NOT RESPOND)
WARFIELD: Mrs. Dinker?
(WITNESS DOES NOT RESPOND)
WARFIELD: Mrs. Dinker, please. I ask you, Mrs. Dinker, is this your daughter Ellie's dress?

Then finally, she'd regained herself, as if suddenly brought back from a trance, her eyes still locked on the dark green dress, but seeing it again as Warfield demanded her to answer: *I ask you, Mrs. Dinker, is this your daughter Ellie's dress?*

To which Mrs. Dinker had given a response at last.

DINKER: I ain't seen it since that day.

Kinley looked up and closed his eyes again, as if giving them a badly needed rest, then let them drop back down to the transcript. He looked carefully at the precise moment Mrs. Dinker's testimony had come to an abrupt and surprising end: *Mrs. Dinker, do you see this dress I'm holding up?*

That had been the instant, the moment her eyes had fallen upon her daughter's dress.

There were many possible explanations, of course, and Kinley had had enough experience to know them all. He'd seen the reality of loss rise out of nowhere, a witness suddenly admitting for the first time that it was not a dream, that the body of the beloved had actually been blasted, carved up, drowned, that it would never rise again. Perhaps that was what had happened to Mrs. Dinker. She'd seen the dress, the blood, and the horror and reality of her daughter's death had swept down upon her like a great black bird.

Or perhaps the dress had done just the opposite, shot Mrs. Dinker back to the past, where, for a brief, dazzling moment, she'd seen Ellie toddling toward her in a soiled diaper, or saying her first word, or blowing out the candles on a birthday cake. Kinley had seen that happen too, seen the sweetness of an unviolated history emerge upon a witness's face. Little Billy Flynn's mother had sat for almost a full minute as she'd stared at the Cracker Jack whistle the prosecutor had held before her eyes, her lips whispering just loud enough for the court reporter to record her words, *Billy Billy Billy Billy Billy*, until the prosecutor had finally touched her shoulder to bring her back to her son's death: *Oh, I'm sorry. It's just that Billy blew that whistle all the time.*

But when Mrs. Dinker had finally returned her attention to the prosecutor, she'd answered differently, and as Kinley concentrated on the words, *I ain't seen it since that day*, it struck him that Mrs. Dinker had never really answered Warfield's question. She had never actually identified the green dress as being Ellie Dinker's. Her answer, in the end, had been a dodge.

Kinley scrolled back up to his original heading and typed his first question under it:

QUESTIONS ABOUT THE INVESTIGATION

1) Why did they not search the well?

Then he paused a moment, and wrote a second:

2) Where is Ellie Dinker's dress?

Twenty-Six

This time Kinley found Ben Wade in an open field, moving like a great, hulking bear through crackling rows of dry corn.

"Marijuana," he explained as Kinley trudged up to him, "they plant it between rows of corn so nobody can find it from the air."

"The air?"

"You know, DEA flights," Wade said. "They're doing them all the time, looking for the stuff."

"It's gotten that bad? I mean, in Sequoyah?"

"Everywhere, far as I can figure," Wade said wearily. "People don't have enough to keep them busy. So, they go for dope to fill the space." He took a sharp left turn, plowing through the bleak brown field, his eyes trained on the ground. "How'd you find me way out here?"

"Warfield's secretary."

"Molly-By-Golly," Wade said with a laugh. "That's what we call her."

"Why is that?"

Wade stopped abruptly and gave Kinley a pointed look. "Why do you think?"

Kinley nodded. "Oh."

Wade smiled silently, then started out through the corn again, slamming through it thunderously, as if he were trying to destroy the fields.

"I came up with another angle on the Dinker case," Kinley began cautiously, hoping he had not begun to wear out his welcome as far as Wade was concerned.

"Well, there's probably a million of them," Wade said. "That's usually the way it is in a murder case."

"The dress," Kinley said. "You're the officer who found it."

Wade nodded. "Sure did."

"How did that happen?" Kinley asked.

"I went up in the woods and there it was," Wade answered matter-of-factly.

"Where exactly in the woods?" Kinley asked. "There weren't any graphics in the record."

Wade stopped and looked at him quizzically. "Graphics?"

"Drawings," Kinley explained, "of the murder scene and other relevant locations. You know, plotting distances and directions, that sort of thing."

Wade shook his head exasperatedly. "Hell, man, this was way back in 1954, in some little one-horse Southern town." He laughed. "Graphics, my ass."

Kinley shrugged. "Anyway," he said, "I was wondering where you found the dress."

Wade gave him a penetrating look. "Well, look, Jack, between two old crime buffs, let me tell you something that you need to know about this case."

"What's that?"

"The victim was not a princess, you know what I mean?"

"Not exactly."

"All right, let me spell it out," Wade said grimly. "We kept a lot of stuff under wraps. You know why?"

235

"No."

"Because the Dinker kid was not much more than a teenage whore."

The brutality of the words struck at Kinley like small lead pellets.

"But we didn't want that to come out," Wade went on. "Nobody did. She was an only child, and somebody had killed her, and as far as we knew, her mother thought she was pure as the driven snow." He gave Kinley an amiable, "good ole boy" smile. "Let's just say that we acted like Southern gentlemen. We protected the ladies, both of them. The dead girl, and her mama." He shrugged. "Besides, Warfield thought that no matter how the Dinker girl might have lived her life, that didn't mean somebody had the right to kill her. So he laid down the law. Keep your mouth shut about her, that's what he said. If Talbott wanted to get into Dinker's background, let him, but as far as the DA was concerned, Ellie Dinker was the flower of Southern womanhood."

"And Talbott never brought it up," Kinley said.

"No, he didn't."

"Did he know?"

"If he did, he didn't let on about it," Wade said. "But as far as the Sheriff's Department and the DA's Office were concerned, Ellie Dinker's life was off limits. So if there are some holes here and there, if we looked here, but didn't look there, well, that was the reason for it. We didn't want to dig too deep, because we already knew what we were probably going to find."

"And that's why the prosecution never really had a theory about why Ellie was killed?" Kinley asked.

"Yeah," Wade said, "because we knew why she was killed."

"Why, then?"

Wade looked at Kinley as if he were teaching a small child the tricks of the trade. "Ellie Dinker was a tramp, Jack," he said. "She probably even took a few bucks for her services once in a while. So, the way we figured it,

236

Overton had probably arranged to meet Ellie on the road for a quick fix of jelly-roll. And you've lived in the big city, Jack, you know what happens sometimes in a situation like that. Somebody makes a smart remark, maybe gets a little bitchy, or maybe it's just a dispute over the fee. Anyway, at the end of the day, the girl is dead.''

Kinley struggled to gain a picture of the scene, Ellie Dinker on the ground, laughing mockingly at the breathless old man on top of her. ''Quick fix,'' he said after a moment. ''That's what it would have to have been.''

''Out in the open like that?'' Wade asked. ''You bet.''

''So she would have just pulled up her dress, wouldn't she?''

''Up with the dress, down with the panties,'' Wade said, as if it were a line from a ribald poem.

''But you never found the panties,'' Kinley said.

''The way we figured it,'' Wade replied, ''a girl like Ellie Dinker might not have been wearing any.''

''We?''

''The people who worked on the case.''

''Riley Hendricks?''

''Well, maybe not Riley.''

''How about you?''

''Yeah, I figured she'd been to a few parties in her life,'' Wade said bluntly. ''But I was like everybody else on the case. I didn't think that gave Charlie Overton the right to kill her.''

''Are you still sure he did?''

''Yes,'' Wade said, ''and you're not?''

''No, I'm not.''

Wade grinned knowingly. ''You will be,'' he said confidently. ''You just need to get a little perspective, that's all. You're too close to it.'' He hesitated before delivering the next remark. ''Maybe too close to Dora.''

Kinley could still feel the force of her hand on his face. ''That's not it,'' he said.

Wade stopped and looked at him closely. ''What is it,

Jack? What's bothering you? It bothered Ray, too. But he never told me what it was."

"I don't know for sure," Kinley admitted, "just a feeling."

A curious sympathy came into Wade's large, round face. His eyes narrowed, and a single light-brown eyebrow arched upward. "All right," he said quietly, "what do you want from me?"

"Just to see what you saw," Kinley told him.

"You mean where I found the dress?"

"Yeah."

Wade shook his head wearily. "All right, Jack," he said. "Damn, you Yankees sure are pushy."

They reached the mountain road a few minutes later, Wade pulling his car over to the right shoulder, Kinley nosing in behind him.

"This is where I went into the woods," Wade said as he strode back toward Kinley's car. He turned and pointed to a small break in the forest. "I went right up that trail." He glanced down at Kinley's shoes. "You're not exactly wearing your hiking boots, boy."

"I wasn't planning on doing any hiking when I came down here," Kinley replied.

"Well, you won't have much of it to do," Wade said assuringly as he turned sharply and headed across the road. "I found her dress just a little ways up the trail."

Kinley followed along behind as Wade jumped a narrow gully, crawled quickly up a short, red clay embankment and entered the mountain forest at the same break in the undergrowth he'd pointed out only seconds before.

"I was alone," he said as he moved up the slender trail that led in a somewhat winding route through the forest depths. "Even Riley wasn't with me."

"Why not?" Kinley asked as he trudged behind, slapping thin, low-slung branches from his path.

"Maddox needed him for something," Wade said. He

238

chuckled softly. "Riley had actually been to college, and I think that bothered Sheriff Maddox a little."

"What do you mean?"

"He liked to give Riley shitwork once in a while," Wade said. "Maybe to make him humble, you know." He thought about it for a moment. "But I think that college degree intimidated Maddox a little." He shook his head lightly, then returned to the subject. "Anyway," he said, "Riley was busy doing something, so I came up here by myself. We didn't exactly have a big law enforcement community at that time, so people were scattered around pretty good during the time we were looking for her."

"So you often worked alone during the search?"

Wade shook his head. "No," he said lightly. "Just that one time."

The trail swung to the right, through a thick stand of pine, and as he walked, Kinley could hear the crunch of the needles beneath his feet, and he remembered how, as a boy, he'd loved to lie on the ground and cover himself in them, sleeping through the long afternoons until he'd finally open his eyes and see his grandmother looming over him, her hands stretching down and his stretching up, grasping.

He felt his hands repeat the motion and plunged them quickly into his pockets, as if to hide them from Wade's searching eyes.

"Right there," Wade said suddenly as he came to an abrupt halt on the trail.

Kinley stepped to his side and watched as Wade lifted his arm toward a tall tree which stood in a small clearing in the distance.

"It was hanging from right there," Wade said quietly. "I'll never forget it. Just hanging over a limb, like somebody had tossed it up there."

They made their way to the clearing, and Kinley stared at the lone tree while Wade, breathless from the climb, eased himself down on a large gray stone.

"It must have been quite a sight," Kinley said after a moment.

"Yeah, it was," Wade told him. He shook his head, remembering it. "It was just hanging there, like I said, bent over a limb, like it was . . ." He stopped, and Kinley turned to look at him. His face had taken on a deep wonderment, and behind his eyes, Kinley could see a mind powerfully and passionately at work.

"Like it was what?" Kinley asked.

Wade's eyes lifted toward him, the wonderment now turned to a dark questioning. "Like it was waiting for me," he said.

Kinley stepped over to him. "Was it?"

Wade stood up and flung his large arm over Kinley's shoulder. "How about a drink?" he asked. "It's been a hard climb."

They went to a small bar at the south end of town, the kind Kinley had come to know well in his work, remote, honky-tonk bars where people sat around nursing their grudges against whatever it was they'd come to blame for the way things had turned out.

Wade ordered, then, puffing on a cigarette, waited somewhat impatiently until the drinks arrived. "All right," he said, when they came. "Here's to letting it loose."

Kinley lifted his glass, but said nothing.

"Okay, here it is," Wade said after the first quick sip. "A few things always bothered me. Riley never knew that, and Ray didn't either." He sat back slightly. "But get one thing straight, as far as the Dinker girl, what I said before is the God's truth. She was a tramp. Nobody made that up. As far as meeting Overton, that may be true, too. If he needed some, and she was able to provide it, why not? Besides, his old lady was pregnant, big as a house. Who knows, maybe he needed a little something to get him through the last few days."

240

Kinley nodded. "So what bothers you?"

"The well, that always bothered me," Wade said. "But according to Ray, that came up a crapper."

"Yes, it did."

Wade looked at him questioningly. "You found that out by your own self?"

"Yes."

"You mean, you went down in the goddamn thing?"

"Yes," Kinley said, "and there was nothing down there. I know what to look for, and it wasn't there."

Wade looked at him admiringly for a moment, then went on. "Okay, so one down," he said. "The next thing was the way the investigation went. Warfield didn't have much to say in it. Maddox took it over."

"What's wrong with that?"

Wade gave a quick, dismissive snort. "Floyd Maddox was a fucking rube, Jack," he said. "He was a court house guard dog. He didn't know the first thing about how to handle a murder investigation."

"Who did?"

"Warfield," Wade said. "And Felix. Felix James, the Sequoyah Chief of Police."

"Then why didn't they handle it?"

"I think Warfield wanted to," Wade said. "He kept his eye on it. Maybe for political reasons. It's an old road. You go from District Attorney to Attorney General to Senator or Governor or whatever your dick gets hard for."

Kinley nodded. It was a familiar path.

"So, just for the political clout, I guess Warfield wanted to keep his hand in things," Wade went on. "Of course, he was going to get the limelight for the prosecution anyway. So, really, he didn't have anything to worry about."

"Unless no one was arrested," Kinley said.

"Yeah, well, he wouldn't have wanted that," Wade said. "So, maybe for that reason, he hung around a lot."

"But the Chief didn't?"

Wade shook his head. "No, he didn't. He just sort of bowed out of it."

"Do you know why?"

Wade smiled. "You know, I got to hand it to Riley. He's sort of kept at this case in a way. And, you know, about five years ago, just before Felix died, they were at a meeting somewhere, the school board or something like that, and damned if old Riley didn't come up and ask the old Chief flat out. 'Why didn't you stay on top of the Dinker case?' That's what Riley asked him." He laughed at the brazenness of it. "Right to his goddamn face."

"Did he get an answer?"

"Well, the Chief was pretty well gone with cancer by then," Wade said, "but, yeah, he had enough left of him to spit out an answer. He looked at Riley, and he said, 'It was out of my hands, Deputy.' Then he walked away, and that was the last time I ever saw Felix James alive."

"What do you think he meant by that?"

"I think he meant that it was a technical matter," Wade said, "of law enforcement, I mean, a jurisdictional thing."

"What do you mean, jurisdictional?"

"The murder was probably committed on the mountain above Mile Marker 27," Wade explained. "Which means that it was beyond the Sequoyah city limits. That made it Sheriff Maddox's jurisdiction."

"I see," Kinley said.

"So, in that case, it was the Sheriff's business," Wade added, "and that's the way it went down. The Chief just went on writing speeding tickets during the whole thing."

"So what was unusual about him bowing out?"

"Just that he didn't usually do that sort of thing," Wade said. "He was more like Warfield, ambitious. With a murder case, you'd have thought he'd have hung in there. But he didn't."

Kinley nodded quietly and took a sip of beer. He was somewhat disappointed, since nothing Wade had told him really amounted to much that could be followed up. It was speculative, subjective, the sort of testimony he'd spent hours gathering, then tossed aside like bunting gathered up after the parade had gone by.

"And one other thing," Wade said suddenly.

Kinley lowered the glass and waited.

"The dress," Wade told him. "It disappeared."

Kinley felt his hand crawl up, grasp the notebook he kept nestled in his jacket pocket and draw it out. "The green dress? Ellie Dinker's dress?"

Wade nodded. "Vanished."

"But it was at the trial," Kinley said, astonished. "Warfield held it up for the jury to see."

"Oh, yeah, it was at the trial all right," Wade said. "It didn't disappear until after that."

"Do you know when?"

"About five years ago," Wade answered. "We'd always kept it in a box in the courthouse basement. All the physical evidence was kept down there—the tire iron, the dress, the shoes, everything."

"Were the tire iron and shoes there?"

Wade nodded. "Yeah, they were still there," he said, "but the dress was gone." He took another sip of beer. "Anyway, I was rummaging through some stuff down there, and I came upon the box all the Dinker case stuff was kept in, and the flaps were open. I started to close them, and as I was doing that, I glanced in, and I could see that the dress was gone."

"And that was about five years ago?" Kinley asked, as he wrote it down in his notebook.

"Had to have been between May and August, too," Wade said. "Because I'd been down in the basement in May, and I can tell you one thing, the flaps weren't open on that box."

Kinley wrote that down, too, then glanced back up at Wade. "It was during the time that Mrs. Dinker was always coming to the courthouse to read the transcript of the trial," he said.

Wade nodded solemnly. "Yeah, I know," he said

243

softly. "And that's what made me start thinking that maybe something went wrong in the case way back then." He drained the last of the beer, then lowered the glass to the table. "One thing about that dress, it didn't get up and walk out by itself."

Twenty-Seven

All the way back down the mountain, Kinley continued to think of the various, somewhat disconnected, things Ben Wade had told him. Most of them could be explained. It was possible, for example, that Chief James had only acted professionally in withdrawing from a case that was not in his jurisdiction. As for Sheriff Maddox, his actions could be put to nothing more sinister than the limited intelligence and organizational skill he had exhibited during his long tenure as Sheriff. Even Ray had commented upon it from time to time. "He was a bumbler, Kinley, a political hack," he'd told him not long after Maddox had died, and just before he had decided to run for the office himself. "He just did what he was told by the local bosses."

But neither James's professionalism nor Maddox's incompetence could explain the most essential of Ben Wade's revelations, the disappearance of Ellie Dinker's dress.

As he continued down toward the valley, driving

slowly along the curving mountain road, he could see all of Sequoyah spread out before him, a narrow stretch of lights which ran for almost three miles down the slender green valley. He had spent his youth watching it from the great height of his own mountain home. It had been the "big city" then, or as much of a big city as he had yet experienced, or ever expected to experience before the Yankee researchers had discovered him, and he'd thought of it as a strange and indecipherable place, a random, haphazard collection of stores and houses, churches and factories, presided over, perhaps kept in check, by the overhanging wall of the courthouse façade.

But now, as he continued to drift down the mountainside, his foot pressed firmly on the brake, Sequoyah seemed small and vulnerable, even innocent when he thought of Boston or New York, its corruptions more or less harmless, a quick five spot from a local bootlegger, another five to fix a traffic ticket. Compared to the epic graft of Manhattan, Sequoyah's trivial venalities seemed little more than the time-honored way of doing business, a form of friendly chicanery.

Except for Ellie Dinker's dress.

He saw it in the fervent detail of his imagination, first as it shifted along Ellie Dinker's thin, white legs as she made her way toward the mountain road, then as it waved in the summer breeze before Ben Wade's astonished eyes, still later as it hung from Warfield's determined fingers, and finally, as it was yanked from the dark box by hands Kinley could not see.

He glanced down toward the scattered lights of Sequoyah once again. Over the roofs of the shops and houses, and even higher, past the pointed spires of the Protestant churches, he could see the lights of the courthouse, some of them still burning on the top floor. One of them was in the exact place where Ray's desk rested on the second floor. And as Kinley's eyes focused on its tiny square of light, he could almost see Ray's pale face pressed against the tiny window as he peered sleeplessly

246

into the night, his ghostly eyes fixed on the mountain, a car moving down the mountain road, his old friend Kinley behind the wheel: *It's better to know, don't you think? No matter what the cost.*

He sat down at the desk and typed out the list of people who'd thus far become associated with the case, placing the names in two columns, the living and the dead.

LIVING
1) Riley Hendricks
2) Ben Wade
3) Horace Talbott
4) Dr. Stark
5) Helen Slater
6) Dora Overton

DEAD
1) Chief James
2) Sheriff Maddox
3) Thomas Warfield
4) Martha Dinker
5) Ellie Dinker
6) Charles Overton
7) Sarah Overton
8) Ray Tindall

CONDITION UNKNOWN
1) Betty Gaines
2) Luther Snow
3) David Halgrave

Once the names had been typed into the file, he returned to Martha Dinker's testimony, and suddenly, with his knowledge of the missing dress now included in the data his mind had rearranged, Mrs. Dinker's action on the stand became utterly clear, the halting phrases, and particularly the repeated references the court reporter had made in the record to what Kinley now saw as Mrs. Dinker's mute alarm: *WITNESS DOES NOT RESPOND.*

But she had responded, Kinley realized, as he looked at the single page of testimony Mrs. Dinker herself had gazed at for so long as she had sat hunched over the gray metal desk outside the evidence vault. She had powerfully responded. She had gone speechless, and as his eyes bore into the transcript for what he knew would be the final time, Kinley could visualize the whole terrible moment in his mind:

WARFIELD: Did you actually see Ellie head up the mountain?
DINKER: Yes, sir.
WARFIELD: Do you remember what she was wearing?
DINKER: A pair of black shoes and a green dress.
WARFIELD: What was it made of?
DINKER: Cotton.
WARFIELD: Was it dark green or light green?
DINKER: Dark green. And it had a little white lacy collar that I made for her.
WARFIELD: Mrs. Dinker, did you ever see your daughter again?
DINKER: No, sir.

At that moment, Warfield had walked to his desk and displayed the dress Ben Wade had found hanging like a headless, limbless body in the trees above the mountain road.

In response, Mrs. Dinker had stared silently at the dress for a moment, then mumbled something the court reporter had found inaudible.

But as Kinley could sense now, Martha Dinker had no longer been in the courtroom as Warfield fired his questions. Her mind had been whirling, as her eyes bore down upon the dress. And as the seconds of her unexpected silence lengthened, the court reporter had finally had no choice but to write into the bleak history of the trial that to the prosecutor's insistent question Martha Dinker had given no answer whatsoever. Instead, she had stared mutely at the dress hanging limply from Warfield's long white fingers, until, under the barrage of his insistent demands, she had finally responded: *I ain't seen it since that day.*

Kinley held his eyes fixedly on Martha Dinker's final, explosive response to Warfield's question, then got up, poured himself a scotch from the bottle he'd bought the day before and walked out onto the front porch.

The feel of the wooden swing against his back was firm and reassuring, something hard and steady in a world that seemed to be dissolving, the old Sequoyah with its rooted notions of how the world should be, how people should behave within it, of where a human should stand amid the swirling chaos of the years, all that ancient, solid ground seemed to be shifting subtly beneath his feet.

He took a sip from the glass and leaned back, his mind returning to the courtroom, to Martha Dinker's stunned silence as she'd gazed at her daughter's dress. She had seen something which had silenced her, stopped her completely in the onward rush of her testimony, stopped her as fully and completely as if a hand had suddenly pressed itself against her mouth.

But what?

He was sure it was in the transcript somewhere, on that single page somewhere. By now he had read it a sufficient number of times for his mind fully to have recorded it, and as he sat on the dark porch he replayed it in his mind, once again moving to the abrupt halt in Mrs. Dinker's testimony as Warfield had lifted the dress to display it before her.

What had she seen at that moment?

With the dress gone, he realized that he might never know. It was one of the worst kinds of dead ends for an investigation, a solid, black wall that seemed beyond penetration. The dress was gone, and he had no way of knowing where it was, or even what it might have looked like, other than that it was dark green with a lacy collar Mrs. Dinker had made herself.

He took another sip of scotch and let his legs press back against the wooden floor, swinging himself gently in the dark air, his mind wandering amid the welter of accumulating detail, as he always allowed it to do when he confronted what appeared to be an insurmountable difficulty. At times it had been a productive maneuver, and suddenly, out of nowhere, a lost item or misspoken word flared up from the mound of ashes and sent him whirling again. At other times, however, it had come up empty, and there were moments when those failures rose to haunt and disconcert him. He had never found Billy Flynn's little plastic ring, and for all he knew Mildred Haskell had swallowed it the day she murdered him. The strange girl in the red bell-bottoms whom Daphne Moore had seen with Willie Connors only minutes before he kidnapped her remained a black, featureless silhouette. Why Colin Bright had lied about coming north toward the Comstock farm remained a mystery, as did the reason Alley Short had called the police to report a murder she had herself committed.

He pushed back roughly, almost angrily, his feet once again flying out, sending the swing further back, so that when he swept forward again he could feel a breeze riffle through his hair. It was cooler than the air had been only seconds before, and because of that Kinley knew that a layer of high air had suddenly descended from the mountain's heights, moving in a broad wave down its steep slopes, rustling through the leaves, branches, vines.

His eyes opened quickly as the idea struck him, the single slant of light which might still pierce the dark wall that separated him from Ellie Dinker's dress.

He stood up, walked back to Ray's office, opened the bottom drawer of the file cabinet and drew out the file marked "O," the one which Lois had returned to him several days before, and which had contained only a series of newspaper articles and photographs about the case.

Meticulously he went through the contents of the file across the desk, staring at each photograph. After a moment, he leaned back again, his eyes moving randomly across the desk, the energy of their earlier mission now lost in failure. There had been no photograph of Ellie Dinker's dress.

But as his eyes shifted from article to article, Kinley noticed that the entire case had been covered by a single reporter, the same one who'd journeyed to the state prison and written so evocatively of Overton's execution. The name appeared at the top of every article and at the bottom of every picture the paper had published about the case.

Kinley glanced up at the still illuminated computer screen and wrote in the name under CONDITION UNKNOWN.

It was number 4: Harry Townsend.

Then he did what he'd learned to do first in trying to track someone down. It was an entirely obvious strategy, and it had always surprised him how often it paid off. He pulled the Sequoyah Telephone Directory down from its place on the shelf above the desk and looked Townsend up. He was there, complete with home address.

Kinley wrote both into his notebook, then returned to the computer screen and made the necessary adjustment, erasing the name under Condition Unknown, and typing it out again, as if, with Godlike power, adding Townsend's name to the Book of Life.

The computer screen was still shedding its blue light into the room when, several hours later, he heard a soft knock at the door, rousing him from the sleep that had finally overtaken him. He pulled himself up, blinked the remaining slumber from his eyes, walked into the foyer and opened the door.

"I'm sorry," Dora said quietly.

Kinley nodded.

"May I come in?" she asked.

He let her pass in front of him.

In the living room, she eyed the bottle of scotch, now about a third empty. "Be careful," she said, as her eyes drifted back to him.

"I've always kept everything under control," Kinley said, a little stiffly.

"Are you leaving soon?"

"No, why?"

"I thought that because of . . ."

"It's not that simple, once you start."

"Have you found anything?"

"Nothing of importance."

"You don't have to keep going, you know."

He looked at her determinedly. "Yes, I do," he said.

"I came to say I'm sorry," Dora said, "and to let you know that if you wanted to drop everything, it would be . . ."

"I don't," Kinley told her.

She nodded curtly, then started toward the door, moving briskly past him, as if in flight.

He wanted desperately to let her go, but he found that he could not. "There's some scotch left," he whispered, without turning around to see her.

She stopped. "Yes, I know."

He turned toward her slowly, the sudden admission like a revelation, something known for years, but never fully revealed before. "I don't want to be alone," he told her.

She did not seem convinced, but for the moment at least, she appeared willing to put aside her bitter doubts. "I guess, in the end, no one does," she said.

"Will you stay?"

She shook her head. "No," she told him. "Not in Ray's bed. But if you want, you can come with me."

Twenty-Eight

He was up early the next morning, once again staring at the fog. Dora lay beside him, equally awake, but her eyes focused differently, as if on a separate world.

"How did you get out?" she asked as she turned toward him, propping herself up on her elbow, her lips nearly touching his.

"Didn't Ray tell you?" Kinley answered with a slight smile. "The Yankees rescued me."

"They didn't make you leave," Dora said. "You did that."

Kinley shook his head. "I always wanted to leave."

"Even when you were young?"

"For as long as I can remember."

"Why?" Dora asked. "Ray always said you had it pretty well."

"My grandmother loved me," Kinley said. "That's what Ray meant."

"But you left her, too."

Kinley nodded. "There was always something driving

me," he said, remembering it as a heated rod, or a whip at his back. In his youth, it had even taken the form of a harsh, determined voice: *Getout! Getout! Getout!*

He sat up. "I have to leave early."

She made no effort to stop him but simply watched silently as he dressed himself.

"I'll call you tonight," he said as he opened the bedroom door.

She smiled at him indulgently. "For a genius, you don't have a very good memory."

"What?"

"Don't you remember, Kinley?" she asked. "I don't have a phone."

As he glanced down at his notebook, then up again at the matching address on the old tin mailbox, Kinley hoped that he hadn't arrived too early to expect a decent welcome. His experience had long ago taught him that dragging people from their beds was not the best way to get their cooperation. Even Colin Bright had preferred the afternoon, his eyes always faintly clouded in the morning light.

It was a small, wooden house on a street that looked as if it had seen better days. Still, it was neat, and freshly painted, the typical retirement home, Kinley thought, of an old-age pensioner. The life inside the house was not difficult for him to imagine. There'd be empty soup cans in the kitchen waste basket, an orange hot water bottle hung over the shower stall, and in the medicine cabinets and scattered across the bed night tables, scores of pills, ointments, mentholating creams. His grandmother had been the only old person he'd ever known who'd managed to avoid such indignities.

He returned the notebook to his pocket, got out of the car and walked toward the door.

He knocked lightly when he reached it, heard a small groan from a distant room, then saw an old man lurch ponderously toward him, his ghostly white hair luminous in the surrounding shadows.

"Coming," the old man said, but without the gruffness Kinley had often encountered in old people, the pains of age working insidiously to undermine even the most determined manners.

Within seconds, he was at the door, his white face pressing close to the screen. "Everything I need, I got," he said, though not irritably, but merely as a point of information, as if to save the traveling salesman the energy of his pitch.

Kinley offered a quick smile. "I'm looking for Harry Townsend," he said.

The old man nodded. "That's me."

"You used to work for the Sequoyah *Standard*, I believe," Kinley added.

" 'Til I retired," Townsend said. He brought his face still nearer to the rusty screen and squinted harshly. "Lost my sight just about," he said. "No place in this world for a blind reporter."

He was a reporter all right, and Kinley had seen quite a few of them in his time. The old man who stood before him seemed almost made from the original mold, small and wiry, with a thin mouth and restless eyes, a young man now grown old in that way which made age seem more the product of too much experience than the listless passing of the days.

"I'm a reporter, too," Kinley told him, "not with a newspaper, though."

The old man nodded, unimpressed. "Magazine features?"

"Books."

He nodded again, still unimpressed. "What you want me for?" he asked, his voice as direct as Kinley imagined it had been years before when he'd sat in Judge Bryan's courtroom, his pencil scratching across his notebook as Warfield marched before him, or Overton slumped defeated in a chair six feet away.

"I'm working a story now," Kinley said, "investigating it."

The eyes squinted hard again. "Which one?"

"Ellie Dinker," Kinley said, expecting the old man's face to lift thoughtfully, as if trying to retrieve something only faintly impressed upon his mind.

"Oh, yes," Townsend said softly, with the strange sense of a prophecy fulfilled. "I knew that someday someone would."

They sat down in a small room adorned with plants that were slowly dying of thirst.

"My wife used to water them," Townsend said quietly, by way of explanation, "but she's gone now."

He did not elaborate on where his wife had gone, whether to the islands, distant relatives or the grave, but Kinley made no effort to nail it down.

"You covered the story from the beginning," he said as he drew his notebook from his jacket pocket.

The old man nodded. "The only one who did."

"Why was that?"

"Local thing," Townsend explained, "nothing Atlanta or Birmingham or Chattanooga would have been interested in. Besides, it got solved too fast. There was no buildup."

Before coming over, Kinley had done his homework thoroughly, as he always did, carefully reading the stories Ray had complied on the case. "Were you the main reporter then?" he asked, by way of moving into a direct line of questioning.

Townsend snorted roughly. "Way back then, the Sequoyah *Standard* was nothing much but a little country printing press," he said. "We reported when some bigwig got married, and when Miss Addie's son came home from Vanderbilt. That was about it."

"Until the murder."

Townsend nodded. "Until the murder, that's right,"

he said. "Reporting that case the way we did, that's what turned the *Standard* into a real newspaper. After that, we got an itch for stories, real stories, not just tidbits from the local social calender." His eyes swept over to the room's large, dusty window. "It was strange, that case," he said, "from beginning to end."

It was the perfect opening, and Kinley seized it.

"That's how I'd like to hear about it," he said, "from beginning to end."

The old man turned toward him. "It's not a pretty story," he said, then shrugged lightly, as if divesting himself of the one small bit of incontestable knowledge his long experience had taught him, "but then, the good ones never are."

"When did you first hear about it?"

"Well, that was the first odd thing," Townsend said, "because it took a long time for anybody to hear about it."

"What do you mean?"

"Well, she'd been missing a couple days before I knew anything about it," Townsend answered. "It wasn't on the police blotter, you might say. The report, the one Mrs. Dinker made to the Sheriff's Office, it wasn't recorded anywhere."

"Why not?"

"Well, things were run sort of haphazardly in the Sheriff's Department back then," Townsend said, "but still, they had these little forms . . ."

"Incident Reports," Kinley said.

"Yes, that kind of thing," Townsend said, "and when Mrs. Dinker came down to tell about Ellie being missing, nobody filled out a form."

Kinley quickly scribbled the information into his notebook. "Mrs. Dinker talked directly to Sheriff Maddox, didn't she?"

"Yes, she did."

"And he launched an investigation."

Townsend shook his head. "No, not really," he said,

257

his voice suddenly low and grave. "He later testified that he did, but I checked on his movements after Mrs. Dinker talked to him, and, really, he didn't go looking for that little girl at all."

"What did he do?"

"Mostly hung around the courthouse and let his deputies handle everything," Townsend said. "Of course, he had reason to do that. They were planning a big celebration, and there was a lot going on."

"Wouldn't that be enough to explain what Maddox did?" Kinley said. "Or didn't do?"

"Maybe for the first day," Townsend said, "but not the second. He didn't do much of anything that day either."

"He set up the roadblocks."

"Only because Chief James made him," Townsend said. "James told Maddox that if he didn't get moving, then the City Police would take over."

"Why did James withdraw from the case later on?" Kinley asked. "Ben Wade thinks it was just a question of jurisdiction."

"There never was a true jurisdiction in this case," Townsend said, "because nobody knows where the murder took place. It could have been inside the city limits, or it could have been outside."

"So why did he bow out?"

"To let the cronies handle everything."

"What cronies?"

Townsend ticked off the names without hesitation. "Thompson, Warfield, Maddox, Mayor Jameson, and a few others, mostly from the courthouse crowd," he said.

"James wasn't in that group?"

"Chief James wasn't in any group."

"Why was that?"

"Because he was from the south side of town," Townsend said. "His daddy was nothing but a drunkard, and his mama worked in the cotton mills." He smiled bitterly.

"He was strictly from white trash as far as the others were concerned."

Kinley nodded. "I see."

Townsend shrugged. "Anyway, once Maddox started working the case, the Chief just bowed out."

"When did Maddox start working it?"

"Not till late on the day after the girl turned up missing," Townsend said. "Before then, he didn't do shit."

"July 3," Kinley said as he wrote it in his notebook.

"That's right," Townsend said. "Maddox really got hopping late that day."

"And by that afternoon?"

"It was over like that," Townsend said, snapping his fingers softly, "like magic."

Kinley continued to read through his notes. "They did the roadblock on the afternoon of July 3," he said, reciting its details, "found a witness who fingered Overton . . ." He flipped another page. "Then Wade found Ellie Dinker's dress."

"And twenty-four hours later Charlie Overton was in jail," Townsend said.

Kinley looked up from the notes. "Dumb luck?"

"Maybe."

"You don't think so?"

"No, I don't," Townsend said, "but it's not just how quickly things came together that last day, but the way the whole day broke down."

"What do you mean?"

"Well, for one thing, Maddox suddenly didn't want much to do with me," Townsend said. "He claimed he was too busy every time I showed up at his office. He was always rushing out." He laughed to himself. "Floyd Maddox was a big old fat boy, not too smart. He didn't rush anywhere."

"Unless he had something to hide?"

Townsend nodded grimly. "I was sorry when that old boy died," he said. "You know why? Because I always

259

figured somebody would finally come around and start looking at this case, and that if they looked deep enough, they'd get Floyd eventually, they'd nail him like he nailed Charlie Overton."

"You don't think Overton had anything to do with Ellie Dinker's murder?" Kinley asked.

Townsend shook his head determinedly. "Not one thing."

"How can you be so sure?"

"Well, for one thing, Overton didn't have a motive."

Kinley's mind did its trick, flashed Luther Snow's testimony onto its black screen. "Well, at the trial . . ."

Townsend waved his hand dismissively. "Luther Snow," he said disgustedly. "All that bullshit about woman trouble. That was a load of crap. If Charles Overton had woman trouble, it didn't have anything to do with Ellie Dinker."

"You think Snow just made it up?"

"That sorry bastard," Townsend said harshly, the old reporter's deathless idealism suddenly rising, as it sometimes did, to insist on the preciousness of certain vital things. "A man gets on the stand, he ought to say something that makes sense, that has some facts in it. All this woman trouble stuff, that didn't add up to a hill of beans as far as evidence goes."

Kinley refused to be swept away by the old man's relentless manner. "How do you know this 'woman trouble' wasn't about Dinker?"

"Well, look at what he said."

"That Overton had talked about . . ."

"Implied," Townsend said, cutting Kinley off. "Snow didn't really *say* anything. He just implied it."

"That's right."

"Woman trouble? Overton?" Townsend asked. "With Ellie Dinker, a young girl, only sixteen years old?"

Ben Wade's equally reliable face swam into Kinley's mind: *Ellie Dinker was a tramp.* "I've been told that Ellie Dinker didn't have a spotless reputation."

Townsend nodded. "She knew more than she should have, a girl her age," he admitted, "and God knows that child didn't die a virgin, but that's just looking at it from Ellie Dinker's side of things."

"What does it leave out?"

"The other half."

"Overton?"

"Overton," Townsend said flatly.

In his mind, Kinley saw Charles Overton as Townsend's own grainy photographs had portrayed him, poor, broken, spiritless, a sheep walking passively into the slaughterhouse. "He didn't seem the type who'd be having a fling with a teenage girl," Kinley admitted.

Townsend stared at him evenly. "It wouldn't have mattered if he was."

Kinley felt his fingers close around the narrow shaft of the pen. "What do you mean?"

"He was a wounded man," Townsend said softly, "in his spirit, but not only there."

Kinley looked at him quizzically, but did not speak.

"Talbott made this speech at the end of the trial," Townsend said. "It was about as good as Talbott could do, I guess. He was trying to save Overton's neck, and so he brought out the fact that he'd been in the war, wounded in the war, that sort of thing."

Kinley nodded.

"Well, after the trial, Old Man Jessup, the owner of the paper, told me to do a profile on Overton," Townsend went on. "Just look into his life, check out a few things, so we could run a nice full story on him after the execution."

Townsend stopped suddenly, and his face grew oddly full of wonder, as if the mystery of life did not reside in the extravagances of birth or death or the long line of accidents that stretched between them, but in the weird instances of sudden, miraculous discovery.

"Well, I was just a hireling, so I did whatever Old Man Jessup said," Townsend continued after a moment.

"I did the routine things, looked into the public record to see what he owned, what he didn't, whether he had any kind of criminal record before the murder." He stopped and took a deep breath, as if the very telling of his story had begun to exhaust him. "And just as a way of covering all the bases," he continued finally, "I wrote the Army for a copy of Overton's war record."

Kinley could feel it coming, sense it like a primitive man might have smelled the air and sensed the approaching storm.

"Charlie Overton had been in the war, just like Talbott said," the old man went on, "and he'd been wounded, too. It had happened right at the end of the war, in some little tussle near the Rhine. But what Talbott left out was that Overton had been wounded in the groin, the genitals, that he'd lost any capacity whatsoever to handle, or even want to handle, a sixteen-year-old girl."

Kinley's mind shot back to Sarah Overton, big with a child in 1954, a full nine years after the war, big with a daughter she named Dora.

Townsend shook his head slowly. "What it added up to was that there was no way Overton could have had any kind of relationship with Ellie Dinker, and certainly not one like Luther Snow described, one that would get him into some kind of 'woman trouble' with her."

Kinley felt his hands tighten, but retreated into his profession, focusing on the story, pushing Dora from his mind like a small girl from a speeding train.

"Did you tell Warfield this?" he asked.

Townsend nodded. "I told the person I thought would do the most with the information."

"Horace Talbott," Kinley said.

Townsend nodded. "And he did nothing with it," he said grimly. "As far as I can tell, he buried it just as deep as somebody buried Ellie Dinker."

Kinley looked at him intently. "Why?"

"I don't know."

"Did you try to find out?"

"No," Townsend said, as if admitting that with this failure he had reached a lost region of himself. "And, within a few weeks, Overton was dead." He looked away for a moment, his eyes settling on the drooping petals of a dying flower before returning to Kinley. "I tried to do him one last service, though," he said. "I kept everything I came up with on the case." He smiled softly. "I was waiting, you see," he added. "And I knew that you would come."

Kinley thought of Ray, the locked drawer in his small desk at the courthouse. "Was I the first one to come here?" he asked.

Townsend shook his head. "No," he said. "Ray Tindall did."

"Did you tell him everything you told me?"

"Yes."

"And you gave him all the information you had?"

"I gave him everything," Townsend said. He shook his head contemptuously. "But he didn't do anything with it, either." He glared at Kinley contemptuously. "I'd always thought better of Ray, but the way he acted, I figured he was just another one of that courthouse crowd." He shook his head disgustedly. "At first I thought he was really trying to get to the bottom of this Overton thing, but later, I knew that was wrong."

"What was he doing?"

"He was working for the big boys," Townsend said authoritatively. "Whatever they did back then, Ray was trying to cover it up."

Kinley looked at him, astonished. "How do you know that?"

"Because he brought it all back," Townsend said, "all the papers I'd given him. All the stuff I'm giving you. He brought it all back, every single bit."

"When did he do that?"

Townsend smiled approvingly, as if some measure of justice had been done. "The day the bastard died," he said.

Twenty-Nine

Kinley did not wait to return to Ray's house on Beaumont Street before going through the large yellow envelope Townsend had pressed into his hand before he left.

Instead, he drove directly to the town park, pulled over to the curb and spread the papers out on the front seat. It was not a great deal of material, and most of it, pictures and newspaper clippings, Ray had already gathered in his own file on the case. Still, the slender stack of documents which Townsend had given to Ray was critical. For there, nestled among the yellowing newspaper articles Townsend had written for the Sequoyah *Standard*, was also the official report he'd received from the United States Army regarding the final disposition of Corporal Charles Herman Overton, all the accumulated material regarding his medical discharge in 1945.

It began with an official statement dealing with the circumstances under which Overton had been wounded. As a report, it was exactly what Kinley had become accustomed to, succinct and emotionless, even when it detailed circumstances of the deepest imaginable feeling:

On March 12, 1945, while on routine patrol near the west bank of the Rhine, Corporal Overton's unit approached a group of civilians. The men gathered along a rural byway. Acting according to established military procedure, Captain Carlos P. Santiago began to carry out his assignment of gathering all relevant intelligence regarding previous, ongoing or future enemy action in the area.

During the course of that operation, the report continued:

The unit was fired upon from the surrounding woods. In the ensuing engagement, the unit sustained heavy casualties. Corporal Overton was severely wounded in the legs and groin, and as a result of those wounds, Corporal Overton was later hospitalized for three months in a military hospital in Belgium.

Townsend had stapled a second report to the first, this one written by Dr. Paul J. Rosenberg, a United States Army Surgeon, stationed in London. In the usual clinical language, Dr. Rosenberg briefly detailed the procedure by which Charles Overton's testicles had been removed due to the "irremediable trauma suffered by the designated organs."

Under the heading "Prognosis," Dr. Rosenberg had written candidly that "following surgery, patient should recover completely within a period of two months, though loss of sexual function is complete and irreversible."

Kinley folded the report and let his eyes sweep out over the park, imagining Overton fully. Broken, emasculated, he had offered "no resistance," just as Maddox had testified. It was easy for Kinley to envision it now, a man already horribly wounded, suffering through the inexplicable pregnancy of his young wife, and now, at the end of a long, torturous road, accused of murdering a young girl. Under such conditions, burdened by such past experiences, he had finally embraced a fatalism which resisted nothing because it had already come to accept the unacceptable again and again. No wonder he had looked disoriented as he'd shuffled across the cement floor to the electric chair; no wonder, at such a moment, he'd had nothing whatever to say.

Kinley shifted his eyes to the far side of the park. It was still early, but a few old men could be seen scattered among the benches of an area the town had long ago designated as "Whittler's Corner." Beyond them, Sequoyah's single main street had begun to come to life as well, its small clothing stores now dotted with browsing customers, its old routine entirely in place.

For a time, Kinley sat in perfect stillness and watched the morning unfold before him, its iron routine unchanged from his youth. Perhaps, he thought, this changelessness had been its principal allure, the life raft of daily predictability which even Ray had finally clung to, and which he'd wished, above all else, to keep out of harm's way.

He was working for the big boys. Whatever they did back then, he was covering it up.

Kinley glanced down the main street to where he could see the red-striped awning of Jefferson's Drug Store as it fluttered softly in the distance. Inside, he was seated at the small marble table once again, his eyes first on Ray, then on Mrs. Dinker, then back to Ray, his ears listening keenly to his old friend's words: *It's better to know, don't you think? No matter what the cost.*

Kinley tried to imagine what could have been powerful enough to change Ray's answer to so deep-seated a question. For a few minutes, he concentrated on the town, his eyes fixed on its main street, as he worked desperately to see Sequoyah as he thought Ray must have come to see

266

it. Perhaps, in Ray's final vision, it had not been a town at all, Kinley thought, but a frail organism, infinitely vulnerable, living on faith alone, a gossamer patchwork of church spires and flagpoles, Ray's own bizarre version of Never-Never Land, a myth he'd decided to protect at all costs.

In an instant, Kinley felt his vision shift radically, this time focusing on the mountain, the granite ledge upon which Overton's house still sat perched above the town, its unpainted wooden frame glaring down at Sequoyah, a slumberless gray eye.

"Dora," Kinley thought. "Maybe it was Dora." As a hypothesis, it seemed reasonable enough. Perhaps Ray had returned Townsend's papers because he knew that to go any further in his investigation would mean that he would have to tell Dora that Charles Overton was not her father.

But if Charles Overton were not Dora's father, Kinley wondered, his mind reasserting its dominion, its purely technical inquiry rising to close him off from all other forms of speculation, who was?

"Complete and irreversible," Kinley said, his eyes still on the solid immobility of Horace Talbott's face.

"You knew about Overton's condition," Kinley added, when Talbott failed to respond.

Talbott continued to stare at the Army report, his fingers moving up and down one side of the paper, as if trying to make it disappear.

"You knew it before Overton was executed," Kinley said bluntly, the accusatory tone now unmistakable. "Harry Townsend told you all about it."

Talbott's eyes lifted slowly toward him. "Yes, he did," he said, "but I knew it before he told me."

Kinley was surprised, not only by Talbott's quick admission, but by the fact that he'd amplified it, deepened his complicity in Overton's death.

267

"During the trial?" Kinley asked, unbelievingly. "You knew during the trial?"

"Even before the trial," Talbott said bluntly, his head now fully erect, as if the truth, even so lately disclosed, had served to liberate him.

"How did you know?" Kinley said; then, before waiting for Talbott's reply, answered the question himself. "Mrs. Overton. She worked for you."

"Because of my wife," Talbott explained. "She was very ill for many years."

Kinley said nothing, instead relying on the old device of letting the dam break of its own pent-up waters.

"Sarah was only twenty-nine years old when she came to work for me," Talbott said. "And she was quite beautiful at that time." He smiled appreciatively. "Like Dora is now," he added, "very attractive, as you know."

Kinley's mind flashed the pictures of Mrs. Overton that had been published in the Sequoyah *Standard*. She had been pregnant by then, a large woman wrapped in thick layers of winter clothes, her face strained with worry and fatigue, her beauty lost behind her circumstances.

"That was in the fall of 1950," Talbott went on. "My wife had been sick for many years by then. Multiple sclerosis. She was deteriorating very rapidly. She couldn't walk or feed herself." He shrugged. "For as long as I could manage it, I took care of her by myself," he continued. "She had been very independent at one time, and her disease embarrassed her. Of course, after a while, I had to get help. That's when I hired Sarah."

"That was in the fall of 1950, you said?"

"Yes," Talbott answered. "And as I said, she was twenty-nine." He smiled. "She had reached that fullness, you know, that a woman reaches at a certain age. She wasn't so young you felt like her father, and she wasn't so old you felt like she was your sister. She was just the right age to be . . ." He stopped, as if unable to go on, not because the story was painful to him, but because it was sweet and beautiful, and he did not want to damage it by telling it too quickly. "Anyway, with my wife, it had been so long." He stopped again. "And Sarah, she was . . ."

In the moment of silence which fell between them, Kinley studied Talbott's face, noting the dark, slightly oval eyes, the strong set of his jaw, the look of force and authority he had bequeathed, along with the oval eyes, to Dora.

"You have to understand about Sarah," Talbott continued finally. "She was not some poor, country bumpkin I took advantage of." He shook his head. "She knew exactly who she was, and what she wanted."

Again Kinley said nothing, but merely waited, listening, for Talbott's voice to begin again.

"She was married to a man she hardly knew," Talbott said. "They'd been married only a few weeks before the war. She'd only been sixteen, a girl. When he came back, she was in her twenties, and Overton was even more of a stranger than he'd been when she married him." He paused a moment, looking for the best way to say it. "And of course, there was the other problem." He lifted the paper he still held gently in his hand. "As you know," he said as he let it slide from his fingers to the desk.

"What happened when she became pregnant?" Kinley asked.

"We thought of an abortion," Talbott said. "But it wasn't easy in those days. It was a very serious step." He shrugged. "Still, if Sarah had really wanted it, it could have been arranged. I knew people. I could have gotten it done."

"But she refused?"

"We both refused," Talbott said. "Sarah knew that I would do my best for the child, whatever the circumstances." He looked at Kinley helplessly. "I don't expect you to believe this, but I actually offered to marry Sarah. More than that. I wanted to marry her. But Sarah didn't want that."

"Why not?"

Talbott looked at him pointedly. "Well, you know Dora, don't you? I mean, how determined she can be."

Kinley nodded, remembering the last few days. "Yes."

"Sarah didn't want to marry," Talbott went on. "She wanted to divorce Overton, and I think she would have eventually." He took in a long, weary breath. "But she felt sorry for him. Time went by, but she still couldn't decide what to do."

"Then Overton was arrested," Kinley said.

Talbott gave Kinley a stern look. "She didn't think of that as a solution, if that's your theory," he said flatly.

"Did you?" Kinley asked.

Talbott did not seem surprised by the bluntness of the question. "No, I didn't," he said. "But I don't expect you to believe that either."

"With all the information you had about his war wound, why did you keep it out of the trial?" Kinley asked, this time less as an accusation than a point of information.

Talbott's answer was unequivocal. "Well, for one thing, because Overton never told me about it, and I could hardly tell him how I knew. That would have made it clear just how close Sarah and I had become."

"What about Sarah? Didn't she want you to use that kind of information?"

"Yes, she did. But not without her husband's approval."

"And he wouldn't give it?"

"No," Talbott said. "His problem was humiliating enough, but he also had a pregnant wife." He looked at Kinley pointedly. "And a child was on the way. A child who needed a father, even if it were a dead one. At least, that's the way I think Charlie thought about it."

"So Overton never mentioned his war wound to you at all?"

"Never," Talbott answered, "And I gave him a few opportunities. I mentioned rape, the fact that if they found Dinker's body, it might show she'd been raped. I thought he might say, 'If it does, then I'm free,' but he never did." He plucked a pencil from his desk and began to run it smoothly back and forth between his fingers. "You can't make a case out of thin air." The pencil returned to the desk. "I did my best with what I had."

Kinley said nothing, letting his silence cast doubt on Talbott's defense.

"But even if he had told me about the war, I don't think it would have mattered," Talbott said.

"Why not?"

"Because it was more or less irrelevant," Talbott said.

"Irrelevant to what?"

"The murder of Ellie Dinker," Talbott said authoritatively. "Because the fact is, Charlie Overton murdered Ellie Dinker. I never really doubted it. The evidence was overwhelming. Overton was positively identified as being with her on the mountain not long before she died. Then they found the girl's shoes in the back of his truck. Not to mention the tire iron they found there, too. There was blood all over it, of course, and Dr. Stark testified that the blood was the same type as Ellie's. Everything pointed to Overton, and nothing pointed away from him."

"Except the motive," Kinley reminded him.

"You mean what Luther Snow said?"

Kinley nodded.

"That's the one question I've always had," Talbott said. "I never really doubted that Charlie did it. He was half a man, with a beautiful young wife who was suddenly pregnant by someone else." He looked at Kinley fiercely. "Can you imagine the rage?" He tapped a single index finger on the top of his desk. "That was the motive, you know. The rage he must have been feeling. Then, all of sudden, Ellie Dinker comes prissing up to him, maybe teasing him a little, because, as you've probably found out, she was that type of girl. Anyway, he just finally broke. It's happened before. It'll happen again." His eyes took on a strange darkness, as if his face had suddenly retreated into the shadows. "Some men hate women, you know," he said, "hate them all their lives."

"And you think Overton was a man like that?" Kinley asked, "that he hated women?"

"No, not all of them."

"Just his wife, then?"

"No, he loved Sarah," Talbott said. "That's why he couldn't hurt her. But Ellie Dinker? She was a stranger. He could do anything he wanted." He plucked the Army report from the top of his desk and thrust it toward Kinley. "Which he did."

"So she was a stand-in for Sarah Overton?" Kinley asked.

Talbott nodded. "Ellie Dinker was every bitch who'd ever betrayed Charlie Overton, every nurse who'd ever giggled outside his hospital room."

"So you never believed that Overton and Dinker had planned to meet on the mountain that day?" Kinley asked.

"No."

"Or had any kind of relationship before the murder?"

"Absolutely not," Talbott said. "Charlie Overton was a withdrawn man. He went from his job to his house, and once he was in his house, he never went out again. The world scared him, and he stayed away from it as much as possible."

"Then why did Luther Snow testify that Overton knew Ellie Dinker?" Kinley asked.

Talbott shook his head. "I don't know. I've wondered about that myself, but I've never found an answer." He looked at Kinley with an unexpected attitude of encouragement. "Maybe you can," he said.

Kinley said nothing, but merely let his eyes settle on

Talbott, studying his features once again, Dora in ghostly pentimento behind them.

"Are you going to tell Dora?" Talbott asked after a moment.

Kinley did not know the answer to that question, and so dodged behind a question of his own. "Should I?"

Talbott stared at him. "Ray didn't," he said.

Kinley leaned forward slightly. "Ray got this far? He found out this much?"

Talbott nodded slowly. "He came just like you did," he said.

"And you told him everything you told me?"

"Everything," Talbott said.

"When was that?"

"About six weeks before he died," Talbott said. "He had the same information you had, but I thought he was going to do something else with it."

"What do you mean?"

"Well, I asked him the same question, about whether he was going to tell Dora about me," Talbott said. He smiled thinly. "And I was very encouraged by the answer."

"What did he say?"

"He was very firm, very decisive, the way Ray always was," Talbott said. "He looked me straight in the eye, and he said, 'Absolutely.' Just like that, without any hesitation. 'Absolutely.'"

Kinley nodded silently, Ray's face once more in the forefront of his mind, the same old Ray, with the same old answer and the same old reason: *It's always better to know, isn't it? No matter what the cost.*

"And so I expected him to do it," Talbott added. "To tell Dora the truth, that I'm her father." He glanced down toward his own gnarled, aging hands. "She's my only child, you know," he said. His eyes lifted slowly toward Kinley. "I see her almost every day. I go to that little bar she works in, and I have a glass of wine. We chat

273

about this and that.'' He let out a breath so slowly his chest seemed to empty, as if it were his last. ''I thought Ray would tell her, and maybe, if he did, I'd be able to take her in my arms just once before I die.''

But Ray had never told her, and during the early, predawn hours of the following morning, as Kinley lay sleeplessly entangled in Dora's arms, he was not at all sure that he would ever tell her, either. He was not even sure that the truth was what he'd always thought it to be, something high, exalted, worth pursuing at all costs. Perhaps it was something evil, too, just another knife that could be used to open up our veins.

''Are you all right?'' she whispered.

He looked up at her. ''Yes.''

She let her open hand move softly down his arm. ''You're sweating.''

''I sometimes do.''

''At night? In the fall? For no reason?''

He told her his first lie. ''Yes.''

Thirty

He left her a few hours later, the early morning fog still thick around him as he drove down the mountain road to Sequoyah. He did not want to return immediately to the house on Beaumont Street, to the tiny office lined with Ray's books, to the lingering smell of the funeral flowers. He did not want to return to *Ray*, to what Ray had learned, or why he had learned it, or even what he had done with the information after he'd received it, all of which now burdened Kinley with unexpected and unwanted questions his other investigations had never posed. In a sense, he felt a bleak nostalgia for all his former investigations. At least they'd possessed the comfort of the impersonal, and he'd been able to conduct them in the anesthetized atmosphere which seemed extraordinarily appealing to him now. The insistent ache he felt for Ray and Dora had been absent from all his earlier inquiries, and he could sense that some unregenerate part of his character yearned for the old numbness to envelop him again, return him to the safety of purely academic cares.

* * *

The little diner on Sequoyah's main street was the only place open, so he pulled into its small, gravelly parking lot, and went in. He sat at one of the booths at the front window, and waited, his hand grasping and releasing first the fork, then the spoon. He'd squeezed the napkin into a crumpled mass by the time the waitress appeared.

She was somewhat chubby and seemed to roll forward rather than walk, but she took his order with an unreproachable professionalism which Kinley admired. She was quick and cool and had no time for idle chatter, and he gave her his order in the same functional manner.

"Coffee. Black. No sugar," he said.

She returned with it promptly, then vanished down the aisle.

He took a quick sip, his eyes following the still somewhat drowsy movements of the awakening town. The early birds were the same in every place he'd ever been, the deliverers of life, laden with their milk and bread. Behind them came the eager office workers, and after them, the people who worked the retail trade, filling their registers with money doled out to them from the manager's steel safe. In a sense, he thought, it really was a kind of organism, just as Ray might have come to envision it, but one that had something brooding darkly at its core, something that he couldn't ignore, any more than a doctor, observing an otherwise robust and healthy patient, could ignore a murmur of the heart.

It was almost eight o'clock, and Kinley was on his third cup of coffee when William Warfield came through the door, spotted him, and strode down the aisle toward him.

"Good morning," he said as he stepped up to the

276

booth. He glanced about the restaurant. "Looks like business isn't too brisk this morning."

Kinley nodded and gave him a polite smile. "No, not too busy," he said.

Warfield nodded toward the empty seat across from Kinley. "Mind if I join you?"

"No."

"Just my usual coffee, Dottie," he called to the vanished waitress as he pulled himself smoothly into the booth. "How's the book going?"

"Book?"

"On the Overton case," Warfield said. "Aren't you writing a book on it?"

"Just looking into a few things," Kinley answered. "It's not a book yet."

"Yeah, Ben Wade said you'd talked to him," Warfield said. "So did Ella."

"Ella?"

"Ella Hunter, the Court Clerk," Warfield explained.

Kinley nodded. "Oh yeah."

"Anyway," Warfield went on. "How's it going? The investigation, I mean."

"I'm running into a few roadblocks," Kinley told him. He shrugged, unwilling to go further. "But that's not unusual in an investigation."

"No, I guess not," Warfield said, then looked at him curiously. "What kind of roadblocks?"

Kinley kept the more important ones to himself, but offered Warfield the one he thought closest to the District Attorney's own professional concerns.

"Well, as a matter of fact," he said, "some of the evidence is missing."

"Missing?"

"Disappeared."

Warfield looked at him worriedly. "Evidence? Missing? In the Overton case? Disappeared from where?"

"From the courthouse basement," Kinley said. "Right out of the box it had been kept in."

Warfield's concern deepened instantly. "From *my* courthouse?" he asked incredulously, his guardianship suddenly under serious challenge.

Kinley nodded.

Warfield looked at him doubtfully. "Are you sure about that?"

"Yes, I am."

"How do you know?"

"Ben Wade told me."

The source of the information seemed to convince Warfield. "What evidence are we talking about exactly?"

"Ellie Dinker's dress."

Warfield stared at him, thunderstruck. "Are you telling me that Ellie Dinker's dress is not in the evidence box?"

"That's right."

"I don't see how that could be true," Warfield said. "All that stuff is very carefully inventoried."

Kinley said nothing.

"It's also very carefully monitored after that," Warfield added. "I instituted that system myself."

"What system?"

"There's a log," Warfield explained. "Ella Hunter keeps it. Anybody who goes down into the basement has to sign in and out. We don't just let people wander about, you know. We run it like the jail, everything and everybody accounted for. That's the system I insisted upon."

"When was that policy established?" Kinley asked.

"Ten years ago," Warfield said. "We'd had a few things disappearing. Mostly drugs that had been confiscated and were being held for evidence. To stop that sort of thing from happening, I started this sign-in system. It's been in place ever since."

"How far back do you keep the logs?"

"All the way," Warfield said without hesitation, as if pleased by such thoroughness. He gave Kinley a piercing look. "Do you know the date when the dress disappeared?"

"Within about three months, I do."

278

"And when was that?"

"Between May and August of 1986."

Warfield looked at him quizzically. "Are you sure about that?"

"Ben Wade is."

"Well, we have a problem, then," Warfield said, "because that was the time when the courthouse was being renovated."

"Renovated?"

"Done over, top to bottom," Warfield explained. "Everything bought new for the whole place. We did it floor by floor, and I remember very well that they did the basement that summer."

"Which means what?"

"That the basement would have been closed to the public," Warfield said. "The actual room would have been locked, because we didn't want any of the people who work at the courthouse getting into the evidence."

"So you locked it up?"

"Tight as a drum," Warfield said. "Padlocked for three months."

"And no one went in?"

"Just the people in my office and the maintenance people."

"Would they have had to sign the log?"

Warfield shook his head. "No, they're the only people who don't."

"How many people are we talking about?"

"Not many," Warfield said. "Six or seven, something like that."

Kinley drew his notebook from his jacket pocket. "You remember the names?"

Warfield hesitated. "Well, you have to understand something, Mr. Kinley. If something's missing from the courthouse, it's my job to track it down and find the people responsible. It's not your job to do that."

Kinley smiled quietly. "But it might be easier for me," he said.

Warfield was not convinced. "How do you figure that?"

"Well, I wouldn't be a threat to them," Kinley explained. "You would."

Warfield said nothing.

"The point is to get the dress back," Kinley added, careful not to give Warfield the impression that he was trying to do his thinking for him. "That would put everything back in shape, wouldn't it?"

It was an argument he'd used before, and it had never failed to be effective when dealing with a bureaucratic mind.

"That way, it would all be an internal matter," Kinley said, putting on the finishing touch. "The way it should be, a purely private investigation."

"You know, I think you may be right about that," Warfield said, after considering it a moment. "If I started barrelling in, firing a lot of questions, they'd figure they were looking at a formal prosecution somewhere down the road."

Kinley nodded. "Yes, they would."

"Okay," Warfield said, "but you have to let me know whatever you find out."

"Absolutely," Kinley assured him.

Warfield's eyes rolled to the ceiling. "Well, there was myself, of course, and Ben Wade." He stopped, as if a thought had suddenly struck him. "And there was Ray, too. He was the Sheriff then, so he had access."

Kinley continued to write down the names.

"Chief James, of course," Warfield went on, "but he died during that time." He thought a moment longer. "And I guess that was about it, except for the cleaning staff."

Kinley nodded. "And who would that be?"

"There were only two of them at the time," Warfield said. "We'd had a labor reduction."

"Who were they?"

"Lila Trumbull," Warfield said. "But she mostly

worked the upper floors. She moved to Atlanta in late March. That left all the cleaning to Betty Gaines.''

Kinley glanced up from the notebook. ''Betty Gaines?''

Warfield nodded. ''Yeah. Betty worked at the courthouse for about two years.''

''Before that, she worked for Thompson Construction, didn't she?''

Warfield's eyes widened. ''My goodness, you are learning a lot about Sequoyah.''

''She was working for Thompson Construction when Charles Overton was working there,'' Kinley added.

''She was?'' Warfield asked. ''I didn't know that. Back in 1954?''

''That's right,'' Kinley told him. ''Is she still around Sequoyah?''

''Yeah, she is,'' Warfield said. ''Betty lives over in the old factory district. You know, where the old textile mill was, over there by the railroad tracks.''

Kinley wrote it down. ''I might start with her,'' he said, his eyes staring at the other names on the list. ''At the very least, she had a connection to the trial.'' He looked back up at Warfield. ''She testified for Overton,'' he said. ''She was one of the few witnesses who did.''

Warfield looked at Kinley with a sudden, unexpected intensity. ''What do you mean by that?''

''Well, there wasn't much of a defense,'' Kinley told him.

''No, there wasn't,'' he said, ''but how could there have been?''

''Well, even character witnesses,'' Kinley said. ''There were only two of them, and one of them was his wife.''

''That's because Overton was a loner,'' Warfield said. ''At least that's the way my father described him. Very solitary. He hardly ever spoke.''

''So your father did talk about the case from time to time,'' Kinley said.

"Not often," Warfield replied, "but it was a murder case. It was the first one he'd ever had. And, in addition to that, of course, it was a capital case. A man died. Even if the man's guilty, it's not something you forget, putting a man in the chair." He leaned forward. "My father certainly never forgot it."

Kinley saw the elder Warfield in his mind, his fingers drawing the green dress from its cover. "What was he like, your father?"

"He was good," Warfield answered. "He was kind." He looked at Kinley solemnly. "I'll tell you something no one else knows about my father and that case," he said. "After the trial, he gave some money to Mrs. Overton."

"Money?" Kinley repeated, unbelievingly.

Warfield nodded. "To help her out," he explained. "You know, because she'd just had a baby. Anyway, he gave her some money. He funneled it through Horace Talbott."

"I see."

"It's true," Warfield said, though Kinley did not doubt what he'd just been told. "I don't guess Mrs. Overton ever knew where the money came from, but it came from my father." He looked at Kinley with a knowing smile. "I guess that sort of thing doesn't happen in New York, does it?" he asked.

Kinley shook his head slowly. "No," he said, "I don't think it does."

Thirty-One

The old textile factory loomed like a great fortress over the iron rails of the tracks which separated it, along with Sequoyah's working poor, from the other, far more prosperous part of town.

Even as a boy, Kinley had recognized the demarcation as unbridgeable and severe. The boys who drank whisky and the girls who got pregnant belonged to a dim netherworld of factory gates, shift sirens and billowing, sulfuric clouds that hung over the south side of Sequoyah like a great yellow curtain. From time to time, by some quirk of zoning which would be corrected by the following year, a teenage boy or girl from the factory district would actually wind up at Sequoyah High rather than South Side, the old Depression-era brick schoolhouse which had been set aside for their kind. Girl or boy, short or tall, they would always look the same, either thin and bony from too little food, or fat with the bloated excess of their starchy diets. Their behavior was similarly of a piece, and they would slump listlessly in a back-row seat while the teacher droned on about the Lost Cause or geometric proofs which were about as useful to them as the Rosetta stone. They were never at parties, proms or football games. They never sought elective office or campaigned for anyone who did. Their names never appeared on the rolls of the social or academic clubs, school publications. They were similarly absent from the sports rosters, and on the days designated for class photos, they did not show up to stand with their fellow students, so that, in the end, the history of Sequoyah High hardly recorded them at all.

Betty Gaines had to have been one of these, Kinley thought, as he drifted up the narrow street of cotton mill tenements which fronted the old factory on Cotton Mill Row, his eyes trained on the rusty metal mailboxes which lined the street.

Betty Gaines's name was painted in crude black letters on the one which stood near the middle of the block. The small wooden house which rested behind it was built on a cinder-block foundation. Its original wood façade had been covered with sheets of asphalt siding, and even from the road, it had the look of a place which had been left to its own devices. The arched tin roof slumped forward slightly, angling down toward the grassless frontyard strewn with rusting auto parts.

An unsteady chicken wire fence lined the sidewalk, its gate held closed by a loop of clothesline. Kinley tugged the line from its mooring, then headed up the short span of wooden steps which led to the front door.

He knocked once, waited a moment, and knocked again. He could hear a body shuffling about inside, but it took almost a minute for the door finally to swing open.

The woman who stood behind the torn screen looked very much as Kinley would have imagined her, small and somewhat bent, her hair now gray rather than the raven black of the newspaper photographs. It was as if her youth had been squeezed from her violently, rather than having seeped away year by year at its own inevitable pace. There was something in the aridity of her face, the downward curve of her body, the rounded slump of her shoulders, that suggested heavy weights long applied, visible and invisible burdens.

"Betty Gaines?" Kinley asked softly.

She nodded.

"I'm Jack Kinley. You don't know me."

She stared at him through the rusty screen.

"I'm a reporter," Kinley added. "I'm looking into an old murder case."

She nodded gently, her pale lips parting somewhat, as if she'd been about to speak and had thought better of it.

"You testified in the case," Kinley went on. "For Charles Overton."

She remained silent.

"Do you remember that?" Kinley asked.

"I remember it," she said. "Long time ago."

"1954," Kinley reminded her.

"I worked for Old Man Thompson then."

"Yes, you did."

"So did Overton."

"Yes."

"On the courthouse," she said, her head shifting slightly to the right, as if she were attempting to get a glimpse of its towering gray walls.

"That's right."

"Best job I ever had," she said. "Didn't have one that good later on."

Kinley felt his hand crawl toward the notebook in his pocket. "Could you spare a few minutes to talk about those days?" he asked quietly.

For an answer, she simply opened the screen silently, and let Kinley in.

The front room looked like a stage set for some socialist drama of the thirties, all yellow light, worn furniture and uncarpeted floors. An enormous, pre-war radio sat brown and bloated like an overweight guest in one corner. A small table rested beside it, its surface powdered with an array of sewing needles and spools of colored thread. There was a wooden rocker, a tiny, threadbare settee, and between them, another small table, this one covered with an assortment of empty plates and cups, the bleak droppings, as Kinley had noticed, of people who lived alone.

He thought of Maria Spinola, her living room dotted with a dusty, down-at-the-heels assortment of mock French provincial flourishes, lamp shades with gilded fringes hanging limply in the smokey light. Spinola's decor had been the New Bedford Portuguese version of the room which surrounded him now, but with the same mood of listlessness and overall abandonment.

He turned toward Betty Gaines, shaking Maria Spinola from his mind, and asked his first question. "Had you known Charles Overton very long?"

She leaned back slowly in the rocker, her short legs dangling over the side, her feet barely scraping against the floor. "Maybe a couple years," she said, "ever since he started working for Thompson."

"Did you ever talk to him?"

"Just business."

"So you didn't know him personally?"

She shook her head. "I knew Luther, but not Charlie."

"Were they friends, Luther and Charlie?"

"Not that Luther mentioned much," she said. "They didn't live too far from each other. Luther's place was up on the mountain, too. He did some bootlegging way back then." She smiled with an odd maliciousness. "They caught him for it a few times."

"Who did?"

"The Sheriff."

"Sheriff Maddox?"

She nodded. "He run whisky, Luther did. That's the truth, too. You can look that up. He's been caught a few times. He didn't have no still, though. It was strictly bonded, what he sold.''

"Was Overton ever involved in anything like that?" Kinley asked.

Betty waved her hand, her face drawing together, as if in response to the absurdity of the suggestion. "Naw, he didn't do stuff like that,'' she said. "He was a family man. All he did was work and go home.''

"How did you happen to end up testifying at Overton's trial?" Kinley asked.

"Well, I felt like I had to.''

"Why?''

"To straighten things out.''

"What things?''

"What Luther had said.''

"You didn't believe his testimony?''

"No, I didn't,'' Betty said. "Besides, I'd seen Charlie that morning. He was working at the courthouse just like I told the jury, and he come over to me, and you could see that he was sick. He looked real bad off. He was holding to hisself.'' She wrapped her arms around her stomach. "Like this.'' She shook her head. "Sick as a dog,'' she added emphatically, "in his stomach.''

"What did he say to you exactly?" Kinley asked.

"Stomach trouble,'' Betty said flatly, "like he was going to throw up.''

"And he asked if he could go home, is that right?''

"He said he had to go home,'' Betty told him, "that he couldn't work no more.''

Kinley's mind swept back through the pages of the trial transcript, and he heard the voice of Luther Snow.

SNOW: I dug the foundation, and I poured the cement for the whole place, everything from the flagpole to the courthouse steps. Charlie was a sort of a regular lift and haul man. He didn't have no special trade, like a mason or a carpenter or something like that.

"But Snow and Overton, they did work together, didn't they?" Kinley asked.

"At the courthouse, they did," Betty said, "but Overton was just hired for that job. He wasn't no regular employee at Thompson's. He just did what Luther told him to."

Once again, the transcript played in Kinley's mind.

WARFIELD: And did you and Mr. Overton sometimes take lunch breaks together?

SNOW: Yes, sir.

WARFIELD: And you sometimes talked to each other, isn't that right, the way men do?

SNOW: We talked a lot.

WARFIELD: Did you get the impression that Mr. Overton liked and trusted you?

SNOW: Yes, sir.

WARFIELD: And did he discuss what you might call his "private life" with you?

SNOW: Sometimes he did.

Kinley stared at Betty Gaines, hoping that her mind could reach back far enough to draw a subtle conclusion. "Were Overton and Luther Snow pretty close?" he asked.

She did not answer, but the small, blue eyes seemed to cloud strangely, as if misted over by a sudden change of air.

"Snow testified that he was a friend of Overton's," Kinley added, his mind now concentrating on the exact words Warfield had used to describe their relationship. "Is that true? Would Snow have known about Overton's private life?"

Betty remained silent, but Kinley could see the clouds lifting somewhat, as if driven upward by the warmth of a rising wind.

"He said they talked a lot," Kinley went on. "He gave the impression that they were close friends."

Betty's body tensed slightly as she pressed herself back against the spokes of the rocker, her small feet scraping roughly against the floor. "They were nothing to each other," she snapped suddenly, as if a small explosion had gone off in her mind. "They just worked together, that's all."

Kinley felt his fingers tighten around the upright pen. "Why would Snow have said what he did?" he asked. "Why would he have said they were friends?"

Betty shrugged. "To please the boss."

"The boss?" Kinley asked. "Who's that?"

She looked at him, astonished by his lack of knowledge. "Wallace Thompson," she answered. "You don't know who Old Man Thompson was?"

Kinley shook his head.

"He owned the company," Betty told him, "the one that was building the courthouse, Thompson Construction. He ran the whole thing. From top to bottom. He was at a site when he died, that's how close he kept his eye on things."

"And he asked Luther Snow to testify against Overton?" Kinley asked, quickly jotting Thompson's name into his notebook.

"That's the way I see it," Betty said. "I know this much: I seen them two talking to each other not long before old Luther said what a great friend he was to poor old Charlie."

"They could have been talking about anything," Kinley said warily. "How do you know it was about Overton?"

" 'Cause Luther wouldn't do nothing the old man didn't tell him to," Betty said. "The way it was, Old Man Thompson was Luther's protection, and Luther, being the way he was, a bootlegger and all, he needed all the protection he could get."

"What kind of protection?"

"From the county cops."

"Maddox?"

"Thompson kept a tight leash on Floyd Maddox," Betty said, "and since Old Man Thompson and the rest of them liked the taste of bonded once in a while, he didn't want Maddox closing Luther down."

"The rest of them?"

"Old Man Thompson and the other bigwigs in town," Betty explained. "Maddox and Warfield and Mayor Jameson, the whole crowd used to hang around together. They were always going out in the canyon to camp out and hunt, or whatever it is they used to do out there." She shrugged. "It was the whole courthouse crowd. They had a little lodge or something way out somewhere, and they'd all go out there, everybody but Chief James. He wasn't one of the group."

Kinley nodded. It was not the first tale of chicanery among the local elite he'd ever heard, and it still seemed to bear relatively little on the Overton case. "What would any of this have to do with Thompson asking Luther Snow to testify against Overton?" he asked.

" 'Cause it was Maddox that had arrested him," Betty said without hesitation, "and it was Mr. Warfield that was prosecuting him."

"His cronies?"

Betty nodded. "They needed a favor, I guess," she said, "and so they come to Old Man Thompson." She shook her head. "And he give them Luther." She smiled cynically. "That's the way it was with them guys."

Once again, Kinley's mind retrieved a section of the trial transcript, but this time it was the testimony of Betty Gaines, the halting, unsure texture of her words.

"Why did you testify for Overton?" he asked.

She waved her hand, as if unwilling to discuss it.

"You were afraid, weren't you," he said. "On the stand, I mean."

She shrugged. "When you're a young woman, things can scare you."

"Things or people?"

"Well, in this case, it was people."

"Thompson?"

Betty nodded. "He had a mean streak in him," she said. "I seen him hit his daughter once. He knocked her all the way across the room."

Once again, Kinley's mind flashed back to the transcript.

"When Snow talked about Overton having woman trouble, implying that it was with Ellie Dinker," he asked cautiously, "could he have been talking about Wallace Thompson instead?"

Betty nodded determinedly. "I know this much, Old Man Thompson knew Ellie Dinker," she said. "I know he did."

"How do you know that?"

" 'Cause when he found out I was going to testify for Overton, he told me to keep my mouth shut and not to go against him, because he knew what happened, and Overton was going to pay for it."

"Knew what happened?"

"That Overton done it," Betty said. "That he killed that little girl." She rocked back in her chair, her small feet scraping against the floor. "And when he was telling me this, he said, 'Ellie Dinker was a little whore, Betty, but it's got to be set right.' "

"A little whore?" Kinley repeated. "That's what he called her?"

"Them's his exact words," Betty said emphatically. "And I remembered them, too, 'cause when Old Man Thompson spoke to you, you listened."

"From what you knew of Charles Overton, could you have thought that Thompson might be right, that Overton had killed Ellie Dinker?"

Betty shook her head. "Not from what I saw," she said. "He was sort of a weak type of man, you know. Like his insides had been scooped out of him."

"So you never believed that Overton killed Ellie Dinker?" Kinley asked.

"No, I never did," Betty said. " 'Course, everybody else did."

"Except his family," Kinley added.

"And Mrs. Dinker," Betty said.

Kinley leaned forward slightly. "Mrs. Dinker?"

"She didn't believe Overton done it," Betty said. "Didn't believe Overton had killed her little girl."

"How do you know that?"

" 'Cause she come to me about it," Betty said. She nodded toward the small space between the front door and the enormous radio. "She stood right there and told me that there was something wrong in the whole story."

"Why did she think that?"

"Because of the dress," Betty said. "She told me there was something wrong with the dress."

Once again, the scene replayed in Kinley's mind, and he saw Warfield lifting the dress from the box, Mrs. Dinker staring at it, locked in that inexplicable silence which had suddenly closed around her, and from whose grip for a moment she had been unable to break: *WITNESS DOES NOT RESPOND.*

"The dress?" Kinley asked. "What was wrong with the dress?"

"She wanted to see it," Betty said. "She wanted to look at it."

"So she came to you?"

" 'Cause I was working at the courthouse back then," Betty said, "and she figured I could get it."

Kinley's vision climbed up the short white arms he'd only seen in his imagination before, only watched in his mind as they silently opened the box and plucked the green dress from it.

"So you got it for her," he whispered in a kind of awe at Betty Gaines's passionate outlawry, her capacity to do something without regard to consequences, to respond immediately, even recklessly, to a distant plea.

"Well, I figured it wasn't doing no good where it was," Betty said dully, "just going to mold down there

292

in the basement. Besides, the way I looked at it, that dress passed on to Mrs. Dinker when the girl died.'' She shrugged. ''I thought it might help ease her mind, but it didn't. Matter of fact, she sort of went nutty after that. Started poking around in people's yards and wandering all over the place at night. Then she just started to hanging around on the courthouse steps. Not long after that, they took her away.''

''What did she do when you gave her the dress?''

''She just spread it out on the table right there,'' Betty said, nodding toward it, ''and run her fingers over the chest part. She didn't say nothing after that. She just left it right there.''

''Left it?''

''For me to take back,'' Betty said. ''But I never did.''

''You still have it?''

Betty nodded. ''Folded up somewhere.''

Kinley felt himself rise to his feet suddenly, as if pulled up by invisible hands. ''Could I see it?''

''I guess so,'' Betty said as she drew herself to her feet, then disappeared into the other room.

She returned almost immediately with a bundle wrapped in brown paper. ''Here it is,'' she said as she handed it to Kinley.

He laid the bundle down very gently, reverently, as if it were Ellie Dinker's last remains, then folded the paper back to reveal what looked like nothing more than a small green pillow. Using the same gentle motions, he spread the dress out on the table, his eyes moving silently from the hem to the shoulders like a glider passing over a flat green field.

As he looked at it, he heard Warfield's voice asking Mrs. Dinker to describe the dress, then her answer, that it was green and had a lacy collar *that I made for her*.

At that moment, his eyes still fixed on the dress, Kinley realized precisely what Mrs. Dinker had seen as she'd stared uncomprehendingly at the dress which had hung from Thomas Warfield's hands. He glanced up from the dress and settled his eyes on Betty Gaines's face. "Where's the collar?" he asked.

She stared at him silently.

"Mrs. Dinker said she made a collar for this dress," Kinley added. "A white lacy collar."

Betty's eyes fell toward the dress. "I can see where it was," she said. She took a short, slightly trembling finger and ran it up a line of barely visible white stitching. "Right there's where it was sewed on."

It was a seamstress's eye, clear, sure, unfailing, and Kinley immediately saw the dress as Betty Gaines saw it, the small white threads rising like tiny, flying spirits from a broad green plain.

"Somebody cut it off," Betty said. Her finger moved from one severed thread to the next. "See," she said, "they've all been snipped with scissors."

"Snipped?" Kinley asked. "Not torn?"

"Torn?" Betty said. "You mean like somebody tearing it?"

Kinley nodded.

Betty shook her head with the certainty of a woman who had made a thousand dresses in her time, just as Martha Dinker had, and who saw just as clearly what Martha Dinker must also have seen as she'd stared at the green dress in Thomas Warfield's hand.

"Cut," Betty Gaines said, in a voice whose authority and expertise in such things Kinley could not doubt. "Cut clean. Cut with scissors. That's the only way you don't get a rip when you're pulling something off."

Thirty-Two

"I found it," Kinley said as he spread the dress over Warfield's desk.

Warfield stared at it, astonished. "Good work," he said as he glanced back up at Kinley. "Who had it?"

"It doesn't matter," Kinley said.

Warfield looked at him grimly. "Privileged information, is that it?" he asked. "An unidentified source?"

"Yes."

"That wasn't our deal, as I recall," Warfield said firmly.

Kinley dropped into a professional language he thought Warfield would understand. "There was no criminal intent."

"But there was a criminal act," Warfield told him, "and I believe in prosecuting people for such things."

"We're talking about an old person," Kinley said.

"Mr. Kinley," Warfield said, his voice cold and full of the law's immovable purpose. "I would prosecute the dead if I could bring them back to life."

"Look," Kinley told him, now abandoning his ineffective legal jargon. "At some point, I'll tell you. I give you my word. But for now, there's something else I want to show you." He pointed to the small white threads which ran in a broad crescent along the front of the dress. "There was once a collar there," he said.

"How do you know that?"

"It's in Mrs. Dinker's testimony," Kinley said. "She described it to your father."

"And this collar, it was torn off, I guess," Warfield said, unimpressed with the finding. "She probably fought back, and Overton ripped it off."

"Normally, that's what I'd think, too," Kinley told him.

Warfield looked at him quizzically. "But in this case, you don't?" he asked.

Kinley shook his head.

"Why not?"

Kinley let his fingers move over the line of white threads. "I had a seamstress look at it," he said. "The collar was cut off. With scissors. It wasn't ripped or torn."

"As it would have been in a struggle," Warfield added as he glanced back up at Kinley.

"Yes."

Warfield drew his eyes down to the dress. "It gives off a feeling, doesn't it?" he said. "Something someone died in, their clothes, or just the room, sometimes, it gives off a feeling about them."

Kinley nodded. "Yes, it does." He remembered all the early tools of his trade, the lengths of soiled rope, the torn skirts and bras, the lead pipe caked in blood and earth, the snub-nosed pistol on the tabletop. The locations, too, closets fitted with pulleys, beds fitted with straps, windows painted an impenetrable black, boxes with no windows in them, arrayed with leather thongs.

"I remember the first time I got that feeling," Warfield said. "It was a pillowcase that had been used as a gag, all balled up and stained with this and that. Sheriff Maddox just sort of tossed it to me.'' His eyes drifted up to Kinley. ''It had been stuffed so far down this old man's windpipe that he'd suffocated.'' He took the dress and lifted it slowly, as if the ghost of Ellie Dinker was still living invisibly inside.''We'll put it back where it belongs,'' he said.

Without further word, he rose and walked out of the room, the dress still in his outstretched hands, as Kinley followed him into the elevator, then rode silently down to the basement.

''It's my museum,'' Warfield said, as he walked into the small room lined with brown boxes marked by the names of the cases whose evidence they held. He pulled out the one labeled OVERTON and returned the dress to its interior darkness. ''I know most of them,'' he said, glancing from one box to the next. ''CRAWFORD, a drug peddler; DICKSON, one of his best customers; SHEFFIELD, a wifebeater; CARSON, a pedophile . . .''

''Overton,'' Kinley said abruptly, then looked pointedly at Warfield. ''I think he was innocent, Mr. Warfield.''

Warfield whirled around to face him. ''Do you really believe that?''

''Yes.''

''Why?''

''Things I've found out.''

''Did Ray think he was innocent, too?''

''I think so.''

''Then why the hell didn't he come to me?''

''I don't know.''

''Or to you, Mr. Kinley,'' Warfield added. ''Why didn't he come to you? You're a writer. You could have gotten exposure for the case, couldn't you?''

''Probably.''

''Then why didn't he tell you about it?''

Kinley shook his head. ''I don't know.''

''Something's wrong,'' Warfield said darkly. ''There's something wrong in the way Ray handled this.''

"Maybe he just wanted to do it alone," Kinley offered, still avoiding either of his other choices, misplaced loyalty or love, along with that third possibility which Kinley found he could not entirely exclude from his mind any more than he could block the memory of his ears: *He was doing it for the big boys. Whatever they did back then, he was covering it up.*

Warfield looked at him doubtfully. "Why would he want to do it alone?" His face suggested that it was a question he'd already answered. "To impress Dora Overton," he said. "The Lone Ranger rides again."

"I don't think he was like that."

"Then why did he keep everything to himself?" Warfield demanded. "How much did he find out about this case—if anything—and why did he take it to the grave?"

It was a question which Kinley was still asking himself later that night as he sat in the swing on Beaumont Street, the glass of scotch once again cool in his hand. He thought of Dora for a moment, suppressing the urge to bolt to his car and tear up the mountain to her house. If he did that, he knew that he would be lost for the night, that the urgency he had come to feel for his investigation would inevitably be drained away by this other, newer passion. It was part of the irreducible contradiction of life, that one force seeped life from another, that focusing on one scene required that others be covered with blinders.

Kinley, are you . . . ?

Again, he saw Ray on that last afternoon, the rain falling upon him mercilessly as he trotted, already exhausted, beside the train. He could see Ray's chest heaving as he'd labored briefly to keep up with the train, then given up suddenly, his great arms dropping helplessly to his sides like vanquished fighters sometimes let their arms collapse, as if to take the final punch and get it over with.

Kinley, are you . . . ?

What?

Kinley took a sip from the scotch, leaned back, and let Dora ease Ray from his mind, as if escorting his dead friend silently and without resistance from the room. He thought of her in her small house, or by the window, or out alone on the rim of the mountain, her eyes trained on the lights below, searching for the one on Beaumont Street.

It's better to know, isn't it?

And it was Ray again, resisting now, relentless, determined, his mouth moving in the coffin's darkness, his hands squeezing together rhythmically as Kinley's own hands so often did, obsessively, tirelessly, as if driven by devils of their own.

Another sip of scotch went down slowly, warmly, soothingly as he fought to keep his mind on Ray. It was clear to him now that Ray had continued with his investigation even after he'd caught up with Talbott, learned about Dora, and then chosen to keep it to himself. He had gone on with it, tracking down other leads, nosing into the brown box where Ellie Dinker's dress should have been.

He had gone on with it, then stopped abruptly, scooped the contents of his locked drawer into a yellow envelope and walked out of his office.

Where had he gone?

Kinley let his eyes move down Beaumont Street, its double rows of small, matter-of-fact houses, plain as the town itself, neat and functional. There was something homey in the tiny square lights which faced him from the house across the street. Through its single picture window, he could see the people who lived there as they passed back and forth across the living room, and for a moment, Kinley allowed himself a certain, distant envy for the life he thought they led. It was settled and routine, rooted in the firm clay of predictability, as he imagined Ray's own life had been before Dora.

Now she was with him again, a shadowy outline in his mind which he struggled to squeeze out. He concentrated

299

on Ray instead, his last days alone in the house, then his last hours, also alone, but traveling somewhere with the yellow envelope tucked securely beneath his arm.

His mind shifted again, this time to the last witness, the one his investigation had finally come down to, the last lead: Luther Snow.

There was no listing for Luther Snow in the Sequoyah phone directory, but it had taken only a brief phone call to Ben Wade to track him down, and within a few minutes, Kinley found himself bumping down a deserted logging road which shot off to the left of the same secondary mountain road which, had he continued to follow it, would have led him to his grandmother's house on the brow of the canyon.

It was familiar territory, and even in the bluish moonlight, its details filled his mind with the days and nights he'd walked with her, talked with her or simply sat and listened hypnotically to her voice as she led him down the long trail of blood and mayhem the *Police Gazette* provided, it seemed now, for his instruction.

Luther Snow had been forty-four years old at the time of the trial, a slender, sharp-featured man with a large, pointed nose and small round eyes. Even in the pictures Kinley had seen in the Sequoyah *Standard* clippings, he had given off the same sullen, criminal atmosphere that Kinley had noticed in men who'd done far more desperate things than committing perjury in a murder trial. He'd noticed it in Mildred Haskell and Fenton Norwood and Colin Bright, and as he thought of them, their faces rose like masks before him, grim, silent, as close as he would ever come to the *manus maleficiens* of medieval understanding, the hand that knows no good.

The man who opened the door only seconds after Kinley rapped softly at it struck him as the object lesson in how effectively time could soften the hard angularity of

300

an evil face. Luther Snow looked almost lovable as he stood squinting behind the screen, his slick black hair turned to a nest of silver fibers by the light from the room behind him.

"Luther Snow?" Kinley asked.

The old man nodded. "I don't see too good," he said, still squinting. "Are you the Fowler boy?"

"No."

"Didn't come for nothing, then?"

"Well, not exactly."

Snow's eyes tightened into narrow slits. "What you want?"

"I'm a writer," Kinley said. "My name's Jackson Kinley. I'm working on a story."

Snow watched him uncomprehendingly, as if the word "writer" was one Kinley had suddenly snatched from a foreign language.

"I'm working on the Overton case," Kinley added.

"Overton?"

"Charles Overton," Kinley told him. "The murder trial back in 1954."

The old man's face suddenly hardened, all the youthful menace Kinley had seen in the newspaper photographs instantly and miraculously called back to life, as if evil, even in old age, still remained on call, a demonic army waiting in reserve. "I ain't got nothing to say about that trial," Snow said coldly. "It don't mean nothing to me."

"Well, I just wanted to . . ."

"I got nothing to say," Snow repeated. "Now get on out of here."

Kinley could see the old man's hand as it crawled slowly toward the small steel latch and eyebolt on the inside of the screen.

"Get on out of here," Snow snapped brutally, his hand still moving stealthily, a white spider crawling up the unpainted wooden jamb. "I ain't got to talk to nobody about nothing."

Kinley grabbed the handle of the door and pulled it open slightly. "I think you should talk to me," he said firmly.

Snow's hand descended immediately, its long, skeletal fingers now fiddling witlessly at the leg of his trousers. "I ain't got nothing to say," he repeated.

Kinley took a chance. "It's not too late, you know," he warned, his own voice now as menacing as Snow's.

The old man seemed instantly to understand. "It's years past," he said roughly. "It ain't nothing of interest to nobody."

"It is to me," Kinley said. "And it was to Ray Tindall."

Snow's eyes widened slightly. "He's dead, ain't he?"

"Yeah," Kinley said, "but Warfield isn't."

Snow laughed. "He's been dead for years."

"I mean his son, William Warfield," Kinley said, "the District Attorney."

"What's he got to do with it?" Snow demanded. "It ain't nothing to do with him."

"Perjury is his business," Kinley told him. "A man was executed. It's not too late to look into something like that."

Snow's eyes suddenly began to dart about, as if moving from one place to another on Kinley's face. "Kinley," he whispered. "Kinley. Ain't you that little boy that . . ."

Kinley nodded. "Yeah, I used to live around here."

"With the old woman."

"Granny Dollar."

Snow smiled. "Oh, yeah," he said, almost to himself. "Yeah, I remember you." His eyes drifted down toward Kinley's hands. "I remember you."

"I used to play around here," Kinley said, hoping to move Snow gently into conversation. "I used to roam the woods all around this part of the mountain."

Snow's eyes rose slowly and settled on Kinley's face. "You look like her."

"Who?"

302

"You growed up to look like her."

"My grandmother?"

Snow said nothing as his hand moved once again toward the latch and eyebolt.

And as he watched the hand ascend, Kinley found that he could not stop it as it continued on, higher and higher, until it stopped suddenly, then pressed forward, closing the door, almost gently, in his unmoving face.

Again, like always, he was moving through the woods, his small body plowing wildly through the heavy undergrowth, plunging blindly and at terrific speed into the impenetrable darkness. Someone was pulling him along, jerking his hand violently as he stumbled through the grasping brambles. He could feel the snare of the vines as they tangled around his bare legs, but the hand continued to wrench him forward mercilessly, dragging him brutally toward the dark stone cliff. He could hear his own heart pounding frantically as he neared its jagged edge, and he could feel something emptying inside, as if scooped out, and his hands thrust out to pull it back, to scoop it back into his body, as if it were the air, the very breath of life, which was rushing from him, rushing as he grasped for it with an animal urgency, his fingers snatching desperately at the invisible night.

She opened the door briskly, as if she had not been asleep.

"I'm sorry," he said, "I know it's late."

"I didn't expect you."

"I had a bad dream," he said, then laughed awkwardly. "I feel like a child."

She nodded slowly as she stepped back to let him come inside. "We all do sometimes," she said.

Thirty-Three

The next morning they had coffee in Dora's small kitchen, the two of them together at the tiny aluminum table by the window.

"I used to do this with my mother," Dora said after a moment. She smiled, remembering it. "We'd sit by the window and look out over the mountain. Then one morning, she didn't come out of her room."

"How long ago was that?"

"Ten years."

Kinley nodded. "My grandmother went the same way, I guess. Very suddenly. They found her sitting in her chair on the porch, just staring out over the canyon."

"They?"

"Actually, it was Ray who found her."

Dora looked at him quizzically. "Ray?"

"He never told you that?"

"No," Dora said. "Did he visit her a lot?"

Kinley shook his head. "I don't think so."

"Then why was he up there?"

Kinley realized that he'd never asked Ray that question, that he'd simply taken the fact that he'd found his grandmother dead as a matter of course, something natural, part of the scheme of things. "I don't know why he was up there that particular day," he said.

"Maybe he just went up to talk to her."

Kinley looked at her curiously. "About what?"

"Whatever was on his mind, I guess," Dora said lightly.

Kinley's mind shot backward, moving through Ray's activities during the week preceding his grandmother's death. "Your father was on his mind," he said quietly. "He was very busy looking into the case at about that time."

Dora took a sip from the coffee, then let her eyes shift toward the window, the high mountain fog still thick behind the window pane. "I like it like this," she said.

"The fog?"

She turned toward him. "Having coffee with someone in the morning."

He took in a long, slow breath, choking back what would otherwise have been his immediate and spontaneous response: *Me, too.*

He left her a few minutes later, driving slowly down the mountainside, this time without glancing to the right where the town rested in its misty silence below him. He stared straight ahead instead, his eyes focused on the road while he tried to find a new foothold for his investigation, some tiny indentation in the wall that would allow him to cling to Sequoyah a little longer, to Overton and Ray, and more than anything, he realized, to Dora.

Once back on Beaumont Street, he walked to Ray's office and took a seat in front of his computer. He called up various files, stared at the questions he'd posed, quickly rearranged them in the order his mind demanded now, and typed in the answers he'd been able to track down so far.

QUESTIONS ABOUT THE INVESTIGATION

1) Why did they not search the well?
   ANSWER:
   Incompetence of Sheriff Maddox? Dinker not in well.
2) Where is Ellie Dinker's dress?
   ANSWER:
   Stolen by Betty Gaines on behalf of Mrs. Dinker, and later returned to the District Attorney's Office.

QUESTIONS CONCERNING ELLIE DINKER

1) Why did Ellie Dinker want to meet at the Slater house instead of her own, which would have been much closer to their ultimate destination, the courthouse in Sequoyah?
2) Why did Ellie Dinker leave for Helen's five hours before she needed to?
3) Why did Ellie Dinker move in a direction opposite to the one she should have taken if she'd been planning to go directly to the Slater house?
4) Why did she stop on the mountain road?
5) Why did she approach Overton after his truck broke down?
6) Why did she ask him what was wrong with the truck and how long it would take for him to fix it?
7) Why did she appear "nervous-like"?
   ANSWER TO I THROUGH 6: because she was planning to meet someone.

Only a moment's further thought unearthed the answer to Question 7, and he immediately typed it in: *Because she did not want the man she'd planned to meet at Mile Marker 27 to be recognized.*

306

But who would have recognized him? Overton? Was it possible, Kinley wondered, that Overton would have known whoever it was that Ellie Dinker had planned to meet that day, and that because of that she was "nervous-like," demanding immediate answers to her questions before walking as far up the road as she could without entirely leaving her point of rendezvous?

Kinley fixed his eyes on the console, making sure there was nothing else, then typed in his last remaining questions, their letters burning like small hot coils on the monitor's bright screen:

8) Who was Ellie Dinker waiting for?
9) Where is Ellie Dinker now?

For a moment, he thought that these might be the only questions left in the case. Then, slowly, as if inching its way cautiously into his mind, yet demanding to be gathered within the circle of the others, a third and final question rose insistently: *Why did Ray come to my grandmother's house?*

He waited for Serena in front of Lois's house, the cold fall chill of late afternoon already gathering around him by the time he saw her emerge from the building.

"I wasn't sure you were still in town," she said as she approached him.

"I'm still looking into a few things."

She did not seem surprised. "I'm glad," she said and left it at that.

"As a matter of fact," Kinley added, "I was hoping you might help me a little."

Serena looked excited at the prospect, as if she'd just been asked to join a trek into other, more adventurous worlds.

"It's about Ray," Kinley went on. "Just a few questions about him."

Serena nodded. "Sure."

"Good," Kinley said. He shivered slightly. "It's a little chilly out here," he said. "Why don't we find a place inside?"

They found it on Beaumont Street, and after a few, brief pleasantries about how things were going at the high school and Serena's plans to return to college the following week, Kinley moved directly into the matter at hand.

"Ray was working very hard on an old murder case," he said, "the Overton case. Have you ever heard of it?"

Serena shook her head.

"It happened in 1954," Kinley told her, "and Charles Overton was sentenced to death. I think Ray had come to think that Overton was innocent."

Serena smiled sweetly. "That sounds like him."

Kinley nodded. "You mentioned to me at one point that you and Ray had grown apart not long before his death," he said. "Do you remember exactly when that was?"

Serena thought for a moment, then answered. "It hadn't been very long," she said, "only about a month before he died."

"Around late July or early August then?" Kinley said.

"Yes."

"How did he seem?"

"Worried," Serena answered. "Preoccupied." She thought a moment longer, as if trying to find the most precise word to describe him. "Suspicious," she said finally. "He'd started locking things up. His office. His desk. Those file cabinets."

"But they were unlocked later?" Kinley asked.

"They were unlocked the day he died," Serena said.

"Not before then?"

Serena shook her head. "No. That's what made me think that someone had been in Daddy's office. But it didn't look like anybody had broken into anything. The only thing I noticed were the missing files."

308

Kinley's mind produced the relevant letters instantly. "S, O and D."

"Yes," Serena said. "Have you found them yet?"

Kinley shook his head, unwilling to tell Serena that her mother had taken them in order to conceal Ray's relationship with Dora Overton.

"That's the key," Serena said flatly. "That's the key to what happened to Daddy."

Kinley returned to his original question. "So, Ray was suspicious, you said?"

"Yes."

"Of what, did he ever give you any hint about that?"

"No," Serena said. "I just know that he was always locking things up and that he was spending a lot of time reading transcripts."

"Trial transcripts?"

"Yes."

"Of the Overton case?"

"I don't know," Serena said. "But there were lots of transcripts in his office."

"Lots?"

"Volumes and volumes."

Kinley's mind immediately flashed to the short stack of transcripts which Overton's brief trial had generated. "Volumes and volumes?"

"That's right."

"How long did it take him to read them?"

"A couple of weeks, I guess," Serena said. "He was reading during his spare time. Mostly at night. In his office."

"When did he stop?"

"Around the middle of July, I think."

"Which is when he started locking things up," Kinley said, as if to himself.

Serena nodded. "Yes, at that same time."

"Do you know what the transcripts were about?"

"No."

"Or where they came from?"

Serena shrugged. "The courthouse, I guess."

"You mean here in Sequoyah?"

"Yes," Serena told him. "He'd load them into the back of his car and bring them home. He spent hours in his office. He was always taking notes."

"Notes?"

"On legal pads," Serena said.

"Do you know what he did with the notes?"

Serena's face turned very solemn. "He burned them."

"How do you know?"

"I saw him do it," she said. "I just dropped by after school one day, and he was doing it." Her mind seemed to drift back slowly, drawing in upon the moment. "He was standing by the fireplace. All his papers were in a big box, and he was feeding them into the fire." Her eyes moved reflexively toward the fireplace. "He was standing there. He didn't have a shirt on."

Kinley looked at her quizzically.

"Because it was so hot," Serena explained. "It was in the summer. As a matter of fact, I know exactly what day it was because we'd just gotten out of school for the holiday weekend."

"Which holiday weekend?"

"The one for the Fourth of July," Serena said. "It was that Wednesday."

"July 3," Kinley said.

Serena nodded.

Kinley glanced toward the fireplace, but saw the one in his New York apartment instead. It had never worked, and so he'd put a planter in it, then watched over the next few days as the plants had wilted and died from lack of attention. He'd been trying to revive them that same afternoon when the phone had rung suddenly, marking the date forever in his mind. He'd been surprised to hear Ray's voice at the other end: *Sorry, Kinley, but it's Granny Dollar; I found her dead this afternoon.*

* * *

310

The courthouse was still open when Kinley arrived a few minutes later. In the large room which led to the evidence vault, Mrs. Hunter was busily straightening up the day's disarray, neatly shelving books to make the office presentable for the following day.

"I have a favor to ask," Kinley said as he moved down the corridor toward her.

Mrs. Hunter glanced at the clock. "It's about quitting time," she said.

"It's very important," Kinley told her.

Mrs. Hunter gave him the weary nod of the exasperated but dutiful civil servant. "Well, I'll do what I can," she said.

"It's the log," Kinley said. "The one you use to keep track of things in the vault."

Mrs. Hunter nodded.

"I'd like to look at it," Kinley said.

Mrs. Hunter looked relieved that so little was being asked of her. "Well, I can do that for you, I guess," she said.

Kinley followed her to the front counter and watched as Mrs. Hunter retrieved the same vast ledger in which he written his own name several days before. "Here it is," she said.

"How far does it go back?"

"We start it over once a year."

"So this goes back as far as last January?"

Mrs. Hunter nodded. "Yes, sir. Do you need to go back further than that?"

"I don't think so," Kinley told her.

"Well, go ahead and look at it then," Mrs. Hunter said. "I'll just finish up a few things." She glanced at the clock. "You've got about fifteen minutes before the office closes."

Kinley quickly turned to the front of the book and began going through the ledger, searching for any entries for Ray Tindall, any notation of anything he'd taken from the vault.

311

He found the first one on February 19, only six weeks after he'd met Dora. It was for the Overton trial, the same transcript Kinley had already pored over, and Ray had checked out each of its six volumes over the next three weeks.

Ray's next withdrawal from the vault, on March 1, was the first two volumes of Case Record 217394-C, the final code letter "C" indicating, as Kinley knew, that it was a criminal case.

Over the next two weeks, Ray had checked out the remaining three volumes, returning all five of them on April 1.

Kinley quickly wrote the case number and dates in his notebook, then returned to the log, leafing slowly through its wide pages, his eyes now intent on every withdrawal.

He found the next one on April 24, Case Record 641739-A. Kinley noted immediately that the "A" was a general designation, which meant that it was a civil action, rather than a criminal case, the parties in the dispute having finally taken their irreconcilable differences before a judge.

Again, Kinley wrote the number into his notebook, then began moving through the log again, his eyes bearing down more and more intently on the pages as spring passed into summer, each day moving steadily toward that moment when Ray had taken all his accumulated notes and fed them into a blazing fire.

He stopped at May 15. On that day, Ray had checked out yet another transcript, this one for Case Record 217560-C, another criminal proceeding.

Kinley scribbled the number into his notebook, then continued through the book, turning through the rest of May, then all of June, and finally the first week of July.

Nothing.

"Would it be possible to look at these transcripts?" Kinley asked as he handed the open notebook to Mrs. Hunter.

She looked at the numbers unbelievingly. "All of them?"

"I have the whole night," Kinley explained. "And all of tomorrow." He shrugged. "Whatever it takes."

She considered it for a moment. "Well, Mr. Warfield said to help you any way I could," she said at last, "but you'll have to carry them yourself."

Thirty-Four

Mrs. Hunter had been right. The accumulated volumes of trial transcript had been a formidable burden, and Kinley had had to make several trips back and forth from the courthouse to his car before the last of them were loaded into the backseat.

The process had been repeated when he'd arrived at the house on Beaumont Street, and within a few minutes, the transcripts sat in a ragged pile beside Ray's old metal filing cabinet.

Kinley had arranged them in the same order in which Ray had checked them out, and as he plucked the first one from the stack and brought it over to Ray's desk, he felt again the odd sensation that he was following a well-worn path, that Ray's broad back was always in front of him, leading him on, just as it had been in front of him that first time so many years before, when they'd gone down into the canyon together to find the little shack behind its wall of vines.

He looked at the first volume without opening it, his

hand peculiarly resistant, as if he were opening the dark lid of his old friend's coffin.

As an act of discipline, he pressed his hand down on the cover, as if feeling for a pulse, his eyes drifting up to the wall behind Ray's desk, the little note he'd hung there, a call to urge him on.

In an age of mass death, the mystery remains the final redoubt of romantic individualism in its insistence that one life, unjustly taken, still matters so much within the human universe that the failure to discover how and by whom that life was taken contains all we still may know of romantic terror.

Kinley glanced back down to the transcript, opened it and read what was written on its title page: *State of Georgia v. Luther Lawrence Snow*.

The trial of Luther Snow for the illegal sale of alcoholic beverages had begun on May 3, 1946. The prosecutor was Thomas Warfield, who'd just been elected District Attorney the previous November, and as he read Warfield's opening remarks to the jury, Kinley was surprised at how clumsy they were.

WARFIELD: The State will prove that Mr. Snow sold liquor in this county, and he has sold it a great deal, you may be sure—and maybe he never made liquor in the county—but he's not being tried for that. He's being tried for illegally selling whisky in the county, and we don't allow that here.

From this opening statement, Warfield had gone on to construct an equally inelegant case, calling witnesses in a random order which, Kinley guessed, had pretty much kept the jury off-balance for the entire trial.

First, he'd called a nineteen-year-old boy named Wendell Peeples, who'd purchased liquor from Snow. Under Warfield's unsteady leadership, Peeples had wandered in circles through his testimony, continually backtracking, until Peeples himself had finally balked at continuing down such a winding route:

PEEPLES: What's that?
WARFIELD: You know, I was asking about what time it was you left your mother's house.
PEEPLES: You mean, you want me to tell that again, Mr. Warfield?
WARFIELD: Oh, no. You're right. I'm sorry. Let's go on to something else.

Next Warfield had called Floyd Maddox, the equally youthful and newly elected County Sheriff, and for a time, the two of them had staggered through the somewhat crude sting operation Maddox had devised against Snow.

As a scheme it had certainly skirted the edges of entrapment, a circumstance which Snow's attorney would doubtless have noticed, except that it was 1946 and Snow had not been given an attorney to represent him in the case.

For a time, as Kinley read first one volume, then another, the atmosphere which rose from the proceedings had an almost comical effect, a bumbling Keystone Kops affair, with Warfield stumbling through his witness lineup and Maddox grandly revealing the previously secret details of a law enforcement operation that was hardly more complicated than a bait-and-switch con game.

It was not until the final volume that the mood abruptly changed.

Luther Snow took the stand in his own defense, declared that he had no questions for himself, and then, in what could only be thought of as a wild and brilliant maneuver, turned himself over to Warfield for cross-examination. *Come and get me, Warfield. I'm waiting.*

At the reading of that single grim, determined line,

Kinley saw the old man before him, younger and more resourceful, but with the same small eyes, musty odor and look of malignant self-control.

SNOW: Come and get me, Warfield. I'm waiting.
WARFIELD: How are you, Mr. Snow?

To this question, Snow returned a steady and unflinching glare which the court reporter noted in the same succinct phrase she'd used to describe the silence of Martha Dinker: *WITNESS DOES NOT RESPOND.*

WARFIELD: You've pled not guilty to this indictment, haven't you, Mr. Snow?
SNOW: Yeah.
WARFIELD: Which means that you're denying that you sold any whisky to Sheriff Maddox, isn't that right, sir?
SNOW: Not guilty.
WARFIELD: So now, for the jury, and the people here . . . and for the record, you're pleading not guilty, isn't that right?
SNOW: To the thing, I am.
WARFIELD: Thing?
SNOW: Whatever you called it.
WARFIELD: You mean, the indictment?
SNOW: Whatever's wrote on the paper, that's what I ain't guilty for.
WARFIELD: Selling whisky?
SNOW: Ain't nothing wrong with selling whisky.
WARFIELD: Nothing wrong?
SNOW: Across the state line, over there in Tennessee, they got stores on the main street that's selling it all day long.
WARFIELD: But we're not talking about Chattanooga, are we?
SNOW: No.

WARFIELD: What are we talking about?

SNOW: Money. How to get it.

WARFIELD: And one way is by selling whisky?

SNOW: Whatever way, it don't matter to me.

WARFIELD: So you'd do anything for money, Mr. Snow?

SNOW: Anything.

WARFIELD: So I could rely on that, couldn't I?

SNOW: Till your dying day.

It was a grim exchange, and Kinley had read a great many others like it. Mildred Haskell had talked like Snow, and Colin Bright—ghostly, disembodied voices, perfectly modulated for their refined malignancy.

WARFIELD: Are you married, Mr. Snow?

SNOW: Yes.

WARFIELD: What's your wife's name?

SNOW: Bertha.

WARFIELD: Where is she right now?

SNOW: Hospital.

WARFIELD: How'd she get there?

SNOW: I gave her a whipping.

WARFIELD: You beat her up, isn't that right?

SNOW: I needed quiet.

WARFIELD: And that's the way you get it?

SNOW: A man's got to do what a man's got to do.

At that point, Snow must have said it with a sneer, or perhaps a thin, sinister grin, because the spectators had laughed so loudly that the judge had called a halt to the proceedings until order could be restored.

Then, with the laughter trailing off, the cross-examination began again.

WARFIELD: Have you ever been in prison, Mr. Snow?

SNOW: Yeah.

WARFIELD: Whereabouts?

318

SNOW: All over.

WARFIELD: In Alabama, for car theft?

SNOW: Yeah. A blue Olds, anybody would have wanted it.

WARFIELD: In Alabama for burglary?

SNOW: Big house. Some fat old plantation man.

WARFIELD: Way out in Texas, for assault.

SNOW: Yeah, and he needed stopping, too.

WARFIELD: Nothing in Georgia.

SNOW: I guess I'm turning soft in my old age.

Again the courtroom spectators had laughed, and again the judge had found it necessary to caution them against any further outburst.

By now Warfield was getting scared. Luther Snow was talking circles around him. In the mountain country, prosecutions for boot-legging were never easy, but Snow was turning everything against Warfield, mocking him, ridiculing him, making him look like a fool, and Warfield's own shakiness under the assault was undermining his case almost as effectively as Snow's determined outlawry.

As for Snow, he knew he was winning, and he went in for the kill.

SNOW: You know what I think?

WARFIELD: It's not your place to . . .

SNOW: I think you had a drink last night. Maybe before that, too, and, hell, I bet you up and had another one the day before that.

WARFIELD: Mr. Snow, I'm not the one who is on . . .

SNOW: And it went down warm and easy, like it does on everybody.

WARFIELD: Mr. Snow, you cannot continue to . . .

SNOW: Because everybody likes a drink when things are a little hard on them.

WARFIELD: Mr. Snow, you . . .

SNOW: And that's what I give them.

WARFIELD: Your Honor, I would ask that you direct the . . .

SNOW: Not that rotgut they make in the hills, but bonded whisky.

WARFIELD: . . . the witness to please stop . . .

SNOW: Just like you got, I bet, at your little bar at home, Warfield.

WARFIELD: . . . talking.

SNOW: I've already stopped, Your Honor.

WARFIELD: Well . . . well, I . . .

COURT: Do you wish to rest your case, Mr. Warfield?

WARFIELD: Well, I . . . Yes. Yes, Your Honor, I do.

If Snow had conceived of his own cross-examination as a ploy, it had worked brilliantly, Kinley realized as he turned to the last page of the transcript. For later that same afternoon, a jury of poor, hardworking country people had considered the bloated hypocrisy of Thomas Warfield, heir to all the Warfield fortune, so young his skin still held its infant sheen beneath the courtroom lights, and compared it to the snarling, belabored, but unrepentant visage of Luther Snow, and found Snow innocent of the charges which had been brought against him.

It was almost seven in the evening before Kinley completed his reading of Snow's trial. He made himself a quick dinner before going on to the next case.

By eight he was in the back room again, his hand turning to the first page of Case Record 641739-A, the court proceeding Ray had checked out nearly two weeks following the Snow trial transcript.

It was a civil case, as Kinley already knew from the code, but the names of the plaintiff and the defendant were surprising: *County of Sequoyah v. Thompson Construction Company.*

The case had been brought to court only two years before, in the fall of 1989, and as Kinley read on through the testimony, he found it difficult to imagine why Ray had been so interested in it.

It was a very common legal suit for the retrieval of funds on a charge of professional negligence. According to Wallace Wainwright, the County Attorney, Thompson Construction had failed properly to reinforce certain areas on the courthouse grounds when various structures had been erected in the summer of 1954, notably one section of the cement stairs leading to the courthouse entrance and the flagpole, which rose over the front lawn. The pole had been mounted in a granite foundation that was now sinking to the left, causing it to lean northward at an angle of eighty degrees, or, as Wainwright put it colorfully in his opening statement to the judge, "enough to cause a perfectly fine set of eyes to have to look cross-eyed at our country's flag."

As for the county, it asked only that the stairs be recemented, and that the flagpole, along with its original granite mount, be unearthed, its foundation reinforced, and the entire assembly returned to its original resting place.

As for Thompson Construction, now in the hands of Leonard Thompson, the founder's son, it remained adamantly unwilling to accept any responsibility for either the mangled steps or the sloping flagpole, as the company's attorney, John Billings, brought out repeatedly in Leonard Thompson's testimony:

BILLINGS: So, as far as your own responsibility is concerned, you see none on the part of Thompson Construction, isn't that right?

THOMPSON: That's correct.

BILLINGS: Would you tell the Court why that is, Mr. Thompson?

THOMPSON: Because my father advised against it.

BILLINGS: And that was back in 1954?

THOMPSON: Yes.

BILLINGS: But county officials weren't willing to go along with that, were they?

THOMPSON: No. They were in a hurry to get everything finished at the courthouse. It was brand-new, and they wanted everything all fixed up for the celebration. So on the night of July 3, 1954, we sent three men down there, a foreman, a crane operator and a regular workman, and they worked pretty much all night. I've got the names right here. It was Lonnie Adcock and Charles Overton worked that night. Adcock worked the crane. The foreman on the job was Luther Snow.

BILLINGS: And did they complete the flagpole that night?

THOMPSON: They sure did. It took them all night, but they did it.

Kinley looked up from the transcript and let his mind do its routine calculations. On July 2, even summer school had been dismissed so that students could come into Sequoyah to help spruce up the city, and to attend a small patriotic rally in front of the courthouse that afternoon. Earlier that day, Ellie Dinker had headed up the mountain toward Helen Slater's house. At around twelve-thirty, Charles Overton, complaining of a stomach ailment, had left the courthouse construction site and headed up that same mountain toward his home. At around twelve-forty on the mountain road at Mile Marker 27, the two of them had met, probably for the first time. Late on the afternoon of the following day, Luther Snow had telephoned Wallace Thompson and told him that the county wanted the flagpole completed by the following morning. A few hours after that, Snow, Overton and Adcock had gathered at the site and begun the long night's work.

Kinley let his mind wander on through the names that

had so far been mentioned in the case, the inevitable toll of the years once more pressing down upon him. Wallace Thompson was dead. Overton and Dinker. Snow would not talk. Kinley's eyes bore down upon the one remaining name: Lonnie Adcock.

Thirty-Five

Once again it was the rootedness of small-town life which had come to his rescue, the fact that people remained in place, holding down the same jobs, occupying the same living spaces, Ray's organism endlessly reproducing itself.

The space Lonnie Adcock occupied within Sequoyah's scheme of things was a moderately large single-story ranch house on the north end of town. It was in the area's only commercial housing development, and as he wound gently to the left before coming to a stop at the end of a circular cul de sac, Kinley was reminded of the identical prefabricated neighborhoods that peppered the flatlands of the North.

Lonnie Adcock was surprisingly young, as Kinley noticed when the door opened, and to accommodate this new information, his mind envisioned a young man standing awkwardly in the thick summer darkness of July 3, 1954, his fingers playing edgily at the controls of the crane, while he waited for Luther Snow to tell him what to do.

"I don't mean to bother you," Kinley said to the

middle-age man who smiled politely from his place in the open door. "My name's Jack Kinley, and I've been looking into the Overton case."

Adcock's face registered nothing.

"Charles Overton," Kinley added.

The face brightened. "Oh, yeah, Charlie Overton," Adcock said. "Of course, when it comes right down to it, I didn't know him very well."

"I just have a few questions," Kinley assured him.

"Well, come on in, then," Adcock said amiably as he opened the door more widely. "I was just sitting around anyway."

Kinley walked through the door and into a small, green carpeted living room which looked even smaller because of the huge rear-screen projection television that rested like a great wooden altar at the far end.

"My son gave it to me," Adcock said, referring to the television, "but I don't like it that much. Picture's too fuzzy."

Kinley took a seat on the sofa while Adcock settled into a yellow Naugahyde recliner.

"Like I told you," Adcock repeated, "I didn't know the man very well. We worked together some, but that's about all." He picked up a bowl of generic nuts and lifted it toward Kinley.

"No, thank you."

Adcock popped a couple in his mouth. "I was barely twenty at that time," he said, "and the older guys, they didn't really pay much attention to me."

"The older guys?"

"That worked at Thompson's."

"You mean, Luther Snow."

"Snow and Peabody and Quinn," Adcock said, ticking off the names. "And Overton, of course. He pretty much kept to himself."

"He and Snow weren't friends?"

Adcock's lips curled downward. "Snow wasn't nobody's friend."

Kinley reached into his jacket and took out his pen and notebook. "Do you remember the night of July 3?" he asked. "That was the night you put up the flagpole."

"Oh, yeah," Adcock said. "It was just the three of us that night. Me and Snow and Overton. We didn't have no other help. The next day, I was really sort of bitching about how hard it had been."

"Snow just wanted you and Overton for the work that night?"

"I guess so," Adcock added, "but he was wrong on that, because it was a hell of a job for three men." He shook his head, remembering it. "And besides, it was raining."

"Raining?"

"That's right," Adcock said. "What they used to call 'a real toad stringer.' "

"But you put the flagpole up anyway?"

"We sure as hell did," Adcock said proudly.

Kinley's mind moved slowly through the black, rainswept night, focusing on the long gray line of the pole, still horizontal on the courthouse grounds, its granite foundation waiting silently by the open hole.

"It was a bitch, let me tell you," Adcock added. Another handful of nuts disappeared into his mouth. "Worst night of work I ever had."

"When did you get to the courthouse?" Kinley asked.

"Around nine," Adcock said. "That's when Snow told me to show up."

"And that would have been after dark?"

"Damn right," Adcock said. "It was already pitch dark when I got there, and Snow was already in the pit."

"Pit?"

"The hole that had been dug for the base of the flagpole," Adcock explained. "Snow knew the ground wasn't ready, so he was in there trying to shore it up." He reached for another handful of peanuts, then continued. "We kept the hole covered with a tarpaulin when we wasn't working. That was supposed to keep it dry, and when I got there Snow was under the tarp shoring up the pit. I could hear him smacking at the ground with his shovel, like he was packing it down.''

"In the dark?''

"Just like a rat in a hole,'' Adcock said. "He didn't even have a flashlight down there.''

"What happened then?''

"He came out, and we waited for Overton to show up,'' Adcock said. "He got there about ten minutes later.''

Kinley could see the yellow lights of Overton's battered truck as it wheeled into the courthouse parking lot, the summer downpour pelting at it mercilessly as Overton eased himself out of the cab and headed for the other men, a hunched, faceless figure, a shadow in the rain.

"When he got there, we started to work,'' Adcock said. "We worked all night, pouring cement under the tarp and smoothing everything out.''

"Were you always together?''

"Most of the time.''

"But not always?''

"Yeah, always, except for when Snow went to get us some food.''

"When was that?''

"Around one or two in the morning, something like that,'' Adcock said. "We were all tired and needing a break, so Snow told us to sit down a spell, and he walked over and took Overton's truck and went and got us some sandwiches and coffee.''

"He took Overton's truck?''

Adcock nodded. "Yeah, he did,'' he said. "I saw Charlie give him the keys, and after that Snow went up and got in and drove away.''

"And he never left again?''

Adcock shook his head. "No, we worked side by side until around eight the next morning. We were all dead tired by then. Especially Overton.''

"Why Overton?''

"Because he was sick at his stomach," Adcock said. "He threw up a couple times that night." He shook his head. "I felt sort of sorry for him, the way he looked. White as a sheet. He said he'd tried to get some help for it the night before, but it hadn't done him no good." He shook his head. "Overton really shouldn't have been on the job that night. I don't know why Snow wanted him there."

Kinley felt his pen stop on the page as the certainty dropped into place in his mind, its conclusion carved on to it as certainly as words in stone: *I do*.

Back in the tiny office on Beaumont Street, Kinley glanced through the old photographs of Sequoyah that Lois had found in the file marked "S." They'd seemed irrelevant before, nothing more than part of Ray's lifelong mania for gathering the facts of local history. Now they were the key to everything.

For what he thought must be the last time, Kinley replayed the initial stages of the crime itself. He saw Overton's truck as it drifted to a stop, then Ellie Dinker's black shoes scrambling toward him, her green skirt slipping through the tall summer grasses, then moving away again, back up the mountain road until she passed Mile Marker 27. By then she must have been beyond Overton's view as he lay beneath the truck, his shirt already soiled with the greasy slime and roadside dirt that Sarah Overton would later testify about at the trial.

At some point not more than a few minutes later, Snow must have picked Ellie up. Ellie had not lived a careful life, and as Kinley thought of it, Snow was the perfect candidate for her less than discriminating eye. She'd gotten into the car with him, and disappeared up the road to some location which had never been discovered, and there, in the forest, or in some shack, or along the canyon rim, Snow had murdered her in one of the many ways

Kinley had come to know, with a rope, or a stone, a pipe, a pistol or a fist.

With Ellie dead, Snow had then turned desperately to a solution. He needed to conceal the body, and he needed someone else to pin the murder on. Overton must have emerged almost immediately as the perfect candidate. Since other people had no doubt seen Overton and Ellie together, he was the perfect fall guy, and in a single malicious instant, Snow must have realized that by framing Overton he could accomplish both ends at once. He could bury Dinker's body beneath the courthouse flagpole, and then, while using Overton's truck to get sandwiches, plant the bloody tire iron and Ellie Dinker's shoes behind the seat.

Almost to escape his own grim meditations, Kinley returned his eyes to the photographs Ray had gathered together in the ''S'' file.

In the first, the courthouse stood in all its gray magnificence, the steps in place, the motto already affixed above its great carved doors, the grounds thoroughly seeded, the rich summer green already on the lawn, everything in place, even the august crowd of county servants and politicians who posed before the building, smiling brightly at Harry Townsend's camera. Everything was in place except for the long gray flagpole and its granite mooring. It stood several yards from the open pit which had already been dug for it, its green tarpaulin cover fluttering slightly before the beaming line of county officials. On the back, Ray had written the date in his own tiny script, ''July 2, 1954.'' By looking at the slender shadow cast by the courthouse as it appeared in the photograph, Ray had been able to calculate the time of day at which it had been taken, ''midday to early afternoon, July 2, 1954.''

In the second photograph, the courthouse grounds were empty, all the officials now in their offices or behind their counters, the steps vacant, the courthouse doors securely closed. Now the flagpole stood erect and unbending in the morning sun. Beneath the photograph, the newspaper had written its own stirring caption: *Our flag on high. Independence Day in Sequoyah. July 4, 1954, 8:00* A.M.

Kinley glanced up suddenly as something caught in his mind. He snapped the first picture up, turned it over and looked at the date and time again: July 2, 1954, between twelve noon and early afternoon. Within those slender bounds Ellie Dinker had already arrived at Mile Marker 27. By then Charles Overton's truck had ground to a halt on the shoulders of the mountain road, and she had stridden down the road to flutter about Overton's racked body, firing her questions before darting away, ''walking on a little ways,'' as Overton had said, before she stopped. By any possible scenario, between midday and early afternoon, Ellie Dinker had been picked up, murdered, and her body hidden for later burial.

Quickly, Kinley turned the picture over and stared closely at the figures who had assembled on the courthouse steps to smile dutifully for Townsend's picture. He could see Wallace Thompson standing between Sheriff Maddox and Chief James. He could see their respective deputies arrayed on either side, Ben Wade, Riley Hendricks, all of them together in one military line, and to their left, the courthouse construction crew, Adcock and two other men whom Kinley imagined to be Quinn and Peabody. Overton, of course, was missing because he'd gone home sick only minutes before. But of the five-man construction crew, Overton was the only absent one. For standing grimly on the courthouse steps, his hands folded around the handle of a clay-encrusted pick, standing there where he could not have been if all Kinley's earlier assumptions had been right, standing there where he could not have been if Ellie Dinker were to die by his hands within the meticulous time frame Ray, himself, had established, was Luther Lawrence Snow.

Kinley felt his lips part silently, a short breath rush in as his mind took over, concentrating its considerable

330

attention on the line of men who stood together on the courthouse steps, searching for a shadowy afterimage, rather than a man, a face that occupied the dark reverse of Snow's unexpected presence, missing in body, but spiritually there, as Kinley suddenly saw it, the name printed on a campaign poster as if to take up the otherwise vacant space of his catastrophic absence: Thomas Warfield for Criminal Court Judge.

Thirty-Six

It was nearly midnight by the time Kinley got there, but a small yellow light was still burning in Snow's front room. Once on the porch, Kinley could see the old man inside. He was sitting at an angle from the door, his eyes trained on the fire that flickered softly in the small brick hearth.

Kinley knocked lightly at the door, waited a moment, and was about to rap again, this time as loudly and insistently as he felt the need, when suddenly the door creaked open and the old man stood before him again. He looked older than the day before, though not in the least frail.

"You back?" Snow said flatly.

Kinley paused just an instant for dramatic effect, then cast the most clever lure he had, the one that usually initiated an immediate and spontaneous defense. "There's no statutory limit on murder," he said.

Snow stared at him unflinchingly. "What murder?"

"Ellie Dinker."

Snow snorted. "I didn't kill Ellie Dinker," he said coldly.

"I know you know what happened to her," Kinley told him evenly.

Snow opened the door and stepped out onto the porch. For a moment the two of them stood in the chilly silence, the moonlight pouring softly over them. "I'm nearly eighty now. You think I give a shit what comes out on me?"

"At first, I thought you killed her," Kinley added. "But you didn't, did you? You couldn't have done that. You were at the courthouse when it was happening."

The old man walked to the edge of the porch and peered out at the dark landscape. Far in the distance, through a screen of trees, the diffused light of Sequoyah could be seen as it swept up from the valley below. "You best be on your way," he said.

Kinley did not move. "Who did kill her?" he asked as he stepped over to Snow. "And why?"

Snow did not answer. He kept his eyes fixed on the rim of the mountain and the distant grayish light that ascended from the valley town below.

Kinley shifted to the right and came up on Snow's side, standing shoulder to shoulder. "It was Warfield, wasn't it?" he asked tentatively.

Snow remained silent. His arms crawled upward and wrapped around his chest, as if to protect it from the cold. "I hate the way the winds always whip up from the canyon."

Kinley turned toward him, his eyes on Snow's immobile face. "Was it Warfield who framed Charles Overton?" he asked.

Snow's eyes slid over to him. "He's dead. What difference does it make?"

Kinley decided on a different direction. "Where did it happen?" he asked. "Where was she killed?"

Snow snapped a pack of cigarettes from his pocket, lit

one and took a long, slow inhalation, as if fortifying some inner part of himself against the encircling cold. "That's what the big cop wanted to know."

"Ray Tindall?"

Snow laughed. "Chief James," he said. "Poor old Cousin Felix." He grinned at the irony of it. "When he didn't have nothing, he come to me. He thought it being blood between us, I might tell him something about the goings on up here." He shrugged, as if giving in to the randomness of life, the way it came at you suddenly from around the corner, like a man snarling in your face. "But I told him to forget it. I said, 'Blood don't mean nothing to me. I got a friend or two, but blood, it ain't nothing to me.' "

"And he left it at that?" Kinley asked.

Snow smiled. "He didn't have no choice. He was boxed in. It was me or nothing." He shrugged. "So it was nothing."

Kinley decided to play his trump card. "You buried her," he said bluntly. "You must know what happened."

Snow inhaled a long draw on the cigarette. He did not seem troubled by the accusation. "Where'd I bury her then?"

"Under the flagpole down at the courthouse."

Snow took another pull on the cigarette, then released it in a sudden burst. "Well, that's a new one on me." His eyes returned to the dark valley and the distant cloudy light which seemed to rise from it persistently, like smoke from a still-smoldering city. "Something happened, but don't nobody know what it was." A slender grin crawled onto his face. "That's the glory of it," he said, almost wonderingly, as if in the presence of an epic criminality. "That Felix tried, and Warfield and Sheriff Tindall, he tried. But ain't nobody got the whole story of what happened to Ellie Dinker." He tossed the cigarette into the darkness, as a small, hard laugh broke from his lips. "Under the flagpole?" he scoffed. "You think that's where Ellie Dinker is?" He seemed to consider it a moment. "Well, hell, why don't you look?" His laughter pierced the air again as his eyes shifted back to Kinley, utterly still and penetrating, but with the same disturbing sense of demonic teasing that Kinley had noticed at the end of their last meeting: *You look like her.*

Kinley gave him a penetrating look. "You're bluffing," he said determinedly.

Snow lit another cigarette. "If she's under the flagpole," he said smugly, "then why don't you go dig her up?"

"I intend to," Kinley told him firmly.

Snow pulled himself to his full height and headed back to the front door. "You don't plan to do no such thing," he said contemptuously as he closed it, leaving Kinley alone on the dark porch. " 'Cause you're just like all the others. You don't want to know."

Once back at the house on Beaumont Street, Kinley slumped down in the front room. It was still a long time until the courthouse opened for business, but he knew he would not be able to sleep. Instead, he let his eyes wander over to the charred interior of the fireplace.

You're just like all the others. You don't want to know.

In his mind, he saw Ray burning the yellow sheets one at a time, sending up in flames all that he'd been working to assemble, the black ashes rising like tiny question marks into the blank, overhanging sky. He wondered if Snow were right about everyone, Warfield, Maddox, Ray and himself, everyone but old Chief James from the wrong side of the tracks, excluded from the inner circle, yet probing relentlessly at his dark edges, trying, against all odds, to find out what had happened to Ellie Dinker.

He stood up, walked to the office and took his seat once again at Ray's desk. Ray was there, too, permanently fixed in his mind, no longer the young red-headed boy in the corridor of Sequoyah High. Nor was he the young man crouched over the little marble table in Jefferson's Drug Store, his eyes trained on the black figure of Martha Dinker. He was not the local lawman, either, strong and incorruptible, the lone pillar of righteousness upon whom depended the innocent and the just. Instead, Kinley found that he could envision him only as he'd appeared in their final dwindling seconds together, a slightly overweight middle-aged man, running breathlessly by the train, the rain pelting him fiendishly as he struggled forward, trying with all his fading strength to utter one last word: *Kinley, are you* . . . ? Kinley felt his eyes drawn down toward the still unopened volumes of the third transcript Ray had checked out of the courthouse vault, then heard, as if it were whispered directly into his ears, the last of Ray Tindall's words, *Kinley, are you . . . sure?*

He opened the transcript at once and read the title page: *State of Georgia v. Edna Mae Trappman.* The trial had occurred in the spring of 1954, and once again, as in the case of Luther Snow, the prosecutor had been Thomas Warfield. The defendant, however, was not whom Kinley might have expected. She was young, only nineteen at the time of her arrest, and she was charged with a crime he'd never run across in any of his other cases, practicing medicine without a license, a charge brought on an accusation by none other than Dr. Joseph Stark.

As Kinley began reading, it was clear that in 1954, Stark had come to think of himself not only as the mythical village doctor, kind, gentle and certainly all-knowing, but as the guardian of Sequoyah's medical ethics as well. Trappman, he told the court, had broken those ethics by ministering to the ills of the gullible, the hopeless, the mindlessly in need.

WARFIELD: Now, Dr. Stark, when did you become aware of Edna Mae Trappman?
STARK: You mean, when did I first hear of her?
WARFIELD: Yes, sir.

STARK: I have my notes right here. That would have been in April of 1953.

WARFIELD: About a year ago, then?

STARK: Yes, sir.

WARFIELD: And could you tell the Court the circumstances of that entry in your notes, Doctor?

STARK: It was a conversation with a patient who had been suffering from an inoperable tumor.

WARFIELD: And this person had been treated by you?

STARK: To the extent that she could be treated, yes. But she was terminal. There was very little that could be done.

WARFIELD: Were you her only doctor?

STARK: I had always thought so.

WARFIELD: Did something come up in that conversation with—let's call her Patient X—did something come up in your conversation with Patient X to convince you otherwise?

STARK: It most certainly did. She—Patient X—told me that she'd been seeing someone else. A woman.

WARFIELD: And did Patient X name that person who had been treating her?

STARK: Yes, she did. She said her name was Edna Mae Trappman.

WARFIELD: Now, Dr. Stark, did you conduct, what we might call, a private investigation of Miss Trappman?

STARK: Yes, I did. At least as much as I could. I asked other patients about her, and I found that a few of them had heard of her. Some had even been treated by her.

WARFIELD: Treated. How?

STARK: Medically. She gave them things.

WARFIELD: Medicines?

STARK: If you can call them that. Mostly plants from the woods up there on the mountain. One concoction was made of some wildflowers that grow down in

337

the canyon. There were pieces of bark in it and sprigs of vine.

WARFIELD: And to whom did she give these—well—we can't really call them medicines, can we, Doctor?

STARK: Certainly not. She gave them only to the dying. They were her special clientele, you might say. Desperate people. They'd buy anything.

WARFIELD: But terminal cases, they were not her only patients, were they, Doctor?

STARK: Well, no. She had other treatments, if you can call them that. Anyway, she claimed that she could do a great many things.

WARFIELD: What things, Doctor?

STARK: Well, for one, that she could get rid of a child, things like that.

WARFIELD: Get rid of a child?

STARK: She was an abortionist.

WARFIELD: Did you verify any of these other things, Dr. Stark?

STARK: Not on my own, no, sir.

WARFIELD: You came to me instead, didn't you, Dr. Stark?

STARK: Yes, sir, Mr. Warfield. Since you were the District Attorney, I came to you.

Warfield had subsequently conducted his own investigation, assigning Ben Wade to go under cover by posing as a man with a recurrent and undiagnosable "stomach growth."

WARFIELD: And that's all you told her, wasn't it, Mr. Wade, that you had stomach trouble?

WADE: That's right. I said I'd had it a long time, and that it was killing me. I told her I'd been everywhere trying to get help, and it wasn't getting any better.

WARFIELD: And as a result of these conversations, did Edna Trappman agree to treat you for this condition?

WADE: Yes, she did.

WARFIELD: And did that treatment, in fact, take place?

WADE: Yes, it did.

WARFIELD: Could you describe it for us?

WADE: We met at this house on the mountain. When I first talked to her, she said that she was planning on leaving Sequoyah in a few days, and that if I wanted a treatment, she'd have to do it right away. I said that was fine with me, and we set up an appointment.

WARFIELD: And pursuant to that appointment, you met with Miss Trappman, didn't you?

WADE: Yeah, I did. We met at this place on the mountain. She didn't live there, but she sort of used it sometimes, I guess.

WARFIELD: Used it?

WADE: Like a home base or something. I couldn't quite figure it out. It was just a shack, more or less, but done over pretty well.

WARFIELD: When did you meet with Miss Trappman?

WADE: The first time was on February 4. It was at night. We always met at night. I guess she liked it better. Anyway, I drove up the mountain to the place she said she'd be at.

WARFIELD: And you found her waiting for you?

WADE: Yes, sir. She was standing along the canyon rim, and she was wrapped up in a long shawl that went almost to the ground. The wind was blowing hard, and she had long black hair, and it was really whirling around her head. She looked real strange. It gave me the creeps.

WARFIELD: But you didn't run away, did you, Ben?

WADE: No, sir.

WARFIELD: What happened after you got there?

WADE: I kept the car lights on, and they were shining right on her. She didn't come toward me. She just stayed there on the rim of the canyon, like she was about to jump off of it or something.

WARFIELD: All right, go ahead.

WADE: Well, I came up to her, and I told her who I was,

and she didn't say anything. She just handed me a little bottle, and I gave her some money.

WARFIELD: How much did you give her?

WADE: Five dollars.

These were not the last of the county funds turned over to Edna Trappman, however, for during the next two months, as she returned sporadically to Sequoyah, then moved on, Wade continued to request treatments, then receive and pay for them.

WARFIELD: So, finally, you shelled out close to two hundred dollars, didn't you, Ben?

WADE: Yes, sir.

WARFIELD: Well, after all that money, did your stomach get any better?

The laughter which subsequently broke over the courtroom at Warfield's facetious question had prevented the court reporter from hearing his answer: *INAUDIBLE*.

The laughter stopped immediately, however, when Trappman herself took the stand, and even within the bare, black-and-white minimalism of the transcript pages, Kinley could sense the tension that had arisen as Warfield began to question her. For there was something in her voice that penetrated and electrified the otherwise unadorned lines of the transcript, an eerie, crystalline clarity which Kinley always associated with an overmastering intelligence.

WARFIELD: For the record, would you state your name and address, please.

TRAPPMAN: Edna Mae Trappman.

WARFIELD: And your address?

TRAPPMAN: I live where I am.

WARFIELD: You have no address?

TRAPPMAN: I don't live any particular place.

340

WARFIELD: You're a drifter, isn't that right, Miss Trapp-
man, an itinerant?
TRAPPMAN: I live in lots of places.
WARFIELD: You live out of a car, isn't that right?
TRAPPMAN: Sometimes.
WARFIELD: Mostly peanut butter from the glove compart-
ment, is that it?

Trappman did not respond, but Warfield chose not to
pursue the point.

WARFIELD: All right, fine, we'll let the address go. We
know where you are right now, that's the main thing.
Well, let me ask you this, Miss Trappman, do you
have a job at this time?
TRAPPMAN: No.
WARFIELD: Well, how do you manage to keep that car
moving on down the road, then?

Rather than retreating into silence at Warfield's question, Edna Trappman rallied suddenly and gave a remarkable answer.

TRAPPMAN: I perform miracles.

The courtroom spectators had reacted with uneasy
laughter, but rather than waiting for the court to intervene,
Trappman had followed a remarkable response with an
even more remarkable action. She had quieted the court
herself.

TRAPPMAN: Silence!

It was one of the few times Kinley had ever seen a
court reporter use an exclamation point to describe the
emotional pitch of a witness's voice, and it must have
been in response to the sound of that single word, or the
look in her eye at the moment she'd delivered it.

SILENCE!

And from the transcript, Kinley could tell that the courtroom had fallen silent instantly, for without any intercession on the part of the judge, Warfield had immediately resumed his examination. But now he seemed ill at ease, perhaps shaken, as if by the same hard demeanor that had imposed silence on the court.

WARFIELD: Well, I . . . I have a few . . .
TRAPPMAN: Questions?
WARFIELD: Yes, a few more for you to . . .
TRAPPMAN: Ask, then.

She was now in full command, and the force of her control seemed to rise like a lingering smoke from the pages of the transcript.

WARFIELD: Well, about making a living . . .
TRAPPMAN: It's all in your head.
WARFIELD: What?
TRAPPMAN: What you see.
WARFIELD: You mean . . .
TRAPPMAN: When you look at me.
WARFIELD: I don't know what you . . .
TRAPPMAN: Looking for a cure.
WARFIELD: . . . mean when you . . .
TRAPPMAN: Looking for a way out.
WARFIELD: Are you saying that you . . .
TRAPPMAN: I provide the way.
WARFIELD: . . . are guilty?
TRAPPMAN: Yes.

And there, in that instant, the trial had ended. Warfield had immediately asked that Trappman's spontaneous confession of guilt be accepted by the court, and the court had done exactly that. Minutes later, it found Trappman guilty on a charge of practicing medicine without a license, adjourned for two hours, then reconvened, at which time the court asked the accused if she had anything to say before it pronounced sentence.

She did. It was plain-spoken, rather than eloquent, and it was clearly the voice of a person who'd had little formal education, but Kinley marvelled nonetheless at her intelligence and moral agility, her ability to turn everything around.

TRAPPMAN: I will say this, and nothing else. There is no way out. All the roads are blocked. There are just voices. Everything is in your head. You can feel them sometimes, things crawling through you. Tiny feet. They aren't real, these little animals. But we listen to them. We beg them. We pray to them. We want a way out of what is grinding us to death. It doesn't matter what it is. A cancer. Polio. People tell their children. They say, "Don't drink water when you are too hot. If you do," they tell them, "you will get polio." Is this practicing medicine? Or is it saying to a child, "Don't be afraid. I know the way out. You don't have to be afraid of getting polio and being crippled all your life. There is a way out, and I know what it is. Just don't drink water when you're hot, and then you'll be all right. You'll never get polio." And children, they take this, and they go play, and get hot, but they don't drink water, and polio, it doesn't scare them anymore. They think they know the way out. It isn't real. Nobody knows anything. It's only a wish that gets you through. I don't practice medicine. These people that come to me, they don't want medicine. I practice magic. And sometimes, when it's a problem in their heads, I give them magic for that, too. And when they can't get over something, I show them how. I show them that everything's a shadow. You see, they are all tied up in knots. They think it's all solid. Their troubles are like stones. But even a stone can disappear. You just pick it up and throw it in the river.

And, like magic, it's gone. There's no harm in any of this. Find what harm I've done, and make me pay for that. That's all I got to say.

A few minutes later, at a time the court reporter set at 2:37 P.M., the court did just that. It found the harm she'd done, and it made her pay.

COURT: Edna Mae Trappman, you have been found guilty of practicing medicine without a license, an act which has offended the good order and dignity of the State of Georgia. Accordingly, it is my duty to sentence you to three months in the County Jail, sentence to begin immediately on this day of April 2, 1954.

That was it, nothing more, and as he closed the transcript and dropped it onto the stack beside Ray's desk, Kinley let his mind roam through the details he'd gathered from his own investigation. Through each of them, it seemed to him now, he had solved some small part of the puzzle. But the whole still eluded him. If Warfield had murdered Ellie Dinker, why had he done it? Why had the body been hidden? Why had Overton been framed?

He could see Snow's eyes staring motionlessly toward him: *That's the glory of it. Ain't nobody got the whole story of what happened.*

Perhaps Snow was right, Kinley thought, now posing other questions of his own. If Warfield had felt he needed a motive in his case against Overton, Kinley now felt that he needed one in his case against Warfield. But there was no one left from that distant time. Maddox. Thompson. Warfield. Martha Dinker. Sarah Overton. Even Chief James. All of them were dead, all of them silenced. No wire still connected a single living person to the case.

Except one, of course, and as Kinley considered his next move, it struck him that this final living witness had

344

also entered the story an inordinate number of times. He was always there, lurking in the background, never in the forefront, always a witness, but never a participant, and yet, always somewhere near the action, as if to leave his fingerprints throughout the murder room.

Thirty-Seven

It was a Saturday, and so Kinley waited until the middle of the afternoon before pulling up to Dr. Stark's large, colonial-style house. It rested on a spacious lawn, presided over by great magnolia trees and bordered by a towering wall of dark green shrubs. Stark had lived there for as long as Kinley could remember, the kindly village doctor who'd delivered half the seniors of his own graduating class, Ray Tindall included.

Dr. Stark did not look surprised to see him when he opened the door. "Ah, Jack," he said amiably. "Nice to see you again." He stepped out of the door and motioned Kinley into a wide foyer, its high white walls hung with portraits of the ancestral dead.

"How's Serena?" Dr. Stark asked as he closed the door.

"Fine, I suppose," Kinley answered, his eyes fixed on one portrait, a man in a great red chair, his long white fingers folded over a black quill pen.

"He was a writer, like you," Dr. Stark said. He smiled quietly. "My great-grandfather." He walked across the foyer and opened another door. "We can talk in here," he said as he disappeared inside.

Kinley followed behind him, then took a seat in one of the room's large black leather chairs. "I've been doing a lot of work," he said.

Dr. Stark nodded as he settled into the identical chair which rested opposite Kinley. "So Billy tells me."

"Billy?"

"Billy Warfield," Stark said. "I still call him by the name he had when he was just a teenage boy." He smiled quietly. "Anyway, he's part of the country club grapevine, you might call it. We sometimes do a round of golf together. I'm not much competition to Bill. I think he more or less humors me. You know, an old man, a friend of his father's." He looked at Kinley significantly. "For Southerners, such attachments remain strong," he said, as if pointing out that Kinley could no longer number himself among his former compatriots, that his Yankeeness had now entirely consumed him.

"What did Mr. Warfield tell you?" Kinley asked.

"That you were looking into the Overton case," Dr. Stark said. "So, I knew you'd end up here at some point."

"Why?"

"Because I was a witness in that case," he said.

"I see."

"And because you'd already come to talk to me about Ray's death," he added.

Kinley nodded.

"And because Ray had come here, too," he said pointedly. "Came here with the same questions."

"What questions?"

"About Ellie Dinker."

"What about her?"

"He'd read in the transcript about my having been her

347

doctor," Stark said. "He wanted to know more about that." He smiled thinly. "For some reason he'd come to believe that Overton was an innocent man."

"Why did he think that?"

Stark shook his head. "I don't know."

"But he was asking about Ellie Dinker?"

"Yes," Stark said. "I think he wanted to establish some sort of connection between her and Overton. Either that, or with someone else."

Kinley reached for his notebook. "What did you tell him?"

Stark hesitated a moment, eyeing the notebook. "Sequoyah's an awfully small town, you know. People have to deal with each other carefully."

Kinley said nothing.

"We're talking about something that happened a long time ago," Stark added. "Most of the participants are dead."

"So there'd be no reason to keep anything back, would there?" Kinley asked.

Stark smiled. "That was Ray's argument."

Kinley offered him his warmest down-home grin. "Did it work?"

To Kinley's surprise, Stark nodded. "Yes, it did." He shrugged. "I liked Ray. He had a way of putting people at ease."

"What did you tell him?"

"Everything I knew," Stark answered bluntly, "which wasn't much, when you came right down to it. Just that at the time of her murder, Ellie Dinker was pregnant."

Kinley's pen froze in place.

"She came to me," Stark added. "I had always been her doctor."

"For prenatal care?"

Stark laughed. "No, Jack, for an abortion," he said. "You have to understand something. Ellie Dinker was not an average teenager. She'd been around, if you know what I mean, and she was very, shall we say, frank girl."

348

"Meaning what?"

"That she asked me straight out," Stark said. "She came into my office. I examined her and told her she was pregnant, and before I could get another word out, she just said, 'Can you get rid of it?' Just like that, without another thought." He walked over to a small liquor cabinet and opened it. "It's late enough in the afternoon, don't you think?" he said. "Will you join me?"

Kinley shook his head.

Stark poured himself a drink, talking again as he did so. "Of course, something like that was out of the question. It was 1954, after all. Performing an abortion was illegal. If I wouldn't do one now, I certainly wouldn't have done one then."

"But you never mentioned any of this at the trial," Kinley said.

"No, but I mentioned it to Tom Warfield," Stark said, "and he told me it was irrelevant."

"Irrelevant?"

Stark's face darkened slightly. "I reacted the same way. I mean, it was Overton's motive. At least that's the way it seemed to me."

"But Warfield didn't think so?"

Stark shook his head. "Absolutely not," he said. "He never brought it up when he questioned me, and since it was a medical confidence, I didn't tell anyone else." He took a short sip, then returned to his seat, rubbing the glass rhythmically between his hands. "But privately, it gave me what I needed to put my own doubts at rest."

"What doubts?"

"About Overton," Stark said. "I mean, I had the whole story. Overton had gotten that girl pregnant. That was the whole story, the key to everything. She was pregnant, and it was Overton's child, and she'd probably gotten awfully difficult about it." He shrugged. "It was easy to see what happened after that. They got into an argument, and Overton killed her. I guess he thought it was the only way out."

"Because he was the father of the child?"

"Of course."

"Were you Overton's doctor?"

"No," Stark said. "He never came to me about anything. Even that mythical stomachache he'd gotten at work the day of the murder."

"So you had no medical knowledge of him?" Kinley asked.

"None whatever."

"Well, I can tell you that Overton could not have been the father of Ellie Dinker's child."

The glass stopped dead in Stark's hands. "Why not?"

"He was wounded in the war," Kinley said. "In the groin. He couldn't possibly have gotten Ellie Dinker pregnant."

Stark watched him unbelievingly. "How did you know that?"

"From an Army medical report," Kinley said. "Ray saw it, too."

Stark nodded thoughtfully. "I guess that's why he asked those odd questions."

"What questions?"

"Well, once I'd told him about Ellie Dinker being pregnant, he started asking a lot of other questions," Stark said. "He wanted to know who else Ellie might have gone to."

"For an abortion?"

"Yes," Stark said. "And, to tell you the truth, at first I couldn't think of anyone, but he kept at it, and finally I remembered something."

"Edna Trappman," Kinley said.

Stark looked at him, surprised. "Yes, that's right."

"You testified at her trial back in 1954," Kinley added.

"Yes, how did you know that?"

"Because Ray read the transcript of that trial," Kinley told him. "Just a few weeks before he died."

Stark looked puzzled. "Why?"

"I don't know," Kinley admitted. "But what do you know about her?"

Stark's answer was unequivocal. "A terrible woman," he said. "The coldest person I ever met."

"I didn't know you'd ever met her," Kinley said. "I mean, face to face."

"Well, it wasn't exactly a meeting," Stark said, "more an observation."

"What do you mean?"

"I actually went to see what she looked like," Stark said. "I don't know why. Maybe I was just curious." He fell silent for a moment, his eyes narrowing, as if trying to get a view of her again. "She was very tall, very thin. She didn't look well, herself, but she looked . . ." He stopped, still trying to collect the varied elements of his observation. "She looked . . . the way she moved . . . it was like there was no one else in the world."

"No one else?"

"That's right," Stark said. "She was the sort of person who only uses things, but never really connects with them."

"Where did you see her?"

"Well, I'd seen her in court, of course," Stark said. "But never before the trial."

"But you saw her after the trial?"

"It must have been a day or two after she was released," Stark said. "It was only a glimpse, but it was enough." His eyes lifted slightly, as if trying to find a picture of her in his head. "I'd seen her in court, of course, but to see her out in the open, free again, it was different. It made you feel . . . vulnerable, as if there was something loose out there, an animal on the prowl."

"Where did you see her?"

"It was in early July," Stark answered. "She couldn't have been out of jail for very long, and I was heading home from my office. It must have been around ten o'clock. I was going slow, because it was raining.''

Kinley's mind was now in Stark's car, moving slowly through the darkness and the rain.

"I saw her get out of a car," Stark continued. "She got out and started walking up the sidewalk in the rain. She was drenched. Her hair was hanging down all over her." His eyes shot over to Kinley. "Like Medusa. I remember thinking that.''

Kinley could see her, a dark figure moving with a kind of slow, hypnotic motion through the rain. Her back was to him, but he could see her, as if through a screen of falling water, and in his own imagining, she floated in an unlighted and unpeopled world, a figure without a landscape, her feet rooted in nothing but the ebony air.

"Where did she go?" he asked softly.

Stark shook his head. "I don't know," he said. "She was carrying a bundle in her arms, and she couldn't have gone far. She never even turned off the headlights. I could see them disappearing behind me as I drove on down the street.''

"But you never saw her again?" Kinley asked with a strange urgency. "Never at all?"

"No," Stark said. "That was the last glimpse I ever had of her. Just moving down the sidewalk."

"Toward what?"

Stark shrugged. "Toward nothing," he said. "All the stores were closed by then. But that wouldn't have mattered. They were several blocks away anyway. There was nothing on that hill but the courthouse, and it wasn't even finished yet.''

Kinley glanced down at his notes. "Early July?" he said. "It was opened on the fourth."

"Then this must have been the day before," Stark said. "Because they were still working on it. I know, because I saw old trucks in the parking lot, and the crane was moving.''

Kinley closed his notebook, his mind now suddenly transported to the courthouse grounds, to where Overton toiled in the rain, to the granite slab which Adcock's crane was lowering into its unready pit.

"Did you tell Ray all this?" he asked.

"Yes, I did," Stark said. "And then he just got up to leave. 'I'll let you know what I find out,' those were the last words he said before he left." Stark looked as if a second thought had struck him suddenly. "And as it turned out, they were the last words he ever said," he added, "at least, to me."

Back in the office on Beaumont Street, Kinley thought of the last words Ray had spoken to him. *Kinley, are you sure?*

Since he'd never heard the last word, it was a question Kinley himself had put in Ray's mouth, but now it seemed no less real for his imagining it. He remembered how they'd faced each other that last time, Kinley on the train, Ray running breathlessly beside it. To answer the question, he'd gone to the last of the transcripts and found nothing but a vaguely interesting defendant in a less than interesting case. After that, he'd tried the last living witness and done no better. There seemed no place else to go, and he thought that perhaps he would have to live forever with a single eerie picture in his mind: Edna Trappman moving toward the courthouse with a bundle in her hand, the tire iron, perhaps, and Ellie Dinker's shoes.

Kinley, are you sure?

He picked the transcript's single volume up again, flipped to the front page, then the second, third, until he'd read it all a second time.

Still there was nothing more than the names. He started with Trappman, looked it up in both the town and county phone directories on the off chance that she might actually have settled down after her release from jail. But there was no listing for any Trappman in either Sequoyah or its surroundings.

Kinley leaned back in his chair, wondering if, perhaps, he had at last come to the end of the line. Within the body of the transcript itself, there seemed nowhere else to go.

Kinley, are you sure?

Once again, slowly and tediously, the minutes crawling into hours, Kinley concentrated his attention on the single volume of the transcript, reading it word by word until he had finished it entirely.

He rubbed his eyes tiredly when he'd finished.

Nothing.

Kinley, are you sure?

The voice was faint now, barely audible in Kinley's mind, but it was enough to draw his attention back down to the final page of the transcript once again, his eyes lingering on the Judge's sentence:

COURT: Edna Mae Trappman, you have been found guilty of practicing medicine without a license, an act which has offended the good order and dignity of the State of Georgia. Accordingly, it is my duty to sentence you to three months in the County Jail, sentence to begin immediately on this day of April 2, 1954.

Kinley, are you sure?

Now the voice was gaining strength, as if Ray's lifeless body had twitched inside his tomb, his green eyes fluttering beneath the closed lids, as Kinley's own eyes bore down upon his last hope.

In his imagination, he saw her being led away, just as Overton had been led away, the bailiff's hand on her elbow as he escorted her into the waiting arms of Sheriff Maddox and his jail. He saw the door close behind her, blocking her from his view, and for a fleeting instant, he felt a shudder as he whispered his two-word answer within the empty room.

Kinley, are you sure?

"Not yet."

Thirty-Eight

The County Jail was a single-story brick building whose basement had been converted into a kind of windowless dungeon for the county's incorrigibly disreputable, but more or less harmless, offenders. As Kinley had learned over the years, serious criminals were rarely kept in such facilities except for the relatively brief time during which they were being tried for their crimes, after which they were invariably transferred to far more secure institutions. As a rule, then, the county jails served as little more than unsightly, and usually unhygienic, holding pens for people on short time.

From the trial transcript, Kinley knew that Edna Trappman had been sentenced to three months. He also knew that most jails kept visitor's logs. Such logs were kept by the Jailer himself and rarely thrown away, since they were heavy and cumbersome, and most jailers, as Kinley had discovered, were immensely sedentary men, the type who found it easier to shove something into a backroom closet than take the more complicated steps necessary for the destruction of official county documents.

The County Jailer did not fit this stereotype, and for a moment, as Kinley glimpsed the short, wiry, continuously animated old man behind the receiving desk, he was afraid that the logs had been discarded altogether, that there would be no record left of the short time Edna Trappman had spent there.

"My name's Jack Kinley," he said as he stepped up to the desk.

The old man nodded peremptorily. "We don't allow visitors till afternoon," he said.

"I'm not a visitor," Kinley explained. "I'm just trying to run a few things down."

The old man looked at him as if he could not exactly make out what the phrase "run a few things down" meant.

"It's an old case," Kinley began slowly. "A woman was kept here back in April of 1954."

The old man nodded. "I was Jailer back then, too," he said as if to impress Kinley with his longevity.

"Her name was Edna Trappman."

The old man's face stiffened. "Oh, yes," he said quietly. "I remember her."

"She was sentenced to three months."

The old man nodded. "Something about medicine," he said, "some little thing."

"Little?"

"Compared to what she'd done."

"Like what?"

"I don't know for sure," he said. "But I've been a jailer for fifty years, and sometimes you get somebody in here, and they're not like the rest. They got this other feeling about them." He shivered slightly. "Creepy."

"And she had that?"

"More of it than anybody I ever had in this jail," the old man said. "Man or woman, she had more of it."

357

"Did she have visitors?"

"Yeah, she did," the old man said. "A few."

"Did you keep a visitor's log in those days?"

The old man nodded. "We've always kept one," he said, then added before Kinley could ask him, "You want to see it?"

Kinley smiled softly. "Yes, I do."

The old man disappeared for a moment, then returned with a large ledger. "This is '54," he said. "You should find every name listed." He opened the book, then explained how it worked. "Over there, that's the inmate's name," he said, his finger nearly touching the far left-hand column of the book. "And over here," he added, the finger drifting to the right, "that's the visitor's name."

"Okay, thanks," Kinley told him.

"Glad to do it," the man said but remained in place, watching as Kinley turned to April of 1954 and began moving his finger down the long line of names, his mind producing a story for each name he saw, all the drunks and small-time larcenists, hustlers and wife-batterers, the whole host of what New York cops called "grifters," the petty, back-alley street scum who lacked the sheer animal intelligence or courage to do something either masterfully cunning or heroically evil.

Edna Trappman.

The name appeared for the first time on April 2. On the same night she'd been sentenced, another woman had come to see her, signing her name in a minuscule black script: Ludie Rae.

Kinley took out his notebook, recorded the name, then turned the next page, his own finger moving as the old jailer's had, down the list of names which formed a long column on the left-hand side of the page.

Edna Trappman.

It was three days later, on April 5, and the visitor was once again Ludie Rae.

Again, Kinley recorded the name and date, then contin-

358

ued down the list, his finger moving in toward the page, nearly touching it, but held back, as if involuntarily, refusing to go too near.

Edna Trappman.

Three weeks had now passed, and Ludie Rae had come again, this time with someone else, a man who'd signed in, too: J. K. Creedmore.

Kinley jotted the names into the notebook, the finger moving again down the gray precipice of names, turning one page after another as the weeks passed and no one came to visit the lone dark-haired woman in cell number four. For a time, as he continued through the book, Kinley saw her in his mind, sitting in the dank, concrete cell, its steel door open, the cell itself stripped and unoccupied, its wire-mesh cot now bare of the single thin mattress which normally rested upon it, the seatless, rust-stained toilet only a few feet from the bed, as if to remind the sleepless of their soiled and degraded state.

Edna Trappman.

It was the middle of June now, and at last someone had arrived. It was Ludie Rae again.

Kinley noted the visit, then rushed on through the rest of June and into the first days of July, and finally to the afternoon of the second of July, when Trappman had been released, signing out on the prison log, her three-month sentence served.

Kinley shook his head disappointedly. According to the prison log, Thomas Warfield had never dropped in on Edna Trappman a single time during her three months of incarceration.

The old man seemed to grasp Kinley's mood of weariness and frustration. "Didn't find what you were looking for?" he asked.

Kinley shook his head.

"What was it you were after?"

"A particular name," Kinley told him as he closed the book. "Thomas Warfield."

The old man laughed.

Kinley looked at him quizzically. "What is it?"

"Well, hell, man, Tom Warfield didn't have to sign the log," he said, amazed by Kinley's political naivete. "You don't ever ask the District Attorney to do things like that. They're above procedure. Always have been."

Kinley pressed his hands down on the book and leaned into them slightly. "Are you telling me that Thomas Warfield did visit Edna Trappman?"

The old man nodded.

"When?" Kinley asked.

"Toward the end, as I recall," the old man said. "The last month she was here, he came down a couple times."

"Do you remember the dates?"

"Just the last one," the old man said.

"When was that?"

"The day she got out," the old man answered. "Warfield came down to get her, and they left together."

Kinley quickly opened the log again, racing toward the time and day of her release. He found it almost instantly: July 2, 12:31. He recorded the numbers, then turned back to the Jailer. "Do you know where they went?"

"Just that they got in Warfield's car," the old man said. "Then Warfield pulled off, and they headed up the mountain." He shook his head at the oddity of it. "That was strange, too, because there wasn't nothing happening up on the mountain, but we were having a big celebration down here."

Kinley eased himself back, then let the flow of the swing sweep him forward. Despite the late fall chill, he felt warm, finished, satisfied.

He had it now. Everything. The whole story, the one that had eluded everyone from Martha Dinker, still searching for her daughter among the wells and vacant lots of Sequoyah, to Ray, tormented by his own relentlessness, burning his notes out of what Kinley now understood as unbearable frustration.

360

He was still contemplating the intricacies of the plot when Dora arrived almost an hour later. Without a word, he led her into the house, poured her a drink, then made a small fire in the hearth, before joining her on the sofa by the window.

"I think I know it all now," he said.

She nodded. "Then you can go home soon."

"Yes."

"Good," she said. "You must miss it."

"Yes, I do," he said without apology. "I hope you'll come up and . . ."

She waved her hand sharply. "Please, don't say it."

"I'm sorry."

She took a sip from the glass, straightening her shoulders somewhat, as if preparing to hold her ground. "Well, what did you find out?"

"Ellie Dinker wasn't murdered," Kinley said. "At least, I don't think she was." He waited for Dora to ask a question, then went on when she didn't. "She was pregnant, and Thomas Warfield was the father. He arranged for an abortionist to do the work on Ellie, and my guess is, she died during that procedure."

Dora said nothing. Her eyes drifted over to the fire.

"He had a body on his hands," Kinley went on, "and since an autopsy would have discovered both that Dinker was pregnant and that she'd died because of a botched abortion, he hired Luther Snow to get rid of the body." He shook his head, still amazed at the audacity of it. "Ellie Dinker is buried under the flagpole on the courthouse lawn."

Once again, Dora said nothing, but only took another sip from the glass, her eyes still level on the fire.

"Warfield framed your . . . Overton," Kinley told her, his own odd code of truth stopping the word "father" before it could escape his mouth. "Then prosecuted him."

"He murdered my father," Dora said softly.

Kinley nodded, thought of Talbott alone in his big

house, of the impossibility of telling her all he knew. "I think so," he said.

"What are you going to do now?"

For a moment, Kinley thought she'd asked the question in the same sense he'd been asking it of himself before she arrived, then realized that she meant something different altogether: what was he going to do with all he knew.

"I want Overton cleared," he answered. "And the only way I can do that is by telling William Warfield what I know."

Dora nodded slowly. "Did Ray know all this?"

"I don't know, Dora," Kinley answered. "I don't know how much he really found out."

"Because he wouldn't tell me anything," Dora added. "Why?"

"Maybe he didn't get far enough to be sure."

"And you have?"

"Yes," Kinley said, then felt his hands twitch involuntarily, as if grasping for some final truth. He pressed them flat against his legs, stopping their movement with a single brutal thrust. "Yes," he repeated. "Absolutely."

"Good," Dora said.

Throughout the long night that followed, as he noticed in the morning, she said hardly another word, and as he rose to prepare himself for his confrontation with William Warfield, Kinley wondered if she'd been right in what she'd said days before, that to know for sure was not the highest value, and mystery not the terror Ray had surmised, but only the cagey, cunning route by which each life managed to evade for as long as possible its inevitable arrest.

Thirty-Nine

William Warfield welcomed Kinley into his office early Monday morning, and for a slender instant, his openness and amiability made Kinley feel the urge to make a quick about-face and disappear down the corridor as Ray Tindall had, leaving the body dead and buried in the ground.

It's better to know, don't you think?

Once again, Kinley nodded silently to his old friend's question, then took a seat, his eyes following Warfield's slow descent into his own chair, noting the trouble that seemed to gather like a gray web across his face.

"You look very solemn," Warfield said. "I hope you haven't found anything too distressing."

"Mr. Warfield," Kinley began very softly, "there are a few things I have to tell you."

By late that same afternoon, the backhoe was in place, and Kinley stood with Warfield, Ben Wade and a few other casual observers as it went to work on the court-house lawn.

For almost an hour, Warfield remained nearly motionless in place, his body in a gray winter coat, his hands folded together, as if holding on to something small and precious. Kinley stood beside him, his eyes trained on the hoe's heavy metal scoop as it sank deeper and deeper into the ground, slowing steadily as it neared the mark.

Finally, it halted altogether, and two workmen climbed into the open pit to do the last of the work with hoes and shovels.

For a long time, Kinley watched them as they dug further and further down, their heads disappearing beneath the dry grass, until nothing at all could be seen of them except the tools of their trade and the large clumps of reddish earth they tossed in all directions as they continued down.

Suddenly, they stopped, and Kinley heard Warfield suck in his breath and hold it tensely until the word came, a voice out of the pit.

"Mr. Warfield, could you come over here?"

Kinley looked at Warfield knowingly. "They've found her," he said.

The two men moved over to the pit, both of them staring down at the men inside, red with clay.

"We've hit solid rock," one of them said, "and we ain't found nothing yet."

Kinley stared, thunderstruck, into the red mouth of the pit, his eyes fixed on the granite slab upon which the workmen stood.

"Well, Mr. Kinley," Warfield said pointedly. "Satisfied?"

Kinley felt his shoulders slump.

Warfield continued to gaze at him irritably. "Well, what now?"

Kinley shook his head distractedly. "I don't know," he said.

* * *

He met Dora late in the afternoon, the first blue shade falling around them as they sat together on her front steps.

"I can't prove anything," he said. "I know Ellie Dinker was pregnant. And I know that Thomas Warfield left the courthouse with an abortionist named Edna Trappman. I even know they headed up the mountain road to where Ellie Dinker was waiting for them by that road marker." He shook his head. "But I can't get any farther than that."

Dora thought a moment. "Maybe you should start from the other end," she said.

"What do you mean?"

"Maybe you should work back from Ellie Dinker's death." She paused, her eyes concentrating on his. "Or from Ray's," she added.

"In the canyon, you mean?"

She nodded.

"But there's nothing down there," Kinley said. "At least not where they found him. I know that place. It's just in the woods by the river. There's nothing that . . ."

"But he must have been down there for some reason," Dora told him insistently.

Kinley recalled his old friend, the strength he'd used up in the long haul down to the canyon floor, his heart pumping against its own frail walls as he'd struggled forward through the undergrowth.

"Yes," he said finally, "there must have been a reason."

Minutes later he was in the car, driving the rest of the distance across the mountain's broad plateau, toward the most desolate stretches of the canyon. He could feel his old exhilaration building as he continued on. In part, it was the sense that he wasn't finished yet. But there was something else as well, a feeling that he could soon make good his escape from the confines of something he'd never understood, but had always felt each time he'd returned home to Sequoyah. It was the same feeling he'd had when he'd left Sequoyah the first time, heading north for his education, the same feeling he'd had every time he'd left from one of his brief visits to his grandmother's after that. It was even the same feeling, he understood now, that he'd had on the train that day as he'd looked down at Ray's face in the rain.

Kinley, are you . . . ?

He pressed Ray's question from his mind, crowded it out, first with thoughts of New York, then of Boston, and finally of Walpole CI, the prison where Fenton Norwood remained, waiting for him, his latest specimen. Repulsive as Norwood was, with his fat face and reptilian eyes, Kinley realized that he could hardly wait to get back to the little green room where they'd faced each other, his tape recorder whirring softly as he watched Norwood's pudgy, pink face. In a sense, he thought of it as a haven, one of those Old Testament cities of sanctuary his grandmother had read to him about. He remembered her eyes on those occasions, the irises shaded so faint a blue that in a certain light the shading had seemed to disappear entirely, leaving her eyes blank and lusterless, two pale orbs with nothing but the black hole of their pupils peering down at him.

He was still thinking of her as he drove toward the rim of the canyon. He passed the turn that would have taken him to Ray's grave, but found he couldn't do the same as he approached a second turn a few minutes later, this one to the left, a narrow dirt road that few people ever ventured down anymore, but which he knew better than any other area around the canyon.

In his own distant way, he'd already said good-bye to Ray and his grandmother, but with both of them now gone, he felt compelled to add one last good-bye to the old house he'd lived in for almost his entire childhood.

He made the turn slowly, then nosed the car through the thickening brambles that stretched out from along both sides of the road. Long, green tendrils reached toward him like bony, rotting fingers. He could hear them slapping against the sides of his car until they slowly drew back as the road widened once again, and he pulled into what was left of his grandmother's frontyard.

As he got out of the car, peering across the weedy lawn, he was not sure why he'd decided not to sell it himself after his grandmother's death. Instead, he'd simply left the whole business to Ray, along with all the old woman's things, to do with as he saw fit. "Don't you want anything?" Ray had asked him, and he'd answered with nothing more than a crisp, "Just whatever you get for it." A check for seven thousand dollars had come not long after that, part from the sale of the property, part from some cash Ray had found in a biscuit can on a high shelf in the kitchen. That had been the last of it, and Kinley had gladly turned the rest of Granny Dollar's modest possessions over to Ray, all her papers and artifacts, even down to the great moldering stacks of the *Police Gazette* she'd piled into the potting shed behind the house, and which he assumed Ray had tossed, with almost everything else, into an open fire.

The old house was still standing as sturdily as it always had, though the weeks since her death had already begun to give it a look of abandonment. A scattering of fall leaves dotted the once-pristine front porch, and a fallen branch rested diagonally across the front stairs, so that, overall, his childhood home already looked as if it were now inhabited by nothing but spiders and field mice. And yet it had been his home for many years, the place where Granny Dollar had rocked him through one asthmatic night after another, her voice dark and sinister as it moved through the grisly tales of the *Police Gazette*. He could still hear that voice as he had heard it then:

The earth that covered her body was loose and from its shallow covering Detective Fletcher could see a single white hand as it rose from the dark earth, half-eaten by animals but still bearing upon its ravaged fingers the jade rings of Madame Poissant.

He allowed himself a short laugh at the weirdness of it all, then walked out to the canyon's edge. Far below, and several miles to the north, Ray Tindall had clutched his heart, stumbled forward and died on the canyon floor. He had fallen face down, his fingers grasping at the ground in that way Kinley could feel his own fingers grasping, first at his trousers, then at thin air, the way they often did, as if reaching for an invisible hand.

To stop them, Kinley lifted his hands to his face, then curled his fingers forward, closing them into a fist, before, in a single, shivering instant, he froze, his eyes riveted on his own fingernails.

dark earth

His memory was his great ally, faithful in everything, beyond escape once a fact or impression had entered it.

dark earth

He remembered the exact words of Dr. Stark's autopsy report. "Fingernail scrapings revealed the presence of a moist reddish clay."

But now, as he stared down into the canyon, his eyes riveted on the wildly rushing river, he realized that there was no red clay along its winding, churning banks. As far as it stretched along the canyon floor, the river cut instead through a dark, pebbly earth. The red clay of the area lay further back, perhaps half a mile from the river's edge. With the kind of heart attack Ray'd had, it would not have been possible for him to have walked more than a few feet from where he had been stricken.

As he stood on the rim of the canyon, poised motionlessly above it, Kinley tried to recall the pictures Deputy Taylor had taken of Ray's body as it lay, with one arm outstretched, as if reaching for an invisible treasure. His shirt and trousers had been fully in place, no violence done to them either before or after death, his hair neatly combed, his reading glasses had still been tucked into his pocket.

Reading glasses, Kinley thought. In Ray's case, that had been exactly what they were. Quickly, Kinley recalled all the times he'd ever seen Ray in the open since he'd first gotten his glasses almost ten years before. Since that time, they'd hunted a few times, fished and rambled the woods together. On none of those occasions, Kinley remembered, had Ray ever taken his glasses. Instead, he would drop them in the little wooden tray beside the door. But on the day of his death, Ray had taken them with him. What, in the middle of the forest, beside a tumbling stream, at the bottom of a distant canyon, had Ray Tindall needed to read not long before he died?

He glanced back at his car, then at the old house, his eyes concentrating on the porch where Ray had found his grandmother, bolt upright in her chair, her gray hair draped across her wide, unbending shoulders. Suddenly, a wild array of images began to swirl chaotically in his mind, Ray's reading glasses tumbling in space, but not alone, the sprig of vine Ray had pressed into a book tumbling with it, along with a swarm of faces: Granny Dollar's, stone dead on her porch; Ray's breathless in the rain; Ellie Dinker's, stern and inflexible, demanding to be rid of her unwanted child; Charlie Overton's, ashen and disoriented as he shuffled toward his death.

He felt his hands again, twitching in their spasmodic dance. Reflexively, he moved to stop them, then released his grip, as if compelled to do so by deeper and more urgent needs.

Kinley, are you . . . ?

Suddenly he felt as if his mind had released some strange grip it had had upon him for as long as he could remember, a sense of being held back, closed off, as if some part of him had been shut up in a box or strapped down in a chair. For an exhilarating moment, he felt unbound, and he sensed it as an entirely new experience.

He moved forward effortlessly, as if carried by an immense, invisible hand, down the bleak, wintry trail that led into the canyon. He did not know where he was going, except that it was toward where Ray's body had been found, his new starting point. He could feel the earth turn smoothly beneath him, as if he were suspended in air, the globe rotating under him, waiting for his appointed destination to roll into position at his feet.

When he reached it, he touched the ground, then lifted himself again. He knew he was exactly there, standing between the same trees he'd seen in the police photographs of Ray's body. He'd recognized the place the first time he'd glimpsed it in Taylor's pictures, and even at that moment, it had seemed to him that he and Ray had been there many times, though actually it had been only once, a late summer day only a week before he'd left for college.

Now, as he stood beside the river, he could see the large stone they'd rested on, hear the conversation they'd had:

Well, Kinley, you may not be back down in the canyon for a long time.

No, I guess not.

Maybe never.

Maybe.

That's what you want, in a way, isn't it?

What?

To leave forever. To be rid of it.

I think so.

Kinley, are you sure?

The stone was bare now, and as Kinley watched it from the bank, the river seemed to churn madly, tossing its white foam, as if beneath the green roof of its surface millions of angry spirits clamored to be free.

He turned away and glanced at the dark earth beneath his feet, the same that should have been beneath Ray's fingernails, instead of the red clay Dr. Stark had found there.

370

For a moment, Kinley tried to reorient himself, to use as his final destination that unknown place where Ray's fingers had clawed the ground. Dr. Stark had told him that Ray's clothes had been clean except for the forest debris they'd gathered when he fell. There'd been red clay beneath his nails, but none of it on his clothes. The shovel, he thought, remembering the night he'd gone down into the well. He'd looked for all the necessary tools before his descent, but had not found a shovel. His mind shifted instantly into its trusty logic: *He took a shovel. He was going to bury something. No. He did bury something. He buried it in red clay.*

He turned away from the river and moved deeper into the surrounding woodlands, toward the nearest stretch of indigenous clay, so red, moist and malleable that he'd often thought of it as the flesh of earth itself. In death, Ray had lain facing south, and if he'd been returning from whatever mission had sent him into the canyon, forced him down into it at the risk of his own life, his heart no more than a clogged and sputtering chamber of tubes and valves, then he'd accomplished his task to the north of where his strength had finally deserted him.

Walking northward, then, still the servant of his mind's relentless logic, Kinley moved rapidly, his pace increasing his velocity with each step, his eyes fixed on the ground, meticulously searching it for the subtlest changes in color and texture.

Slowly the ground began to give up its darker hues, growing brown beneath Kinley's feet, then, as he continued on, lighter still, but with the first thickening orange that he knew would turn to a moist and glistening red.

Within half a mile, the last hints of the orange had been leached from its bed of dark, engulfing red, and Kinley stood, as if on a distant but disturbingly familiar beach, his mind reeling within the transformation of the scene, pictures reverberating like echoes in his mind. The shadows were now darker as the canyon wall hung over him, and the trees seemed to fling themselves upward from the depths of an even denser foliage, gray and leafless, but consuming nonetheless, as if it were a tropical forest that had gone to ruin, leaving nothing but its gray, contorted skeleton behind.

He headed north again, his mind now moving backward, as if in opposition to his body. He could feel the atmosphere thickening, as it had in the well, and he stopped for a moment, breathed in a long, hard breath and let his eyes lift tremblingly toward a light he hoped for, but could no longer see beyond the bony tangle of the trees.

He dropped his eyes again, resigned to the canyon's choking air, then moved on, more slowly now, apprehensively, as he thought Ray must have moved as well, the old legends of the canyon coming to life in his mind, gory tales his grandmother had spun as she'd rocked him through the night, and which had seemed even more grisly than the ones she'd read from the *Police Gazette*.

Long time ago, in the canyon, there was this house . . .

He stopped, cocked his head to the right, as if listening to her voice as it filtered through the trees, his mind diving further and further back, like a creature struggling breathlessly through thick black water.

Long time ago, in the canyon, there was this house surrounded by vines.

He glanced around, his eyes searching for some way out of the suffocating air. He could feel his lungs heaving in that aching, airless way he remembered from his asthmatic childhood, his ribs like a vise pressing in upon his life.

The vines were green and thick, and there was no way to get through them.

He remembered the sprig of vine Ray had pressed into the book, his only gift to him, presented, it seemed to Kinley now, like a twisted legacy.

No way to get through them but to slash and slash and slash.

372

He started moving again, straight ahead, northward, as if in defiance of the earth's unfeeling tilt, north against the eternal flight of migratory birds, the bankless channels of the wind and the unbending sway of rivers, mountains, ice, north as he had always gone, against the course of nature.

He speeded up, hurrying like a panicked child, desperately toward home, his feet scurrying over the flat red earth, the limbs slapping at his face and chest, the thickening vines twining their reptilian tentacles along his feet and legs.

Getout!Getout!Getout!

He slammed against a tree, breathing now in short, painful gasps, the choking asthma of his childhood clogging his lungs with the same terrifying fury he could remember through all his stricken nights.

He spun around the tree, his hands at his throat, and stopped, his eyes fixed on the place before him.

It was there, like a vision, but real. A small house in its solitary ruin, surrounded by a dense circle of vines, thick and barbed, but their grim geometric perfection now broken by a crude, jagged rift.

The shovel Ray had used to slash his way through the vines lay like an arrow in Kinley's path, the sharp point of its red-caked scoop pointing to the house a few yards beyond it, silent in the gray light, its door flung open and half-unhinged. At the bottom of the front stairs, he could see a shallow hole, a mound of red clay poised beside it. As he stumbled toward it, he saw that the hole was empty, as if Ray had changed his mind at the last minute.

He glanced up into the house, his eyes lighting on the solitary table at the center of the room. He could see a small box on top of it, and he realized that it was the tin biscuit box his grandmother had kept on a high shelf, beyond his grasp, and that Ray must have retrieved it when he'd cleared out the old woman's things.

He moved up the stairs, and as he passed through the

door, he could feel his breath miraculously returning to him, as if he were entering a less constricted atmosphere.

He stopped just inside the door, then paused a moment to take in the room. It was furnished with only a few dusty chairs and the single wooden table that rested at its center. The walls were blank and unadorned, except for a few hanging lanterns which seemed to cling to them like the dried husks of gigantic insects. There was no back entrance to the house, but to the right a single closed door led to an adjoining room.

As he walked to the table, Kinley felt his body tighten, as if his skin had suddenly contracted, squeezing in upon his bones. He glanced toward the door to his right, felt an odd shudder, and let his eyes drop toward the table, as if aimed with a terrible precision upon the little tin box and the small white candle that rested beside it, half-burned, but still erect, its slender white shaft now turned yellow by long years of disuse. Initials were carved in the wood of the table: WT, AJ, TW, FM, JS.

He remembered something Betty Gaines had told him, that Thompson, Warfield and others of the city fathers had had a place in the canyon, and he realized that this shrouded little house he and Ray had stumbled upon so many years before had been that place in its abandonment. AJ was Andrew Jameson. FM was Floyd Maddox. JS was Joseph Stark. It was here they'd come to drink the bonded liquor Snow had sold them, to tell their exploits and war stories. He thought of Ellie Dinker. The place they'd brought their women.

His eyes bore in upon the tin box. He could remember seeing his grandmother draw it down from time to time, but always secretly, so that once, when he'd raced into the room, she'd slammed its top down noisily, her lips twisting rudely as she screamed at him:

Getout!Getout!Getout!

But all those days were behind him, and so Kinley shook his head against the voice's harsh command, pressed his hands against the sides of the box and slowly opened it.

He could see a small stack of papers, along with a single sprig of vine which rested on top of them like a grim adornment. As he drew it from the papers, Kinley recalled the almost identical strand that Ray had placed inside the book he'd told Serena to give him, and he realized suddenly that it was the one clue Ray had left behind to guide him into the canyon.

He dragged the candle nearer to the box, lit it quickly, then lifted the papers from the box. The first was a single square of notepaper exactly like the one Ray had hung over his desk. This time, however, the message was different:

Dear Kinley:

I found these papers when I cleaned out Granny Dollar's house. I'd planned to burn them along with everything else. But I couldn't. I thought I'd bury them here, but I couldn't do that either. So I left them in plain sight, in case you want to know. If you've found them, I know it's because you've looked very hard.

Ray

Kinley laid the note aside, Ray's voice still whispering softly in his mind, then put the other papers flat upon the table. For a moment, he hesitated, as if he were a suicide, the pistol barrel already at his head, the finger squeezing down upon the trigger until it reached that last lightning interval between the precipice and the void.

It's better to know, don't you think? No matter what the cost?

He leaned forward and stared down at the papers. He knew that Ray would have arranged them in the order in which he wanted them to be read.

The first was a birth certificate which had been issued to George and Bertha Kellogg on May 7, 1900, in Waycross, Gerogia. It was little more than a small square of crumbling yellow paper, and it recorded the birth of a daughter, Ludie Rae Kellogg.

Kinley's mind shot back to the jail log, to the short list of visitors who'd called on Edna Trappman, to the Ludie Rae who'd signed her name in that tiny, nearly indecipherable script which signaled, according to his own light acquaintance with graphology, an intensely powerful mind.

He turned to the next page, his eyes moving intently over its brief contents. It was a marriage license, issued in Chattanooga, Tennessee, on September 5, 1927, to Samuel P. Dollar and Ludie Rae Kellogg, and it was bound by a rubber band to a second document, this one a death certificate which recorded the death by "locked bowels" of Samuel Dollar on June 10, 1929.

Kinley's hand clutched at the document, crushing it slightly before he willed his fingers to open and release it once again. So it was Granny Dollar who'd come down the mountain to visit Edna Trappman in her cell, he thought.

But why?

Quickly, he turned the page facedown on the table, then fixed his eyes on the yellowing paper which rested beneath it. It was a second birth certificate, this one also issued in Chattanooga, and dated August 9, 1932. It recorded the live birth of a female child whom its unwed parents, Ludie Rae Dollar and Ernest Trappman, had named Edna Mae.

"Her daughter," Kinley whispered, unbelievingly. He felt a blue, arctic wind rush over him, lost and frozen. In his mind he could see his grandmother as she sat rigidly in her chair with his own small body in her arms, staring down at him with eyes that were like his, passionless and aloof.

You look like her.

He heard Luther Snow's words in his mind.

You look like her.

But he didn't look like Granny Dollar, Kinley thought, defensively, imploringly, as if arguing the merits of some cause he couldn't understand.

You look like her.

He stepped back from the table, his eyes darting about desperately. Suddenly, the room seemed to expand in all directions, the ceiling shooting up to a great height above his head, the walls reeling outward, turning the small room into a great chamber, as the air inside it thickened and grew warm with summer heat.

He could feel his own body shrinking as the room swelled to its former immensity, and he knew his mind was returning him to his earliest years. He could feel his small lungs struggling painfully for breath as he searched the face that hung above him, so much younger than all his other visions of it, still unlined, the hair only slightly streaked with gray. *Granny Dollar.*

He was in her arms now, his eyes moving urgently over the contours of her face. Voices sounded softly around him, and he knew that they were not alone. He could sense shadows all about, feel his own tiny body twisting in his grandmother's arms, always afraid, always watchful, but trying to see, hungry for every detail, his ravenous mind working desperately even then to order and retrieve, while his eyes locked on the shadows that danced around him.

A face swam toward him from the maze of shadows, a white dot perched on a tall green hill, with a voice that was more like a bark, harsh, bitter, animal-like: *This your little boy?*

He did not hear an answer, but only saw her mouth jerk down, as if repulsed by the sight of him, then another face draw near him after hers had retreated, a different face, young and brown and warm, peering at him softly from the black tangle of her hair.

You look like her.

"Mother," Kinley breathed. He could feel her as he had felt her then, as he had felt her that day in the small house, while still in Granny Dollar's arms, but reaching out to his mother needfully, his small, white fists clutching at her hair while his eyes clung to her fiercely, trying to draw her more clearly into view.

But she drew away again, dissolved into the smoldering summer haze, even as he fought to get her back, his eyes shooting left and right frantically as he worked to locate her among the shifting shapes and voices, men, women, a clutter of forms.

The voice barked again: *Did you tell your precious little boy about this, Mr. Warfield? Huh? Did you tell Billy?*

A column of white swept over to the small green mound, its voice softer, deeper, male: *I don't think that's necessary, Ellie.*

Be a good joke though, wouldn't it? Just to spring it on him while he's getting ready to go off to college. Just say, "Hey, Billy, you know that little tramp you screwed in the canyon? That Dinker girl? Well, I found out you knocked her up, but don't worry, I handled it for you."

Billy will never know anything about this.

Yeah, well, that's the way it is with you people. You can always fix things up. But I . . .

Silence!

It was his mother's voice, rising from the welter of the others, harsh and commanding as he sometimes heard it. Then silence, until her face swept up to him, her eyes on the old woman who held him tightly to her arms. "Take him up to the house, Mama. We'll be up when it's over."

Then she floated away from him languidly, her hair a dark, ragged sail. But he could still smell her skin like warm bread, and his hands reached out for her achingly as she grew small in the vast distances of the smokey room, and he realized that he was moving away from her, toward the open door, then down the stairs and through the encircling vines in a rush of green that led

378

him upward steadily, his breath loosening as he rose, until he felt himself mounted on a high gray shelf, the tops of the trees stretching up from the ground below him, his grandmother's arms cradling him gently as she spoke:

Long time ago, in the canyon, there was this house surrounded by vines.

Kinley grasped the edges of the table in front of him, his fingers clutching at it in quick, uncontrollable spasms as his mind hurled him backward, groping through its lightless chamber for that slender ribbon of nerve and tissue that still bore the shadowy image of what his eyes had seen and his ears heard so many years before. It was as if he could feel the actual, physical churning of his brain inside his skull, its wild, electric pulse, building ominously, heedlessly, explosively, until, in a single, miraculous instant, it opened like a dark bud, and he was in his mother's arms, his face nestled sleepily in her hair despite the hard, frantic pace of the rocker as it slung him back and forth, its harsh, rhythmic squeak orchestrating his mother's low, murmurous chant, her words like drops of rain in the humid, summer air:

I need more time, more time, more time.

We don't have more time, Edna. Creedmore's gone. It's up to us.

Good riddance. Makes me ashamed I ever used his name.

We got to do something soon, Edna. She's dead, and it's just a matter of time before Warfield finds out about it.

It's the way he always wanted to settle things. Get rid of it. Get rid of it. He wanted me to do it, too.

He felt her arms tighten around him, her voice in his ear: *Never.*

That's passed. Now we have to do something else.

I need more time, Mama, to find a way out.

It passed like a flock of birds, the hours like black shadows sweeping across the weedy yard, until, from the depths of his sleep, he heard the grind of the engine as the old truck staggered into the yard, its dusty cab shuddering as the motor died.

From over his mother's shoulder, he could see Granny Dollar as she talked to the ragged, dusty figure who crouched brokenly beside her, groaning pitifully, his arms wrapped around his stomach.

He was gone in only a little while, the remedy given, the money exchanged, and as the old truck departed, he'd seen his grandmother move toward him through the hot, suffocating air, move like a phantom glimpsed beyond the black tangles of his mother's hair, heard her voice sound firmly over the rocker's dreadful, aching cry:

You heard him, Edna. He seen that girl on the road this afternoon, before you and Warfield picked her up. People must have seen him with her.

You know him?.

He works with Luther. I could find out about him.

The old woman continued forward, her hand moving up under her dress, drawing a long, black snake from beneath her apron, curved, but unbending, a dark, frozen shape. She waved it softly in the thick night air. *I got this from the back of his truck while you were giving him the treatment.*

The black curtain of her hair shifted softly as she nodded.

We have a way out now.

He felt her rise from her chair, then his body float forward into his grandmother's wiry grasp, his place in his mother's arms now taken by the black rod she nestled at her breast.

He was moving again, his eyes searching the darkness, trying to keep his mother's shape in view, his hands grasping for the shifting tangles of her hair until she finally stopped again, the great room spreading out around her. Her face turned toward him. He reached for it, but she drew back.

Leave him in here.

He was on the floor now, his hands pressed down upon the bare floor, as he watched the door to the other room open, then close. He leaned backward, his tiny hands grasping at the table leg as he pulled himself up, then tottered forward uneasily, his ears tuned to the odd, hollow sound he could hear beyond the door: *Fump. Fump. Fump.*

Suddenly the door shot open and he felt himself soar upward into his grandmother's arms, his eyes staring over her shoulder and into the room, where his mother's shadow danced on the wall, the slender bar falling a final time upon the shapeless mass which lay on the bed beneath it: *Fump.*

And it was morning again, the long night remembered as no more than a passing shadow as he rested in his mother's arms, the two of them together on the porch, the other woman dissolving into the green woods, the even greener dress folded in her arms.

After that, there was only rain in great thundering sheets, falling with the night, battering at the roof while they wrapped it all in quilts, the slender white arms already tied with a strip of white cut from the mound of green, a pillowcase drawn over the blackening face before they lugged it heavily to the waiting car.

Do it right, Edna. Just plant the stuff in his truck, then take the body across the state line. And don't come back here until I tell you.

The engine groaned to life, loud as the hard drum of the rain upon the hood and windshield.

I'll be back to get him, Mama.

The rain swept across his face, slapping at his eyes. They closed tightly against it, and when they opened again, she was gone. But all through the passing hours his hands still reached for her, grasping frantically for the vanished face, its wreath of thick black hair, while the long night stretched numbly into day, and the air along the canyon rim so clogged his lungs with smoke and dust and loss that the old woman finally took him up in terror and amazement: *My God, Kinley, you're turning blue.*

Kinley drew in a long, unencumbered breath, then let his eyes wearily descend to the last document Ray had left for him.

It was a newspaper clipping about a fiery automobile accident which had occurred during the rainy, early morning hours of July 4, 1954. It had happened at the southern end of the canyon where its dark, jagged tip stretched into the neighboring state of Alabama. The car had exploded on impact with the canyon floor, the charred remains of two women found inside, burned black and unrecognizable.

"Mother," he said softly.

Beneath the last of the documents, there was a single yellow envelope, slightly bloated with its secret contents. Kinley opened it wearily and drew out the stack of dusty papers Ray had placed inside, the final revelation.

Kinley read the first of them, then the second, then down through the long years of their steady accumulation, the whole story unravelling before him until it came to rest, entirely revealed. "At last," he whispered exhaustedly as the last bit of paper drifted from his fingers.

Forty

She was beautiful in the dawn light that swept over her from the eastern rim of the mountain.

Her eyes widened, as if alarmed. "Kinley, you look . . ."

He raised his hand to silence her. "I know now."

"Everything?"

"Yes." He turned and walked out to the edge of the cliff. Below, Sequoyah remained shrouded by a bank of gently floating haze. Within a few hours, he knew, the last gray wisps would be burned away.

She came up to him softly. "Well, are you going to tell me?"

"Yes," he said, his eyes still trained on the valley's clouded depths. He drew the envelope he'd found in the canyon from his pocket and gave it to her. "Everything."

Dora took the envelope, opened it and pulled out the large stack of cancelled checks Ray had put inside. "They're all made out to your grandmother," she said wonderingly. "All from Thomas Warfield?"

"Yes."

"So much money," Dora said as she continued going through the checks. "Over so many years."

"All the years I was growing up," Kinley told her. "All the years I was in those expensive special schools, then Harvard after that."

"He was paying her during all that time?"

"Yes, he was," Kinley answered.

"Why?"

Once again, Kinley heard his mother's voice: *Never*. "Because he had no choice," he said. "At least, not after I was born."

Dora looked at him quizzically.

"He was my father," Kinley told her.

Dora started to speak, but he raised his hand to stop her, his mind moving through the list of people he would have to tell about all he'd discovered: Lois, Serena, Talbott, Stark, Warfield . . . Dora.

"It's better to know, don't you think?" he asked her.

She nodded determinedly. "Yes."

He looked at her a moment longer, glad she didn't live in the town, but far above it, on the mountainside, certain that when he returned from his mission in the valley, she would still be there.